Praise for *Lady Sophie's Christmas Wish*

"An extraordinary, precious, unforgettable holiday story… An unconventional storyteller who knows exactly how to touch a reader's heart and reach deeply into the soul."

—*RT Book Reviews,* Top Pick, 4½ Stars

"My Christmas wish for you is that Santa brings you this book…a joyful, sensual read."

—*USA Today Happy Ever After*

"Shines with love, sparkles with humor… Breathtaking."

—*Long and Short Reviews*

"Supremely sexy, emotionally involving, and graced with well-written dialogue…a fascinating, enjoyable read."

—*Library Journal*

"Yet another outstanding Regency romance featuring the Windham family…each book is a treat that shouldn't be missed."

—*Night Owl Romance* Reviewer Top Pick, 5 Stars

"A gem of a read! A rapturously entertaining story that warms the heart just in time to bring in the holiday season with yuletide cheer."

—*Romantic Crush Junkies*

"Grace Burrows gives us yet again a magical delight that I, for one, will carry in my heart for years to come."

—*Dark Diva Reviews*

"Rarely does an author come along that really grasps the essence of the Regency period the way Grace Burrowes does... She gives readers a novel that will pull at their heartstrings and renew their faith in miracles."

—*Debbie's Book Bag*

"Grace Burrowes has given us the most romantic story of Christmas miracles...a touching story that takes time to peel back all its layers and reveal the hidden delights of true humanity."

—*Yankee Romance Reviews*

"A delightful holiday story of longing, hope, and love... Sweet, but ever so tantalizing."

—*Anna's Book Blog*

"Burrowes's style of writing is compelling in its gracefulness, in the tempo of the book, and in the absolutely readability of the text. No one else...has that kind of mellow tempo and fluidity...whilst still having sizzling chemistry between the characters."

—*Reading Adventures*

"The perfect feel-good, sigh-inducing romance read for the holidays—or anytime, for that matter."

—*Book Lover and Procrastinator*

Also by Grace Burrowes

LADY LOUISA'S
Christmas Knight

GRACE BURROWES

sourcebooks
casablanca

Published by Sourcebooks Casablanca, an imprint of Sourcebooks
P.O. Box 4410, Naperville, Illinois 60567-4410
(630) 961-3900
sourcebooks.com

Originally published in 2012 in the United States of America
by Sourcebooks Casablanca, an imprint of Sourcebooks.

Printed and bound in Canada.
MBP 10 9 8 7 6 5 4 3 2 1

This book is dedicated to my brother, Tom, one of those rare people who can say the exact kind, honest thing you badly needed to hear that you didn't know you needed to hear. Whatever you're dealing with, Tom can bring both humor and wisdom to the situation. Chicky, you were right: the peep-peeps do poo poo all over.

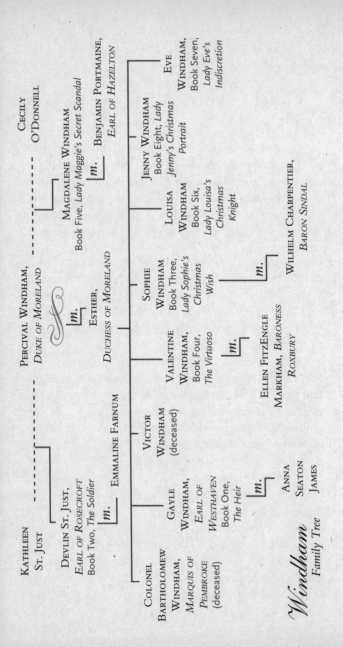

Windham Family Tree

KATHLEEN ST. JUST - - - PERCIVAL WINDHAM, *DUKE OF MORELAND* - - - CECILY O'DONNELL

DEVLIN ST. JUST, *EARL OF ROSECROFT*, Book Two, *The Soldier*

MAGDALENE WINDHAM, Book Five, *Lady Maggie's Secret Scandal*

m. BENJAMIN PORTMAINE, *EARL OF HAZELTON*

EVE WINDHAM, Book Seven, *Lady Eve's Indiscretion*

EMMALINE FARNUM

m. ESTHER, *DUCHESS OF MORELAND*

JENNY WINDHAM, Book Eight, *Lady Jenny's Christmas Portrait*

LOUISA WINDHAM, Book Six, *Lady Louisa's Christmas Knight*

m. WILHELM CHARPENTIER, *BARON SINDAL*

COLONEL BARTHOLOMEW WINDHAM, *MARQUIS OF PEMBROKE* (deceased)

VICTOR WINDHAM (deceased)

VALENTINE WINDHAM, Book Four, *The Virtuoso*

m. ELLEN FITZENGLE MARKHAM, *BARONESS ROXBURY*

SOPHIE WINDHAM, Book Three, *Lady Sophie's Christmas Wish*

GAYLE WINDHAM, *EARL OF WESTHAVEN*, Book One, *The Heir*

m. ANNA SEATON JAMES

One

SIR JOSEPH CARRINGTON ACQUIRED TWO BOON companions after doing his part to rout the Corsican. Carrington was accounted by no one to be a stupid man, and he understood the comfort of the flask—his first source of consolation—to be a dubious variety of friendship.

His second, more sanguine source of comfort, was the Lady Ophelia, whose acquaintance Carrington had made shortly after mustering out. She, of the kind eyes and patient silences, had provided him much wise counsel and companionship, and that she consistently had litters of at least ten piglets both spring and autumn could only endear her to him further.

"I don't see why you should be the one moping." Sir Joseph scratched the place behind Lady Opie's left ear that made her go calm and quiet beneath his hand. "You may remain here in the country, leading poor Roland on the mating dance, while I must away to London."

Where Sir Joseph would be the one led on that same blighted dance. Thank God for the enthusiasm of the local hunt. Riding to hounds preserved a man from at least a few weeks of the collective lunacy that was Polite Society as the Yuletide holidays approached.

"I'll be back by Christmas, and perhaps this year Father Christmas will leave me a wife to take my own little dears in hand."

He took a nip of his flask—a small nip. Unless he spent hours in the saddle, or hours tramping the woods with his fowling piece, or a snowstorm was approaching, or a cold snap, his leg did not pain him too awfully much—usually.

"I honestly do not know how you manage it, my dear. Ten piglets, twice a year, for at least as long as I've had the pleasure of your acquaintance."

She apparently hadn't caught yet this season, though, and winter had arrived. This was worrisome on a level a man not yet drunk didn't examine too closely. Ophelia's fecundity provided reassurance of a fundamental rightness about life—reassurance far more substantial than that held by Sir Joseph's flask.

"Get me some piglets, your ladyship." He switched ears, and his friend tilted her heavy head into his hand. "Get me the kind of babies I can sell at market and grow rich on. Richer. For Christmas, a litter of twelve would do nicely."

Her record was eleven, and every one of them had lived. That had been two years past, when Sir Joseph had been desperately in need of some kind of positive omen.

A groom whistling the aria "He Shall Feed His Flock" in the manner of a holiday jig let Sir Joseph know that his mount was ready. The lad would not intrude on a private audience between Sir Joseph and

Lady Ophelia, not when the groom could abuse poor Handel without mercy instead.

"I'm off. Say a prayer for Reynard."

With a final pat and a scratch, Sir Joseph left his porcine friend to join his neighbors.

Hunt meets reminded Sir Joseph of the army on parade: all the finery was visually impressive and the great good cheer and bonhomie on both occasions fueled in part by nerves and liquor. The agenda of the day in both cases was ostensibly virtuous, and yet, if all went according to plan, somebody not of the assemblage would die a bloody death.

That the somebody was a fox—mere vermin—and outnumbered by the hounds often thirty-couple to one never seemed to bother anyone but Sir Joseph. Even amid the great good cheer of a December hunt meet, he knew better than to share his sympathies for the animal with another human soul.

❧

"The Little Season is a great pain in my backside."

Lady Genevieve Windham hadn't bothered to speak quietly, which her sister Louisa found surprising. True, grumbling to one's sister ought always to be a safe thing to do—Louisa had no use for the Little Season either—but riding in at the back of the third flight, they could come within earshot of their neighbors.

"We've missed all but the last two weeks of it," Louisa pointed out. "Thank God for Papa and his hunt madness."

"It's like hunting grouse," Jenny said, letting her mare drop back farther from the other riders ambling toward the hunt breakfast. "Lent ends, and the husband hunting begins, the mamas beating their charges forward into the waiting guns. I don't know how many more years of this I can take, Louisa."

"One grows used to much of it." This was not quite a lie, though Jenny's rare moment of low spirits required the kindness of…prevarication, at least.

"You've been at it a little longer than Evie or I, and I should not be complaining to you. I do apologize, Lou."

Jenny's tone was genuinely contrite for she was truly good, truly considerate, things Louisa had long since stopped aspiring to. Jenny had angelic blond good looks to go with her generally cheerful disposition, in contrast to Louisa's dark hair. In a despairing moment, Her-Grace-their-mama had called Louisa's features bold.

Alas, that was no lie at all.

In the meadow below, other riders were straggling in from the morning's hunt. A group of bobbing feathers caught Louisa's eye: two pheasants, a peacock, and an ostrich plume dyed—may the sainted bird never learn of it—pink.

And clearly, those feathered hounds were following a scent. Louisa scanned the meadow, her pleasure in the morning's hunt evaporating when she saw their intended prey.

"Jenny, I feel a charitable impulse about to overtake me." For of all men, Sir Joseph Carrington did not deserve to have the pack descend upon him.

Jenny stopped fiddling with the single tuft of mane unbraided over her mare's withers. "You haven't yielded to an impulse in at least five years, Louisa. Logic is your sole guiding… Oh dear."

"The hounds are running riot," Louisa muttered. "The poor man can't even see them coming."

A single rider mounted on a black gelding walked his horse across the meadow on a loose rein, while above and behind him, the four ladies trotted their horses in pursuit.

Louisa had been stifling impulses successfully for eight years, did Jenny but know it. She wasn't going to stifle this one. "Blame my recklessness on the approaching season. Sir Joseph doesn't stand a chance against all four of them at once."

The prospect of a decorated veteran, a knight of the realm no less—also a widower and a *papa*—being swarmed by Isobel and her band of marriage-mad minions wasn't to be borne.

Louisa nudged her mare into a canter, cutting over a stream, two logs, and a stile, with Jenny bringing up the rear. Sir Joseph Carrington had served with her brothers Bart and Devlin on the Peninsula, which further assured his place in that class of men whom Louisa respected without question.

He also had no sisters, cousins, or aunties who would rescue him from the fate trotting up behind him. None of the fellows riding in would dare lend assistance either, of course, lest they be drawn into the affray and find themselves dancing with every unmarried lady in the shire at the evening's ball.

Louisa knew what it was to contend with one's fate in isolation, knew the loneliness and exhaustion of it. She suspected Sir Joseph might too, and if she could spare him this small ambush, she would.

"Sir Joseph," Louisa called as her mare cut in front

of the other four riders by two dozen yards. "Good morning! Excellent final run, wasn't it?"

Sir Joseph glanced back toward Louisa, which allowed her to see the moment when he realized his peril. "Lady Louisa, Lady Genevieve. Good morning."

He didn't quail at the pack closing in on him. He tipped his hat in casual greeting then faced forward again. Devlin had said Sir Joseph was a demon on dispatch—brave and unflinching. His battle instincts were apparently still in working order.

From the corner of Louisa's eye, she saw Isobel Horton of the pink plume glowering a sentiment not at all in keeping with the approaching Yule season.

Happy Christmas to you too, Isobel. "Jenny, weren't you looking for some help with setting up the hunt breakfast?"

Jenny's smile as she came up on Sir Joseph's off side could have graced a saint. "So, I was. Sir Joseph, if you'll excuse me?" She turned her mare. "Oh, ladies! Isobel, Elspeth, I am ever so glad to see you. And Isobel, that is the most cunning hat…"

Sir Joseph watched this maneuver, a hint of a smile hovering on his dark features. "Neatly done, Lady Louisa, and please thank Lady Genevieve when next you see her."

Louisa inclined her head, lest he catch *her* smiling.

Carrington's voice did not lie easily in the ear. His bass-baritone growl lacked the plummy vowels and aristocratic musicality of either public school or university. Louisa liked this about him, liked that he wasn't all pretty manners and mincing vocabulary. She liked even more that he knew exactly what had just transpired and didn't pretend otherwise.

"Care for a nip?" Sir Joseph held out a silver flask engraved with an unfurled rose bud. The thing looked incongruously small and elegant in his black-gloved hand. "And in case you're wondering, there's a combination of rum and hazelnut liqueur in here. It warms the bones."

She accepted his flask, appreciating the gesture, though he likely would have made the same offer to Isobel or Jenny. In the hunt field, there were frequent stops to "check one's tack" or let the horses blow while the hounds were cast. When the weather was brisk, these pauses invariably involved a tot of whatever was in one's flask. Even the ladies were permitted a discreet nip—Louisa had drained her flask before the second run.

"That is…good." Bracing, even. The brew itself was warmed by Sir Joseph's body heat, giving the spirits a mellow fire when imbibed. Louisa took a second sip and passed the flask back.

A very agreeable combination, indeed.

Sir Joseph helped himself to a swallow, and the flask disappeared into an inner pocket of his hunt coat. "I admit to some puzzlement, my lady: you are a bruising rider, well able to keep up with the hounds, even to leading the first flight, and yet you lurk at the back with the inebriates and the timid. You have piqued my curiosity."

Piquing a man's curiosity was not a good thing in Louisa's experience, though the part about being a bruising rider was lovely coming from a former cavalry officer.

"I keep my sister company."

"Ah."

Men had the ability to mock with a single syllable. Certain men. Louisa's five brothers had been born with this ability, and yet, she didn't think Sir Joseph meant to make fun of her.

"Lady Genevieve rides quite well," Louisa admitted. A good lie was based as much as possible on truth. Her brothers had taught her that too. "She is softhearted though, and does not like to risk being in at the kill."

"I see." The smile was back, very subtly. Louisa wanted to stare at the man to see if that smile ever broke forth into the genuine article.

Staring would not do, however. Louisa gained a moment's pause to think up another conversational gambit when Sir Joseph's horse began to passage. The animal was far from dainty, and yet, when it collected itself like that, quarters lowering, trot steps becoming elevated and cadenced, man and beast each looked elegant and elementally...attractive.

"Enough of this nonsense. Settle, you."

When Carrington spoke to his horse, his voice was different—purring and affectionate, not growling. The horse relaxed back into a walk while the rider stroked a hand over its mane.

"He is quite an athlete, Sir Joseph, and yet I noticed you also avoid the first flight."

"Sonnet is anxious for home now. He and I are alike in that regard—most comfortable among familiar surroundings. To reply to your observation, Lady Louisa, all I can say is that war has changed the way I view blood sport, to the point where I find the term an oxymoron. Will you be going up to Town before Christmas?"

Louisa knew what oxymoron meant, along with onomatopoeia, synecdoche, and anthropo-morphism—for starters. Perfect gentleman was an oxymoron. *Perfect lady was too.*

"For the next two weeks, my sisters and I will remove to Mayfair with Their Graces."

"Do I surmise that this is *not* a cause for rejoicing?"

Louisa turned her head to regard him and found his gaze was serious—too serious? "Are you teasing me, Sir Joseph?" Her brothers—brave men each—used to tease her, before her schoolgirl arrogance had taken one of their dares to a disastrous conclusion. She did not miss their nonsense whatsoever.

Sir Joseph leaned a little closer in his saddle and glanced around, as if imparting a great confidence. "I am commiserating, I think."

He straightened, swiveled his eyes front, and kept speaking. "I go up to Town in spring and autumn and each time wonder if I'm not becoming more like my great-uncle Sixtus. For the last forty years of his life, he never once set foot in London, and each decade, he professed to be happier than the one previous."

"This would be the fellow from whom you inher-ited your property?"

"My farm."

His *farm* was thousands of acres. According to His Grace, they were very good acres, and Sir Joseph took excellent care of them. Lucky man, to be able to rusticate where one could see stars at night and go for a pounding gallop come morning.

Ahead of them now, Jenny and her companions were chattering back and forth, no doubt weaving a conversation about watercress sandwiches or something equally riveting.

"London isn't so bad," Louisa said. London was tedious, crowded, and full of people with a bewildering ability to talk much, say little, and apparently enjoy themselves in the process. "Christmas will see us back out to Morelands in a very short while."

"Two weeks can be an eternity."

He said this with something like resignation. Louisa saw him put his reins in one hand and fish inside his hunt coat for his flask, though he neither withdrew it nor imbibed any more of his personal brew—more's the pity. She could have used another tot. Two weeks was, after all, one million two hundred nine thousand six hundred seconds.

Perhaps he could have used a tot too. His expression was bleak, but then, Sir Joseph's expression was usually bleak. He was not a classically handsome man—his features were saturnine, his brows a trifle heavy, his nose not quite straight, though bold and a bit hooked. He yet managed to be attractive to Louisa for she *had* seen him smile.

Just the once, he'd smiled at his small daughters one day in the church yard, but Louisa had never forgotten the sight. His smile, full of warmth, humor, and affection, made him very attractive indeed.

"Will you be attending the hunt ball, Sir Joseph?"

"One does."

Yes, one did. Louisa suspected this was more of his unflinching bravery at work. "Shall I save you a dance?"

She regretted the impulse as soon as the words were out of her mouth, though not for herself. Dancing was one social activity she enjoyed, provided her partner was halfway competent. She regretted her question for him. Sir Joseph limped, and Louisa wasn't sure the fellow was even capable of dancing.

He petted his horse again, a soft stroke of black leather down a sleek, muscular crest. "I can manage the promenade. A sarabande or old-fashioned polonaise is usually within my abilities early in the evening. I haven't attempted waltzing in public in recent years and hope to die in that state of grace."

"The promenade, then."

As they approached the hunt breakfast, Louisa tried not to think of Sir Joseph growing old without ever again knowing the pleasure of sweeping a lady around the ballroom to the lilting strains of a waltz. If Louisa dwelled on such thoughts, she'd be at risk for pitying Sir Joseph. A man possessed of unflinching bravery, an excellent seat, and a half-full flask would have had no use for her pity whatsoever.

Louisa Windham had preserved Joseph from enduring the company of Miss Fairchild and her giggling familiar, Miss Horton, for the duration of the hunt breakfast, and possibly at the hunt ball as well. They'd been looking for him all morning, like a couple of hounds on the scent of the fox: eyes bright, yipping inane compliments to each other, their gazes searching the first flight for their prey, then the second...

While Joseph had the company of a pretty woman with no designs on his person, his purse, or his pork.

He assisted Lady Louisa from her horse, which

allowed him the realization that she was not as substantial as her height might have suggested. When she slid to the ground, he collected one other little fact about her: despite the morning's activity, the scent of citrus and cloves clung to her.

Expensive, and in the brisk air of a bright winter morning... Christmassy. He liked it.

He liked her, in fact, though he would never burden the lady with such a confession. In the two years since he'd been turned loose on the local Kentish gentry, he'd spent considerable time on the edges of drawing rooms and dancing parlors, visiting in the churchyard, and tending to the neighborly civilities.

From what he'd observed, Lady Louisa went her own way, as much as such a thing was possible for a duke's unmarried daughter. She spoke her mind and had a saucy mouth.

Also a saucy bottom. He particularly liked her saucy bottom. He enjoyed the way her riding habit revealed a bit more flare at the hips than was fashionable, and the way she made no effort to hide the Creator's generosity with her fundament.

She was a woman a man could get his hands on...

"Sir Joseph?"

He stepped back from her while grooms led their horses away. "May I fetch you a plate, Lady Louisa? Something to drink?"

How long had he been standing there, contemplating her backside in the midst of their neighbors, the hounds, milling horses, and bustling servants?

"I could use some sustenance."

That she did not demur and swan off in search of

her sister surprised him and pleased him. "As could I. Shall we?" He winged his arm at her, more willing to remain at her side than a gentleman would admit.

Though if he again thanked Louisa Windham for using her superior social standing to rescue him from certain capture, she'd likely give him a puzzled look, change the subject, and forget she'd promised him the opening dance.

Which he was looking forward to, oddly enough.

From several places ahead of them in the buffet line, Timothy Grattingly and some other young fellow started arguing about the ideal breeding for a morning horse.

"They would not appreciate Sonnet," Joseph murmured as the lady added apple slices to the plates he held. "He's good English draft on the sire's side, and pure Spanish on the dam's. A woods colt who saved my life more than once."

Louisa Windham aimed an impatient glance at the young men and their escalating disagreement. "Sonnet has a good set of quarters on him, good bone, and he's sane. I don't see that much else matters. Where shall we sit?"

Where the hounds would not find him, where he could enjoy more of Louisa Windham's tart common sense and sweet fragrance. "A little quiet wouldn't go amiss, in the sun and out of the breeze." The weather being nippy, even in the sheltered environs of their host's stables.

She shot him a tolerant smile, suggesting the lady had divined his strategy. "There," she said. "That bench."

Louisa had chosen a wooden bench flanking a dry fountain and a bed of dead asters. While Joseph remained standing with their plates, Louisa set their drinks on either end of the bench, unpinned her hat, rearranged her skirts, and otherwise caused the kind of fuss and delay natural to women.

He ought to have resented it, as hungry as he was, as much as his leg was starting to throb. Instead, he noticed that when Louisa pulled loose her hat, a lock of her dark hair abandoned its intended location to coil along the column of her neck.

She did not seem to notice or care, while he could not stop noticing.

Perhaps a trip to Town—to the fleshpots of Egypt, as it were—was not entirely a bad idea. A gentleman farmer who'd behaved himself the livelong year could do with some recreation at Christmas, after all.

"I'll take those." She reached up and plucked both plates from Joseph's grasp, gesturing with her chin for him to sit.

His preoccupation with the flawless, pale, and possibly clove-scented skin of her neck, or the exact feel of that fat, dark curl of hair against his fingers vanished as he realized he was going to have to get his arse on the bench beside her. A graceless moment awaited him. After he'd ridden for several hours, the joints of his right leg were not strictly reliable in their functioning.

He managed. It was a matter of moving stiffly, stiffly, then for the last few inches, nigh collapsing onto the bench, like an old man too stubborn to make proper use of his canes.

"Does riding bother your injury?" Lady Louisa started munching on a slice of apple after delivering her inquiry.

"There's a balance. If I ask too much, it worsens; if I ask too little, it worsens."

"And nobody asks you about it, do they? Care for a bite of apple?"

He enjoyed apples. He wasn't sure he enjoyed talking about his injury—now that somebody *had* inquired.

"War wounds are old news." He accepted a slice of apple from her hand. They'd removed their gloves to eat, of course, which meant he noticed the contrast: His hands were calloused and bore a scar, a white slash that made a hairless track across the backs of all four fingers of his right hand. Her hands might have belonged to a Renaissance tapestry virgin stroking some fool unicorn's neck.

She frowned at his hand as a three-legged hound went loping past, sleigh bells jingling merrily on its collar. "Another injury?"

"An attempt by a French soldier to relieve me of the reins. He was not successful."

Thank God. Joseph slammed a mental door on the memory—something he'd become adept at—and accepted another bite of apple from the lady beside him. "Are you ever bored, Lady Louisa?"

She paused in a rather purposeful effort to clean her plate, glancing up at him with a puzzled frown. "What brought that on?"

No tittering reply, no simpering or casting lures, and the lady had both a kind heart and a lovely appearance. Better still, Joseph would open the evening's dancing with her for a partner.

Joseph waved his scarred hand. "Talk of injuries puts me in mind of boredom, perhaps. The recovery was a greater challenge than the initial harm. One does wonder what a duke's daughters find to amuse them."

"I have wondered the same thing. We make calls, we have charitable endeavors, we correspond with our sisters, sisters-by-marriage, and cousins. We attend social functions, and when in Town, ride or drive in the park. It's all quite…"

She fell silent, leaving Joseph with the sense he'd just glimpsed a hurt that wasn't healing all that well. He patted her knuckles. "I read."

Another look, much more guarded. "One assumed you were literate."

He read to his pigs, more often than not. "I read more than just the journals and classics, Lady Louisa. I am left to my own company a great deal, and winter nights are long and cold."

She perused the contents of her plate, which spared him any more inquisitions from dark green eyes. "They are. Jenny spends them sewing or painting—she must create. Sophie was our chief baker until she married Sindal, Eve is Mama's boon companion for the social calls, and Maggie frolics with her account books when she's not making calf eyes at Hazelton."

"I correspond with your-sister-the-countess regarding business matters." He also noted that Louisa's little recitation included no activity of choice for herself.

"With Maggie?" Another pause in her eating. "She would be so bold as to correspond with a single gentleman and no one the wiser. *Droit du spinster*, she'd call it. I used to think Mags had a pound sign where her heart was supposed to be. Little I knew."

She tore off a bite of Christmas stollen with particular focus, suggesting there was Family Business lurking at the edges of the conversation. Joseph took a sip of his punch then set the glass aside.

"Drink with caution, my lady. There's some turned cider somewhere in the recipe."

She studied her bite of holiday bread. "It's always like this, isn't it? At the hunt meets we bundle up in our finest, slap on our company smiles, fill our plates, and yet, there's always something…sour punch, a horse that has to be put down, a neighbor retching in the bushes while his half-grown son tries not to look hopeless." She put her mostly empty plate aside. "I'm sorry. I should perhaps find my sister."

Joseph had never considered himself more than passingly bright, but his powers of observation had been sharpened by the inactivity occasioned by his injury. Pretty, kind, titled, and well dowered Lady Louisa was dreading her next trip to Town, maybe all her trips to Town. She had no hobbies or pastimes she'd mention in public, and both of her older sisters were married.

And yet, she'd ridden to the rescue of a man she barely knew, perhaps because she heard the hounds in full cry all too often herself.

Joseph got out his flask. "Life can be like that, tarnished around the edges."

Mostly to divert her, he reached over and tucked the errant curl behind her ear, finding her hair every bit as silky and pleasing to the touch as he'd imagined. He could write a sonnet to that single lock of hair.

Perhaps he would.

"It's true as well, my lady, that we're both in good health, we have friends and neighbors who will miss us when we're gone, we have food to eat and warm beds to sleep in, and Christmas will soon be here." He did not mention that they'd be sharing the promenade.

She hadn't flinched at his touch. She studied him from serious green eyes. "You learned this while at war too, didn't you? You learned to be grateful."

"Perhaps I did." He'd learned something—how to content himself with agriculture, solitude, and good literature, perhaps. Almost.

"His Grace says you are also leaving for Town tomorrow, Sir Joseph, though one wonders why."

Her query was too insightful and made him abruptly reassess her with her serious, *pretty* green eyes, lovely scent, and silky hair. "The same reason we all go up to Town. I must socialize occasionally if I'm ever to find a spouse. Would you care for another nip?"

"Yes." She accepted his flask and held it to her lips. While Joseph again admired the graceful turn of her neck, she tilted the flask up, as if she were intent on draining it of every last drop.

"Why would Sir Joseph Carrington be in need of a wife?" While she spoke, Louisa accepted a mug of mulled wine from one of the footmen circulating around the ballroom. There were little bits of cinnamon floating on top, a display of holiday extravagance on the part of the family hosting the hunt ball. Mistletoe hung in the door arches, and wreathes festooned the doors. The fragrances of evergreen and beeswax lurked under the scent of too many bodies that hadn't bathed since the morning's ride.

Eve waved the footman away without taking any wine for herself, though Jenny was too polite to decline.

"Maybe Sir Joseph seeks a wife because he has children," Jenny volunteered. "Little girls need a mother."

"Maybe because he's lonely," Eve suggested. "He's a comely man. He can't be much more than thirty, and Maggie says raising swine is quite profitable. He doesn't seem inclined to the usual male vices, so why not have a wife?"

Louisa sipped her wine, recalling Sir Joseph at Sunday services with the two little minxes who called him Papa. "You think he's comely?"

Eve Windham, the youngest of the ducal siblings, rarely ventured an opinion about any member of the male gender. She collected hopefuls and followers and even proposals with blithe good cheer, but never gave a hint her heart was engaged by any of them.

Eve's gaze traveled across the ballroom, to where Sir Joseph was in conversation with the plump, pale Lady Horton. The woman's two eldest daughters flanked him—penned him in like a pair of curious heifers would corner a new bull calf.

"I like a man who isn't silly," Eve said. "I like a man who will be able to provide for me and mine; I like that he's a papa—though he'll want sons to pass along all that wealth to—and a pair of broad shoulders on a fellow doesn't exactly offend, either."

Jenny's blond brows rose. "From you, Eve, that's a ringing endorsement. Were he not a mere knight, I'd be passing your notice along to Mama."

"It doesn't matter that he's a mere knight," Eve said, though her rebuke was mild. "Is the libation any good?"

Louisa wrinkled her nose. "Too sweet. Some people must use the holidays to inform all and sundry of their wealth."

"You're cross tonight," Jenny said. "I know something to cheer you up."

Eve's lips quirked, and the look that passed between Louisa's sisters was conspiratorial and mischievous. Eve and Jenny shared more than blond beauty, though Jenny was willowy and Eve was a smaller, curvier package. Louisa's remaining unmarried sisters both had a sort of gentleness to them, a warmth of spirit toward all in their ambit that Louisa lacked.

And envied, truth be known.

"I can use cheering up," Louisa said, picking up the thread of the conversion. "My evening starts out promenading with Sir Joseph, and my dance card is empty thereafter. Sindal will no doubt take pity on me, but he fairly heaves one off the dance floor in an effort to return to dear Sophie's side."

"Deene would dance with us were he not in mourning," Eve observed.

"But he *is* in mourning." Which was a shame. The Marquis of Deene was tall enough, a fine-looking fellow, and more family friend than anything else, which meant for Louisa's purposes he was safe.

"Lord Lionel Honiton is not in mourning," Jenny said, "and he's just now coming down the steps."

Hence the knowing sororal glances. Louisa did not look up as she set aside her glass of too-sweet, lukewarm wine punch. "He declined to ride today. I wasn't sure he was coming."

Nor had she missed him, though that hardly need be said.

"Too busy choosing his attire for the evening," Eve replied. "I swear he outshines the ladies."

Lord Lionel was all golden good looks, with brown eyes that put Louisa in mind of Her Grace's spaniel. When Louisa glanced over Eve's shoulder to take in his lordship's progress down the stairs, she saw he had as usual troubled over his turnout.

A handsome man who knew how to wear lace was a beautiful creature, regardless of his other attributes. Lionel sported just a touch here and there—his throat, his cuffs—but it was golden blond lace, which complemented his fair coloring and his blue-and-gold ensemble marvelously. His cravat pin would be something perfect—sapphire or topaz set in gold, perhaps—and the sleeve buttons at his cuffs would match it.

"Louisa's saving her supper waltz for Lord Lace," Eve murmured. "I declare that man wears more gold for a hunt ball than I have in my entire jewelry case."

"He maintains standards," Louisa said. Town standards, even Carlton House standards—assuming the jewelry was real, which Louisa doubted. "And he dances well enough."

Louisa knew of what she spoke, for she'd had the pleasure more than once. When one danced with Lord Lionel, there was a sense of the entire room pausing to watch. That he seemed to know it was only to be expected.

She considered that he chose her as a dance partner because she was, first and foremost, of suitable rank—a duke's daughter could dance with a marquis's son—and because her dark coloring set off his golden male beauty. Then too, she was a good dancer.

"He's coming this way," Jenny said, peering into her still-full glass. "I'd say he's about to speak for your supper waltz, Lou, and before he's done much more than greet the hostess."

"Good evening, my ladies."

Louisa stifled a groan of relief at the growled salutation. "Sir Joseph, good evening." Her sisters offered their curtsies, and Jenny—bless her—launched into the civilities.

"Marvelously mild weather today for the holiday hunt, wasn't it?"

Sir Joseph, severely resplendent in dark formal attire, appeared to consider Jenny. "One wonders if Reynard shares that opinion. He probably starts praying for nasty winter weather no later than April of each year."

"In spring," Louisa said, "he and his vixen are likely concerned with family matters."

Sir Joseph's lips twitched while Eve and Jenny both managed to look pained. Family matters—*what* had she implied? Louisa stared at the cinnamon bits floating on her awful drink.

"Perhaps he is," Sir Joseph said. "Perhaps he thinks of going up to Town early so he might confer with his tailors before the Season advances. Rather than discuss the sartorial habits of the fox, Lady Louisa, might I remind you that you've promised me your promenade? The orchestra is tuning up, though I shall certainly understand if today's exertions left you too fatigued to allow me the privilege."

He was giving her a way to decline their dance. Behind Jenny, Lord Lionel had paused in his progress across the room to speak with Isobel Horton. The girl had refined the simper to an art and was clinging to his arm like a barnacle. He gave Isobel his undivided attention, those brown eyes of his turned on the woman as if she were the light of his existence.

What would it take to inspire Sir Joseph to look at a woman like that?

"Louisa rarely passes by an opportunity to stand up," Jenny said. There was an urgent note in her voice, as if Louisa had missed a conversational cue.

"Jenny's right." Louisa shifted her gaze from Lord Lionel's peacock splendor to Sir Joseph's sober face. "The more I'm on my feet, the less I'm left trying to make small talk, which as you've no doubt surmised, is not one of my gifts."

"Nor mine." He winged his elbow at her. That's all. As overtures went, it had a certain compelling simplicity.

While Lord Lionel scribbled on Isobel Horton's dance card, Louisa took Sir Joseph's arm. She assumed her place at his side among the other couples preparing to stroll their way through the opening of the evening, and was assailed by a troubling thought: Was Sir Joseph partnering her because he thought *she* was in need of rescuing? Was this charity on his part?

The possibility was not as lowering as it should have been. Louisa instead found it…intriguing.

She could not marry, not while the threat of scandal

hung over her like a blighted sprig of mistletoe, but she ought to be allowed to stroll the perimeter of a ballroom on the arm of a handsome man, shouldn't she?

Two

"I CAN RECITE POETRY TO YOU," SIR JOSEPH SAID WHEN Louisa had walked with him halfway down one side of the room. "Poetry would preserve us from silence and yet require no thought on anybody's part."

Poetry? Louisa's heart tripped. "Are you teasing me?"

"Oh, perhaps. You could nod occasionally or beat me on the arm with your fan, and no one would know we're ducking the obligation to converse. I have a friend who's partial to the Shakespeare sonnets." He paused while Louisa cast around for something—anything—to say, but he spared her by launching into a quiet, almost contemplative recitation: "'That time of year thou mayst in me behold, when yellow leaves, or none, or few do hang on boughs which shake against the cold…'"

Across the room, Isobel Horton smacked Lord Lionel's arm with her closed fan.

Louisa *adored* that sonnet, which Sir Joseph had begun with just the right balance of regret and warmth. "Why don't you instead tell me why you're hunting a spouse, Sir Joseph?"

He grimaced. Her question was graceless, but there was no calling it back. "Hunting? Striding about in my gaiters, my blunderbuss primed and ready to take down some unsuspecting little dove in midflight? I suppose the image is not inaccurate. I require a wife for two reasons."

He *required* a wife. Women longed for a husband, they dreamed of children to love. They were not permitted to *require* a husband. Brave he might be, and possessed of marvelous taste in poems, but Louisa wanted to smack Sir Joseph, and not with her fan.

"Two reasons. Please explicate."

They were forced to a halt by the couple before them, who appeared too busy flirting to manage even forward steps in time to the music.

"First, I am responsible for two girl children, and the influence of an adult female in the maternal role is desirable on their behalves."

In the part of her brain that reveled in language, that regarded every spoken sentence as aural architecture, Louisa noticed that Sir Joseph managed to allude to being a parent without acknowledging any relationship. He did not say, "My daughters need a mother," nor did he say, "I am in want of a wife to mother my children."

He fashioned a job description, though an accurate one under the circumstances.

"The second reason?"

He glanced around. He waited until the lovebirds ahead were moving along, proceeding as a three-legged unit, heads bent so close as to ensure talk. Louisa wanted to smack them, as well, perhaps with the butt end of Sir Joseph's blunderbuss.

"There is a title."

She forgot the lovebirds and nearly forgot Lord Lionel halfway across the room, suffering the press of Miss Horton's udder against his arm.

"I beg your pardon?"

"There is a title." He sounded weary as he spoke, his voice barely above a whisper. "The barony has been in abeyance for more than two hundred years, and God willing, it will remain in abeyance."

Abeyance. Abeyance could keep a title dangling just out of reach on a family tree for centuries. Abeyance befell the old baronies, when the holder of the title left only female descendants, who increased and multiplied and were fruitful, making it impossible to choose to whom the title ought to descend, because various heirs had equal claim on it.

"You do not sound pleased about this." He sounded horrified, in fact.

"I am in fervent hopes a fourth cousin, Sixtus's descendant of the same name, the only other contender, will shortly be in expectation of a happy event with his young wife. Each year, I await his Christmas correspondence, hoping a new little cousin of the male persuasion will have arrived in the preceding year."

"You don't want a title?"

They stopped perilously close to a dangling spray of mistletoe, and he…shuddered. The broad-shouldered, plainspoken man who'd been knighted for bravery shuddered. "Consider, Lady Louisa, that our regent is nigh profligate handing out titles. What if he took a notion to elevate the title above a barony? What if he recalled that my knighthood was earned in combat?

What if his great capacity for sentiment should affect his generous heart, and…a knighthood is bad enough. A barony would be nigh intolerable, and anything worse than that enough to send a sane man to Bedlam."

Perhaps Sir Joseph's courage was not limitless. Louisa's certainly wasn't. "You would be Lord Somebody, Sir Joseph. You'd sit in the Lords, you'd have your pick of the debutantes."

She managed to stop herself from pointing out that even his hog farming would be overlooked. Farming was not trade; it was solidly agricultural. Bacon, ham, lard, and leather being necessities, every title in the land probably raised some swine.

Louisa also did not ask the man what he thought of dukes—or dukes' daughters—if baronies were nigh intolerable. "You must marry in part because of this title."

Sir Joseph huffed out a sigh then moved them away from the Mistletoe of Damocles. "I did not say I *must* marry. I am not averse to the notion because of the girls, and then there is this remote, distant, though not quite theoretical business of a title. Titles come with responsibilities, and my cousin is not young."

A duke's daughter grasped his point: he'd need an heir. A title should not languish for two hundred years in abeyance, only to fall into the Crown's greedy clutches through escheat immediately thereafter.

"Perhaps this year, your cousin's union will be fruitful."

"One offers prayers to that effect, though this is his third union."

The couple before them was whispering, heads bent so close the young man might have stolen a kiss with less impropriety.

"Sir Joseph, I find I'm thirsty. Would you be offended if we abandoned the promenade and sought some refreshment?"

He said nothing. He fairly yanked her out of the line of other couples and headed for the table where more poor quality, not-quite-warm, gaggingly sweet wine awaited them both. She went along with him and pretended to sip her drink, though the evening stretched before her as an interminable exercise in appeasing seasonal social obligations and evading strategically hung boughs of mistletoe.

Meanwhile, across the room, Miss Horton pressed, Lord Lionel laughed, and the orchestra played on.

❧

"The secret to a short and successful courtship is to pick a desperate woman."

Lord Lionel Honiton's cronies laughed predictably at this sally from one among their number. Lionel took a sip of good brandy—Petersham was hosting, and he was still too new to Town to understand that those who drank his brandy and fondled his housemaids were not necessarily his friends.

"You miss the mark," Lionel drawled to the wit lounging in a cushioned chair near the hearth. "A desperate girl is the secret to a short courtship ending in marriage, I'll grant you, but better still if *her parents* are desperate, in which case the settlements will see the thing done *successfully*."

A round of right-hos, hear-hears, and what-whats followed, along with another circulation of the brandy decanter.

"And then"—the wit held up his glass as if to toast—"there's the wedding night."

More hooting and stomping, because the hour was growing late, and the decanter was seeing a great deal of action. These same fellows would cheerfully call one another out over a slur to a woman's honor before dinner. Four hours later, they were degenerating into the overgrown schoolboys they were, ready to hump anything in skirts and to cheer one another on in the same cause.

While the assemblage began to debate just how many Seasons it took to create desperation in a decent young woman, much less in her parents, Lord Lionel topped up his glass.

"You'll regret that in the morning," said a voice to his right.

Lionel held the glass in both palms, letting the heat of his hands warm the liquid. "I will do no such thing. You are far too sober, Harrison, if you think I'll even be abroad during anything approaching morning."

Harrison was visually appealing, lounging against the mantel, a lean, dark contrast to Lionel's own Nordic coloring. He was also serious to a fault, which allowed Lionel to appear the wit by contrast. All in all, a useful association—for Lionel.

"You'll be abroad in daylight." Harrison's tone was mocking, condescending even.

"Perhaps I'll be making my way home in the morning, as the term technically applies past the witching hour, but as for the broad light of day"— Lionel paused for another sip—"heaven spare me."

"You'll be about because Lady Carstairs's Christmas

breakfast is tomorrow, and very likely, all three Windham sisters will be on hand. You've been currying the favor of that trio all year."

"Have I?" Lionel yawned, scratched in the general area of his...upper thighs, and peered at his drink. "Three of them, you say?"

Harrison's dark eyes narrowed.

Elijah Harrison was a hanger-on. He painted portraits, which meant he wasn't even a gentleman, though he was somebody or other's heir, so he was titled and tolerated. Then too, the Regent fancied himself quite the patron of the arts, and Harrison enjoyed a certain cachet with the Carlton House set.

"Moreland has three unmarried daughters," Harrison said. "All pretty, all well dowered, and you're just trying to decide which one will be the least work."

If Harrison's tone had been accusatory, Lionel might have been alarmed, but Harrison spoke as if merely stating facts, and boring facts at that.

Boring, *accurate* facts.

"You're trying to decide which one is vain enough to insist on having her portrait painted," Lionel replied. "Or you might be thinking of approaching His Grace about doing all three, as it were."

He let the innuendo hang delicately above his spoken words.

"I have never found it attractive in a man to pursue a woman publicly, while privately maligning her. Smacks of...desperation." Harrison eyed the glass in Lionel's hand. "Desperation and dishonor. I bid you good night, my lord."

He wafted off, all elegant good looks and sly innuendo, making Lionel long to lift a foot and plant it in the encroaching bastard's backside. He resisted this urge not because Harrison was right—Lionel *was* growing desperate and had seldom regarded honor as more than a convenient disguise for bad motives—but he was also intent on having some fun with one of Petersham's plump, giggling upstairs maids. A public row with a nobody of a painter would queer the chances of that altogether.

~

Sir Joseph dawdled for two days. In those two days, he visited regularly with Lady Opie, scribbled off several notes to his London house steward, rode out with his land steward, called on his tenants—again—and otherwise put off a journey he did not want to make.

But had to. His peculiar discussion with Louisa Windham had stuck in Joseph's mind like the proverbial burr under his saddle. Until he'd spoken the words aloud to her—he required a wife—the need hadn't been exactly pressing, though it had been nagging. Now, like a sore tooth, it seemed never to leave his awareness.

"When will you be back?"

Amanda, scrambling around on his lap, made the last word into a whine of at least five syllables. "Baa–aaa–aaa–aaa–ck?"

"Yes, Papa." Fleur clutched his riding jacket in grubby little mitts and started scaling his left knee. "*When* will you be back?"

"I do not recall inviting either of you to roost upon

my person." Though there they were, each plunked down on her territory of choice, and each smelling of soap, lavender, and something else—mischief perhaps.

"You always go away," Amanda opined. "But if you didn't go away, you'd never come see us at all anymore."

Fleur chimed right in with the chorus. "You *used* to tuck us in."

"You used to be infants. Quiet little things who neither slid down banisters nor begged a man for ponies the livelong day."

Amanda turned big brown eyes on him. "You could bring us ponies for Christmas. We've been ever so good."

"We have," Fleur concurred. "Nurse hasn't needed her salts since Monday!"

"Allow me to point out that it's Tuesday morning." Joseph gently stopped Fleur from putting her thumb in her mouth. "Don't get your hopes up that I'll bring you ponies for Christmas. You're both too young, and winter is no time to learn to ride."

Fleur's chin jutted in an unbecoming manner. "If we were boys, we'd have ponies by now."

Amanda nodded vigorously, dark curls bouncing. "Fleur is right. If we were boys, you'd listen to our lessons."

"If you were boys, you could inherit a damned title."

The words were out, muttered, but far too inappropriate for tender ears to have missed a single syllable.

"Papa said *damn*." Fleur slapped her hand over her mouth as if to hold back her giggles. "*Damn* is a bad word. We're not supposed to say *damn*, or *damn* it, or God *damn* it to hell, or—"

"Cease." Joseph wrapped an arm around her to put his much-larger hand over her mouth. He was outnumbered, though, and Amanda started up immediately.

"Or bloody *damn* or *damn* and blast. If we were boys, you'd *teach* us how to swear and even belch, and we'd know how to far—"

He ended up with two little girls wiggling off his lap, their giggles cascading behind them as they scampered a few feet away.

"Enough, the both of you." He rose to his full height and scowled down at them. "This is no way to earn anything but a lump of coal in your stocking. When I return from Town, I'll expect perfect deportment from each of you, glowing reports from the maids and Miss Hodges both, and no more of this riot and insurrection."

They quieted immediately at his tone, their smiles turning to looks of uncertainty aimed at him and then at each other.

Joseph felt again that sinking in his middle that suggested he was not fit to parent these children—not fit in the least—much less another dozen whom he saw only on occasion.

He went down on one knee, unable to tolerate the possibility that those uncertain looks would degenerate into quivering chins and—he shuddered at the very notion—a double spate of female tears. "Give me a farewell kiss, and I'll be on my way. Say your prayers while I'm gone, don't tease each other too mercilessly, and mind Miss Hodges."

"Yes, Papa."

He held out his arms, and the girls advanced, first Amanda—the elder, the one who elected herself in charge of taking risks—then Fleur, the loyal follower. They dutifully bussed his cheek, and he let them go.

"And stay off the banisters."

There being nothing more to say, he left the nursery, mounted his horse, and pointed his gelding in the direction of London. The roads were dry, the weather fair, and Joseph's horse—after about five miles—apparently in the mood to behave, which left Joseph to the task of brooding.

He did not require a wife, but his dependents needed an adult female to take them in hand, and thus a wife he would get. His wife would know what to do with Miss Hodges, whom Joseph had overheard lamenting again the "plebeian" coloring exhibited by Sir Joseph's daughters.

Dark hair and dark eyes hadn't been the least plebeian on King Charles II or his Iberian wife, had they? Females nowadays were held to some other standard, one which maintained that fair hair and fair skin were pretty, while dark hair...

Louisa Windham had dark hair and dark eyes, and on *her*, the combination was...lovely. She was not a restful woman, having about her a faint air of discontent, of boredom, perhaps. But it was to Louisa Windham that Joseph had articulated the need for a wife, and to her he'd admitted that the title was figuring into his thinking.

The title.

Cousin Sixtus Hargrave Carrington had written to warn Joseph that he was not enjoying good health.

To receive the annual letter so many days before Christmas was only to underscore the point: Sixtus did not expect to live out the year.

Any party holding at least a one-third interest in a title in abeyance could petition to have that title bestowed upon him. Hargrave and Joseph, though each held an equal claim, had by tacit agreement declined to petition for a choice to be made between them. Upon either man's death without male issue, the other fellow would be saddled with the title.

And that... Joseph thought of his relief when Lady Louisa had spared him having to clomp and mince through a promenade—or perhaps spared herself. He thought of his offering to recite poetry to give them both a reprieve from his attempts at polite conversation. He thought of his daughters at the mercy of an employee who didn't even approve of their *coloring*—something neither child could help or control.

"My life is not a fairy tale," Sir Joseph informed his horse, "but it's quite bearable. I can provide for my dependents. I have a measure of privacy and can, on occasion, steal away to read to an appreciative audience."

The horse snorted.

"Very well, a tolerant audience."

A mere knight could limp; a lord must waltz. A mere knight could read Shakespeare to his favorite breeding sow; a lord was likely forbidden to *have* a favorite breeding sow. A mere knight could admire a lovely, dark-haired lady from afar, while a lord...

A lord had a title and a succession to attend to, so he must—he absolutely must—have a lady to bear him sons.

Joseph urged his horse from the trot into a rocking canter and put all thoughts of ladies and waltzes from his mind, the better to allow him to pray for his fourth cousin's immediate return to good health.

෴

"My love, I thought you'd be going out this morning." As he spoke, His Grace, the Duke of Moreland, made an instantaneous assessment of the slight frown on his duchess's brow and changed course to join her in her private sitting room. He saw the frown disappear and closed the door behind him.

Whatever was troubling his bride of more than three decades, she was going to try to hide it from him. Silly girl. If the huntsman had blown "gone away," His Grace would not have felt any stronger need to pursue and investigate.

"Is there fresh tea?" he asked, taking a place beside his duchess.

But Her Grace was no fool. She knew that in the duke's eyes, the purpose of tea was to wash down crème cakes. In extremis, tea might serve as an adequate medium in which to stir a generous dollop of brandy on a freezing day.

Tea for its own sake was a lame undertaking, and Her Grace had long since divined His Grace's position on the matter.

"I sent Westhaven and Anna off shopping with the girls," Her Grace said. "Eve tried to beg off, but her sisters wouldn't have any of that."

"Abandoning you to my dubious company." And abandoning him to the dubious offerings on the tea tray: scones and butter, jam, and honey. Not even a hot cross bun or a few slices of stollen. "Whom do you suppose will make our stollen this Christmas, since Sophie has gone to housekeeping with her baron?"

"Just where do you think Sophie got her recipe, Moreland?"

He adored it when she called him Moreland in that magisterial tone. He planted a kiss on her cheek. "From your mother, because your interest in cooking is almost equal to my interest in a tepid cup of tea. What has given you a fit of the megrims, my love? Shall I take you for a drive? Send around to Gunter's for a picnic?"

"Louisa asked me if she might remain at Morelands next spring."

His Grace sat back, trying to shift mentally to that part of his intellect—the brilliant politician and successful former cavalry officer part—that occasionally got him past the rough patches when the papa part was knocked on its backside.

He reached for his wife's hand, needing the subtle information gathered by physical connection with her—and the reassurance. "What is that about, Esther? Louisa is not the least retiring and not the type to mope."

But Louisa was from that vast, unmapped territory known as His Daughters. His Grace loved his five adult daughters and would cheerfully have died to protect them, but as for *understanding* them… He might as well have tried to grasp the mental processes of…another species entirely.

"I have been thinking this over," Her Grace said,

"and you're right. She's not the type to mope. She takes after her papa in that she's more given to action than introspection."

"You have referred to me as a bull in a tea shop in your more honest moments, Esther."

"A handsome bull." She moved closer in that subtle way women had of shifting without being visible about it. "A doting and lovable bull, one who keeps me quite pleased with him, usually."

"Such flattery will have me locking that door, Esther Windham." A quarter century had passed since they'd needed any locked doors in the middle of the day, but mistletoe was showing up all over the house, and standards had to be maintained if his duchess was to be kept smiling a particular smile.

She cocked her head, the beginnings of that smile lurking at the corners of her mouth. "About Louisa."

His Grace understood priorities, for they were the heart and soul of bearing a lofty title. Comforting his duchess involved more than just flirting with her. He slipped an arm around her waist, the better to allow her head to rest on his shoulder.

"About our dear Louisa," His Grace said, pressing a kiss to his duchess's brow. "As pretty a young lady as ever sipped the punch at Almack's. She is worrying you, and thus I must be worried, as well."

"I have grasped her reasoning, I think, but you must tell me your thoughts. I believe, as the oldest unmarried daughter, she thinks to remain at Morelands so as not to overshadow her younger sisters."

His Grace stroked a hand over his wife's wheat-gold hair while he considered her theory. He was careful not to disturb her coiffure—a man married to a duchess learned the knack of such things.

"Your thinking is logical, and Louisa is logical. There are still many people who believe daughters ought to marry in birth order or not at all. I will say again that Louisa should have been a cavalry officer. She has the gallantry for it and the excellent seat."

"Also the outspoken opinions and tendency to take charge of matters outside her authority."

"You can't blame the girl if she takes after her mama in some regards."

Esther sat forward and aimed a glare at him, until he smiled at her ruffled feathers. She smiled too and subsided against him. "Shameless man, and you a duke."

"Also a father. Have you spoken to Louisa about her wayward notions? She cannot be allowed to give up so soon, Esther. Young men are blockheads. This is known to all save young men themselves, and Louisa is not one to tolerate blockheadedness from any quarter."

"Percival, what if Louisa is right?"

The little note of despair in his duchess's voice sent alarm skittering through His Grace's vitals. "Right? To give up the chase after what, only three Seasons? That is rot, utter tripe, Esther, to think—"

She put her fingers to his lips, giving him the scent of roses and the sensation of soft, soft skin against his mouth. "Six Seasons, Percival. Six Seasons, which means for five Seasons she's had to stand around with her empty dance card, secure in the knowledge she has not taken, convincing herself all the while that it's her fault her sisters have not married."

Her Grace was being reasonable. She was at her most dangerous when she was being reasonable.

"Maggie was past thirty when she married, my love. Men are idiots, is the trouble. We need time to mature beyond the screaming demands of our base natures, to appreciate a woman's—"

He fell silent. He'd been such an idiot, and only by the grace of a merciful God and the cleverness of his dear duchess had he been spared the marriage from hell.

"I don't want to give up on her either, Percival, for Louisa has a soft heart and would make a wonderful wife and mother, but to see her tortured, Season after Season…"

Tortured. Tortured was not a word a father liked to hear regarding any of his offspring, but most especially not his pretty, proud, and—facing facts was also part of being a duke—sometimes blunt-to-a-fault daughter.

"She dances well." He needed to defend Louisa, even to her mother.

"With the few who ask her."

"She's fluent in any number of languages."

"So why hasn't she singled out some diplomat? They tend to be from good families, and we've certainly seen enough of them underfoot in recent years."

"She's very well read."

"Appallingly so, some would say."

"She understands mathematics better than any Oxford don."

"Percival, that is hardly an attribute that will secure her a happy future."

His Grace rose from the sofa, needing to pace in the face of such honesty. "It isn't Louisa's fault she's got a brain. It isn't her fault she isn't dainty and blond and simpering. You never simpered, Esther, and no woman of your magnificent height could be called dainty."

Refined, yes—Her Grace managed that easily—but she was not dainty.

"I never asked Lord Hubert if I might try a puff of his cigar, either."

"Hubert is eighty if he's a day. How else is a young lady to flatter and flirt with such a curmudgeon?" Except old Hubert in his cups had a puerile turn of mind, and a puff of his cigar had—several brandies later—turned into a much more prurient innuendo. His Grace shuddered to recall the quiet talk he'd had with the man in the sober light of day.

Her Grace arranged her skirts in a sniffy sort of way. "I never threatened to get my curricle to Brighton in record time, arguing that a woman's lighter frame would give her an advantage of weight not enjoyed by the overfed dandies of the Carlton House set."

"She didn't mean to insult the Regent." And thank God the Regent remained too convinced of his own dashing good form to take it that way.

"Percy, in six years, the young men have not learned to appreciate Louisa, but it's also true that she hasn't moderated her ways much at all."

"She should not have to." He resumed his seat beside his wife. "She is brave, she's intelligent, she's loyal as hell—witness this sacrifice she's trying to make for her sisters. We must find her a fellow, Esther."

The duchess's brows rose, indicating that His Grace had leapt to a different conclusion than his wife had been leading him to. His Grace's gratification was probably akin to what the fox felt when twenty couple hounds went off baying at the top of their lungs after some deer or rabbit.

Her Grace did not take his hand or put her head on his shoulder. "I was thinking more in terms of allowing her to stay with Sophie and Sindal for a bit, or perhaps excusing her from next spring's Season entirely."

"It might come to that, but first, let's investigate the other options, shall we?"

He poured his wife a steaming cup of tea, prepared it exactly to her liking, and passed it to her without pouring one for himself. "We will find her a fellow among those in Town anticipating the holiday season. We must simply apply ourselves. There's plenty enough to choose from—how hard can it be to find one bridegroom between now and Christmas?"

Three

"MAMA ASKED ME A CURIOUS QUESTION WHEN WE were in the park yesterday." Eve was swaying slightly in time with the orchestra as she spoke. "A question about you."

Louisa wanted to sway—she wanted to be out on the dance floor twirling down the room, and in just a few minutes she would be, provided Lionel didn't forget his commitment.

"What sort of question?"

"She asked if you were partial to Mannering or any particular young men."

Louisa resisted the urge to glower at her youngest sister. Shrieking in a crowded ballroom *would not do*. "What did you say?"

Eve's expression was sympathetic. "I said I needed time to consider my answer. What do you want me to say?"

Relief washed through Louisa, and gratitude. Siblings were the best kinds of friends to have. "Tell her I'm considering joining a nunnery, except I can't find one where dancing is permitted."

"Louisa, this is serious."

It was. It was an indication that Her Grace, in the Windham parental tradition, was going to indulge a propensity for meddling. "I will go visit St. Just up in the West Riding."

"There are bachelors in the West Riding, Sister. And long, cold winters."

And St. Just, converted like their other brothers to a firm belief in connubial joy, would offer Louisa questionable sanctuary.

"Tell them… Merciful heavens, Eve, do you suppose they're looking for a list?" Louisa dropped her voice as the music came to an end. She saw Lord Lionel detach himself from his fellows near the door to the card room and start to cross the room.

"A list might not be a bad idea. Two lists, one of possibles and one of impossibles."

"They're all impossible." They were impossible as long as evidence of Louisa's youthful folly was at large for all to stumble upon. Visions of a small, red leather-bound book evaporated from Louisa's mind to be replaced by the reality of Lionel approaching in a lavender-and-gold evening ensemble.

Amethysts, Louisa guessed. Lord Lionel would be wearing amethysts tonight.

"Tomorrow morning," Eve said quietly, "we'll gather in the library to see what might be done. I'll alert Jenny."

"While I, for once, enjoy the supper waltz with a handsome swain." Surely she was entitled to that much diversion?

Eve said nothing while Lord Lionel cut through the dancers leaving the floor, looking like a swan among ducks. His height, his dazzling attire, his aristocratic good looks... Louisa let herself stare at the male pulchritude approaching, let herself enjoy for just a moment that all the other girls were watching as Lord Lionel bowed over Louisa's hand.

Too bad his charm, like his jewelry, was more appearance than substance.

"My Lady Louisa. Lady Eve. I believe my dance ensues momentarily."

"The honor will be entirely mine."

Louisa put her hand over his knuckles, noting that he had, indeed, chosen amethysts to adorn his outfit. An amethyst and gold pin for his lacy cravat, amethyst sleeve buttons, and, if she wasn't mistaken, his watch fob sported a small procession of amethysts along a delicate gold chain.

He bowed, she curtsied, the introduction sounded, and then she was in his arms.

"You wear the rose colors exceedingly well, my lady." Lionel's originality was limited to his wardrobe, for as many men did, he lowered his lashes as if gazing into Louisa's eyes, when Louisa could see he was, in fact, darting glances at her décolletage. "And they go with my own choices tonight very nicely."

Was he complimenting her or himself?

"A pig in a ball gown would look ravishing on your arm, my lord." He blinked, leaving Louisa to suspect her rejoinder hadn't been exactly smooth. Before she could muster any words to repair the damage, the music started.

Lord Lionel was a masterful dancer. He moved decisively; he didn't leave a woman to wonder who was in charge of matters. As they moved down the room, Louisa told herself she ought to like that about him.

He was also tall enough to partner her, and he wasn't afraid to wear amethysts—or faux amethysts. As she one-two-three'd in his arms, Louisa realized that in Lord Lionel, she might have the start of a list of men she might flirt with to appease her parents.

Except, she wasn't precisely certain *how* to flirt.

And this close, Lionel savored rather strongly of cigar smoke overlaid—not too pungently, thank heavens—with both the scent of manly exertion and the scent of patchouli.

Patchouli was not a fragrance Louisa cared for.

She tried to imagine marital intimacies with a man who wore patchouli and concluded it was fortunate she would not be taking a husband. Scents tended to concentrate in the dark.

"I've been looking forward to this dance all evening, my lady, and to having your company in the hour that follows."

"As have I. You've been lurking in the card room, which I'm certain has been a disappointment to every young lady present."

Surely that was an acceptable response? He smiled down at her, or at her bosom. "Gathering my courage, some of it Dutch."

He twirled her under his arm—the scent of exertion being a tad stronger as she passed close to him—and brought her back to waltz position. "Will you be in Town until Christmas, my lady?"

"Not quite that long. Yourself?" And was he, or

was he not, holding her a shade closer than he had been earlier?

"That depends."

Something in his eyes changed, became cooler or hotter—Louisa couldn't discern which. Perhaps Lord Lionel had gas. "Depends on?"

"The company to be had, for one."

Another turn under his arm, and Louisa was wishing the dance would end. "Good company is always a blessing."

"Indeed, it is." His response was inane, but he offered it as if his words were imbued with meaning and resonance, with portents and promises.

When the dance was over and they had filed through the interminably long buffet line, Louisa was aware that being in company with Lord Lionel was an effort, the same as being in company with every other young man of her acquaintance. It was particularly an effort when it earned her the disbelieving looks of women five years her junior.

Then too, there were looks from women five years her senior that were…pitying.

So many looks, which aided neither Louisa's digestion nor her attempts at conversation.

While Lord Lionel ate his supper—he had a peculiar tendency to gaze at her while he licked his fingers slowly between bites—Louisa consumed her food, as well. Every once in a while, she'd look up to find her companion studying her. By the time they'd parted at the end of the meal, she'd found a word to describe the *looks* he'd been giving her.

It wasn't a nice word, but Louisa respected words

when they rang with truth, and the word that came to mind as she considered the way Lord Lionel had looked at her was not "possessive" or "speculative" or even "considering."

The word that would not leave her mind was "covetous." The way he'd regarded her had been covetous.

❧

"Thank God that's over." Lionel slumped into a chair in a corner of the men's card room. "Hardest bit of work I've done since bringing off Lady Ponsonby three times in the same evening."

A few of the older fellows at nearby tables scowled at that bit of indiscretion, but they'd likely done the same yeoman labor themselves, Lady P being of a demanding and inconstant—if charmingly licentious—nature.

"Hear, hear." Grattingly lifted a glass, which Lionel snatched from his hand.

"My thanks." Lionel took a deep drink of Grattingly's brandy—dancing with Louisa Windham was thirsty work. "There should be a medal awarded for any man with the stamina to both waltz *and* dine with a woman who lacks conversation, a sense of humor, and the ability to let her partner lead her down the room."

A chair scraped, and Elijah Harrison emerged from a gloomy corner. He nodded coolly at Lionel and left the room.

"Encroaching toad." Grattingly muttered this observation then looked about as if to canvass the surrounds for seconds. Hearing none, he cleared his throat. "Though I must say, Honiton, you make a damned impressive pair with Lady Louisa. The girl moves nicely."

Lionel smiled. "If she moves so nicely, why am I one of the few to dance with her, particularly when it comes to the waltz?"

He took another sip of brandy—it was free, after all—and wondered if he could tolerate a lifetime of Louisa Windham's hesitant smiles and awkward conversation. Harrison's recent accusation, that Lionel had singled out the Windham daughters as marital prospects, came to mind.

Lionel was in truth trolling for any prospects, any prospects at all that would clear his debts, muzzle his parents, and get his older brothers off his back. The Windham sisters were certainly suitable for a marquis's son, but suitable and desirable were worlds apart.

"The other two sisters are prettier," Lionel observed, taking another swallow of brandy.

"They ain't such bluestockings, either," Grattingly said. "They're golden and cheery and don't spout the Bard at a fellow when he's trying to flirt his way through a dance."

"Yes, but Lady Genevieve is intolerably sweet, the milk of human kindness oozing from her every word. I'd run screaming from her in less than a year, lest she expect me to visit orphanages or some such rot. A man would be lucky to swive her once a week in the dark while she recited Paternosters in his ear."

Grattingly guffawed obligingly, though it was nothing more than the truth. "The little one might make a nice armful, and she's friendly."

Lady Eve Windham was a pretty, lively little

thing, who could often be seen taking pity on pudgy, aging university boys like Grattingly or impoverished younger sons.

"One hears Lady Eve was invalided some years back," Lionel said, finishing his—Grattingly's—drink. "Though the nature of her indisposition remains a mystery. An invalid wife is a curse not to be contemplated, regardless of how robust her curves are at present, particularly if her little indisposition is sporting about on some ducal property in the shires."

"Hadn't heard about that," Grattingly said. Lionel watched while the man's gaze settled on the Windham sisters standing like three goddesses outside the card room door. They were pretty enough, well dowered enough, wellborn enough that all three ought to have been snatched up years ago.

If Lionel had to marry Louisa Windham, then he supposed he could simply gag her when it came time for the marital intimacies. Gag her and blindfold himself—stranger things had been done in the name of securing a succession—or staying out of the sponging house.

"More brandy, Grattingly." He shoved the empty glass at the fellow, who scampered off in the direction of the sideboard. When Grattingly moved, Lionel could see another man who'd been sharing Harrison's poorly lit corner.

Joseph Carrington sat with his leg propped on a stool, rubbing at his thigh with both hands. In the low light, the poor bastard's features had a fiendish cast, all darkness and shadows, almost as if his injury were making him furious.

Perhaps it was. Carrington limped his way through life and would likely never know the pleasure of being able to bamboozle a well-dowered woman to the altar just by waltzing her down the room.

The Duke of Moreland had a conspiratorial streak, one his daughters shamelessly exploited. He loved his political machinations, loved his plotting and scheming in the halls of Westminster, loved pulling strings to make the Lords dance to his tune without him being identified as the piper.

So when he went riding in the park of a morning, he was only too happy to extend his escort to both Louisa and Jenny, provided a groom was brought along, as well.

His Grace drew up under an oak that was still shedding the occasional reddish-brown leaf. "There's young Mannering, out in last night's attire. Not well done. Ladies, you will forgive me if I ride on and spare you an introduction?"

Louisa spoke for both herself and Jenny. "Ride ahead, Your Grace. Jenny and I will take a turn on the Lady's Mile."

The duke saluted with his crop and cantered off, leaving Jenny and Louisa to exchange a smile.

"He's introduced us to any number of young swells still half-seas over from last night's carousing," Jenny observed. "What do you suppose he wants to whisper in Lord Mannering's ear?"

"Maybe he just wants to give us a chance to gallop with only a groom in tow," Louisa said, "and I intend to take him up on it."

She tapped her horse stoutly with her heel and set off toward the Serpentine. Jenny fell in beside her, and when they reached the stretch beside the water, they raced their mounts at a pounding gallop for a few hundred yards before coming back to the walk.

"A good gallop is not enough," Louisa said, patting her gelding stoutly, "but it's better than nothing."

"Especially when the days start growing shorter," Jenny said. "And the mornings can be so very brisk. Who is on that black over there?" A big black horse was passaging its way along a path through the trees ahead, the rider a picture of relaxed elegance.

"I believe that's Sir Joseph. I wasn't sure he'd bestir himself to come up to Town with Christmas right around the corner." Louisa watched for a few more moments while Sir Joseph collected the horse into the more difficult trot-in-place known as piaffe.

"They're quite an accomplished pair."

"Good God." Louisa fell silent as the horse shifted into a controlled rear, a slow rebalancing of its weight down, down onto its haunches until the front end lifted and balanced in a breathtaking display of strength and control.

"Can St. Just teach his horses to do that?" Jenny asked in subdued tones. "I don't even know what it's called."

"That is a pesade," Louisa said, "and no, St. Just's horses can't do it because they're too young to have the requisite strength—and our brother likely lacks the patience to teach the maneuver."

"It's very difficult?"

"I suspect it takes years."

The horse dropped from its impressive pose, and

Carrington thumped the beast on the neck with a gloved hand. Jenny applauded, which had Carrington's head coming up and his gaze slewing around.

"My ladies, I wasn't aware we had an audience. Good morning."

Sir Joseph's voice always took Louisa aback, the rasp of it, the lack of smoothness. One could not forget that voice, try though one might.

"Sir Joseph, good morning," Louisa replied. "My compliments to your horse. That's the same one you had at the Christmas meet, isn't it?"

"The selfsame. Sonnet, say good morning to the ladies." The horse tucked a foreleg back and bowed his glossy head without any visible cue from the rider.

Jenny's smile could not have been brighter. "How marvelous! Louisa, we must expand your list to include Sonnet. He's tall, dark, and handsome, and possessed of both good manners and the ability to dance."

"A list?" Sir Joseph petted his horse again, but this time it seemed to Louisa to be more of a caress down the gelding's crest. "Are you looking for a new mount, Lady Louisa?"

Jenny snorted, the wretch, then turned it into a coughing fit.

"I am not. *Genevieve*, we've had our gallop, so why don't you rescue His Grace from Lord Mannering? I'll catch up in a moment."

Jenny went docilely enough—Mannering was likely in need of rescuing from one of His Grace's harangues about the dignity of the yeomanry—but at a gesture from Louisa, Jenny also took the groom with her.

Sir Joseph watched her canter off, his expression

unreadable. "Mannering is in want of a wife." He did not sound pleased about this.

"How can you know such a thing?"

"Men gossip," Sir Joseph muttered darkly. "And our gossip is worse than women's gossip because we do not limit ourselves to scandal broth. We must exchange our *on-dits* over brandy, port, and worse."

Scandal broth—a cup of tea by any other name. "Shall we walk the horses in the direction of His Grace's last known whereabouts?"

"As my lady wishes."

Louisa turned her gelding to amble along beside Sir Joseph's, wondering as she did why His Grace would be accosting a young man admittedly in need of a wife. "Why would Mannering bruit his marital intentions about in the clubs?"

"Because he, like most men of his age and ilk, permits himself to become a trifle disguised of a night." Sir Joseph's gaze fixed on his horse's mane. "It's said his mother will not permit him sufficient funds to afford the usual Town amusements. So he's willing to marry, at which time he'll have a larger allowance and at least the attentions of a new wife to divert him."

"What you mean," Louisa said slowly, "is that he can't afford a mistress."

Sir Joseph's lips pursed as the horses crunched dry leaves underfoot, and a sad, sinking feeling stole through Louisa's bones. The holidays were a sentimental time, was the trouble. Her melancholia had nothing to do with her unmarried state and the caliber of fiancé her parents might be fruitlessly recruiting for her.

"Shall I answer honestly, Lady Louisa?"

"If you do, perhaps you might call me simply Louisa. I should not have broached the topic of Mannering's personal life."

He didn't ask her to explain why she'd offer such a familiarity, perhaps because he understood no amount of formality would obliterate the blatant curiosity of her question. The desperation of it.

"Tell me about this list your sister alluded to."

"Must I?"

"No." He steered his horse around a rut in the path. "I think I can guess. You're tiring of the whole ruddy business and ready to give up."

She could laugh and dismiss his surmise, tease him about his own situation, change the subject altogether.

Or she could meet honesty with honesty. "Blunt speaking, sir. You're not wrong. I'm trying to convince my family to allow me to retire from the field so my sisters can shop for husbands in earnest." *Convince* was a polite description of inchoate begging, though Louisa would beg if it improved her sisters' chances of finding mates.

"But your doting parents are determined to continue the siege, aren't they?"

There was no judgment in his tone. If anything, he sounded like he was commiserating, despite the fact that his lips were compressed into a flat line again.

"I think they're wavering." At long last, they seemed to be wavering—though His Grace's tête-à-tête with Mannering did not bode well.

Sir Joseph said nothing, which gave Louisa a chance to study him in sidelong glances. His expression was serious, though not a scowl. As Louisa's horse shied half-heartedly at a small puddle, she noticed that Sir Joseph's mouth was more full than she'd pictured it, his lips shaped into a male version of the classically graceful bow.

How lovely. An attractive mouth on a growling man.

"What would make it better, Lady Louisa? What would give you the resolve not to compromise, not to let weariness guide you to a choice you might regret?"

Lady Louisa. He was not going to trespass on the strength of her casual invitation, and—worse luck—he was not going to turn the subject or pretend he saw an acquaintance he must speak to on some distant path. Unflinching courage was an overrated commodity.

"One hardly knows what might make it more bearable. Do I detect a similar weariness on your part, Sir Joseph?"

"Perhaps, but I also have children to consider, and that helps."

She eyed him curiously. "Does that mean you can hold your nose and point to a potential wife with an adequate dowry?" And what sort of wife would he point to?

Those full lips quirked. "To the contrary. It means I cannot make a cavalier choice regardless of how disenchanted I might be with the whole business."

"Disenchanted." She tasted the word and found it…sadly appropriate. "Not all the young men are disenchanting."

"I suppose not, nor are all the young ladies, but the process itself is still unappealing on some level."

They'd reached the point where His Grace had separated from his daughters, and there was no sign of the duke. "Papa has gone off somewhere. If we can't find him, I'll simply make my own way home."

"Not without an escort, Louisa Windham."

Now he used her given name, now when his tone was as stern and uncompromising as the duke's when discussing the Regent's financial excesses. "I did not mean to imply I'd go anywhere in Town without a proper escort. What do you know of Lord Lionel Honiton?"

She lobbed the question at him in retaliation for his peremptory tone, also because he'd give her an honest answer.

"I know he's vain as a peacock, but other than that, probably no more given to vice than most of his confreres." This was said with such studied detachment, Louisa's curiosity was piqued.

"Many young men are vain. Lionel is an attractive man."

"Perhaps, but you are equally attractive, Louisa Windham, more attractive because you neither drape yourself in jewels nor flaunt your attributes with cosmetics, and I don't see you lording it over the ladies less endowed than you are."

He was presuming to scold her, and yet Louisa couldn't help feeling a backhanded sort of pleasure at the implied compliment. "Beauty fades," Louisa said. "All beauty. If Lord Lionel is vain, time will see him disabused of his beauty soon enough." Unbidden, the memory of Sir Joseph reciting Shakespeare came to Louisa's mind: "That time of year thou mayst in me behold, when yellow leaves, or none, or few do hang on boughs which shake against the cold…"

"So it will." Sir Joseph held back a branch for Louisa to pass. "While yours will never desert you."

"Are you attempting flattery before breakfast, Sir Joseph?"

His lips quirked up at her question, a fleeting, blink-and-she'd-miss-it suggestion of humor. "I am constitutionally incapable of flattery. You are honest, Louisa Windham, loyal to your family, and possessed of sufficient courage to endure many more social Seasons than I've weathered. To a man who understands what matters most, those attributes grow not less attractive over time, but more. Will I see you out riding again some morning?"

Now he was changing the subject, after calling her brave, loyal, and honest. He'd told the truth, as well—he had no talent for flattery. None whatsoever.

"I take it you prefer to ride early in the day?"

"Of course. The fashionable hour provides no real opportunity for exercise, and the Sunday church parade is even worse. Then too, there's something to be said for showing old Londontowne at her best, for seeing it when 'all that mighty heart is lying still.'"

She cocked her head. "Is that Coleridge?"

"Wordsworth. 'Composed upon Westminster Bridge.' It makes a pastoral study of even a dank and teeming metropolis, so great is the poet's ability in that regard."

A line of poetry for Louisa was like a shiny lure to a raven, even a line casually tossed off by Sir Joseph Carrington. Maybe especially a line from him. "I don't think I know this poem, and I'm more than passingly familiar with Wordsworth."

While Sir Joseph sat on his black horse, the leaves

shifting quietly against the frozen earth, and sunlight glittering on the Serpentine, he recited for Louisa a sonnet. The poem he gave her described a fresh, sparkling morning in London as something beautiful and precious, even to a man in love with nature and the unspoiled countryside.

When Sir Joseph fell silent, Louisa felt as if the hush of a great city at dawn enveloped them, and in the ensuing beats of quiet, she realized three things.

First, Joseph Carrington's voice was made for poetry. Like a violoncello switching from lowly scales and droning exercises to solo repertoire, when he put his voice to poetry, Sir Joseph spoke lyrically, even beautifully.

The second thing she noticed was an inconvenient and utterly *stupid* urge to cry. Not because the beauty of the spoken word moved her to tears—though occasionally it could—and not because the poem itself was so very lovely. It was a short, pretty sonnet about a single impression of the city gained on a clear autumn morning.

Louisa's ill-timed lachrymose impulse was the result of the third realization: no man had ever recited an entire sonnet to her before, and likely no man ever would again.

❧

Sir Joseph waved the grooms away, muttering the same thing he always muttered at well-intended stable lads, the first thing his commanding officer had taught him on the Peninsula. "A cavalryman looks after his own mount."

The grooms went off to tend to the myriad chores no doubt piling up elsewhere on the pretty little property gracing a corner of bucolic Surrey.

"You will get coal in your stocking for Christmas," Sir Joseph groused at his horse. "You allowed me to sit there, blathering to a woman—a *lady*—about domes and ships and whatnot. When a man recites poetry to a beautiful, intelligent woman, he ought at least to be mentioning roses."

He ran his stirrup irons up the leathers, loosened the girth, and glowered at his horse. "Stand, while I try to find a headstall of sufficient size for that empty noggin of yours. Daffodils would have been an improvement—daffodils and lonely clouds."

He stalked off, finding the halter on its customary hook while Sonnet stood, docile as a lamb in the barn aisle.

"Lambs wouldn't have gone amiss either, though nobody reads Blake except eccentrics."

The horse lowered its head and started rubbing against Sir Joseph's jacket. After a few moments of this, Joseph stepped back. "Filthy beast. I'll smell like horse for the rest of the day."

And that had been part of the problem. Sitting there beside the Serpentine, the early morning light finding coppery highlights in Louisa Windham's dark hair, Joseph had caught a whiff of her citrus-and-clove scent. Even a brief poem had allowed him a few moments to wallow in that unusual, Christmassy fragrance.

"She tolerated my recitation," he said, undoing the gelding's bridle. "At least it was a short poem about towers and theatres."

Sonnet tried to rub again, this time against Sir Joseph's hip.

"Wretched animal, are you trying to knock me on my backside?" He scratched behind the horse's ear, which only served as a reminder of Lady Opie. "She would not have cared what poem was read to her."

Provided she got her slops.

Louisa Windham looked to Sir Joseph like a woman who also enjoyed her victuals. She was...curved. Very nicely curved. Sir Joseph leaned his forehead on the horse's neck.

"I am in a sad case, horse, when I am comparing a lady, a duke's daughter, a woman far above the touch of a common soldier, to my favorite breeding sow."

Sonnet gave a lazy swish of a long black tail.

"You're gelded." Sir Joseph straightened and smoothed a hand down the animal's shoulder. "You are spared untimely lapses into poetry as a result. I'm not ready to make the same trade—yet."

Though watching Louisa Windham sit her horse, as winsome and pretty as the winter day itself, Sir Joseph had experienced a confluence of pleasure and pain as acute as any to befall him. She was so lovely, so unconsciously graceful and unaffected, and while simply *beholding* her was a pleasure, parting from her, and knowing he would always part from her, was the opposite of pleasure.

"Sorrow, perhaps." He considered his nigh-somnolent horse. "A bit dramatic but not inaccurate."

The horse did not argue, not while Sir Joseph removed the rest of the tack, not while he groomed the animal, and certainly not when he led the beast to a stall bedded with fluffy straw.

"I expect I will tarry here most of the day," Sir Joseph said, slipping off Sonnet's halter. "Gorge yourself on hay, have a nice lie down. My leg is telling me we're in for snow, so say a prayer I can get my poetry-spouting self back to Town before the worst of it."

Sir Joseph gave the horse one last behind-the-ear scratching, closed the stall door, and limped off to hang up the halter. It did not bode well when a man was complaining to a horse that he missed a pig.

Not well at all.

Sir Joseph was still pondering this unhappy state of affairs when he walked into the kitchen at the back of the big, three-story manor house in the Surrey countryside.

He'd tarried too long in the barn, and now it was mealtime. A dozen chairs scraped back; a dozen pairs of feet made a soft thunder on the plank flooring. A dozen high, happy voices were raised to the rafters.

"It's Papa! Papa is here at last!"

Sir Joseph was swarmed with fierce embraces; with little fingers grabbing at him, at his clothes, at his hands; and with the good, wholesome scents of well-cared-for children: soap, starch, lavender, a breath of chocolaty warmth where little Ariadne clung to his neck.

He extricated himself carefully from all save Ariadne's grasp—she being the youngest could also be the most tenacious—and tried not to compare the pleasures of citrus and clove to the satisfaction of seeing once again that his children were safe, happy, and well cared for.

Four

"WE HAVE SOME MORE NAMES," EVE WHISPERED AS Louisa pretended to look over a selection of silk handkerchiefs with elaborately embroidered borders. "Tonight after supper, we'll regale you with them, and for once you'll keep your nose out of your books, Lou, and pay attention."

Paying attention to Eve and Jenny's almighty list was proving difficult when Louisa kept hearing instead Wordsworth recited in Sir Joseph Carrington's gravelly baritone. Not a grating voice, but a substantial, definitively masculine voice when engaged in the recitation of poetry. How would Sir Joseph deliver Blake?

"And because I am happy and dance and sing,
They think they have done me no injury…"

"Louisa." Jenny spoke a trifle sternly. "For eleven more days you can at least pretend to take an interest in your own future."

"Eleven days or two hundred sixty-four hours. Also approximately sixteen thousand minutes," Louisa said absently, running her hand over a bright red silk offering with white snowflakes dancing around its edges. *Fifteen thousand eight hundred forty minutes, to be exact.*

"Put like that," Jenny said, wrinkling her nose, "it does sound like an eternity."

Nine hundred fifty thousand four hundred seconds sounded more like an eternity. Louisa's gaze fell on another of the gift shop's offerings, and for a moment, her heart sped up. The volume was the right size, and the leather was the right shade of red, but the little book sported a thin line of gold trim. When Louisa inspected the pages, she found them blank.

"A journal," said a familiar baritone. "Though if I buy one for Fleur, then I must buy another for Amanda, and God forbid I should give Amanda one in a color favored by Fleur or conversely."

Sir Joseph, ruddy cheeked and scowling, regarded the volume in Louisa's hand. A sense of relief coursed through her at the sight of him, incongruous though he appeared in a crowded shop near Piccadilly.

"Good morning, Sir Joseph. Do I take it you're searching for Christmas presents for your daughters?"

He ran an ungloved hand through his hair and glanced around warily. "I've left it too late. They've been good, both of them, within reason. Their governess thinks I spoil them, but they're only children, and they try hard, like recruits new to their posts. A token at Christmas is appropriate, or several tokens, for encouragement. Then too, they will draw me pictures and write me verses, and one doesn't want—Louisa Windham, are you laughing at me?"

She set aside the diary and slipped an arm through his rather than indulge in the absurd impulse to hug him in all his paternal exasperation. "You remind me of His Grace. When I was a girl, he made a cavalry expedition of even a family picnic. We'd mount up at his signal and trot along until he gave the command to charge. I had great fun trying to keep up with my brothers. Now tell me about your daughters."

"They are…" He glanced around again. "Your sisters are motioning to you from the door."

"Bother my sisters." Louisa let Sir Joseph escort her to the door, where to her surprise, she found that Jenny and Eve had a sudden pressing need to nip over to Berkeley Square and drop in at Gunter's, and *nothing* would do but Sir Joseph must join them.

He acquiesced like a man grateful for an excuse to abandon his shopping efforts, and yet, as luck—or a pair of meddling sisters—would have it, Eve and Jenny linked arms and sailed ahead, leaving Louisa to take Sir Joseph's arm and bring up the rear, with the footman and the maid trailing along at a distance.

His limp didn't slow him down, nor did he appear self-conscious about it. He steered Louisa through the throngs of shoppers, which parted for him as if he were Moses dispatching the Red Sea.

"It smells to me like snow," Louisa murmured. The air had a crispness, a sense of tidings in the wind.

Sir Joseph glanced at her as they approach the slightly less crowded environs of Berkeley Square. "That is the scent of coal smoke, Louisa Windham. One is cautioned not to inhale it too deeply."

He leaned nearer to open the door for her, his proximity bringing to Louisa's nose a scent that was anything but coal smoke. Cedar and spice, redolent of Christmas and of…Sir Joseph. The fragrance was pleasant but also…comforting. His daughters would know him by that scent, just as Louisa knew her father's bay rum.

And as yet more luck—or the same two sisters—would have it, Gunter's was enjoying enough custom that no two tables were available side by side, such as would accommodate four patrons together. Eve and Jenny chose a spot near the window, leaving Louisa to take a corner table a few feet away with Joseph.

He seated Louisa with as much decorum as a bustling eatery would allow, then got settled across from her by virtue of bracing himself on the table and lowering himself by inches to the seat.

"It pains you," Louisa observed, then regretted the words at the grimace they provoked.

"To be the object of pity pains me, but you were referring to my leg, weren't you?"

While she cast around for something to say, Louisa had cause to mentally wonder at her sisters' motives. Here she was, stranded for the duration in the company of an eligible if somewhat abrupt gentleman, and every notion of how to converse with him had deserted her.

"I did not mean to call attention again… That is… I wasn't trying…" Louisa fell silent as heat climbed from her neck to her cheeks.

Sir Joseph smiled at her, an expression of breathtaking benevolence that rendered him not simply handsome but also…somehow *dear*.

"Spare yourself the apology, Louisa Windham. I limp, and I am happy to limp. Were it not for your brothers' intervention, the field surgeon would have relieved me of a limb that was merely in want of stitches, the bone-setter, and rest. Now, shall we drop that unappetizing topic and take up the challenge of Christmas gifts for my daughters?"

"Yes, please. Tell me about Fleur and Amanda."

As they devoured a pair of lavender ices and a plate of warm plum tarts, Louisa found herself entranced at her first discussion with a man not of her family about his offspring. Her brothers would speak of their children, Uncle Tony doted on his daughters, her father bragged on his progeny incessantly, but Sir Joseph *fretted* over these two very young ladies.

"They are already females," he said as the waiter cleared the plates. "Almost from infancy, they had female minds and female ways. A fellow who has no sisters and little memory of his mother finds himself…daunted."

Men in Louisa's family did not speak of being daunted, not to her. "Daunted how?"

Sir Joseph's brows twitched down. "Their little minds are at once devious and innocent. They can be obvious in their emotions and also unfathomable. They are passionate and reserved." He left off tracing the grain of the table's wood with his third finger and glanced up at Louisa. "They are already like you, my lady. They have that fascinating, unknowable quality."

Fascinating? Unknowable? Heat that had nothing to do with embarrassment curled up from Louisa's middle.

"His Grace used to call me his abacus." This admission slipped out as Louisa noticed that Sir Joseph was smiling at her again. There was a wistful tenderness in his smile that made it difficult to draw a full breath.

"You are not an abacus, Louisa Windham. Any man with eyes can deduce that."

He sounded wonderfully sure of his point.

"I *am* an abacus. I can do mathematics in my head." That sounded like bragging, so Louisa tried again. "I can't *not* do mathematics in my head, in fact. If you think of a problem involving numbers, it solves itself in my mind before I can write it down. I can write it down, but that takes longer than arriving at an answer by thinking about it."

He cocked his head, his smile fading. "Were you accused of cheating?"

The question was insightful, also painful. Louisa nodded, while two yards away, Jenny and Eve broke into peals of laughter. "When our governess wanted to punish me, my sisters explained to Their Graces that I'd always been able to do math. My brother Victor staged a demonstration for them, and Papa took to calling me his abacus. I don't think Her Grace approved of the name."

She should not have said that last, though Louisa wasn't sure why.

"He meant it as an endearment, Louisa," Joseph said gently.

"I know." Though it eased something to hear him confirm it. "Promise me you won't refer to Fleur or Amanda as an abacus, though."

"Perish the notion." One more smile for her, and then he was reconnoitering, taking in Eve and Jenny's table and the empty dishes thereon. "Shall I take you ladies home? Your guidance has been most helpful, and your sisters appear to be finished with their ices."

Helpful. The notion was interesting. Not brilliant, not insightfully direct, not statuesque, not any of the backhanded compliments Louisa was accustomed to, but simply helpful.

"We can return by way of Regent Street," Louisa said. "You'll get more ideas by inspecting the shop windows."

"This is a female tactic." Sir Joseph rose awkwardly and seemed to test his balance for a moment. "You call it browsing the shop windows. Wellington called it reconnaissance."

He helped Louisa to her feet and draped her cloak around her shoulders, smoothing the fabric in a brisk stroke of his palms over her shoulders. In the next moment, he was tying the frogs beneath her chin, as if she were…

His. His to look after, as he clearly looked after his daughters, his horse, his pigs. With Sir Joseph frowning as if the knot beneath Louisa's chin must be done just so, she envied those pigs.

When he'd taken a step back and was treating Louisa to a visual inspection, she lifted her chin a half inch. "Will I do, Sir Joseph?"

"Put your gloves on, my lady. Your prophecy has come to pass." He nodded in the direction of the windows then shrugged into his greatcoat.

"My prophecy?"

"It's snowing, Louisa. If I were home, Fleur and Amanda would be clamoring at me to hitch up the sleigh."

He sounded so homesick, Louisa felt her heart lurch. For him, for the daughters he was missing, and for herself. As long as the little red book was still at large in any quantity, an impromptu sweet with a man who did not see her as an abacus was as much a Christmas gift as Louisa could hope for.

&

As Joseph ushered Louisa to the door, Lady Eve and Lady Jenny begged a moment to greet an acquaintance. Fleur and Amanda were forever indulging in the same delay with their friends in the churchyard.

"Come along, Sir Joseph. If we keep moving, Eve and Jenny will eventually catch up. If we stand by all patience and good cheer, they'll gossip forever."

Louisa tucked her arm through his and gave him a smile that suggested they were conspirators of some sort, two united against the general ridiculousness of the season.

"You are willing to watch a grown man dither over dolls, spinning tops, and storybooks, then?"

"Better that than watching my sisters dither over Pamela Canterdink's engagement ring."

Well, of course. He considered navigating streets now both crowded and sporting an inch of snow. He and Louisa might not make very good time, but he was in no hurry to part from his companion.

A duke's daughter was far above his touch, and that was a shame. Fleur and Amanda would adore having Louisa as stepmama.

After sharing this pedestrian little interlude with her, *Joseph* adored her. Adored her earnestness when she applied her imagination to what gifts Fleur and Amanda would enjoy most, adored the hint of vulnerability he'd seen when she revealed Moreland's clumsy sobriquet for her.

Abacus, indeed. Proof positive that a lofty title did not give a man one jot of common sense.

"Joseph, just look!" Louisa paused as they gained the sidewalk, a purely happy smile curving her lips. "A snowfall like this makes everything clean and new. It gladdens the heart, especially right before Christmas."

She had dropped the honorific, calling him simply "Joseph." That gladdened the heart too, as did the sight of her, snowflakes catching on her lashes and brows, a smile lighting her eyes. Joseph tipped his face up and saw a sprig of mistletoe some wag had hung over a signboard. On the square, a seasonal street chorus launched into a jaunty version of Handel's "Hallelujah Chorus."

And that gladdened his heart yet more.

Before common sense or some other overrated commodity could stop him, Joseph brushed his lips to Louisa's cheek, treating himself to a goodly dose of cinnamon, cloves, and female warmth. "Happy Christmas, Louisa Windham."

He stole that Christmas kiss for himself—he'd been an exceedingly good fellow in the previous year— though he expected at least a scolding for his troubles.

"Rascal." Louisa ducked her face and led him off down the street, not the least daunted, bless her. "I'm out of practice. When my brothers were underfoot, no one was safe from their infernal kisses this time of year. They will soon be visiting, and I can assure you by the New Year, you'll have to be much quicker to catch me under the mistletoe."

As scolds went, that one did nothing to quell a male flight of imagination fueled by Joseph's moment of presumption.

"By New Year, my lady, the berries will all have been plucked, and the mistletoe will be cast aside."

They shared a smile, one that put a lovely bow on a lovely unplanned outing, and on the lovely unexpected pleasure of spending time with a woman to whom Joseph, were he not a mere knight, would gladly have offered more than a single holiday kiss.

❦

Esther, Duchess of Moreland, poured a steaming cup for her spouse.

"We're having chocolate this late in the day?" His Grace asked. "Not that I'm complaining, of course."

"You bear up heroically for the occasional spot of tea, Percival, but it's a beastly day out, and I need the benefit of your thoughts on something."

"Hence the chocolate cakes." He did not help himself to any, though as a younger husband, he would have been inhaling them at a great rate, manners be damned.

"And the sandwiches and grapes," Esther added. "Why are you looking at me like that?"

He was smiling at her, a gentle, indulgent smile that even after thirty years of marriage, still made Esther's insides flutter agreeably.

"You are intriguing, my dear, in both senses. You intrigue me, and you are getting up to some intrigue. What is all this sweetness and flattery about? It must be something very wicked if you're taking such pains with it."

"Not wicked. Why aren't you off whispering in Prinny's ear today?"

"Prinny is adept at several things," His Grace replied. He accepted his cup of chocolate and took a sip. "He spends money like a young man with his first pretty mistress—begging your pardon for the analogy, my dear—he indulges his crapulous tendencies like an entire regiment on leave, and he hides a great deal more shrewdness than most give him credit for."

"Which does not answer the question." She put several sandwiches on a plate, as well as a cluster of grapes. "Are you avoiding him?"

"Not a'tall. I'm to see him tomorrow, during which interview I will neither lecture him nor exhort him, nor even rebuke him for all the money he wastes on his infernal pavilions and chefs and art collections. I will not hint at the disgrace that the royal exchequer—what?"

"Pity the man, Percy. He has no son like our Westhaven to set his finances to rights. His daughter and his grandchild are lost to him, his marriage is a national sorrow, and his crown is not even his own. In the ways that count, he has no wealth of any significance."

His Grace's expression changed, wry humor twisting his lips. "A hit, Esther. A very palpable hit. I'm no better at managing funds than Prinny is. You are appealing to my better nature, and I hate it when you do that."

"Eat your sandwiches, Your Grace. I need some fellows to make up the numbers at this week's dinner, possibly next week's, as well."

The ducal maw made quick inroads on the first of three sandwiches. "Two dinners? How many fellows?"

"I'm thinking at least a half-dozen fellows, all

unmarried. I want them to have some political conversation, lest anybody think—"

He put a grape to her lips. She met his gaze and slowly, deliberately, let him feed her a succulent bite of fruit. "You want me to host this week's political dinner, my love—yet another political dinner—while we flaunt some prospects before our daughters. Not a bad gambit, Esther."

His Grace would see it as flaunting prospects before the girls, not the other way around. Esther loved him for it and fed him a grape.

"I can think of any number of promising young MPs who can be here on short notice, Esther, but our girls deserve to aim higher."

"MPs often advance through merit and patronage." Their girls deserved love, loyalty, affection, intelligent company, *and babies*. "Your patronage is sufficient to ensure a young man is looked on favorably by the rest of the polite world."

"More flattery." His Grace reached for a tea cake then hesitated and sat back. Esther put two on a plate and passed it to her husband.

"Honest flattery." While she doled out cakes, he went on to name a dozen young men with acceptable political inclinations from good families.

This was a compromise on their parts. Esther knew it, His Grace knew it, but they did not speak of it. Younger sons rather than heirs with courtesy titles, good families rather than the very best families, political dinners rather than a fancy ball with all the trimmings. People would notice that Moreland was widening the search for husbands for his remaining daughters.

They would notice, but they would not talk. They dared not.

His Grace reached for the last chocolate cake. "If we're going to all this trouble, Esther, add Joseph Carrington's name to your guest list."

"Sir Joseph?" Esther went to pour herself another half cup of chocolate only to find the pot was empty. This happened when she shared her repast with her husband. "Is he in Town?"

"He's making the expected rounds. A well-heeled Knight Commander of the Bath can't comport himself as if he's merely gentry."

"He's hardly political, though, so why are we inviting him? I have the sense Sir Joseph would rather lead a retiring life than be subjected to the social whirl."

"Invite him for two reasons. First, I can talk hounds and horses with him, which accomplishment likely eludes all the tulips and MPs we'll be parading past the girls."

Sound reasoning, though it also pointed out that the young men invited lacked an appreciation for the countryside, which did not bode well for their compatibility with the Windham daughters. "What's the second reason?"

His Grace picked up the last cluster of grapes, tore one off, and offered it to his wife. "Carrington has donated generously to Prinny's little projects from time to time. The more the moneyed class takes on the burden of His Royal Highness's wild starts, the less the government will be expected to do so. Carrington's generosity should be rewarded in the usual way, and if I show Sir Joseph my favor, Prinny is more likely to take notice of the man."

He fed her another grape. Given that Esther had accomplished her goal—enlisting His Grace's support for these social overtures on behalf of their daughters—she refrained from pointing out that quiet, unassuming Joseph Carrington was probably the last man who'd want or appreciate the burden of a title.

She ate the grapes her husband fed her and contemplated the seating arrangements for her dinners.

ॐ

"You have to write back to her." Emmie St. Just—she was the Countess of Rosecroft only when the appellation was unavoidable—plucked the letter from her husband's hands, unhooked the glasses from his ears, and leaned down to kiss him where he reclined against the bed's headboard. When she let him up for air, St. Just expected he looked a little dazed.

"Why can't you write to darling Lou?" He used the end of Emmie's blond braid to dab at her nose as she straddled his lap. "You ladies and your correspondence would put Wellington's intelligence network to shame." Wellington himself had expressed the same sentiment.

"You write to your brothers, you write to some of your fellow officers and your men, you write—" Her breathing hitched while he drew her down against his chest, the better to have this little argument with her. A married man soon learned the knack of a good argument with his spouse. "You write to your parents. Why not write to your sister?"

He kissed her temple, catching a hint of her lavender scent. "I write to my sisters."

Was there anything more gratifying to a man than the telltale little pause before the wife in his arms could muster her list of reasons and persuasions?

"You dash off notes, barely legi—legible. St. Just, I cannot think when you rub my back, and Louisa's situation is important."

"Making my wife comfortable is important too. Why do you think Louisa's situation is serious?" St. Just agreed with his wife, though he couldn't quite say why.

Emmie cuddled closer. "She sounds desperate, St. Just. Battle weary, lonely. I can't imagine it's easy for her to ask for sanctuary with you."

Sanctuary not with him—he was a dubious source of safety for anybody—but with him and his wife and children. That proposition was rock solid. He patted the rounded abundance of his wife's fundament.

"Sanctuary with *us*, though Louisa is the last woman to admit a need for assistance. I've never met a woman so self-sufficient and unsentimental when it comes to matters of the heart."

Though in other matters, Louisa had emphatically enlisted her brothers' assistance. That thought gave St. Just pause.

Emmie heaved a sigh that did nice things for where their bodies were tucked so closely together, though it suggested St. Just's wishes would not prevail on the topic at hand.

"You mistake an abundance of logic for a lack of sentiment, St. Just. Louisa has a very tender heart, and I am worried for her. She hasn't asked to visit us before, and certainly not during the spring Season."

The timing of the request was indeed suspicious. "I'm pleased, in a sense, that she'd turn to us, though that's selfish of me."

Emmie raised her head to regard St. Just with an expression any husband would know meant serious study. "You haven't a selfish bone in your handsome body, St. Just. If you want Louisa to spend the spring with us, if you want her to live with us, then we'll make her welcome."

No argument there. St. Just kissed his wife, because those protective instincts she'd lavished on him to such good effect were so easily extended to his loved ones. "I don't think it's time for Lou to blow full retreat. She just hasn't met the right fellow."

"So you're delaying an answer to her." Emmie folded back down to his chest and drew her nose up along his throat. "I should have realized you have a strategy. I'm going to write to her anyway and extend an invitation for an after the holiday visit."

Spring was months away. An invitation might give Lou something to look forward to, and it might never result in a visit.

"And what about an invitation to me, Emmaline St. Just?" He kissed her cheek then her brow. "I could use a little welcome too, you know. You abandon me for the livelong day, go racketing about with our daughters, leaving a man to doubt you even recall—" He paused in his pouting while Emmie settled a little more snugly onto his body. "That is a charming invitation, Wife. I will consider accepting it."

While she laughed at him softly, St. Just made a mental note to dispatch some orders to Carrington—Sir

Joseph, nowadays—to do a little reconnaissance where Louisa was concerned. If anybody could reconnoiter a situation without being detected, it was Carrington, and the man needed the occasional assignment lest he lapse into a fit of brooding.

Emmie sighed against his neck, a breathy gust of pleasure that made him close his eyes and give thanks for the many blessings of peace. "Em, is there any reason in particular you want some adult female company this spring?" Theirs was a retiring life, focused on their children, their horses, and each other. "Are you lonely?"

He cradled the back of her head against his palm and went still while he waited for an answer.

"I'm not expecting again that I know of, St. Just, if that's what you're asking. Though if you're done with all this chattering, perhaps you'll soon put the lie to my words."

"You'd like that?" He closed his eyes, seeing her once again gravid with their child, rosy, pleased with him and life and all it held. The thought made his throat ache and the breath in his chest seize.

"I would adore another baby, Devlin. Almost as much as I adore you." She spoke softly and ran her hand over his hair in the most gentle of caresses.

"If it's your wish to be expecting again, Em, then perhaps by morning, you shall be."

Five

"SWITCH SEATS WITH ME." LOUISA SMILED AT JENNY, a brilliant, false smile that nearly outshone the crowded formal drawing room's chandeliers.

Jenny smiled back and bent her head as if to whisper some juicy gossip in return. "You want me to sit between Lord Lionel and Mr. Samuels?"

That was part of what Louisa wanted, to see her pretty, blond sister flirting and joking the evening away six seats down the table, lest Louisa have to endure more of Lionel's slumberous gazes. "Please."

Jenny nodded and moved off. Across the room, between sunny smiles at a trio of dazzled young MPs in holiday finery, Eve arched an eyebrow. *What were you two just whispering about, and when will you tell me?*

There would be time for explanations later. Louisa spotted her quarry in a corner, the same corner he'd been in ten minutes ago, and his gaze was still intent upon his drink.

"Sir Joseph." Louisa dimmed her smile when he blinked at her. "A pleasure to see you again."

He did not look pleased. He looked startled and uncomfortable. "Lady Louisa, a pleasure, of course."

She'd heard that voice in her dreams, murmuring poetry while the winter breeze waltzed with dead leaves and the sun sparkled on the Serpentine. "Your Grace, will you excuse Sir Joseph? He's to lead me in to supper."

The duke winked at his guest. "Lucky man. We must speak further, Carrington, regarding that other matter. Louisa." The duke bowed to his daughter and withdrew, not before Louisa caught a slight admonitory glare from her father.

"What other matter, Sir Joseph?"

Her escort's lips quirked as they linked arms. Louisa found herself watching his mouth, waiting for his genuine article smile.

"Swine, livestock, if you want a marginally less vulgar word. Gloucestershire orchard hogs, to be specific, and their commercial viability. Not a fit topic to entertain a lady at dinner."

He ran his free hand through his hair. This same gesture was characteristic of Louisa's brother, the Earl of Westhaven, when that worthy was feeling at a loss and exasperated. Louisa leaned a little closer to her escort.

"I considered you were in need of rescuing. Papa does not understand that most of us, those of us who aren't dukes or duchesses, must comport ourselves according to certain rules. He'll accost you regarding your livestock. He'll ask Summerdale if he's gotten his daughters launched yet. He'll shout halfway down the table about how it's too bad Mr. Trottenham's filly lost in the second race at Newmarket."

Some of the tension eased from Sir Joseph's face.

"I might make a passable duke, then. I have no notion which topics are acceptable, which are beyond the pale, which are tolerable among men but not women… Nobody writes these things down so a fellow can comprehend them when he needs to."

Louisa saw the butler in the corner of the room trying to catch the duchess's eye. "I rather like that you don't know, Sir Joseph."

"You like that I'm ignorant. Are you courting a career as an eccentric, Lady Louisa? I would sooner ride unarmed across all of central Spain with Old Hookey's own orders in my shirt than have to navigate one more ballroom, one more musicale."

"I know." The words slipped out, making Louisa wish she had a drink in her hand. A good stout nip of Sir Joseph's flask would serve nicely. "I mean, I know how you feel. Like the hands of the clock will not move, like your spirit has taken leave of your body and is perched up among the cupids on the ceiling, just waiting, waiting, waiting for the evening to be over. And the next night, it's the same thing, as if Christmas is not a holiday so much as the start of a brief reprieve."

"Is all of London in secret dread of the very social gatherings we're told are not to be missed?" He stood close enough to her that they need not have kept their voices down—close enough that she could catch a whiff of his cedary scent—and she did not move away.

"I have wondered the same thing myself. Shall we line up?"

He put his hand over hers where it rested on his sleeve, a small proprietary gesture that made Louisa think of her parents. She'd been right to extract Sir Joseph from His Grace's clutches. Right to subject Jenny to an evening of Lord Lionel's glittering company.

Two couples ahead, Jenny was simpering and beaming on her escort's arm, her blond beauty suiting his own good looks admirably.

The sight should have left Louisa envious—much more envious than she was. Instead she was hopeful. Jenny liked beautiful objects, and Lionel was certainly that. Perhaps Jenny and Lord Lace might find common ground, and then, who knew what might grow from it?

"Tell me about your horse, Sir Joseph. Did you train him yourself?"

He blew out a breath, no doubt mentally rolling up his sleeves for the ordeal that was dinner conversation. "Sonnet is like a small child with too much cleverness. He must be kept entertained, or he gets up to mischief. The tricks, the haute école, the frequent outings are more in the nature of self-defense for the rider than anything else."

The horse sounded like a debutante with an unfortunately lively turn of mind, and Louisa said as much. She managed to keep the topic going through the soup course, but then the going became more difficult. Their neighbors had apparently decided that Louisa had earned the exclusive pleasure of conversing with Sir Joseph—and he with her—though he showed no inclination to pull his share of the load. Perhaps his dislike for the parliamentary dinner exceeded her own, which hardly seemed possible.

By the third remove, Louisa was growing desperate.

"Have you seen the Regent's Pavilion in Brighton, Sir Joseph?"

The question was potentially awkward—the Regent was a gracious host, but his table sat only thirty, and a lowly knight was not likely to be among the royal guests.

"I have, a year or so ago. It's…" He frowned at his wineglass. A discussion with Sir Joseph was punctuated with these pauses, which meant Louisa had consumed more than her share of wine far too early in the evening. "It's magnificent. Unlike any other architectural experience I could describe, each detail planned to delight and amaze the mortal eye."

"You think an eruption of giant onions on the Brighton beach magnificent?"

In part thanks to a random lull in conversation all around them, and in part due to the incredulity Louisa had allowed into her tone, the comment stood out from the general hubbub at the table.

The lull turned into a sag, then into an outright silence.

"More wine, Lady Louisa?" Sir Joseph gestured with the carafe, and she nodded. He poured for them both, while down the table, Jenny asked Lord Lionel whether topaz or Polish amber was a better complement to her coloring, and at the far end, Her Grace remarked on how pleasant it was to have a few mild days when winter had seemed so determined to advance quickly this year.

Louisa did not drink her wine, nor could she manage another bite of her *côte de boeuf aux oignons glacés*.

"I gather," Sir Joseph said softly, "you do not favor Eastern themes in your architecture, Lady Louisa?"

He spoke casually, as if Louisa hadn't just *done it again*.

"England has lovely architectural styles of her own," she managed. "What need is there for the exotic and at such expense?"

He turned his wine goblet by the stem, the glass looking fragile in his scarred hand. "The exotic, the different, the unusual, can have a beauty all its own."

At the head of the table, His Grace cleared his throat. "So what will you be doing with that filly of yours, Trottenham? If she isn't winning and won't be broken to the bridle, it hardly makes sense to breed her, eh?"

Another laden comment, one that had Louisa's face suffusing with color. Trottenham made some reply, Eve piped up with a quip about the colts trying harder to win when a pretty filly was in the field, and the company obliged her sally with polite laughter.

Louisa considered pleading a headache, but withdrawing from the table would only fuel gossip, and perhaps reflect poorly on Sir Joseph, who did not deserve such censure. She could retreat into silence, though, and so she did.

Something warm covered the hands she'd linked in her lap. Looking down, she saw Sir Joseph's scarred fingers stroking slowly over her knuckles, once, twice. He was unobtrusive about it. The person sitting opposite him and even on his other side would not know he'd made such an overture.

Louisa turned her hand palm up, and for an instant, Sir Joseph linked his fingers with hers and squeezed gently. "*Fortran et haec olim meminisse…*"

"*Juvabit.*" Louisa finished the half-whispered quote.

Aeneas, trying to instill fortitude in his men, suggesting that some day it might cause a smile to recall even moments such as this.

Sir Joseph squeezed her fingers again, the shock of it warring with pleasure. Nobody attempted to offer Louisa comfort or reassurance after one of her social missteps. Her family would rally in their way, but to cover up her mistakes, not to console her for them.

Joseph Carrington, without a single word, offered consolation and understanding. Before Louisa could acknowledge his kindness, the moment was over, his hand gone, and the lovely warmth easing through Louisa's middle her only proof the exchange had occurred.

Though the phrase "unstinting bravery" took on new and inspiring meaning in her mind. Louisa pushed her wineglass a few inches away from her plate.

"Save some room for sweets, Sir Joseph. His Grace favors them, so we're sure to have some delightful treats to finish our meal. I wouldn't be surprised if plum pudding were among the offerings."

If he'd been any other man, he would have made some flattering reply: *Your company is treat enough, Lady Louisa. What could be sweeter than the countenance I behold at this moment?*

Tripe, of course. From Sir Joseph, she didn't think she could tolerate tripe.

"I am very fond of sweets. Are you enjoying the recent weather, my lady? I haven't seen you in the park, and yet the past few mornings have been mild. That dusting of snow was hardly here long enough to count."

Not tripe. Sir Joseph had looked for her in the park,

or at least noted her absence. She recalled the sight of him in the sharp morning light, reciting a lovely poem exclusively for her enjoyment. A man who'd give a woman a poem like that was indeed brave.

Also perceptive. Louisa marshaled her inner resources lest she reach for Sir Joseph's hand. The idea that she could—and that he would understand—was fortification enough. "The weather has been lovely, but it cannot last. I've bet my sisters we'll see snow again before we depart for home."

And then, thank God, would come the holidays and the peace and quiet of a return to the country.

                                     ∽

"I lurk here because I'm a brooding artist who cannot be relied upon to make polite conversation. What's your excuse, Sir Joseph?"

Joseph peered into the gloom shrouding the cushioned chair closer to the potted palms. Elijah Harrison—Lord I-don't-use-the-title—sat looking bored and artistically pale in conservative evening dress.

"I can be relied upon not to make polite conversation, as well," Sir Joseph said. "Though in my case, it's despite efforts to the contrary. Why aren't you off in the shires painting some duke's daughters?"

Harrison's lips quirked. "The duke's daughters aren't to be found in the shires just yet. If they're pretty enough to attract a husband, or well dowered enough, they're plying the ballrooms. Do you hide from them here?"

"I do." The drink was making him honest—or uncaring.

Joseph needed a wife—he repeated this in his thoughts regularly, like a commandment—so every night he chose from among his invitations, fully intending to scout the hostile territory of Mayfair for same.

And every night he found himself in the card room, by the fire, swilling brandy in company with the other misfits, inebriates, gamblers, and cowards— unless he'd stumbled upon the gathering that boasted Louisa Windham's presence, in which case he did his brooding where he could torment himself with the sight of her dancing down the room.

"The orchestra is in fine form," Harrison said— apropos of nothing.

Fine form, if a man weren't heartily sick of holiday arrangements. "So why aren't you dancing?"

Harrison shifted lower in his chair. "I schedule sittings for most of the day, sunlight being a necessity for much of my work. Had you any fellow feeling, Carrington, you'd be ignoring me while I doze here in warmth and comfort."

There was a touch of genuine irritability in the other man's words, as if Joseph were truly disturbing him at his much-needed nap. Joseph rose, setting his brandy down by Harrison's elbow.

"Pleasant dreams. If I wanted a portrait of a couple of small children—girls—"

He fell silent. Even in the men's card room, it was perhaps not the done thing to bring up business.

Harrison sat up a bit. "Little girls? How old?"

"Six and seven. They're good girls. They'll sit still if they're told to." For about two minutes. They were growing up so quickly, and a portrait would keep the image of something precious alive when Joseph's memory grew dim.

"Are they in Town?" The man looked to be considering the commission, which was a surprise.

"Kent."

"Whose children are these?"

"Mine." It felt good to say it, good to remind himself of this singular if only legal fact, when for the past week, all he'd done was miss them and their siblings in Surrey.

Harrison's brows rose. "Come around to my studio. We'll talk further."

Joseph nodded and headed for the door. When he reached the corridor, he could hear the orchestra lilting its way through a lively gavotte, two hundred slippered feet pounding along in synchrony. If he went toward the ballroom, he might find Lady Louisa Windham, twirling and smiling and looking elegant on the arm of some dandy.

She'd stand with her sisters between sets, putting their pale prettiness to shame with her more earthy beauty. The young men would approach—a greater variety of young men since the most recent ducal dinner—and to the lucky few, Louisa would grant a dance.

Each evening, Joseph watched this routine for as long as he could before slinking off to the card room, there to silently lecture himself about Cousin Hargrave's poor health and the girls needing a mother.

He tested his leg, which was in truth benefiting

from the spate of milder weather, and then turned his steps not toward the ballroom but toward the peace and quiet—and unobtrusive exit—afforded by the garden.

⌒⌒⌒

Louisa had saved her supper waltz for Lionel—he'd all but asked her to when he'd greeted her for the evening—and yet, there he was, smiling down into the madly batting eyes of Isobel Horton.

Damn and blast.

But then, Louisa had danced last night's supper waltz with Lionel—she was to call him Lionel now, and he was to call her Louisa—and the night before that it had been a polonaise.

Louisa had the impression Lionel was trying to help her scotch the latest barrage of gossip sparked by her criticism of the Regent's Pavilion. This was kind of him, but the idea was still quite lowering.

Louisa's sisters were both taking to the dance floor. A lady did not want to be without an escort for supper, after all.

A lady did not in fact want to be seen lurking at the side of the ballroom, without sisters, gallants, or a potential supper escort. If Louisa lingered much longer, Westhaven would be standing up with her.

That would not do. Her brother danced quite well—for a brother—but his pity was the last thing Louisa wanted to deal with. She set her glass aside and slipped from the ballroom, turning her steps toward the fresh air and solitude afforded by the gardens.

⌒⌒⌒

The orchestra bounced its way through the gavotte, and the stomping and thumping on the ballroom floor came to an end.

Sir Joseph cast a look over his shoulder.

I should just go, before anybody else thinks to escape into the torch-lit shadows of the winter garden.

Though it was already too late. A lone figure emerged through the French doors and stood for a moment, tall, slim, and lovely in the flickering light.

"You should not be out here alone, my lady."

"Sir Joseph?"

"Over here." He stepped closer to the torches positioned near the door, pointedly ignoring the mistletoe hanging from the trellis not eight feet away. "May I escort you back inside?"

"You may *not*." She brushed past him, leaving a hint of citrus and clove on the night breeze. "I need some air."

"There's a bench." He took her by her gloved wrist and led her over to the stone bench in the shadows along the wall. Here in their hosts' walled terrace, the flames of a dozen torches made the night almost temperate. "Get your air, and then I will see you back to the ballroom."

He waited while she sat. Lady Louisa did not lower herself gracefully and make a show of arranging her skirts. She plopped down with a huff and stripped off her gloves. "You might as well join me, Sir Joseph. They'll soon be starting up the supper waltz."

A puzzled-male moment went by until he comprehended the difficulty. "You enjoy the waltz and did not want to sit this one out."

She frowned then wrinkled her nose in a manner that put Sir Joseph in mind of little Fleur. "What woman wants to sit out the supper waltz? Are you going to have a seat?"

So testy, except she wasn't suffering pique or anger. As if he were assessing one of his daughters, Sir Joseph knew instinctively that Louisa Windham was a little hurt, a little unnerved, and a little tired of being hurt and unnerved.

He extended a hand down to her. "I have not danced the waltz in several years, and what memories I have of it are few and dim. Perhaps you'd take pity on a lame soldier and see whether he can recall it?"

He expected her to laugh. On his bad days he *was* lame, and most days he was at least unsound, as an old horse might be unsound. He had not danced the waltz since being injured, had never hoped to again because it required grace, balance, and a little derring-do.

Also a willing partner.

Louisa put her bare hand in his and rose. "The pleasure would be mine." Her lips quirked as she stood, but she didn't drop his hand. "You must not allow me to lead."

He'd watched a hundred couples dancing a hundred waltzes, and had enjoyed the dance himself when it was first becoming popular on the Continent. The steps were simple. What was not simple at all was the feel of Louisa Windham, matter-of-factly stepping quite close, clasping his palm to her own.

"I like to just listen for a moment," she said, "to feel the music *inside*, feel the way it wants to move you, to lift your steps and infuse you with lightness."

She slipped in closer, so close her hair tickled Joseph's jaw. Her hand settled on his shoulder, and he felt her swaying minutely as the orchestra launched into the opening bars. She moved with the rhythm of the music, let it shift her even as she stood virtually in his embrace.

What he felt *inside* was a marvelous sense of privilege, to be holding Louisa Windham close to his body, to have the warm, female shape of her there beneath his hands. Her scent, clean and a little spicy, was sweeter when she was this close.

She wasn't as tall in his embrace as she was in his imagination. Against his body, she fit…perfectly.

And with the sense of privilege and wonder, there lurked a current of arousal. Louisa Windham was lovely, dear, smart, and brave, but she was also a grown woman whom Joseph had found desirable from the moment he'd laid eyes on her.

He waited until the phrasing felt right, closed his fingers gently around hers, then moved off with his partner. She shifted with him, the embodiment of grace, as weightless as sunshine, as fluid as laughter.

"You lead well," she whispered, her eyes half closed. "You're a natural."

He was a man plagued by a bad knee and a questionable hip, but with Louisa Windham for a partner and the music of an eighteen-piece orchestra to buoy him, Joseph Carrington danced.

The longer they moved together, the better they danced. Louisa let him lead, let him guide her this way and that, let him decide how much sweep to give the turns and how closely to enfold her. She gave herself up to the music, and thus a little to him, as well, and yet, she anchored him too.

Dancing with a woman who enjoyed the waltz this much gave a man some bodily confidence. He brought her closer, wonderfully closer, and realized what gave him such joy was not simply the physical pleasure of holding her but the warmth in his heart generated by her trust.

She was dancing with a lame soldier, with a pig farmer, and enjoying it.

All too soon, the music wound to a sweet final cadence, but Louisa did not sink into the closing curtsy. She instead stood in the circle of Joseph's arms and dropped her forehead to his shoulder.

"Sir Joseph, thank you."

What do to? Arousal hummed quietly in his veins, the citrus-and-clove scent of Louisa Windham wafted through his brain, and the voice of common sense started yammering in his ears.

Bow, idiot. Bow over the lady's hand, now.

He stroked a hand slowly down her back, reveling in the contour of her muscles and bones beneath his fingers. "The other night…"

She didn't step back, but he felt the tension infuse her spine. "At dinner?"

"I'm sorry. I've wanted to say that, but I haven't found the moment. I have no conversation, Louisa, and what few manners…" What was he trying to say? He knew arguing with a lady wasn't done, but it was more than that. "Prinny's Pavilion is an extravagance, regardless of how pretty or different, and you are entitled to your very sensible opinions."

He allowed himself to rest his cheek against her hair, trying to memorize each pleasure the moment afforded him:

The pleasure of making reparation for a conversation he had not managed well at all.

The pleasure of her body next to his, warm from their exertions, and yet quiet in his arms.

The pleasure of her scent, clean and sweet and unique to her.

The pleasure of her simple willingness to remain close to him.

She obliterated all those pleasures with one more delight, one he could not have foreseen, could not have envisioned in his wildest imaginings, when she went up on her toes and kissed him.

A woman should practice kissing, lest she miss the cheek she was aiming for, and by purest accident, set her lips against a man's mouth.

Some corner of Louisa's mind marveled that her brain was capable of thought, while another noted that up close, beneath the hint of cedar, Sir Joseph's linen bore the scent of true lavender, the sweet, soft version of the flower that Her Grace kept in sachets to fragrance the Moreland dwellings.

Closer than that, with her lips on his, his kiss was soft, as well. Gentle, sweet, and alluring. She slid her hands up to link behind his neck, for stability.

Even a gentle kiss apparently could threaten a lady's balance—and maybe a man's too. Joseph widened his stance while Louisa leaned into his taller frame. When his hand slid into her hair to anchor at the nape of her neck, Louisa wondered why her impressions of a man were different once he'd been her dancing partner.

Sir Joseph's mouth was luscious against hers, a surprisingly sumptuous tactile bouquet that had vines of sensation trailing into her vitals. His kiss, a slow tasting of her mouth, made her feel both languorous and bold, both cherished and challenged.

Louisa noticed what was absent from this kiss: Sir Joseph wasn't in a hurry. He wasn't fumbling. He wasn't breathing sour wine all over her neck. He wasn't kneading her breasts like so much morning dough.

He wasn't unaffected, either. There was…tumescence. Not slight, or maybe such dimensions were normal for him?

He shifted a little so their bodies were not as close and the evidence of his possible arousal was no longer available for Louisa's investigation. She rested her forehead against his cravat and silently thanked him for exercising some sense when she had none to offer.

Men were odd creatures. The ones with war injuries could ride and dance more gracefully than they walked; the ones who'd never laid an improper hand on her could bestow a first kiss more sweet and intriguing than she'd ever imagined.

The ones who bore the scent of home and happiness could be untitled, socially retiring, and raising orchard hogs in the shires.

She was going to have to work on her aim, lest she encounter more mouths where a freshly shaven cheek ought to be. These realizations were disconcerting, and now Sir Joseph was probably entertaining thoughts about her she did not want him thinking. Worse, she was wondering things about him she should not, and felt a trickle of resentment toward him that this should be so.

He sighed, which made Louisa realize she was plastered to his chest.

His broad, muscular chest.

"My lady, as lovely as this dance has been in every regard, I fear the evening is growing cooler, and I had best escort you back to the ballroom."

Louisa took one more whiff of him, her nose right at his throat, where body heat made the lovely scents—lavender, cedar, spices—pure and strong, and stepped back. Whatever he was trying to tell her—*in every regard*—he was right. In the space of one dance and one kiss, the evening had abruptly grown much cooler, and it was time Louisa returned to her sisters.

❧

"Your Grace." Joseph bowed deferentially in the greenery-bedecked foyer to the Earl of Westhaven's town house, only to earn a scowl from Westhaven's departing guest.

"For God's sake, Carrington, I'd rather you salute."

"No, Your Grace, you would not. If I were saluting, that would mean we were back at war, and neither of us could possibly wish for that."

Wellington's lips quirked. He was a handsome man of mature years, standing slightly less than six feet, popular with the ladies, and capable of charm when it suited him. "Arguing with me, Sir Joseph? Old habits die hard."

"Being honest, Your Grace. To be anything else in present company would be disrespectful, also pointless."

His Grace snorted through the feature that had earned him the sobriquet "Old Hookey." "Spare me your flattery. How goes that little import business of yours?"

This was the problem with having served on the Peninsula. A man might muster out, but he was never entirely excused from the notice of his superior officers. Wellington had frequently referred to his direct staff as his family, and still gathered them together socially in his home from time to time.

"My little business thrives, Your Grace. Thank you for asking."

The duke accepted gloves, top hat, and walking stick from a silent footman. "One wondered if you might lose interest. Some of your fellow officers would have. How's the leg?"

"Serviceably sound."

"As good as can be said of most of us. See that it remains that way. Happy Christmas." His Grace underscored his words with a momentary glower then swept out the door.

"Lord Westhaven will see you now, Sir Joseph, in the library."

Joseph followed the footman into the bowels of the town house, wondering how it was this dwelling should have such a pleasant air even on a dreary, bone-chilling winter day. The house had a glow, a peaceful quality Joseph's various residences did not, and the seasonal greenery, cloved oranges, and wreathes were only part of the reason.

As Joseph was ushered into the Earl of Westhaven's

library, he noted that Louisa Windham's older brother boasted a touch of the same happy, settled quality, though Westhaven was by no means a jovial man. He was a good-looking devil, though: tall, with dark chestnut hair and eyes a more emerald green than his sister's. His nose would serve him well when the ducal title befell him.

"Sir Joseph, a pleasure. Shall I ring for a tray?"

"Not necessary, my lord. I won't take up much of your time."

"Take it up sitting, nonetheless." Westhaven did not assume a seat behind his estate desk, but rather, went to the hearth and poked at a cheery fire. "And you'll humor me regarding the tea tray. His Grace's visit has left me peckish."

While Westhaven's back was turned, Joseph got through the ungainly business of ensconcing himself on a comfortable leather sofa. "Order a tray if you wish, my lord. I won't turn down a cup of something hot."

Westhaven put the poker back in its stand and turned, hands on hips. "Tea, coffee, or chocolate?"

Chocolate was a drink for pampered women…or possibly for happily married earls.

"Tea will be fine."

Westhaven flicked a glance Joseph's way then went to the door to speak with the footman. Joseph used the moment of privacy to massage the muscles of his right thigh, which the abruptly colder weather was literally tying in knots.

"Wellington's visit was a surprise," Westhaven said as he took a comfortable chair near the fire. "I think dukes thrive on unsettling people with their mere presence. His Grace was on his way to Carlton House, and I suspect he unsettles even the Regent when he pops in there." Westhaven seemed amused by this prospect.

"God knows Wellington could unsettle his staff when he was of a mind to." Perhaps this was not respectful, but it was true.

"St. Just has remarked as much. Unsettled the damn Corsican too, once and for all, God be thanked." Westhaven barked admission to two footmen, each carrying a tray. When the servants had departed, he sat forward, frowning at the bounty before him. "Help me eat at least half of this, Sir Joseph, or my wife will be interrogating me at great length about my health when next I see her. She has spies in the kitchen, and I have no secrets from her."

"Nor do you try to keep any."

"I do not."

Sir Joseph watched while Westhaven's handsome features arranged themselves into a smile so beneficent, so *doting*, it took Joseph a moment to recall where he'd seen such an expression previously.

"Has anyone ever told you that you resemble your father, Westhaven?"

The earl paused with the teapot lifted a few inches above the tray. "Resemble Moreland? No, not particularly. How do you take your tea?"

Even in his dismissal, Westhaven was acquiring a ducal quality, which only made Joseph more uncomfortable with the purpose of his visit. The earl served him tea, pushed some warm buttered scones on him, and kept up a patter of political and financial talk until a surprising amount of food had disappeared.

Joseph glanced at the clock and decided if he remained on his comfy sofa by the cozy fire any longer, he'd sleep for twenty years.

"You must be wondering why I arranged this call, my lord."

"I admit to some curiosity."

Nothing more. Joseph resented the man's savoir faire, even as he admired it. "I have received a letter from your half brother, St. Just."

The earl's expression didn't change. "What has my brother to say that brings you here on such a cold and dreary day?"

Not his half brother, his *brother*—a telling correction. "He expressed some concern for your sister, Lady Louisa, and asked me to scout…" Westhaven was not military. Joseph wanted to get up and pace, but that maneuver would be awkward, also rude. And as to that, "scouting" a woman's prospects was not exactly genteel.

"He wanted you to keep an eye on Louisa? Any particular reason?"

Green eyes held steady on Joseph, eyes much like St. Just's, though a shade more reserved. "In St. Just's words, my lord, your sister is organizing a retreat from the front, and he is not inclined to facilitate her decision in this regard."

Westhaven steepled his index fingers and tapped them against his lips in a slow rhythm while Joseph eyed the pot of chocolate.

"Louisa is not a coward," Westhaven said.

"St. Just is not one to indulge in dramatics."

Joseph had considered at length this request from a friend, reminding himself it was *not* an order from a commanding officer. While Joseph *was* inclined to torture himself with time in Louisa Windham's vicinity, he *was not* inclined to report to anybody a list of men with whom that lady danced or conversed—particularly if his own name were to be on such a list.

Westhaven wrinkled his patrician nose. "St. Just frets over his younger siblings. One must make allowances. Why have you brought the matter to me?"

"If the lady's interests need protecting, then aren't her brothers better suited to serve as her champion than I am?"

More lip-tapping, more perusal from green eyes that gave away nothing.

"You haven't any sisters, have you, Sir Joseph?"

"I have neither sisters nor female cousins nor even aunts. I do have daughters." Also sons, though they weren't to be mentioned in polite circles.

"Sisters are vexing in the extreme, also dear." Westhaven poured himself another cup of chocolate while he made his pronouncements. "They require protecting, even cosseting, but they do not allow a brother much opportunity for either. My brothers and I are agreed on this. Sisters are too stubborn for their own good, and in the case of *my* sisters, they are also too damned smart."

"Lady Louisa is a marvelously intelligent woman." Joseph was not going to say more, not to the Earl of Westhaven, but the man had no business complaining about his sisters. None at all.

"Women, in the opinion of most men, cannot be

marvelously intelligent, Sir Joseph. Louisa has grasped this but has decided not to use her wiles to snare herself some harmless fellow as a husband."

Louisa Windham's heart would break did she settle for a harmless fellow. That her own brother did not understand as much was…vexing, and disappointing. Sir Joseph tried not to dwell on how it would leave Louisa feeling.

"Some fellow who is not harmless might seek to snare *her*, your lordship. She and her sisters are rumored to be well dowered."

Westhaven's expression darkened. "My countess has suggested as much, but Louisa, Eve, and Jenny take very good care of one another in social settings. I gather St. Just seeks to reinforce the ranks with your watchful eye?"

"Something like that, but because I dance little and converse even less, I am not the best spy."

He used the ugly word, hoping it would convince Westhaven to act and to spare Joseph from fulfilling St. Just's request.

"A spy." Westhaven smiled a very different smile. Satisfied, calculating—this also brought to mind his ducal father when hot on some parliamentary scheme. "That's it exactly. We need a spy. Surely you can see why my own efforts to monitor the situation would be pointless? Louisa would run me off before the first supper waltz, and Jenny and Eve would abet her. His Grace would be an even more obvious cat among the pigeons, but nobody would suspect *your* motives, Sir Joseph." The smile faded on this last observation, to be replaced by a focused frown. "I really must join my brother in his request, much as it pains me to ask for your assistance."

Joseph rose awkwardly, resenting his damned leg, his damned former commanding officer, and his damned regard for a woman who should never have taken more than passing notice of him. "I will not spy on your sister, Westhaven. Spying on a lady is not honorable, and the lady deserves better from her family. Good day."

Westhaven was on his feet with enviable ease. "Not so fast, if you please. Allow me to rephrase my request."

"You did not make a request, Westhaven. And I really must be going." A dignified retreat wasn't quite possible, not when Joseph's right leg had chosen to seize up painfully. He managed some progress toward the door, only to find Westhaven's hand on his arm.

"All I ask is a moment, Sir Joseph."

A moment in which the man would set a spy on his own sister. Sir Joseph surmised that Westhaven would not back down, and it might be best to hear what the man was planning.

"I'm listening."

"Care for a drink?"

Joseph couldn't help glancing at the sideboard, where a half-dozen decanters and bottles sat in a perfectly arranged bouquet of potation. "Say your piece, Westhaven. I thought somebody in a position to assist Lady Louisa ought to be made aware of St. Just's concerns, not a virtual stranger who could at any point be called back out to Kent."

"You're a neighbor, not a stranger. You served with St. Just and Lord Bart, you ride to hounds with His Grace. Her Grace likes you."

That startling bit of news seemed to make a difference to Westhaven. It intrigued Joseph, as well, but
even the approval of a duchess did not signify.

"Westhaven, I esteem your family greatly, and
your sister Lady Louisa in particular. Do not ask me
to violate her privacy more than I already have by
coming here today."

"Fine, then, don't violate her privacy." Westhaven
dropped his hand and shot an appraising look at
Joseph. "But don't leave her without a champion,
however unacknowledged. I can't assume the role,
if for no other reason than my countess and I will
be rusticating ourselves as of next week before we
join my parents for Christmas. I dare not involve my
father, for he has decided to take a hand in the matchmaking himself. If Louisa knew this, she would be on
the first stage north without taking time to pack more
than a book or two."

The friendly, mostly male political dinner in the
Windham home made more sense to Joseph. Political
dinner, indeed. No wonder Louisa had been discom-
moded by a harmless exchange of views.

"Does Louisa know her father is matchmaking?"

"I doubt he announced his intentions, and Her
Grace is complicit in his schemes most of the time."

God in heaven. The cold outside seemed to take
up residence in Joseph's belly. "Every impoverished younger son not hunting in the shires will be
attempting to ingratiate himself with His Grace from
now until Christmas."

"You see the difficulty."

Westhaven stepped back, letting Joseph's imagination

run rampant over scenes of Lady Louisa being accosted in gardens, under stairways, in anterooms, and private parlors—with mistletoe and holiday punch on hand to aid any young man with the wits to exploit them.

Happy Christmas, indeed.

"She loves to dance," Joseph said, half under his breath.

"Louisa?"

How could Westhaven not know this about his own sister? "Yes, Lady Louisa. She'll not suspect her dance card is full because her papa is putting it about she's looking to marry, not until some idiot says the wrong thing to her."

"Louisa can deal with idiots."

That was not the point—her own brother was an idiot—the point was she'd be hurt when she realized her father's scheming, and not her own appeal, was getting her onto the dance floor.

"I will keep an eye on her, but I will not report to you or to St. Just," Joseph heard himself say. "You will inform neither your father nor your mother, and I will tell Louisa what I'm about."

Westhaven's brows rose. "I wouldn't advise that. She'll take evasive maneuvers and defeat the purpose of your efforts."

"You do not understand your own sister, Westhaven. I'll take my leave of you, and should I have to repair to Kent before the holidays, I'll let you know."

Joseph had the satisfaction of seeing puzzlement, however fleeting, on Westhaven's face. And then another smile, this one sweet and slightly knowing. "My thanks, then. And best of luck."

Joseph bid Westhaven good day and retrieved hat,

gloves, and cane from the footman at the front door. When he might have been tucked up in Westhaven's library, enjoying a tot of fine brandy in some masculine company, Joseph instead limped back out into the dark, freezing winter afternoon alone.

Six

"WHAT IS THIS?" ELLEN WINDHAM PICKED UP THE LITTLE volume her husband had just tossed on the night table.

"Poetry." Lord Valentine lowered himself to the bed and tugged at his boots. "Rather naughty poetry. I'm thinking of setting some of it to music."

Ellen sat beside him and turned a page. "'Venus has reserved exclusively for you her best loving thorn…'" she quoted. "'Cupid without remorse, swirling both love and hatred in a single cup…'" She read for a while longer while Valentine rose and stripped down to breeches and stockings.

"Will you attend me, Wife, or will you disquiet your mind with that prurient verse?"

"Some of it is beautiful. Much of it." She set the book aside and regarded her husband where he stood half-clothed by the hearth. "You are beautiful too."

He smiled at her and held out a hand. "I have to send the book on to Louisa, who collects such things, but you can choose for me the poems you find beautiful, and I'll arrange them."

She came to him, letting him enfold her in his

embrace. "Is there any part of you that wants us to be in Town now, Valentine? Christmas is almost here, and your family is gathered there."

"They're only a day's ride from us in Town, and the compositions flow more easily when I can work out here near you and the baby. Do you worry about this?"

She nodded against his chest. "You love your family. They are part of your music too."

Valentine rested his chin against her temple, which he was inclined to do when feeling thoughtful.

"Their Graces would enjoy more time with the baby," he murmured. "We can leave a few days earlier for Morelands. St. Just is already en route, and Westhaven will be leaving Surrey any day."

Ellen relaxed in his arms, letting go of a subtle tension she hadn't known she was carrying. "I'd like that. If I'm out and about tomorrow at first light, I can start making the arrangements for an earlier departure."

She never tarried in their bed alone of a morning. In the subtle and convoluted language of marital dialogue, she'd just warned Valentine that *he* wouldn't be tarrying in bed come morning, either.

"To bed with you now then, Wife." He slipped his arms from around her. "Let me finish washing, and we'll make an early night of it." He kissed her cheek for emphasis, lingering near long enough to make his point.

On a pleasant little bolt of warmth to her middle, Ellen took his meaning. She *always* took his meaning and obligingly slipped off her robe and climbed beneath the covers to watch her husband's ablutions. Even after nearly a year of marriage, watching Valentine in a state of undress was still of such interest to her that she forgot to ask him why Louisa would be collecting naughty poems, regardless of how lovely those poems might be.

ം

Attempting to coordinate her wardrobe with Lord Lionel's convinced Louisa of several truths:

First, she lacked the quality that allowed most young women to fuss over their clothing and accessories, not just for hours or days, but for weeks, even lifetimes. Such a realization was more in the way of articulating a truth long taken for granted. Boredom alone had prompted Louisa to experiment with predicting Lionel's sartorial choices.

Second, Louisa's father was At It Again, meaning the duke had gotten his sons married off, and now had Louisa herself in his matchmaking crosshairs. Worse, Her Grace was conspiring with the transgressor, merrily planning yet another dinner before the remove to Morelands at week's end.

And the display of mistletoe at the town house this year beggared description.

The third realization, over which Louisa tried to muster some guilt, was that she was unwittingly fostering pointless hope on the part of Lionel Honiton.

He danced well.

He dressed well.

He dished out pretty compliments like he was Father Christmas handing out holiday presents. He smiled indulgently until she wanted to apply her closed fist to his manly chin.

Polite society maintained that sisters should marry

in birth order, so as a theoretical exercise, Louisa had tried considering marriage to Lionel. Even theoretically, the notion failed utterly. Patchouli in the dark, upon closer examination, was a harrowing thought.

Some day in the distant future, a man might come along who could overlook the indiscretions and missteps of Louisa's youth, though they were serious missteps and egregious indiscretions. When those mistakes had faded to twenty years' distance, though, they'd appear in a less disastrous perspective. They might become so insignificant, Louisa could even share them with a prospective spouse and not be rejected roundly for her confidences.

She hoped. Lionel, however, was by no means Prospective Spouse material.

The present challenge had become to gently discourage Lionel without encouraging anybody else, so to the present challenge, Louisa turned her attention.

"You must look to Lord Lionel's friends," Jenny said again, proving she was as relentless as His Grace, though her aim was quite different. "Deene can count both His Grace and St. Just among his friends, Sir Joseph is a trusted neighbor who served with St. Just and Bartholomew, and even Hazelton was on good terms with our family before Maggie married him."

"Hazelton was listening at keyholes and the terror of every polite gathering," Louisa countered.

"You get on famously with him now," Eve chimed in. "Lionel has little to recommend him except a stylish bow and some fashion sense. Word has it his finances are embarrassed."

Louisa lingered with her sisters among the ferns at

the edge of yet another ballroom, though even in their relative privacy, Eve kept her voice down.

"Well, you needn't fret that you'll have Lionel for a brother-by-marriage." Saying it should have been harder—much harder.

Jenny tore the end of a leaf off a fern. "Have you quarreled with him?"

"Not yet." Louisa watched as her sister acquired greenish fingers demolishing the fern leaf. "I hope it doesn't come to that."

"Choose another flirt," Eve said, her tone chillingly practical as she surveyed the ballroom. "It works for me, though I'm better served when I pick three or four each Season. They are less likely to get presuming notions if they're never singled out."

While Louisa cast about for a reply, Timothy Grattingly approached them.

"Mr. Grattingly." Louisa held out her hand. She couldn't quite be glad to see him, though his arrival cut short what was no doubt going to be a grueling interrogation from her sisters. "Is it the supper waltz already?"

"Already?" Grattingly smiled, though it struck Louisa as more of a leer. "I've been counting the minutes, the seconds even! Come, my lady, lest there be no place for us on the dance floor."

Louisa rose, but from the same place in her mind that informed her she would not be diverting herself with Lord Lionel any longer, she made a further decision that she could not turn down the room with this lumbering idiot again either, not even for the ten minutes—or six hundred seconds—generally required for a waltz.

"Might we take some air in the conservatory, Mr. Grattingly? It's too chilly outside, but I confess I have an interest in lining up for the buffet a trifle early."

"You don't care to waltz?" His expression reflected consternation, and it was indeed the first time Louisa could recall declining an offer to stand up.

Beside Louisa, Jenny had stopped fiddling with the fern and put her gloves back on. "If you're intent on dancing, Mr. Grattingly, I can oblige."

Jenny's offer was beyond forward—it was *fast*. Also completely in character for Jenny to the extent she'd be making a tremendous sacrifice.

"Nonsense." Louisa wound her arm around Grattingly's sleeve. "Mr. Grattingly won't mind obliging me."

Except he apparently did mind. They promenaded the ballroom in the opposite direction of the conservatory, stopping to chat with everybody and his or her maiden aunt. They even ran into Lionel, with whom Grattingly exchanged oblique civilities while Louisa attempted to smile and not look bored.

Lionel was in lavender, gold, and white tonight. Louisa's algorithm, with symbolic variables for waistcoat, coat, breeches, and stockings, flitted through her mind. Later in the week, he'd trade waistcoat and stockings to present an ensemble in pink, gold, and white. After that it would be brown, gold, and white…

"Shall we?" Grattingly bowed her through the open door to the conservatory, and Louisa felt the touch of humid, earthy air on her face. The place was reasonably well lit for a conservatory and blessedly quiet, though there were no doubt other couples using it for a respite from the ballroom.

"Shall we take a seat?" Grattingly asked. "Don't mind getting off my feet, myself." He offered another one of his unappealing smiles.

"That bench will do," Louisa said, pointing to the first one she saw.

"How about we find the famous Christmas orchid first? I'm told it's blooming, and the Botanical Society comes trooping around daily to sketch it, sniff it, and refine on its features."

Louisa had seen orchids before, but Grattingly was towing her by the hand deeper into the conservatory. "I wasn't aware our hosts boasted orchids in their collection."

Grattingly stopped at a shadowed bend on the gravel path. "Let's sit here."

He stood so he was between Louisa and the way back to the ballroom. Grattingly wasn't much taller than Louisa, but he was stocky enough standing there in her path that something crawly rose to life in Louisa's belly.

"Mr. Grattingly, while we might tarry in the conservatory in plain sight of the open door, the location you've chosen—ooph!"

"The location I've chosen is perfect," Grattingly said as he mashed his body against Louisa's. He'd shoved her back against a tree, off the path, into the shadows.

"Mr. Grattingly! How dare—"

Wet lips landed on Louisa's jaw, and the scent of wine-soured breath filled her head.

"Of course, I dare. You all but begged me to drag you in here. With your tits nigh falling from your bodice, how do you expect a man to act?"

He thrust his hand into the neckline of Louisa's

gown and closed his fingers around her breast. Louisa was too stunned for a moment to think, then something more powerful than fear came roaring forward.

"You slimy, presuming, stinking, drunken, witless varlet!" She shoved against him hard, but he wasn't budging, and those thick, wet lips were puckering up abominably. Louisa heard her brother Devlin's voice in her head, instructing her to use her knee, when Grattingly abruptly shifted off her and landed on his bottom in the dirt.

"Excuse me." Sir Joseph stood not two feet away, casually unbuttoning his evening coat. His expression was as composed as his tone of voice, though even when he dropped his coat around Louisa's shoulders, he kept his gaze on Grattingly. "I do hope I'm not interrupting."

"You're not." Louisa clutched his jacket to her shoulders, finding as much comfort in its cedary scent as she did in the body heat it carried. "Mr. Grattingly was just leaving."

"Who the hell are you," Grattingly spat as he scrambled to his feet, "to come around and disturb a lady at her pleasures?"

Somewhere down the path, a door swung closed. Louisa registered the sound distantly, the way she'd notice when rain had started outside though she was in the middle of a good book.

Though this was not a good book. Instinctively Louisa knew she was, without warning or volition, in the middle of *something* not good at all.

"I was not at my pleasures, you oaf." She'd meant to fire the words off with a load of scathing indignation, but to Louisa's horror, her voice shook. Her knees were turning unreliable on her, as well, so she sank onto the hard bench.

"What's going on here?" Lionel Honiton stood on the path, three or four other people gathered behind him.

"Nothing," Sir Joseph said. "The lady has developed a megrim and will be departing shortly."

"A megrim!" Grattingly was on his feet, though to Louisa it seemed as if he weaved a bit. "That bitch was about to get something a hell of a lot more—"

Sir Joseph, like every other guest, was wearing evening gloves. They should not have made such a loud, distinct sound when thwacked across Grattingly's jowls.

Lionel stepped forth. "Let's not be hasty. Grattingly, apologize. We can all see you're a trifle foxed. Nobody takes offense at what's said when a man's in his cups, right?"

"I'm not drunk, you ass. You—"

"That's not an apology." Sir Joseph pulled on his gloves. "My seconds will be calling on yours. If some one of the assembled multitude would stop gawping long enough to fetch the lady's sisters to her, I would appreciate it."

He said nothing more, just treated each member of the small crowd to a gimlet stare, until Lionel ushered them away. Nobody had a word for Grattingly, who stomped off in dirty breeches, muttering Louisa knew not what.

Sir Joseph asked no permission. He lowered himself to sit beside Louisa while she fought an urge to tuck herself against him and mutter a few curses of her own.

"Louisa?" The gentleness in his voice was unnerving. "Are you unharmed?"

She nodded, but it was a lie. If Joseph hadn't come along, then that crowd would have seen far, far worse than a disarranged dress or Grattingly dusting dirt off his satin-clad arse.

"You're shaking." Sir Joseph handed her a handkerchief. "Next come the chills. Sometimes I'd cast up my accounts too. Once, to my unending horror, I cried. Fortunately, only my horse witnessed that indignity."

"Grattingly has been trying to kiss you too?"

"Good girl." How could a man put such approval and warmth into two stupid words? "Care for a nip?"

"Your special brew?"

He passed her his flask. "Nothing else is quite as effective. I have to ask again, Louisa: Are you unharmed?"

"I'll have some bruises. Did you follow us in here?"

"I did not. I came here for the warmth and quiet."

He was lying. Making a gallant job of it, but for the first time in Louisa's acquaintance, Sir Joseph was dealing in untruths. Still, with Sir Joseph sitting calmly beside her, and his special brew leaving a bracing heat in her vitals, Louisa began to let that quiet and warmth restore some of her equilibrium. "You aren't actually going to meet that idiot over pistols, are you?"

Sir Joseph took a sip from the flask then passed it back to her. "Grattingly might choose swords, though I can give a good account of myself with either. Wellington required it of his staff in addition to competence on the dance floor."

"I see." She held the flask out to him.

"Keep it. What do you see?"

"My brothers would be off in corners, whispering plans as if their womenfolk had never heard of dueling over a lady's good name. You sit here and casually admit to me you expect to fight a duel on my behalf."

She wanted an argument, with him, with anybody. The need to verbally brawl was another reaction to being assaulted, but knowing that still didn't put Louisa in charity with her rescuer.

"In truth your brothers had asked me to keep an eye on your situation, and I had yet to find a way to gain your permission to serve in that capacity. Here is how I see it, Louisa: Firstly, you would do me an injury were I to pretend you should not trouble your lovely self over this matter. Secondly, your honor was thoroughly slighted before an audience that is already spreading to all the world what few details they observed. I can accept Grattingly's apology, assuming he's bright enough to make one, which will do nothing to rehabilitate your reputation."

"And fighting a duel will?"

"Perhaps not, but it will at least serve to keep *my* honor intact, won't it?"

She turned and rested her forehead on his meaty shoulder, the full import of the situation landing on her like a cold, reeking mudslide. Her breath caught in her chest, and the back of her head started to pound.

"I am *ruined*, aren't I? One stupid turn in the conservatory with that cretin, and years of behaving myself count for nothing. At least if I had committed some sin, I might have the memory of it to entertain me in years to come. But no, none of that. Doubtless I lured Grattingly in here, just as I have lured many a man to his doom in gardens and parlors. For my unending wickedness, I got Grattingly's fetid breath, bruises, and—"

Sir Joseph's arms came around her. By the time her sisters found them, Louisa had almost convinced herself nobody would know she'd been crying her heart out.

Nobody but Sir Joseph.

❧

"I've half a mind to challenge the bloody bastard myself." His Grace, the Duke of Moreland, paced to the window and spun on his heel with military precision. "St. Just is already on his way down from the North, and I know Valentine would heed any summons sent in his direction. This is bad, Carrington. This is very bad."

"It will also be over and done with by this time Friday, Your Grace."

"For you, perhaps, but what about for my Louisa? What about for her sisters?" His Grace groped for the arm of a reading chair, settling himself as awkwardly as Joseph might have settled himself on a particularly cold night. "What about my dear duchess? She's gone quiet. Hasn't scolded me since this happened. When the Duchess of Moreland stops scolding her duke, the natural order is imperiled."

Joseph pushed himself out of his chair and went to the sideboard. He sniffed a couple decanters, decided on Armagnac, and poured the older man a drink. "For medicinal purposes, Your Grace."

Moreland took the proffered glass but merely held it. "If I didn't think my wife would expire with wrath, by God, I would issue my own challenge, Carrington."

Joseph returned to his seat. "Except a duel is intended precisely to stop a grievance from escalating into a feud, Your Grace. Grattingly's family is wealthy enough and ambitious enough that they could make some trouble for the Windhams, and I must admit two of your sons entrusted me with Lady Louisa's welfare."

His Grace raised a pair of keen blue eyes to Joseph's face. "They *asked* you? Without telling *me*?"

Joseph decided a drink was in order after all and gained some time to organize his arguments while he poured out a tot of brandy for himself. "Nasty damned weather."

"Hang the bloody weather, though at least it isn't snowing again—yet." His Grace tossed back his drink in one swallow and held out his glass. "What's this about my boys passing off the job of looking after their sister onto you?"

This was part of the reason Sir Joseph wanted nothing to do with a title. It required dealing with *other* titles, old fellows with high opinions of themselves or young fellows with more influence than sense *and* high opinions of themselves.

"St. Just sent word he'd appreciate my taking an interest in Louisa's social situation in his absence. I reported this state of affairs to Westhaven, though he has since left for Surrey, claiming he had to nip out there before joining the family in Kent."

His Grace dispatched his second drink as quickly as the first. "My guess, and it's only a guess, is Lou threatened to hare off to the North, and St. Just wanted warning if she bolted in his direction. The boy's still a bit jumpy from too many battles. Her Grace worries about him too."

While His Grace was at least looking a little more thoughtful.

"Another drink, Your Grace?"

The duke cast a rueful glance at his empty glass. "Best not. Her Grace takes a dim view of over-imbibing. The situation calls for a clear head."

"It does at that, so let me explain my reasoning to you."

His Grace listened, hearing Joseph out from start to finish without a single interruption. When Joseph had laid his arguments before the duke, a silence descended in the ducal sitting room, one broken only by the hiss and pop of the fire and the soughing of the winter wind against the mullioned windows.

His Grace stopped staring into the flames and turned to regard his guest. "I must discuss this situation with my duchess, Carrington. I was fortunate to make a love match before such a thing was common in good society. It has turned out rather well, and I hope my father and mother are taking note of that from some well-appointed celestial nook. Theirs was a dynastic union."

Joseph understood that warning: assuming he survived to week's end, and assuming the lady in question assented to one of his plans, her happiness on earth could become his responsibility. The prospect was not as daunting as it ought to have been, looming quite to the contrary like a Christmas gift out of all proportion to the receiver's desserts.

"I comprehend your concern, Your Grace. If Lady

Louisa is not pleased with my plan, then I will with-draw the offer immediately."

Another silence, while Joseph bore the scrutiny of shrewd blue eyes.

"Very well, Carrington. I'll send Louisa in to you, but wish me luck with my duchess. If I thought the resulting row would put Her Grace back in form, I'd drain every decanter on the sideboard."

Joseph eyed those decanters while he waited for Louisa to join him. The duke had twelve, while Westhaven's library had boasted six. From a place near the cheery fire, Joseph was considering his own little flask—his spare, for Louisa now possessed the better of the two—when Louisa appeared in the doorway.

"Sir Joseph. His Grace said you were asking to speak to me."

"Actually, I was asking him if I might discuss marriage with you."

He put his flask away and took encouragement from the fact that Louisa did not bolt from the room, screaming for all she was worth.

Seven

"WHAT DO *YOU* WANT?" HIS ROYAL HIGHNESS MADE it sound as if Hamburg, of all the toadying ciphers at Carlton House, was the most offensive. He wasn't, but the little man took perverse pleasure in withstanding royal abuse. The Regent found it easy to oblige him on this freezing, blustery, useless day.

"I do most abjectly beg Your Royal Highness's pardon for imposing, but the year will soon draw to a close, and there is the matter of—"

Prinny waved a hand unadorned with rings, the weather having caused the royal case of rheumatism to take a nasty turn. "The blighted honors list and the peerages. Do you think of nothing else, Humbug?"

"You pay me to think of little else, Your Royal Highness, and as a symbol of the realm's grandeur and enduring nobility, there is nothing that compares—"

"Stow it, man, or I'll pay you even less than I do."

This apparently crossed the line from coveted royal abuse to sincere threat. Hamburg's bald pate turned pink, and his pruney lips pursed into silence.

The Regent lay back on his well-padded chaise and

scanned the long list before him. Drunks and thieves for the most part, and the occasional drunk or thief married to a whore-for-the-cause. A few among them were shrewd enough to donate to various projects before they held their hands out for royal favor.

"I thought I told you to add Joseph Carrington to the list." After suggestions from no less than Wellington *and* Moreland, he had told Hamburg this very thing. Catching the man in his error—if an error it was—brightened an otherwise dreary day.

"Sir Joseph will soon inherit a barony, Your Royal Highness."

The Regent set the list aside and motioned for a footman to pour him another serving of wassail. "What barony? I know the titles with only one heir standing between them and escheat, and there are precious few."

"Sir Joseph's situation is a matter of abeyance, Your Royal Highness. The only other contender is childless, sickly, and quite old."

"Abeyance." Abeyance was tedious, also quite rare. "Why hasn't he petitioned for it, if there's only one other possibility? Why haven't they both?"

"I gather neither party wants to dispossess the other of his chance."

Hamburg took to inspecting the royal quarters, studying portraits and appointments the little weasel had seen on numerous occasions. His hands remained behind his back, and yet the Regent had a clear sense the man was somehow fidgeting.

His Royal Highness waved a hand again, and the four footmen stationed around the chamber withdrew, the last one closing the door silently in his wake.

"Humbug, what aren't you telling me?" The Regent used what he privately termed the Royal Confidences tone of voice, part conspirator, part confessor, part long-suffering paterfamilias. Use of it got a damned sight more done than an entire session of Parliament.

"The seat of the barony, Your Royal Highness…" Hamburg took to shifting from foot to foot, like a nervous penguin.

"Go on, and perhaps you might pour yourself a spot of drink. The kitchen pouts when We neglect Our tray, and you might as well sit. We cannot abide to have people hovering about Us."

Hamburg nodded, sat on the very edge of a red velvet hassock, and when he reached for the china, his hand shook slightly.

"About the barony's seat, Hamburg?"

"Yes. About that." He stared at his empty cup. "It seems there might have been a miscommunication some time back before the day of Charles II, or a mistake, perhaps."

"There were a number of mistakes, regicide among them."

Hamburg peeked up from his teacup, probably to ascertain if he was supposed to laugh at the royal riposte. What resulted was Hamburg's version of a smile, a tentative, sickly thing that came close to upsetting the royal digestion.

"Quite, Your Royal Highness. This was a much smaller error, very small, in fact. In the interregnum, the barony's seat was put to service as a home for urchins, and there being a number of those, the place has seen hard use."

Finding homes for urchins sounded like a dirty, expensive business, particularly since the urchins themselves were a class of royal subject that had proliferated madly in recent years. "Do We support this school?"

"The realm provides some support, but there are charitable patrons, as well. A few."

A pair of crotchety widows who no doubt came sniffing around each Christmas with a crate of moldy oranges. "The Foundling Hospital fell into a very sorry state, relying on the generosity of private patrons, Hamburg. It pains Us to consider such a fate for helpless children."

The Royal Confidences tone was discarded for one presaging a display of Royal Displeasure. Between the yeomen coming to the cities for work and finding none, the soldiers mustering out in the wake of the Corsican's defeat, and the nobility having an allergy to earning coin in trade, charitable patrons were thin on the ground.

Hamburg was back to studying the many paintings on the walls. "One might hope Sir Joseph could content himself with being an absentee landlord. Many do."

"You don't have children, do you, Hamburg?"

He drew himself up on his red hassock. "Certainly not, there as yet being no Missus Hamburg."

For all the debauchery attributed to the royal court, it pleased His Royal Highness to think at least one Puritan remained in his employ, though not a particularly bright Puritan.

"Do you think, Hamburg, that Sir Joseph won't

notice his estate does not prosper? Do you think he won't peruse the steward's reports and see he's being eaten out of house and home? He won't notice that children go through shoes at a great rate?"

"I did not think of that. When I first spotted this difficulty, Sir Joseph was a mere mister serving on Wellington's staff. One could hope the Almighty had a solution to the problem in mind."

"Ghoulish of you, Hamburg, but practical."

While Hamburg had a staring contest with some be-ruffed courtier on the east wall, the Regent considered options. The royal brain was of a practical nature when sober, and a sentimental nature at most other times. His Royal Highness felt about half sober, and more than half sentimental, given the Yuletide season.

"Wellington speaks highly of Sir Joseph. Came singing the man's praises just the other day. The week before that, it was Moreland humming the same tune."

"Wellington is known to hold his former staff in great affection, Your Royal Highness."

Having people agree with simple observations was one of the most tiresome aspects of being sovereign. Had there been a footman on hand...

"Fetch Us the decanter, Hamburg, lest this perishing weather give Us a chill."

Hamburg popped to his feet with the alacrity of a marionette.

"Wellington approves of Sir Joseph—said his marksmanship was without peer—and We approve of Sir Joseph. He raises a mighty tasty pig, and he appreciates fine art far better than most of his titled superiors do. If We cast about for a viscount's title, Sir

Joseph would likely find it in his patriotic heart to take on a few dear little boys and girls who want for some clothes and a prayer book."

Hamburg turned slowly, the decanter and glass on a tray in his hands. "A viscountcy, Your Royal Highness?"

"At least. We quite appreciate Our pork. Now bring me the damned drink, take yourself off, and send the footmen in. When you've some letters patent drafted, you may bother Us again."

The pruney expression was back. Hamburg set the tray at his sovereign's elbow, bowed ridiculously low, and backed from the room, list in hand. His Royal Highness added a dollop more spirits to his wassail—it being the season, and so forth—took a deep swallow of his drink, and lay back while the footmen rearranged pillows under the royal foot.

The scheme under contemplation would benefit a deserving knight, please two influential dukes, and relieve a loyal penguin. This was all very good, but what gave the Regent a glimmer of pleasure on an otherwise worthless winter day, was the prospect of keeping a few dozen English orphans fed, clothed, housed, and safe, as well.

All without spending a penny from the public exchequer *or* the royal coffers.

❧

"You asked His Grace if you might propose to me?"

Louisa tried to keep her voice calm, but it was an effort. Joseph looked more serious than usual, also tired.

"One can hope it won't come to that. May we sit?"

She gestured to the sofa then changed her mind

when she saw Sir Joseph was nigh hobbling. "Your leg is bothering you."

"It is." He didn't dissemble. She liked that about him, despite the ridiculous topic he'd broached.

"Does heat help?"

He cocked his head and regarded her. "It does. This weather does not. Grattingly has chosen pistols, though, so if you're concerned, I might come lame to a battle of swords—"

When Louisa tossed a pair of cushions onto the raised hearth, he fell silent.

"We can sit by the fire, Sir Joseph, while I do you the courtesy of hearing you out."

He offered her a hand, and Louisa got settled on a pillow. His own descent was awkward, requiring that his right leg be kept straight while he lowered himself to the cushion. He turned to face her, which put his game leg in closer proximity to the hearth screen.

"If you're going to ring for tea or otherwise engage in evasive maneuvers, my lady, you might as well be about it."

"No evasive maneuvers, Sir Joseph. Fire when ready." He was direct. She liked that about him too. She also wasn't about to let the ducal staff see her caller sitting on the hearthstones.

"Fire, I shall. Are you in love with Lionel Honiton?"

"*What on earth—?*" The question had been dispassionate, disinterested in an alarming way.

"He's a decent young man, Louisa. I have reason to know this because he is a second cousin at some remove to my late wife. His family's circumstances mean he must make his own way, but he saw enough of what happened in that conservatory and would not hold it against you."

Louisa wrapped her arms around her knees and rested her forehead on her forearms. "Which explains why, in the four days since, Lord Lace has neither called on me nor danced with my sisters, much less with me."

"He has called on me."

Louisa turned her head to peer at Sir Joseph. "You sound surprised."

"Grattingly is his friend, or crony. Drinking companion, at any rate. Lionel wanted me to know that he'd encouraged Grattingly to offer an apology and warned me the man will not delope."

"But dear Lionel is not serving as your second, is he?"

Sir Joseph frowned and rubbed his right hand up and down the length of his thigh. "He is not serving as Grattingly's, either. If I asked it of him, I'm sure he would serve as mine, but the less your future spouse has to do with this mess the better."

"Now this is odd." Louisa watched Sir Joseph's hand as she spoke. "I was under the impression a fellow proposed prior to becoming a spouse, and yet, I do not see Lionel about. Perhaps he's lurking behind the curtains?"

Not that she'd accept Lionel Honiton under these circumstances—under any circumstances. Patchouli aside, he was precisely the kind of spouse who could not weather a wife with scandal lurking in her past, much less in her present *and* her past.

"I certainly hope he's not about. If you're not interested in tea, may I pour you a tot of something from the sideboard?"

"It's my sideboard, Sir Joseph. I can pour myself a drink if one is needed. Are you prevaricating?"

A small smile quirked his lips. "Yes. May I be blunt?"

"Of course."

The smile bloomed a little brighter, making the big, serious man look momentarily impish. Louisa kept her focus on Sir Joseph's mouth rather than watching the hand Sir Joseph used to massage his thigh.

And then the smile winked out, like a candle in a stiff breeze. "If I take an interest in Lionel's finances, I'm confident he could be persuaded to offer for you."

"An interest—" Louisa felt something like a chill, despite the heat radiating from the fire. "You'd buy me a husband?" *Were things as dire as that?*

"Lionel was a favorite with my wife. Call it a delayed sense of familial loyalty on my part."

Try as she might, Louisa could not manufacture a sense of insult. Coming from anybody else, she'd greet this scheme with scorn or rage or—on a good day—condescending amusement. Coming from Sir Joseph, it was the act of an honorable man whom she might, in confidence, admit she considered a friend.

Or perhaps the difficulty was she'd begun—in the privacy of a heart that only grudgingly yielded its insights to her brain—to consider him something more than a friend.

"Am I to marry Lionel, or merely remain engaged to him until my sisters have found husbands?"

His hand went still. "Don't you want to marry him, Louisa? He's handsome, not stupid, and not particularly given to vice. He's of suitable rank—"

Louisa pushed Sir Joseph's hands aside and used the

heel of her left hand to stroke down along the belly of his thigh muscle. Doing something—anything—gave her a focus for the queerest sense of disappointment.

Here was her opportunity to marry a handsome, suitable man, a man who danced well and turned himself out beautifully—a man others would consider a catch for a woman such as her—though he was the wrong man.

She knew this in her bones, knew it with her thinking brain, and knew it in her heart. In which moment the knowledge had come to her, she could not say, but knowledge such as this could not be ignored by brains—or a heart—such as hers.

Lionel was the wrong man. Sir Joseph was…not the wrong man, though marriage now even to him wasn't quite right, either. The image of a little red book popped into Louisa's mind like a mental bad penny.

When Sir Joseph tried to brush her hand aside, she shifted closer. "I can get a better angle than you. I'm not marrying Lionel, and I'd as soon not gain a reputation for being a jilt as well as a jade."

"But your sisters… Louisa, you should *not*— God, that feels good."

"My sisters are not inclined to marry." And Louisa was not inclined to suffer missishness from her caller, so she did not turn loose of his leg. She'd spent years watching her brother Victor die by inches, for God's sake… "You tell Their Graces that Jenny and Eve have shared that confidence with me, and I will put something noxious in your flask, Joseph Carrington. There's a knot, here, above your knee." She used her thumb to fish along the corded length of his quadriceps. "Several knots."

"Louisa, if your sisters are not inclined to marry,

then you could be engaged to Lionel for as long as it takes for the talk to die down. An engagement would preserve you from scandal, relieve your parents' minds, and allow me to tend to a relative in need."

She dug a little harder into the muscle beneath the fabric of his breeches. "My sisters think they do not want to marry, but they *shall* marry."

"You can divine the future?"

His voice sounded off, a trifle strained. Louisa concluded she was hurting him and lightened the pressure. "They are both pining for children, missing our happily married brothers, and contemplating lives tending to aging parents and doting on nieces and nephews. They deserve better."

"And you do not?" He sounded wonderfully indignant on her behalf.

"I have books, Sir Joseph. I have telescopes. I correspond with literary acquaintances. I dabble at writing myself. I study the calculus when I'm particularly bored. My nature is solitary and simple—what?"

He'd covered her hand with his own. "You are not being entirely honest, Louisa. What is your real objection to this scheme?"

Louisa neither withdrew her hand nor removed it from Sir Joseph's person. She also did not meet his gaze, lest he see her frustration. The fire was warming her back; Sir Joseph's hand around hers imparted a different warmth entirely—and the damned man was trying to foist her off on Lionel Honiton.

It wasn't to be borne. "Somebody told Lionel I like poetry. Would that someone be you?"

"It might have been." He shifted so their hands

were joined. Did he think Louisa was going to get up and start pacing? "Many people enjoy poetry."

"Lionel isn't one of them. He accosted me last week—before all this nonsense—in Hirtschorn's mews and started spouting off that naughty piece by Marvel."

"'To His Coy Mistress.'" Sir Joseph sounded puzzled. "I hope you did not suggest it to him."

"Of course not, it's not a decent piece, for all it's charming, persuasive, and to the point. 'Had we but world enough and time, lady, this coyness were no crime…'" He frowned and peered at her. "*Was* it persuasive?"

Louisa permitted herself a sigh, because had Joseph been the one reciting the poem, it would have been persuasive indeed.

"When declaimed like some royal fanfare, it rather loses its impact. It's a poem written for an ardent swain, not for a determined fortune hunter."

"So you're turning dear Lionel down because his oratory skills are wanting? That hardly seems fair. Oratory is fine for the Lords, Louisa, but it won't avert scandal, and it most assuredly won't keep you in finery."

He was gripping her hand firmly as he delivered his scold. Despite her pique, Louisa admitted to herself that she liked the way Sir Joseph held her hand. Nothing tentative or limp about it. If he ever learned of her unfortunate excursion as a published author, he might just possibly be willing to grip her hand like that regardless.

Her heart missed a beat, then sped up as a thought crystallized: maybe more than possibly. She *prayed* it was more than possibly.

"Sir Joseph, my own dowry will keep me in finery.

I am sure the idea behind Lionel's recitation was to keep Lionel in finery."

"You are drawing an important conclusion based on very little information, Louisa Windham. One poem should not a marriage prospect destroy."

And one question should not a marriage prospect create, but given that her entire future hung in the balance, Louisa asked the question anyway.

"What about one kiss?"

⁓

"Sir Joseph is going to present Honiton's suit to Louisa?" Her Grace, Esther, the Duchess of Moreland, did not frown, though a close observer might have said she knit her brow *slightly*.

"That is what he'd have me believe. More tea, my love?" His Grace made the offer automatically—Her Grace adored a strong, hot cup of tea.

"Half a cup. I wasn't aware Louisa was more than flirting with Lord Lionel. His family is certainly adequate, but the boy lacks a certain…" She trailed off, accepting a full cup of tea from her husband. "Thank you, Percival."

His Grace settled in beside his wife, tucking an arm around her shoulders. "What is your real objection to Honiton, Esther? Sir Joseph has a contingency plan, if Honiton won't do."

She set her teacup down and rested her head against her husband's shoulder. "My objections hardly matter, do they? If Louisa wants Lord Lionel, then I will not stand in her way and neither will you. This is not how I wanted to celebrate Christmas, though, Percy."

"You don't think she wants him." More likely, Her Grace knew Louisa's mind on this, though how she gained such insights was a subject a prudent husband did not pry into very often.

"I am not certain, but I saw something last week that leads me to doubt Sir Joseph's generous proffer on Lionel's behalf will be accepted."

His Grace had eaten all but two cakes, and those he decided to leave on the plate lest Her Grace be distracted by his lack of restraint. "What did you see, my love?"

"You will think I should have disclosed this sooner, Percy, but I attached little significance to it at the time."

"Are you sure you wouldn't like the last of the cakes, Esther?"

"How can you think of—please eat them, Percival. The servants will just argue over them otherwise."

The duke popped both cakes into his mouth. They tasted particularly fine, given that his lady had *ordered* him to consume them.

"Percival, I saw Louisa kiss Sir Joseph."

"You saw—? Good God!" Before His Grace was done sputtering and coughing, Her Grace had delivered several stout whacks to the ducal back. "You saw Louisa kiss Sir Joseph? I may be getting old, my dear, but as best I recall from my youth, the thing is usually managed the other way around. The swain kisses the damsel."

She gave him an arch look "Not always."

Well. Various memories of their long-ago court-ship crowded out the immediate consternation of a papa who could see his daughter—who *had* seen his daughter—initiating such an impropriety.

"Esther, you are a naughty duchess. I love this about

you, but what does one kiss days ago have to do with the present difficulties?"

"I saw her face, Percy. She meant to buss his cheek, I think, and yet the kiss turned into something else entirely. Sir Joseph did not take advantage, mind you. He captured *and held* her attention, though. I think he surprised her, and she's been considering that surprise ever since."

"For all he raises swine, Sir Joseph is a damned decent fellow. Louisa could do much worse. I've mentioned him to the Regent now that another honors list is in the offing."

Her Grace was quiet for a moment. There being no tea cakes left, His Grace contented himself with the pleasure of sharing an embrace and yet another parental challenge with his beloved duchess—either of which trumped tea cakes handily.

"So that's Sir Joseph's contingency plan? He'll offer for Louisa himself?"

"He won't expect her to accept. He's thinking it will be a temporary engagement, but I have my doubts."

Another silence, while His Grace enjoyed for once making the dear lady exercise some patience of her own.

"Percival, what aren't you saying?"

"That kiss you saw, between Louisa and Joseph?"

"They had just danced a lovely waltz on a quiet terrace. I caught the end of the dance from a second-floor balcony where I'd gone for a moment of solitude."

"And I was across the terrace, having a private moment at the French doors of the gallery. I saw just a few bars of the dance, but, Esther? Do you recall the ballroom at Heathgate's town house?"

"It has an entire wall of mirrors. Ostentatious, but I take your point. Louisa and Joseph look much like ourselves when they're dancing with each other. I don't think Louisa realizes the potential of the situation."

"From where I stood, I could see Carrington's expression, Esther. Smitten, besotted, head over ears, call it what you will. Louisa might not entirely understand what's afoot, but Sir Joseph does. He looked like a man who'd awoken on Christmas morning to find his every wish come true."

"Then we must trust not only that he sees what's in the balance, but that he has the courage and skill to seize it."

"Just so, my love."

His Grace placed a kiss on his duchess's temple and sent a silent request to the Almighty that if courage and skill didn't sort the young people out, then the more reliable commodities of blind lust, some well-placed mistletoe, and a goodly quantity of holiday libation might see them put to rights.

Joseph tried to resort to the instincts that had saved his life more than once in Spain—the detached, analytical mental functions that took no notice of the simmering arousal caused by the simple touch of Louisa's hand on his breeches.

This was the same part of his mind that wanted to believe he held her hand merely to prevent her from stroking his thigh.

The objective is to preserve Lady Louisa from a scandal she's done nothing to deserve. The preferred plan is to see her safely engaged to Honiton, which will, as you have just explained to her, solve a number of problems all around.

That it would break Joseph's heart to surrender the lady to a loveless match was of no moment.

"You mentioned a kiss, Louisa. If a poor ability in this regard is your objection to Honiton as a matrimonial prize, then may I remind you that decades of wedded bliss will ensure you have ample opportunity to refine his abilities."

She gave him a peevish look. "I'm to spend decades teaching a *not-stupid* man how to kiss?"

"You are speaking in the indecipherable code reserved for females seeking to befuddle males, Louisa. Are you telling me you want to inspect Honiton's kisses before you accept him as a spouse?"

Joseph did not raise his voice, but he was coming perilously close to arguing with a lady. *Again.* Even among mere knights of the swine farms, such a thing was not done. The urge to put distance between him and the clove-and-citrus scent of the daft woman beside him was thwarted only by contemplating the spectacle he'd make trying to get to his feet.

A knot above his knee, indeed.

"I would certainly want to inspect the kisses of any man to whom I'd consider plighting my troth, and don't tell me it's a foolish notion. Your kiss was not at all wanting, in case you've wondered."

She fired this observation at him broadside, putting memories of sweet curves, soft, curious lips, and a private waltz where his determination to see to her best interests ought to lie.

"My thanks for that gracious accounting." He

scooted forward and braced both hands on the hearth-stones. "I should be going, so I will leave you to contemplate the tutelage you will bestow on Honiton that he might merit the same encomium."

A strong grasp seized him about the elbow and boosted him to his feet. "You are as articulate as Westhaven and as proud as His Grace, also as stubborn as the two of them combined, and possibly as thick-headed as all the extant and deceased Windham males put together. Why don't you use a cane?"

Joseph tested his balance while he withstood a glare from the woman beside him. "A cane? You think a cane would preserve my dignity? I'm not that much past thirty years old, my lady, and if it weren't for the damned—excuse me, the dashed—weather, I'd be as nimble as a blessed flea."

He *was* arguing with a lady, and because it was *this* lady, an apology was needed before he took his leave. "I beg your pardon. A cane is an excellent idea."

"Marrying Honiton is not."

Her ill humor had fallen away, and she was peering up at Joseph with earnest green eyes. Her arm was still twined around his, and Joseph could not have moved away to save his soul.

"My dear, living the rest of your life through books and nephews is a terrible idea, as is condemning your sisters to the same fate. Society loves for the mighty to fall, and with your lapse, your sisters' matrimonial prospects have been lamed, if not taken from the race. I am a widower, Louisa. I can tell you that having even a spouse to resent, a spouse to gossip with, is better than this notion you've taken. You have such passion..."

She was watching his mouth, watching the idiot mouth that had nearly whispered those last, achingly sincere words.

"People are talking, then?"

They were gleefully tearing Louisa's character to shreds, the women much more than the men. Joseph nodded and said nothing.

"Papa suggested you had some options to put before me. What have you to offer besides this lunatic proposal that I should join myself to a man who is not much given to vice and not at all given to stealing kisses?"

Now *he* was watching *her* mouth. "The only other option I see, Louisa Windham, is for you to marry me." He braced himself for her to whip away, to laugh, to pucker up with the presumption of it. "Say something, Louisa. I mean you no insult, I hope you know that."

"You think I'd take insult because you raise swine and I am a duke's daughter?"

She still had not moved away, and a distracting olfactory tickle of clove and citrus wended its way into Joseph's awareness. "There is that salient reality, but it's also the case that I must have children, Louisa, there being the matter of that da—deuced title. I could not offer you the cordial union you might seek."

"By cordial, you mean unconsummated."

He managed another nod. Merely standing near her, her arm twined with his, their fingers linked—when had *that* happened?—was wreaking havoc with his composure.

She stared past him into the fire, her brows knit. "I

like children. They're honest. They might lie about whether they stole the pie, but they don't deceive themselves about enjoying every bite. Children love a good story. They don't twitch their noses at a lively tale because it does not 'improve the mind.' Eve and Jenny adore children."

What was she saying?

"Louisa, I am offering a marriage in truth, though I am not the better bargain."

This close, he could see the gold flecks in her green eyes. The firelight brought out red highlights in her dark hair, and it was all he could do not to run his fingers over those highlights, to feel for himself the warmth and softness to be had by touching her.

"We kissed once." She spoke quietly and lowered her gaze. "I esteem you greatly, Joseph Carrington, though I have wondered if my efforts in that kiss were sufficiently unmemorable as to make you regret the occasion."

He was so busy trying to muster the discipline to let go of her hand and take himself off that her words didn't register immediately in his befuddled mind.

She esteemed him *greatly*? "Louisa, your efforts were not…unmemorable."

He saw her drop frosty politesse over the hint of vulnerability in her eyes, felt her spine stiffen fractionally—and knew he'd said the wrong thing. He could not abide those withdrawals, however subtle. "Louisa, since we kissed, I have thought of little else, and I esteem you greatly, as well. Very greatly."

While Joseph watched, a blush, beautiful and rosy, stole up Louisa Windham's graceful neck.

"I have had occasion to consider that kiss a time or two myself," she said. He thought her voice might have been just a trifle husky.

Hope, an entire Christmas of hope, blossomed in the center of his chest. "Perhaps you would like a small reminder now?"

He would adore giving her a reminder. A reminder that took the rest of the afternoon and saw their clothes strewn about the chamber. Twelve days of reminders would work nicely, with a particular part of Joseph's body promptly appointing itself Lord of Misrule.

He would not push her, but he would get a cane, the better to support himself should random insecurity threaten his knees in future.

Louisa lifted her gaze to his and seemed to visually inventory his features. After suffering her perusal for an eternity, Joseph let out a breath when she twined her arms slowly around his neck. He would not harry her. It would be a chaste kiss, a kiss to reassure—

Louisa Windham did not need *any* reminders about how to kiss a man. She gently took possession of Joseph's mouth, plundered his wits, and stole off with his best intentions. His arms came around her, anchoring her tightly against his body. Following in the path of sincere gentlemanly attentions, lust galloped up on a big, fast horse *flattening* his restraint.

It didn't flatten anything else, though. When Joseph would have angled his body away to avoid offending the lady, she tucked herself against him, breasts and hips, leaving nothing to the imagination.

"Louisa—"

The daft woman used his bid for reason to seam his

lips with her tongue. God in heaven, she even tasted like cloves and oranges.

"Kiss me, Joseph Carrington…" She muttered her orders against his mouth, and he obliged. By heaven, he obliged with everything in him—but not with force.

He resorted to stealth, teasing the corners of her mouth with his tongue and sliding his hands down, down to her hips. While she retaliated with a hand tangled in the hair at his nape, he shifted closer, wanting more of the feel of her against him. He loved learning the span of her hips with his hands, loved the womanly shape of her, loved the feel of their bodies pressed so tightly together.

But he cared for *her* too, so he eased away from the kiss and rested his cheek against her temple. She was breathing as fast as he, an observation which yielded him no small pleasure.

"Will you marry me, Louisa Windham? I feel compelled to point out to you that you should not when a better alternative exists."

Eight

LOUISA'S EXPRESSION COOLED, GIVING HER A RESEM-
blance to her mother Joseph hoped was not a prelude
to polite rejection, or worse than rejection, a request
for time to "think."

"Your admonitions are very chivalrous, Joseph
Carrington, but unavailing. You are handsome, intelligent, and I will not have to spend decades teaching
you how to kiss. I'm told these qualities adequately
endorse a man for matrimony."

She had accepted his proposal, she esteemed him
greatly, *and* she thought him handsome and intelligent?

As if to deny that such bounty had been surrendered,
Louisa regarded him with hauteur worthy of a duchess—a
ploy to hide her tender heart, he was sure of it. "You will
not allow Grattingly to harm your person, Joseph. You
have my permission to teach him a lesson, though."

A tender and protective heart, then.

"You're the merciful sort. This is good to know."
He kept his arms around her, content to endure any
number of lectures and scolds if she'd deliver them
while in his embrace.

"I'm practical." She nuzzled his neck, which hardly seemed the gesture of a practical woman. "Oh, *look*, Joseph, it's snowing again."

There was wonder and pleasure in her voice, and it nicely gilded the moment. Joseph glanced over her head to the window, where, indeed, big, lazy flakes of snow were drifting down over the damp garden. "I'd best be going then." He treated himself to a quick taste of her mouth and let her be the one to step back.

Let her. As if he could have.

"You will be careful?" Louisa brushed his hair away from his forehead in a gesture that was positively wifely.

"I'm used to snow, Louisa, and my horse is quite reliable."

Her lips flattened. "I meant with Grattingly. For obvious reasons, I do not trust that man to observe the dictates of honor."

"I will take no chances."

"I also don't like you going out in this weather, Joseph. Could you be persuaded to stay for the evening meal?"

An endless meal where he'd sit beside her, trying to both make conversation *and* keep his hands off her? "Perhaps next week. I'll tend to placing the announcement on my way home."

She looked not pleased, but mollified. "Are we to set a date?"

What was this? "That is usually the lady's prerogative. I am at your disposal in this regard." He considered briefly going down on his knees to beg her to allow him to get a special license. Getting up would be a problem, one he'd willingly deal with if he thought she'd give her consent.

She studied him with some unfathomable female light in her eyes. "The strategic thing to do would be to wait until next spring, to open the Season not with a ball, but with an enormous wedding breakfast."

His brilliant fiancée—who esteemed him greatly— could probably tell him the exact number of seconds between now and any wedding date months hence. "A lot can happen in a few months, Louisa."

"A spring wedding would give your daughters time to get used to the idea, Sir Joseph."

A suspicion bloomed in the back of Joseph's mind, a suspicion that his intended was even more clever than he'd perceived.

"Are you cornering me into admitting I'd like the wedding to take place immediately?" The idea of having Louisa under his roof for the Yule season lifted a bleakness on Joseph's heart that had nothing to do with teaching his daughters to ride in the dead of winter.

"I will lose my nerve, Joseph."

That such a magnificent, brave, and dear woman should make this admission to him was far more compliment than insult. She sounded so plaintive, though, so bewildered.

"Common sense ought to dictate some haste, Louisa. I could end up dead, and as my widow, you'd be shown every courtesy."

She blinked, and before his eyes, she regained her dignity. "You will not end up dead. I will not have it. We will be married at week's end if you can fit a special license and a wedding into your schedule."

Relief warred with a sense of having queered the

moment. "And where shall we marry? I assume we're both members of the parish in Kent."

"I'd prefer St. George's."

"Excellent thinking." Before the holiday exodus, let society see the vindication of her honor right under their noses. "I will leave you to plan the details and trust you to know my own tastes lean toward simplicity and dispatch."

She kissed him—with simplicity and dispatch, also a whiff of cloves and a delectable if fleeting press of her bosom to his chest. "Be off with you, then. I must endure my sisters' good wishes, and for that I need no audience."

She meant it. Her gaze could not have been more stoic had she been a martyr holding her prayer book.

He kissed her cheek lingeringly—he was not a martyr—and took his leave of her. As he swung up on his horse a few minutes later—swung up easily— Joseph noted with some curiosity that in the last half hour, his leg had stopped paining him entirely.

✄

"To a successful marriage." Westhaven touched his glass to his guest's and took a sip of excellent potation. "Though I must say, I do not care for the circumstances engendering your betrothal to my sister."

"I do not want a successful marriage," Sir Joseph said, stepping away and perusing a shelf of books in Westhaven's library. "I want, and your sister deserves, a happy marriage. I believe you would say the same thing regarding your countess."

He would. Westhaven set his glass aside and

considered the man so innocently eyeing some books of poetry.

"Do you doubt Louisa will exert herself toward assuring a happy union?"

Sir Joseph frowned in the direction of a small volume bound in red leather. When he too put his drink aside, Westhaven took up a position leaning against the opposite bookshelf.

"I harbor no doubts regarding my intended. Lady Louisa has a generous heart, for all she shares her mother's ability to view the world dispassionately."

God in heaven. Few outside her immediate family were privy to the Duchess of Moreland's practical nature. "You've made a study of my womenfolk."

"If Louisa marries me, they will soon be my womenfolk too, won't they?"

The conversation was not going at all as intended. Worse, Sir Joseph had chosen the small red volume to pluck at random from the shelves. "This is beautiful."

It was also a disaster bound in expensive leather. "It's just a book, Sir Joseph."

"The poetry is beautiful: 'He sits beside her like a besotted god, watching and receiving that laughter which tears me gently to ribbons…'"

"Turn the page, and it takes a very different tone." Westhaven lifted the volume from his guest's hand—carefully, lest the thing tear. It *was* beautiful poetry, when it wasn't being scandalous as hell. He had read some of it to Anna in the privacy of their bedchamber.

Carrington watched as Westhaven put the book back between its fellows on the shelf. "You enjoy those translations?"

"Some of them. I don't believe the point of our gathering is to recite poetry to each other." Westhaven infused a dose of ducal condescension into the observation—something he was getting quite good at, if he did say so himself.

Carrington's lips pursed. "No, it is not. We gather to discuss settlements, and I must thank you for sparing me from undertaking this exercise with His Grace."

"Because?" Though His Grace was also grateful not to have to deal with the business.

"I am not of your strata, Westhaven, I understand this. His Grace does, as well, and to the extent that among your sort marriage is commerce, the negotiation of it must be made complicated and delicate. I neither need nor want a farthing of your wealth to take Louisa as my wife."

Oh, famous. First the poetry, now the insufferable pride of the merchant class must obstruct Louisa's happiness. "Shall we sit?"

Sir Joseph cast a look toward the blazing hearth, his expression betraying a longing Westhaven found uncomfortable to behold. "Your house is marvelously well heated, my lord."

"My countess will not permit me to suffer domestic discomfort. I expect Louisa will be similarly vigilant with your hapless person. I advise you to resign yourself to it."

"Should that be the case, I shall bear up."

They shared a smile, and as they ensconced themselves in comfortable chairs, Westhaven began to hope that Louisa had chosen well after all. "I will not permit my sister to come to you undowered."

"Oh, of course not." Sir Joseph settled a little lower in his chair. "To do so would be to insult the lady. Make whatever arrangements you like, but be aware that upon our marriage, I will donate a comparable sum to the charity of Louisa's choice."

And now things became delicate, because a man of Sir Joseph's unprepossessing origins was unlikely to understand the magnitude of the figures involved.

"That is very generous of you, Carrington, but might it not suggest to Louisa that you place no value on her jointure and thus none on her?"

Sir Joseph eyed his drink. "It ought to make clear the opposite: I place such value on her, that without any settlement whatsoever, I would be well pleased to marry her."

Westhaven shot a look at the door then pretended to study the flurries drifting down outside the window. What he *wanted* was to confer with his countess—that lady being at present occupied in the kitchen, overseeing Christmas baking, if Westhaven's nose were to be trusted. Anna would know if Sir Joseph's thinking did indeed comport with those peregrinations of whimsy referred to as feminine logic.

Though it was of no moment, given that a gentleman farmer, even one sporting a knighthood, could not possibly adhere to the scheme Sir Joseph propounded.

Years of reading law gave a man a certain facility with prevarication, upon which Westhaven drew shamelessly. "I will draft something and have it sent around to your solicitors, Sir Joseph." With enough trusts, remainders, and legal obfuscations, Sir Joseph's pride ought to be spared much of a beating.

Westhaven did not commit himself to a date, since once the marriage was fait accompli, the dickering could be reduced to the status of a family squabble.

"Please yourself, Westhaven, but send the document to me. A mere knight need not admit solicitors to his personal business. What I want to make plain to you and the entire world is that I would have Louisa without a penny from her family."

"I've been in your home, Sir Joseph."

Sir Joseph stretched out his right leg, his posture a trifle relaxed considering the nature of the call. "So has half the shire, given the nosiness of the typical denizen of the neighborhood."

"We are friendly," Westhaven said. "Cordial."

"A bunch of gossiping titles by any other name. You can't learn one another's business under the vicar's watchful eye in the churchyard, so you must call on all and sundry. What is your point?"

They *were* a bunch of gossiping titles, which was part of the reason Westhaven's home was in Surrey, not Kent.

"My point is, Sir Joseph, had I not seen with my own eyes that your domicile is sufficiently commodious to house a duke's daughter, then I would have concern for this match."

Sir Joseph turned his head slowly to study his host. "Any man who does not regard matrimony in the general case with concern, much less the marriage of his own sister, is an idiot. Might I have a bit more?"

He held out his empty glass.

"Of course. I am remiss as a host, for which you will forgive me." While Westhaven refilled Sir

Joseph's glass at the sideboard—and his own—he also revised his thinking. His Grace was correct: Sir Joseph would be a fine addition to the family. The man wasn't cowed by anything as insubstantial as ducal consequence. Such backbone was a necessity for anybody marrying a Windham.

Sir Joseph shared this quality with no less a person than the Countess of Westhaven, in point of fact.

"Let me revise my toast," Westhaven said, bearing their glasses across the room. "To a long, happy, and loving union, such as I intend to enjoy with my own dear wife."

Sir Joseph accepted the glass but looked hesitant. *Loving* had been pushing the bounds of nascent fraternal bonhomie, but *fruitful* would likely have caused the man to blush. Carrington took a sip of his drink, and silence spread between host and guest.

Dealing with siblings, parents, merchants, and other aggravations, Westhaven had learned the value of silence. Perhaps raising livestock taught a man the same lesson.

"Sir Joseph, was there something more we needed to discuss?"

"Yes." Sir Joseph's lips thinned as he frowned at the snow now coming down in earnest. "I'm thinking you'd best fetch that decanter over here."

A duke's heir did not *fetch* anything, except perhaps his wife's shawl, her embroidery, her favorite book, her hairbrush, or her slippers.

Or her morning chocolate.

"Perhaps you had better enlighten me as to the topic first."

The smile hovering around Sir Joseph's mouth was

almost mischievous, leaving Westhaven to suspect his guest's trespasses against strict decorum had been intentional. Such behavior was worthy of...Louisa herself. When Westhaven again regarded his guest—with somewhat more respectful eyes—the man was no longer smiling.

"I would like to discuss my daughters and my sons, and the fact that I am in need of a guardian for them all in the event of my death."

Westhaven crossed his legs at the knee and straightened the crease of his trousers. "I wasn't aware the blessings of fatherhood extended in your case beyond your two daughters."

"Neither is Louisa, and I would prefer it stay that way for the present."

As a tenet of business, politics, and domestic tranquility, Westhaven believed that when something seemed too good to be true—say, an ideal spouse for his brilliant, bookish, outspoken, pretty sister—invariably it *was* too good to be true.

"And how many times have you been blessed as regards the siring of sons, Carrington?"

"Eight—and they have four sisters similarly situated. These are in addition to the two daughters who share my household in Kent."

Eight. The total number of extant Windham siblings, legitimate and otherwise. Twelve bastard children was... King Charles II had sired twelve bastards. A man had to admit to grudging admiration at the sheer stamina involved. And like His Majesty, Carrington was apparently making good provision for his by-blows.

Westhaven fetched the decanter.

❧

"You have mail." Jenny dropped two letters into Louisa's lap.

Louisa did not reply until the footman who'd rolled in the tea cart had departed. "And it has taken all day to be delivered to me?"

"You've had a busy day," Eve said from her seat by the fire. "Though I must say you've borne up wonderfully under the strain."

"Of shopping?" Her sisters had remained at her side throughout, and kept Her Grace's more profligate notions firmly in check.

Jenny set the tea tray down on the low table before the sofa. "The strain of knowing your intended fights a duel tomorrow at dawn."

An unease that had nothing to do with impending matrimony coiled a little tighter in Louisa's gut. "There is that."

"Read your letters, dearest." Jenny's countenance was serene as she poured tea for all three sisters. "Sir Joseph will acquit himself honorably. That's all that matters."

Eve's mouth screwed up in an unladylike fashion. "This honor business seems to create a great deal more problems than it solves. Women never mention it, and you don't see us blowing out each other's brains at a ridiculous hour over some imagined slight."

"Eve." Jenny's voice was sharp with rebuke.

Louisa scanned her letters, feeling equal parts grateful for and annoyed by her sisters' concern. "She has a point... And I have a letter from Valentine."

"Is it words, or has he sent you a composition again?" Jenny held up a teacup. Louisa shook her head

and scanned her brother's elegant, flowing penmanship. "Words. He felicitates me on my choice of
spouse—as if I had a choice."

Eve shot her a puzzled look. "You did."

"So I did." Though the idea of marrying anybody
but Joseph, for any reason but the preservation of
familial honor—and his honor—had been unthinkable
and remained so. "Ellen is in wonderful health, as is
the baby, and Val sends you two his warmest greet…"
China tinkled, the fire popped out a shower of sparks,
and as Louisa read the next few lines, her insides went
queasy and cold.

"Dearest?"

Eve and Jenny exchanged a worried look. Until his
marriage, Valentine had been their escort of choice,
the brother they confided in, the one who seemed in
greatest sympathy with female sensibilities.

"I must pay a call on Sir Joseph." Louisa folded the
letter carefully and got to her feet. If it was the last
thing she did on earth, she was going to pay a call on
her intended.

"Tonight? Dearest, it's already dark, and if you're
not here when we sit down to dinner…"

"We'll tell Mama you have a headache or the
female complaint," Eve broke in. "Either is perfectly
plausible. I'm happy to go with you."

Jenny pursed her lips. "You can't both have a headache."

"I'll go alone," Louisa said. "I'll go on foot. It's
only a few blocks, and I'll wear a veiled bonnet and
have one of the footmen accompany me. This snow
will keep people off the streets, and Sir Joseph will see
me home."

Her plan was arguably improper, also possibly dangerous.

They didn't stop her. They didn't even try.

∽

Assuming you survive the field of honor, what would you be willing to pay to keep your new wife in ignorance of your profligate adultery in Spain?

Sir Joseph stared at the note, the words printed in a sloppy and unknown hand. The little epistle had been delivered with the day's correspondence, no address, no franking, and it had haunted Joseph for an entire cold, miserable day.

Somebody was determined to poison the marital well for him, and before the ceremony had even been held.

And yet, it wasn't quite a blackmail threat—not yet. The solution was simple, of course. All Joseph had to do was tell Louisa she was marrying a man with more bastards than most fellows had legitimate children—and watch a woman he esteemed greatly flounce off to a life of obscure spinsterhood she did not deserve.

"A young lady to see you, sir."

Joseph glanced up from the ledgers he'd been staring at. His butler, a worthy old hound in demeanor and to some extent in appearance, wore a carefully neutral expression.

"Did she give you a name, Sylvester?"

"She did not, sir. The footman who escorted her was wearing Moreland livery."

"Show her in, and tell the kitchen to send up two trays for dinner."

"Very good, sir." Sylvester bowed and withdrew, only to return shortly with Louisa Windham in tow. Joseph knew a moment's chagrin that she'd caught him in his shirtsleeves, but if they married, she'd find him in far more informal moments than this.

When they married.

"The young lady, sir."

"Thank you, Sylvester. That will be all, and close the door behind you."

While Joseph rose from the desk and folded his reading spectacles into a pocket, Louisa remained standing by the door in a dress of red velvet. Her cheeks were rosy with either cold or self-consciousness. "Hello, Joseph. We should leave the door open."

"In which case, we'll lose all the heat I've spent the past two hours coaxing out of this fire." Joseph crossed the room and took her hand in his, her fingers chilly against his palm. "If you're concerned about propriety, may I remind you that we're engaged, Louisa? Your damp hems suggest you came on foot, and your passage here with only a footman in tow might well have been remarked already."

"We stayed mostly in the alleys."

"Did you?" He wanted to summon her footman from the kitchen and read the man the Riot Act regarding the foolishness of allowing young ladies into London alleyways after dark. But Louisa was cold, quiet, and around her eyes there was a tension Joseph did not like. "Come over by the fire. There's food on the way."

He kept her hand in his and sat beside her on the sofa before the hearth. "If you wanted to cry off, Louisa, you might simply have sent a note."

Her dark brows rose. "You think the night before a *duel*, I'd send along a note breaking our engagement?"

Joseph regarded his intended for a silent moment. Beneath the flush of cold, she was pale, and under her eyes, shadows suggested she was sleeping badly. "I would not blame you if you had sent a note, Louisa. Are you crying off?"

He'd managed to make the question sound causal, but could hardly fathom what else might have sent her out in dirty weather, virtually alone after dark. The idea of losing her...

It should have been a relief. Marriage to Louisa would be a challenge, to say the least, and yet, Sir Joseph did not let go of her hand.

"Do you want me to cry off?" she asked in a careful voice, a voice not at all appropriate to the passionate woman he'd become engaged to.

"I do not, and I am not offering you a gentlemanly platitude, Louisa." Giving her the simple truth was surprisingly easy. He wished all truths were that uncomplicated.

Her shoulders relaxed a trifle. "Well, I'm not crying off. That is, I don't intend to."

He was spared having to reply to that ringing assurance by the arrival of the dinner trays. Louisa eyed hers dubiously.

"Eat, Louisa. You are likely missing supper with your family, and if you're going to brave blizzards at night, you must have sustenance."

"I eat too much."

If she'd burped, she could not have looked more horrified at her own words. Joseph busied himself pouring them each a glass of wine, lest he witness the blush he knew she was suffering.

"If your feminine attributes are any indication, you consume exactly the right amount to fill your figure out to its best advantage. Shall we eat?"

In keeping with his preferences, the kitchen had sent up a simple meal of roasted beef, bread and butter, potatoes mashed with cheddar, and some stewed pears. He should have been ashamed to set such pedestrian fare before her, but if they married—when, *when* they were married—she'd catch him taking a tray in the library on many an occasion.

"This beef is cooked to a turn," she said some minutes later. "Your kitchen takes good care of you."

"They're on their best behavior of late. There's a rumor the daughter of a duke will soon take my humble self and my staff in hand."

He saw she was pleased with the compliment but tried to hide her smile by taking a sip of wine.

"Louisa, as much as I enjoy your company, as flattered as I am by your presence, please tell me why you're here."

Rather than answer, she pushed her pears around with her fork. "I got a letter from Valentine."

Joseph extricated the fork from her hand, speared a bite of pear, and held it up to her lips. "And?"

She took the bite from the fork, holding his gaze as she did. "These are good too." She munched slowly while Joseph made a bid for patience. "Valentine was at university with Lionel, Grattingly, and the fellows they sport around with."

"Because," Joseph said, feeding her another bite of

pear, "it is the stated purpose of Oxford to ensure the sons of the Beau Monde form generational solidarity with one another."

While he pronounced judgment on his alma mater, Louisa slid the fork from his hand and speared another bite of pear.

"Because," she said, holding the fork to Joseph's mouth, "they are of an age. Valentine sent you a warning."

Joseph closed his lips around the dessert and tasted pear, cinnamon, and brandy in an explosion of sweetness on his tongue. "What is this warning?"

He did not relieve her of the fork.

"Grattingly was involved in several duels at university. Valentine seconded two of his opponents."

As Joseph swallowed another bite of pear and heaven, he let his gaze travel over Louisa's hands. Pretty hands, and despite what he faced tomorrow— maybe because of what he faced—he wanted to feel those hands on his person.

"I've been a second myself. Life on the Peninsula seemed to breed displays of bravado like an army bedroll breeds fleas."

She paused, feeding herself a bite of pear from the fork they'd been sharing. She had a pretty mouth too. "You'll tell me about that sometime, won't you?"

"About the fleas?"

"About campaigning under Wellington. Bart's letters made it sound like a jolly lark, but a jolly lark does not explain why Devlin came home in such a deplorable condition."

"One hears St. Just is doing much better now, but yes, Louisa, I will tell you whatever you wish to know about army life. What was Lord Valentine's warning to me?"

Between gorging himself visually on her beauty, letting her feed him a subtly decadent dessert, and awareness of what awaited him in the morning, it took Joseph until the pears were gone to understand something: Louisa Windham—soon to be Louisa Carrington—was afraid.

For him. Fear put the pallor to her complexion, the shadows beneath her eyes, the tension around her mouth. Seeing this, the anger Grattingly's behavior had provoked bloomed into a simmering rage.

For her. For the lady who closed her eyes for a moment every time Joseph fed her a bite of pear.

"Valentine said for both duels Grattingly provided the pistols, and both of Valentine's friends said they did not aim true. They pull left, both men were wounded too, one seriously, while Grattingly suffered not a scratch."

"Interesting."

As if he were already married to her, Joseph draped an arm around Louisa's shoulders and tugged her back against his side. "So if I'm to use Grattingly's pistols, I will compensate by aiming slightly right. I expect we will delope, my dear. You will try not to worry about this."

"I can't help but worry." She remained stiff, as if trying to keep some semblance of authority over her person even as she permitted him his half embrace.

"I'm flattered, you know."

His intended turned to regard him. "You could be *dead* this time tomorrow, and you're *flattered* the woman who has agreed to marry you is *worried*? Joseph, you must not allow that man to do harm to your person."

He kissed her, lest she work herself into a fit of the vapors over something neither of them could control. Rather than turn the kiss into a display of disregard for her anxiety, he offered her a kiss of comfort, of reassurance, and even gratitude for her concern.

"Joseph…" Her hand, no longer cold, cradled his jaw. "This solves nothing."

He tucked a lock of her hair behind her ear. "It settles my nerves and distracts me from the looming ordeal."

"Is it an ordeal?" Concern made her green eyes lambent. Joseph turned his cheek into her palm lest his gentlemanly restraint drown in those eyes.

"Of course not. It's the merest nuisance, but I'm pandering to your tenderhearted nature."

"You're not lying to me? Not trying to set my nerves at ease with prevarication? You must not lie to me, Joseph. Not ever."

"Louisa, I was a marksman for Wellington." He kissed her palm. "I can handle any firearm, crossbow, long bow, or dart you put into my hands, and I give a good accounting of myself with knives, swords, and bare knuckles too."

Her gaze searched his face. "You are very fierce. One would not suspect this, watching you with your daughters in the churchyard."

"That requires an entirely different ferocity." And the ability to withstand a pang of homesickness that even included Lady Ophelia.

"I'm going to like your girls, Joseph."

"And they shall adore you."

This earned him a small but genuine smile. "I had tea with Her Grace."

He wanted to kiss her again, and she was discussing domestic trivialities. "Perhaps *that* was an ordeal?"

"I think Her Grace was giving me advice, or her blessing."

Joseph kissed his fiancée's cheek, catching a Christmassy whiff of cloves that did nothing to settle his unruly imagination. Rather than establish some distance, Joseph lingered near enough to run his nose along Louisa's jaw. "What manner of advice?"

"Kiss me, Joseph Carrington."

With pleasure. He kissed her sweetly and gently, until she was a warm, boneless weight of softly groaning female against his side, and then she kissed him sweetly and nowhere near gently.

By the time she had arranged herself flat on her back beneath him on the sofa, Joseph was neither missing his pet pig nor concerned about any duels. He was, however, in the last corner of his mind capable of rational thought, mightily troubled that Louisa had asked him to not lie to her—not ever—and he had been unable to respond with the promise he longed to give her.

Nine

"WHERE COULD SHE HAVE GONE?"

Only acts of God inspired Esther Windham to audible worry, and His Grace made it his business to know when such cataclysms were in the offing. Fortunately, there were none scheduled for the evening.

"Drink your tea, my dear. It's a fine blend, and it will settle your nerves." He picked up her teacup and held it out to her with his most husbandly smile, though how she could swill so much of the wretched stuff defied explanation.

"Percival Windham," she replied frostily, "you patronize me at your peril."

Much better, though he affixed a chastened expression to his features. "You say Louisa took a footman and headed north?"

Her Grace picked up an embroidery hoop and stabbed the needle through the fabric. "The shops are closed at this hour, Percy, and Louisa is not one to make last-minute holiday purchases. Why would she be heading toward Oxford Street?"

"My love, could she be headed for Sir Joseph's town house? His morning might prove eventful."

"Good God." Her Grace tossed the embroidery hoop aside. "You think she's gone to anticipate her vows? To indulge in melodrama that could leave her in a worse scandal than the one that's afoot if Sir Joseph dies?"

"No, I do not. I believe she's gone to spend some time with her fiancé, a man she's increasingly fond of. Sir Joseph cares far too much for her to put her in harm's way. Let's collect Eve and Jenny and enjoy a pleasant evening meal."

Her Grace rose from the settee, a determined light in her eye. "Louisa's sisters will know where she's gone, and they'll not keep such a thing from us."

The duke patted his wife's hand when she accepted his escort. Her Grace worried about Louisa more than others, having once confided that Louisa was the child she did not *understand*.

Perhaps mothers seldom understood the offspring who most closely resembled them.

His Grace paused at the parlor favored by his daughters and rapped on the door. "Come along, my beauties. We must away to the banquet."

Jenny opened the door. "It is time to eat already?" She was sporting the smile that likely fooled everybody in merry old England except her parents.

"I'm famished," Eve said, appearing at Jenny's side and wearing a comparably mendacious, cheerful expression. "Cold weather always makes me hungry."

"Where's Louisa?" Her Grace asked. To her husband's ear, there was a telltale note of imperiousness in the duchess's voice.

"She has the headache."

"It's a slight stomachache."

Louisa's sisters had spoken simultaneously and then looked anywhere but at each other.

"What a shame," His Grace murmured. "To be brought low by both miseries. We will save her a piece of cake in hopes of her speedy recovery. Come along, my dears."

He ignored the consternation momentarily flaring in his wife's eyes, knowing Her Grace would never take him to task before the children. With her youngest daughters trailing docilely behind, the duchess went in to dinner on His Grace's arm, and true to His Grace's prediction, the meal was quite pleasant.

The duke knew a spark of pride when his duchess even recalled to have a piece of chocolate cake sent up to Louisa's chamber when dessert was served.

❧

"This is not what I had planned for dessert, Louisa Windham."

Sir Joseph murmured the words near Louisa's ear, though she was too enchanted with the feel of his weight above her to argue. "I've never wrestled with a grown man before."

"You had the element of surprise to aid you. When you are my wife, I will not be so easily subdued as to end up on my own hearth rug, regardless of the astonishing pleasures to be found there."

Louisa concluded she'd subdued him thoroughly, for he did not move off her where she lay on that rug.

"Joseph, did you just use your tongue—?"

"I'm tasting you, seeing if you savor of the Christmassy scent you've teased my nose with on so many occasions."

His voice had taken on a purring quality, the sound of it curling straight down beneath Louisa's belly to places low and sweet. "I believe I will enjoy being married to you, sir."

"Hush." He traced the curve of her ear with his nose, which made her shiver wonderfully. "I'm wrestling with my conscience—and, madam, I intend to emerge victorious from at least one struggle this evening—though be assured you shall enjoy certain parts of being married to me a great deal."

"One hoped that would be the—oh, *Joseph*…"

He'd shifted, wedged his body more tightly into hers so she could feel his arousal.

"The lady falls silent. Surely, the season of miracles is upon us."

Louisa closed her eyes, the better to appreciate the marvelous sensations Joseph's hand on her breast evoked. He knew what he was about, handling her gently but with an assurance that had heat streaking in all directions inside her.

"I want my clothes off," she said, squirming into his weight. "I want *your* clothes off." Abruptly, the idea of marriage—marriage to Joseph—had developed a compelling appeal.

Joseph lifted up a little, onto his forearms and knees, and Louisa wanted to screech over the loss of him. "You frighten me, Louisa Windham. Remind me to remove all bindings, knives, riding crops, gags, and blindfolds from our bedroom for our wedding night."

She heard the smile in his voice as she opened her eyes to peer up at him. "You find this humorous? I'm in a passion for a man for the first time in my life, and you're amused?"

The smile died, but the warmth in his eyes did not. "For the *first time*, Louisa?"

She hid her face against his shoulder. "You heard me."

He cradled the back of her head in one large palm and rose up over her, a comforting, arousing abundance of healthy male that blotted out Louisa's awareness of everything else.

"I can give you pleasure, Louisa, but my conscience will not allow me to entirely anticipate our vows."

Louisa strongly suspected Joseph was being decent. She wanted to wallop his dratted conscience halfway to Scotland. "Why not?"

"Because Grattingly uses crooked pistols, and because I esteem you too greatly." He delivered these declarations so gently, they sounded to Louisa like the concluding couplet to a poem, for all she resented the truths they spoke to. The last thing her parents needed was the illegitimate grandchild who could result from a night of passion.

From a single *moment* of passion.

"What is this pleasuring you refer to?"

She felt him chuckle. "You sound so suspicious, Louisa. I allude to the intimate pleasure a man brings to a woman he cares for, a pleasure you can bring yourself, if you're so motivated, and one I will visit upon you often once we're married."

While he made his threats, Louisa stroked her hand over his hair. She had the odd thought she was glad he was dark like she, not a perfect, shining blond god, and though even his voice was dark, his hair was soft beneath her fingers.

"*Do not* lecture me, Joseph. Kiss me."

He fell silent, and Louisa closed her eyes, expecting the pleasure of his mouth on hers. Instead, he used his lips on the place where her shoulder met her neck, a tender, vulnerable location that bloomed with warmth at the touch of his mouth.

"*Do not* be impatient, Louisa."

She'd been *born* impatient, born having to wait for those whose brains could only dawdle and stumble along, but when Joseph used his mouth on her neck again, it was Louisa's brain stumbling.

"I do like that, Joseph."

"How convenient. I rather enjoy it myself."

He sounded smug. She didn't care. While a slow, sweet warmth purred up from her middle, Louisa tugged Joseph's shirt from his waistband.

"In a hurry, Louisa?"

When had a man ever put so much lazy warmth in a simple question? "If you don't want me undressing you, then take it off yourself."

He lifted up, pulled his shirt over his head, and resumed nuzzling her neck in the time it took Louisa to draw a breath.

"Better." Much, *much* better. To feel the warmth of his skin, the exact contour of his muscles and bones beneath her hands was better indeed.

"Then you won't mind some turnabout." He moved again, this time shifting to her side. "Shall I blow out the candles, Louisa?"

He lounged beside her, head propped on his hand, surveying her with a peculiar light in his eyes. She wanted to see all of him but realized he'd then expect to see all of her. Her bold pronouncement about removing clothing had been made by desire galloping well in advance of her courage.

"Yes, please douse the candles."

He moved around the room in just his breeches and boots, leaving Louisa a moment to simply watch him. She beheld abundant muscle, a kind of prowling grace despite the slight unevenness of his gait, and she beheld evidence of his arousal behind his falls.

Or so she suspected. There had been some phrases and words she hadn't been able to translate from the Latin, and her useless, idiot, twitting brothers had found her requests for assistance uproariously funny.

"You can still change your mind, Louisa," Joseph said, lowering himself to the rug and tugging off his boots. "A few days from now, we'll be married, and there will be nothing of the illicit about intimacies even greater than these."

Louisa watched the firelit shadows play over his features. "That always struck me as ridiculous. The same act is a sin in the morning but a sacrament at night, provided you say some magic words and wear the right dress."

"I am marrying a radical and a blasphemer." Joseph tossed pillows down from the sofa and stretched out beside her. "We'll have very lively discussions."

He began to unbutton her dress, which as luck would have it fastened down the front. His hands were large, in proportion to the rest of him, and he had an ink stain on the heel of his right palm.

"I like that you aren't put off easily, Joseph. We *will* have some lively discussions."

"We might even argue, Louisa." He smiled, then leaned down over her breastbone and inhaled through his nose. "I intend to be married to you for quite some time and have not such a store of gentlemanly manners as most of the fellows you socialize with."

"Will we raise our voices to each other?"

He drew a finger slowly over the swell of Louisa's breasts. "I will never raise my voice to you in anger, Louisa Windham, soon to be Louisa Carrington."

She sighed, closed her eyes, and felt a lump rising in her throat. As Joseph slowly, almost reverently loosened her clothing, Louisa had a vision of them both aging amid a houseful of children, rousing discussions at the supper table presaging tender loving in the privacy of their quarters. She had not looked for this, had not thought it could be hers, but lying there while her intended gently acquainted her with his intimate touch, she felt something lovely and sweet stirring along with desire.

She felt *hope*. Hope for herself, hope for this unlikely marriage.

"Louisa, my dear, your intimate apparel is a revelation."

He was staring at her chemise, a red silk creation embroidered along the border with green, gold, and white thread in a holly pattern.

"Jenny makes them for us, and these stays are her design too."

The stays laced up the front, an old-fashioned construction not usually considered appropriate for Town wear. With some maneuvering, they could be put on and taken off without the assistance of a lady's maid... Or *with* the assistance of a fiancé.

Joseph began undoing the laces, causing little pulls and tugs Louisa had felt many times before, though never in a context that made her attend the sensations.

"I wonder if His Grace knows his womenfolk are so enterprising. Lady Jenny could make a fortune with these."

Louisa ran her hand through his hair. "Are you talking to settle my nerves?"

He pushed her stays aside then started on the bows of her chemise. "Is it working?"

"I'm not nervous, Joseph, I'm...restless. Inside."

He kissed her on the mouth. "The things you speak aloud, Louisa. The things I want to do with you..."

She hadn't lied, she *was* restless, but also uncertain of how to go on, which state of affairs she *loathed*. Joseph finished untying the bows of Louisa's chemise, and for the first time in her life, Louisa felt the weight of an adult male gaze on her naked breasts.

"You're staring, Joseph. This is not well done of you."

"You stared at me without my shirt."

"That's different." Rather than belabor the illogic of her observation, Louisa tried to cross her arms over her breasts. Joseph prevented it with gentle implacability.

"Lady Jenny must make you a new set of stays, Louisa. Ones that won't lace up quite as snugly. This will be my first request of you as your espoused husband."

Still he did not take his eyes off her breasts, and Louisa felt his regard like a visual caress. "My dresses won't fit if I use looser stays."

"But, dearest affianced Wife, you will be able to

breathe." He sat up, crossing his legs to perch at Louisa's hip. "The Creator has generously seen to a very attractive distribution of your feminine assets, and we can have an entire new wardrobe made if you wish, but I would have my wife able to breathe—particularly if she's to shout at me on occasion."

He laid his hand on her sternum, his touch warm, his palm slightly calloused. The sensation of it, the immediacy of the contact on such an intimate body part had Louisa closing her eyes. For long, quiet moments, she focused only on his hand as he learned the shape and feel of her breasts, and she learned of pleasures new and strange.

"Should I be enjoying this?"

He didn't stop touching her. "One hopes you are. I certainly am." His tone was contemplative, almost detached. Through the haze of her growing arousal, Louisa felt a spark of determination that he should not remain so thoroughly in possession of his wits.

Without warning, she reached up and explored *his* chest with *her* hand. Joseph's fingers went still in the process of lazily circling her left nipple then resumed their progress.

He had nipples too. If they were susceptible to half the sensations being stirred in the comparable part of Louisa's anatomy…

"I am marrying a bold woman." Joseph grabbed her hand, kissed her knuckles, then placed her palm directly over his heart. "I adore bold women."

Taking him at his word, Louisa levered up and kissed him. She'd learned something from him: holding back just a little in a kiss made the pleasure flare hotter.

And then holding back wasn't possible. She was aware of Joseph lowering her to the carpet with their mouths still fused, aware of his hand trailing down over her belly, and aware of clinging to his shoulders even when her back was securely supported by the floor beneath the hearth rug.

"Spread your legs, Louisa."

The words were a growl as Louisa felt the wet, hot pleasure of Joseph's mouth close around her nipple. His hand on her knee gently reinforced the meaning of his command, and then his fingers drifted through the curls on her mons.

When had her skirts pooled around her waist?

Louisa winnowed her hands in his hair, wondering if this was the real reason she'd come hurrying through the night to her fiancé. Instead of sending a note, she'd been greedy, sensing she could at least have shocking intimacies with him, even if the worst were to happen tomorrow.

The idea that Joseph might not survive the duel intertwined with the conflagration of need rising in her body to create a spiraling urgency.

"Joseph, I want more. I want to be closer."

He said nothing but passed his fingers over an intimate part of her anatomy in such a way as to provoke shocks of sensation that radiated up from her womb. There was pleasure in his touch, but it sparked an awful unrest too.

"Again, please."

He kissed her. "As often as you like."

The damned man was everywhere—his chest pressing against Louisa's breast, his mouth consuming hers, his hand... He'd thrown a leg across Louisa's thigh, anchoring her as she undulated her hips in counterpoint to what he was doing with that hand.

She was suffocating with all his touches and breathing hard too. "I can't… I don't know…"

"I *do* know. Be patient. You're close."

He increased the pressure a lovely, blessed trifle, and things inside Louisa shifted. What had sought to move away from the man beside her could only cling to him, and inside her, what had been straining to fly apart came together more and more tightly in wrenching spasms of pleasure. She thrashed, sank her nails into muscular male flesh, and heard herself letting go of sounds halfway between sighs and moans. All the while, Joseph showered her with a pleasure so intense it bordered on unbearable.

When the sensations ebbed, Louisa was lying on her side amid a puddle of rumpled, disarranged clothing, plastered to Joseph's chest, her leg hiked over his hips, and her face mashed into his throat. Odd bits and phrases of Latin finally made sense to her, while her emotions—her very body—made no sense at all.

"This is part of being married?"

Joseph's hand stroked slowly over her hair, and Louisa thought for a moment he hadn't heard the question—or maybe she hadn't spoken aloud.

"It is part of you being married to me."

There was an implication in his words Louisa was too scattered to parse. Insights—into old passages of verse, into her siblings' marital devotion, into her own parents'—floated in the haze that passed for her thoughts. "Can one do this repeatedly? Successively? Nine times in a row?"

"One can if she's female and has some time on her hands. We fellows would find ourselves challenged to keep that sort of pace—though the attempt would certainly be pleasurable in the right company."

His tone suggested Louisa was the right company for him, which did nothing to restore her composure. "Why doesn't anybody tell a young lady about these things?"

"Young men all over England are whispering to their sweethearts about things like this. Perhaps the old fellows are too, if they're lucky." He shifted his hold, cradling Louisa by her derriere and hefting her up over him, so she straddled him on the rug.

"I am marrying a brute." She cuddled into the warmth of his chest and felt his arms come around her.

"You sound pleased to contemplate it."

Modesty requiring more self-discipline and clothing than Louisa could lay claim to at that moment, she settled comfortably on her fiancé. Through his clothing, his arousal created an intriguing pressure against her sex, one that evoked memories of the sensations she'd just enjoyed.

"I generally do not like surprises, Joseph Carrington."

"I am duly warned."

"I liked this one. I'm falling asleep."

She felt him kiss her crown. "You've earned your rest. When you're sufficiently revived, I'll escort you home."

Louisa sighed gustily, closed her eyes, and took in a big whiff of contentment and prospective husband. She'd thought honor and a thriving property were the greatest assets Sir Joseph brought to the marriage, but she'd been wrong.

In addition, he brought kindness, intelligence, and a generosity in matters of passion that took Louisa's breath away. She even ventured to hope that Joseph Carrington, among all men, might someday have the capacity to *understand* her.

As Louisa drifted off to sleep, she prayed he also possessed a great deal of luck and a steady, accurate aim. If he could manage all that—*and if her youthful indiscretions remained in the past*—then their marriage would exceed her most fervent imaginings.

"Your Grace, need I remind you that dueling is illegal?"

Joseph kept his voice down, though Grattingly had yet to arrive, and the corner of Hyde Park the Duke of Moreland had found his way to was very secluded. "Illegal, is it? What a pity. The pleasures of leaving one's duchess and one's cozy bed in the dark of night and freezing one's parts off aren't to be missed. You look passably rested, Carrington."

"I am." Joseph climbed off his horse, gratified to feel not a twinge of stiffness in his leg, even in the chill of a wintry dawn. If he survived the morning, he'd make it a point to linger half naked with his lady on hearth rugs before roaring fires often and at length.

"Listen, Carrington." With a lithe grace appropriate to a man half his age, Moreland swung down from his glossy bay gelding. "One doesn't want to butt in, and if you insist, I'll toddle along directly, but I received a note from my youngest son yesterday."

"Lord Valentine?"

His Grace nodded and stroked a gloved hand down the horse's neck. "I believe your second approaches."

Joseph followed the direction of the duke's sight to see an elegant town coach tooling up the slushy lane. "Harrison. I told him to bring a damned hackney."

"For God's sake, man, my own coach awaits just past those trees."

"And if I bleed all over your fancy coach, Your Grace?"

"Don't be an ass. Valentine sent you a warning. Sent it by pigeon and by post, so take heed: Grattingly's pistols, at least the ones he was using ten years ago, pull left. They're heirlooms, so Valentine is of the opinion he'll still be using them."

"Lord Valentine's warning reached me yesterday, Your Grace. I appreciate your ensuring I received it."

"For God's sake, you are as bad as Louisa."

Joseph took his gaze from Harrison's fancy town coach—and what was a mere portraitist doing with such a rig?—and surveyed Moreland's features. "I beg your pardon?"

"Your affianced wife, Louisa. She's incorrigible. The girl has loving family on every hand, *every hand*, and yet she must make her own way. Has always had to forge her own path, and I suspect she's met her match in you, so to speak."

The duke was trying to communicate something, while Joseph was trying to make out the crest on Harrison's coach. "Your presence here is still not well advised, Your Grace. Hanging felonies will likely be committed."

Moreland thwacked a riding crop against gleaming field boots. "Listen to me, young man: You have no father, no brothers, no uncles, not even a damned third cousin to see you through this. If a prospective papa-by-marriage is all you've got, then by God, that's what you'll take."

There was something heartening and familiar in the way Moreland delivered a scold. Warmth, unexpected and welcome, bloomed in Joseph's chest. "Your Grace, may I say first, thank you, and second, you are as bad as Louisa yourself."

"Where do you think she came by it? One wonders what you'll have to say to Arthur if he ever bestirs his bones to leave his carriage."

The fancy coach had drawn to a halt, and at the mention of "Arthur," Joseph comprehended whose crest he'd been admiring. "Did you send for him?"

"Me?" His Grace's look of innocence was a work of thespian brilliance. "Wellington's ability to gather intelligence is rivaled only by that of my duchess. I would certainly never attempt to involve a peer of the realm in such shady dealings as these."

"Of course not."

Wellington alighted from his coach, caught sight of Moreland, and smiled hugely. "Your Grace! A fine day for an outing, though our purpose here is hardly in keeping with the approaching Yule season. Carrington, good day."

Moreland and Wellington indulged in a riot of ducal bonhomie while Joseph saw with relief that a hackney was disgorging the soberly attired person of Elijah Harrison. A second man alit from the cab, dressed in somewhat finer style than Harrison.

"Splendid," Moreland said. "Lord Fairly is joining

us to ensure the medical necessities can be tended to." Fairly was tall, blond, and carrying a black bag Joseph did not allow his gaze to dwell on.

"My lord. Harrison." Joseph bowed to the stranger, though perhaps the bow included that ominous little bag too. "My thanks for joining us. Your Grace, may I make known to you—"

"No need for that," Moreland interrupted. "Fairly's a family connection of sorts. Wellington, I'm pleased to introduce David, Viscount Fairly, and, Harrison, I believe we're all familiar with you as a fixture in the dim corners of various clubs. Sir Joseph, if your opponent would see fit—ah! The rascal is going to post after all."

There was a benefit to having a pair of dukes invite themselves to one's first duel in many years. Moreland took control of not just the introductions, but inserted himself into the discussion of where the field ought to lie and how many more minutes they should wait before the sun climbed over the horizon. Wellington dogged Grattingly's seconds at every turn, leaving Fairly to chat Joseph up.

"Nervous?" Fairly put the question quietly, though they were downwind of Grattingly, suggesting the doctor wasn't a complete fool.

"Would I admit such a thing to a stranger?"

"You don't have to. There's tension about your mouth and eyes, your breathing is shallow, and you've been pushing the snow around with the toe of a riding boot that deserves better treatment."

Joseph turned to regard the man. "If your medical acumen is commensurate with your powers of observation, perhaps my nervousness is misplaced."

"I can also tell you that Grattingly's breath reeks like a gin whore's when the fleet has docked. He's very likely still the worse for drink from last night's excesses."

"Which makes him unpredictable."

Fairly nodded and said nothing more.

Moreland came churning across the snowy ground. "I believe all is in readiness, unless that buffoon's seconds can talk him into a last-minute apology."

Wellington flanked Joseph's other side. "I've conferred with the family, Joseph. Your opponent is a weasel who discredits vermin throughout the realm. Do as honor compels you, and even his fellow weasels will not lament the loss."

Joseph looked about himself to see at least three titles, possibly four if Harrison's dubious antecedents could be counted, all out in the cold dawn air to risk their reputations on his behalf.

"Gentlemen, I have never enjoyed defending a lady's honor more. Who's to give the count?"

"That honor falls to me," Harrison said. "Grattingly's second has the pistols."

A look passed among the men surrounding Joseph.

Joseph asked the ticklish question. "Somebody has inspected them?"

Harrison looked grim. "I have."

"Well," said Moreland, "I have not. Arthur, come along."

A-duking they did go, over to the folding table where Grattingly's matched pistols sat in an open velvet-lined box.

"To the naked eye, they look sound enough," Harrison muttered. "I could think of no reason to use another pair that wouldn't get us both called out all over again."

"Would that be another pair of pistols or dukes?"

As Joseph offered his rejoinder, Moreland's foot slipped, sending His Grace careening into His Other Grace, and the both of them pitching forward. The folding table collapsed, and the pistols tumbled out of their cozy box and into the snow.

"Oh, well done," Fairly said softly. When Joseph cast him a curious look, the man shrugged. "I don't hold with using antique weaponry for such serious matters. Appearances are well and good over the drawing room mantel, but this is not a drawing room affair."

The seconds conferred, and while Grattingly sputtered curses and cast Joseph withering looks, both dukes repaired to their coaches and brought forth boxed sets of dueling pistols.

Things moved along quickly from there. Grattingly chose Moreland's set of Mantons, Joseph took his place back-to-back with his opponent, and Harrison began the count.

The snow, Joseph later concluded, saved his life—if Their Graces hadn't already done so. Harrison's voice rang out, tolling the steps, but one shy of the turn, Joseph heard the snow beneath Grattingly's feet crunch off-rhythm, two steps where there should have been one.

A shot to the back was marginally less likely to be lethal than a shot to the chest, so Joseph did not emulate Grattingly and turn early. Grattingly's pistol discharged before the count ended, and Joseph felt the bullet whistle past his ear.

When Joseph turned, Grattingly was on one knee, his right arm still extended with the smoking pistol dangling from his grip.

"Foul!" Harrison called from the direction of the coaches. "Foul on Mr. Grattingly for firing early."

"He slipped!" Grattingly's second called, but the man's words lacked conviction.

Wellington's crisp voice cut across the frosty silence. "Take your shot, Sir Joseph."

Joseph aimed, inhaled, exhaled partway, and when he should have taken his shot—a clean bullet through Grattingly's black heart—there arose in his mind an image of Louisa Windham curled onto his chest in sleepy abandon. She had given Joseph permission to teach Grattingly a lesson—and only to teach him a lesson. Joseph adjusted his aim and fired.

The pistol went sailing from Grattingly's hand, while a few yards away, Moreland accepted a tenner from Wellington.

&

"I owe Your Grace a new set of pistols." Joseph kept his gaze from where Grattingly's hand was being wrapped in bandages by the physician. No blood had been drawn, but Grattingly's middle finger had been dislocated when the gun had been shot from his grasp.

"Consider this set a wedding present," Moreland said. "You'll come back to the house for some breakfast, won't you?"

Breakfast. Joseph envisioned himself at his desk in his drafty library, tea getting cold at his elbow, cold eggs on a plate with some cold buttered toast completing the picture.

"Breakfast wouldn't go amiss. Does one invite one's seconds and any chance-met dukes to breakfast after a duel?"

Moreland's white brows rose. "Arthur will take Harrison and Fairly to the club for a beefsteak. Let them listen to his glorious tales of India and Spain. I'm sure you've heard him prosing on as many times as I have."

Wellington was not particularly given to prosing on, but Joseph wasn't inclined to argue with his prospective father-by-marriage. He was, however, inclined to get his arse out of the freezing dawn air before the cold made his leg seize up into uselessness.

Moreland signaled to his coachman. "I'll tend to the civilities. You'd best be having a nip. You look a trifled peaked, and we mustn't be alarming the ladies with unnecessary dramatics."

Joseph extracted his flask from an interior pocket and took the duke's excellent advice. Moreland marched off to say something to the physician, while Wellington appeared at Joseph's elbow as if…on cue.

"So you're acquiring a wife for Christmas, Carrington."

"Your Grace has no doubt been invited to the wedding. I won't be offended if you decline the invitation, though."

Wellington shook his head at the proffered flask. "*Decline?* And put dear Percival in one of his legendary pets? Not bloody likely. Besides, I'll probably be able to get on Esther Windham's dance card at the wedding ball, and one doesn't pass up such an opportunity lightly. Does the young lady approve of your import business?"

In tone, this was a casual question from a man who could be brusque, direct, and blunt to a fault—all qualities Joseph liked about him. It was also an inquiry from a military duke who took the welfare of his officers seriously.

"The matter hasn't come up yet, Your Grace."

"Hmm." Wellington looked Joseph up and down. "Ladies don't like surprises, Carrington. My own duchess has informed me of this on several occasions."

"This is no doubt true in the general case, sir." But not true of certain ladies regarding certain surprises.

"When my duchess bestirs herself to offer an opinion, she is rarely wrong. Ah, yon Percy is done glowering at Grattingly. What an unworthy display the boy made. Pissed himself like the greenest recruit, I'm guessing, or he wouldn't be keeping that coat buttoned up. See you at the wedding, Carrington!"

Wellington bustled off, while Joseph took another nip and waited for Moreland to rotate into the post of ducal nursemaid.

"Let's be off," Moreland said, swinging up onto his bay. "My duchess is holding breakfast for me, and I do not keep her waiting lightly."

When they reached the Moreland mews and the grooms had taken Sonnet's reins, His Grace gestured toward a gate in a high brick wall. "This way, unless you want to go sashaying around to the front door at this hour? Word of the duel's outcome will be making the clubs by noon if some brave soul braces Arthur on the matter directly. Fairly will see to it if Wellington is having an inconvenient attack of discretion, and I imagine Harrison will stick his oar in if need be."

So there was strategy even to a duke's breakfast beefsteak. The notion was daunting.

Joseph followed Moreland past a snowy garden, through an unprepossessing door, into a dimly lit back hallway. The scent of baking bread hit Joseph's nose like an olfactory benediction.

"Moreland." Esther, the Duchess of Moreland, paused as she rounded the corner into the hallway. "And Sir Joseph. I hope your morning ride was pleasant?"

Their morning ride?

A footman slipped Joseph's greatcoat from his shoulders while the duchess performed a similar service for the duke. She passed the coat off to the footman and studied His Grace, clearly awaiting an answer.

"Utterly uneventful, my dear."

While Joseph looked on, and before the footman had withdrawn, Moreland brushed a kiss to his wife's cheek. "We ran into Arthur in the park. You're to save him a waltz at the wedding ball, or I'll never hear the end of it. I expect the bride had best do likewise, or Joseph will be the one His Grace plagues with sighs aplenty and public innuendo. Fairly sends greetings, and Sir Joseph is famished."

Her Grace's green-eyed gaze swiveled to take in Joseph in his riding attire. "An early outing can leave one with an appetite, particularly in this brisk air. Sir Joseph, if you'd like to freshen up, Hans will show you to a guest room."

Hans being yet another footman who'd appeared from thin air. Joseph let himself be led above stairs, though watching Their Graces had been a fascinating exercise in…marital code, Joseph decided. Her Grace knew damned good and well what had been afoot this morning, knew Wellington had been recruited to the scene…

Hell, it had probably been Her Grace's idea to send for reinforcements.

A door opened to Joseph's left as the footman—*Hans*—continued a stately progress through the house.

"Joseph."

He turned to see Louisa silhouetted in a doorway. She was attired in a plain green velvet day dress, her dark hair in a simple bun at her nape. Her expression went from surprised to smiling—brilliantly, magnificently smiling.

"My lady, good morning." He could not help but smile back.

He was calculating how much of a bow his hip and knee could tolerate, when she launched herself at him. "Please tell me you are unharmed. Please tell me all is resolved and you sustained no injury."

Footman be damned. Joseph brought his arms around his intended. "I am unharmed." He was at risk for being suffocated and knocked on his backside, but that did not matter. It did not matter in the least.

"And all is well?"

She was asking something more, something he'd figure out just as soon as he let himself enjoy for a moment the warmth and feminine abundance of Louisa Windham in his embrace, her clove scent winding into his brain and her smile scattering his wits.

"All is—"

"You won't have to hare off to the Continent? *We* won't have to?"

"Grattingly stoved a finger, I'm told, and the demands of honor are met. There will be no hasty departure for France." And she'd assumed if there had been a need to flee from the law, she'd be fleeing with him—an intriguing if wrongheaded notion.

"He stoved a finger?" Louisa shifted, tucking her hand into the crook of Joseph's elbow and moving alongside of him. "How is that possible?"

Joseph did not think of prevaricating. "He fired early, and when I took my shot, I shot the gun from his hand. Your father gave me the set of pistols as a wedding present." Louisa paused in the act of walking him down the corridor, her smile becoming, if anything, yet more incandescent.

"*You shot the gun from his hand?* That is, that is… *famous. Brilliant.* St. Just will be jealous. All of the boys will be jealous. *I* am jealous. *You shot the gun from his hand.* I am so proud of you, Joseph. Well done. Brilliantly well done."

They resumed their progress toward soap, water, and towels—heated water, scented soap, and warm towels as it turned out—while Louisa continued to deluge Joseph with a bewildering spate of approval. She also stayed near him, if not touching, for the duration of a hearty hot breakfast and insisted on walking with him to the mews when the meal had concluded.

"I wanted to kiss you," she said as they waited for Sonnet to be brought out. "When I saw you this morning, whole and healthy. Did you want to kiss me?"

In the bright morning sunshine, Louisa's green eyes sparkled like spring grass wet with dew, and energy fairly crackled around her.

And this magnificent, gorgeous woman—who was to be his wife—was confessing to a thwarted urge to kiss *him*. The grooms were busy in the stable, and the alley was deserted enough that Joseph could be honest. "I find, Louisa Windham-soon-to-be-Carrington, that I am constantly in readiness for your kisses. This state of affairs brings me back to boyhood Christmases, to the sense of excitement and...glee that hung over my holidays. As if delightful developments were always awaiting me."

He didn't sound gleeful to his own ears, but seeing his fiancée's smile, feeling her hand close around his several times under the breakfast table, he'd felt glee. Glee, relief, warmth...

And desire, of course.

Louisa smoothed a hand down his lapel. "If we were not standing in plain view of a half-dozen neighbors, Sir Joseph, I would comport myself very gleefully indeed. Did you know we're to have a ball after our wedding breakfast?"

He'd hoped she would kiss him. Instead, he caught her fingers in his and brought them to his lips. "If you don't want a ball, Louisa, I can probably put a stop to it. Where are your gloves?"

"Where are yours?" She made no move to retrieve her hand. "I think the ball is for Her Grace, a grand gesture to quiet the tabbies and gossips. Then too, Mama and Papa haven't hosted such an event or even a house party for some time now."

He tried to decipher her meaning. "So you want to have a wedding ball?"

Her expression dimmed. "Would you mind?"

"Come with me." He led her by the hand—she had warm hands, even in the morning chill—to a bench outside the stable. He took the place beside her, which meant ignoring the oddest impulse to sit her on his lap. "The question is not would I mind a ball, Louisa, it's do you want one?"

"If Mama and Papa want one, does it matter?"

"It matters to me. If we're having a ball merely to quiet gossip, a lavish if hastily arranged ball, a ball following an equally lavish wedding breakfast and a well-attended ceremony at St. George's, then we're tacitly confirming all the gossip, aren't we?"

She worried her lower lip with her top teeth, which gave her a girlish and uncharacteristically tentative air. "There's no good choice, is there? If we make a splash, we're trying to face down scandal. If we don't make a splash, a hole-in-the-corner affair practically announces a scandal."

Seeing that Louisa fretted, seeing that gossip and scandal preyed on her peace of mind, Joseph realized something he could not say to her, though keeping it to himself didn't quite amount to a lie.

She was marrying him to avert scandal. He was lucky to marry her, however, on any honorable terms he could find. That was why he felt like Christmas approached whenever he was near her, because she was dreams come true, unattainable wishes granted, and hope restored.

He kissed her cheek just for the chance to catch a

whiff of her scent. "We will have that ball. Wellington is already angling for a place on your dance card."

Louisa dropped her forehead to Joseph's shoulder, her relief evident. "He's a good dancer and something of a wit."

They remained there on the hard, cold bench until Sonnet was led out. Joseph swung up and parted from his fiancée, thinking that when next he saw her, it would be on the occasion of their wedding.

As he rode off into the chilly morning air, he had to smile at the thought of the greatest hero in the land being referred to as "a good dancer and something of a wit."

But then the smile died. Even Wellington's offer to dance with Louisa was likely a tactic undertaken to scotch gossip and scandal. What on earth would the new Lady Carrington think if she learned her knight in shining armor was father to no fewer than twelve bastard children?

Ten

"THIS IS A DISASTER."

"Don't clench your teeth, dearest." Jenny's pencil paused in its movement across the page. "What is a disaster?"

Louisa stomped into Jenny's drawing room—it really was a *drawing* room, not a withdrawing room—and tossed herself onto the sofa beside her sister.

"I'm to be married tomorrow. What is the worst, most indelicate, inconvenient thing that could befall a woman as her wedding night approaches?"

Maggie, arrived to Town for the wedding, took a pair of reading glasses off her elegant nose. "Somebody put stewed prunes on the menu for the wedding breakfast?"

Louisa couldn't help but smile at her oldest sister's question. Since childhood, stewed prunes had had a predictable effect on Louisa's digestion. "Eve made sure that wasn't the case."

"We're to have chocolate," Eve said, "lots and lots of chocolate. I put everybody's favorites on the menu too, and Her Grace didn't argue with any of them." She was on a hassock near the windows, embroidering some piece of white silk. Maggie had the rocking chair near the fireplace, where a cheery blaze was throwing out enough heat to keep the small room cozy.

"It's your monthly, isn't it?" Sophie leaned forward from the hearth rug and lifted the teapot. "The same thing happened to me after the baby was born. Sindal looked like he wanted to cry when I told him. I was finally healed up after the birth, and the dear man had such plans for the evening."

An admission like that from prim, proper Sophie could not go unremarked. "You *told* him?" Louisa accepted the cup of tea and studied her sister's slight smile.

"Have the last cake." Maggie pushed the tray closer to Louisa. "If you don't tell him, then it becomes a matter of your lady's maid telling his gentleman's gentleman that you're indisposed, and then your husband comes nosing about, making sure you're not truly ill, and you have to tell him anyway."

Louisa looked from Maggie to Sophie. Maggie was the tallest of the five sisters, and the oldest, with flame-red hair and a dignity that suited the Countess of Hazelton well. Sophie was a curvy brunette who nonetheless carried a certain reserve with her everywhere, as befit the Baroness Sindal.

They were married, and they spoke to their husbands about…things.

"Why can't a husband just understand that indisposed is one thing and ill is another?" Louisa thought her question perfectly logical.

Sophie and Maggie exchanged a look, but it wasn't a superior, "we're married and we understand these things" look, or even an older-sister look. It was more of a "how does one say this?" look.

"Sindal and I share a bed," Sophie said. "You'd be surprised how easy it is to discuss certain matters when the candles are blown out and your husband has just taken you in his arms."

They shared a bed, the implication being they shared a bed *every night*. Jenny's head bent a little closer to her sketch pad, and over by the window, Eve practically had the embroidery hoop against the end of her nose.

"Hazelton and I share a bed, as well. Always have," Maggie said. "The issue of monthlies hasn't come up yet, but carrying a child has indelicate consequences of its own."

"And you discuss these things with him?"

"Our parents share a bed." Eve spoke quietly, her mouth screwed up as if she puzzled over some complicated stitch. "I know they have adjoining chambers, but have you noticed the maids almost never change the linen in the duchess's bedroom?"

"It's the same at Morelands," Jenny said, glancing up from her tablet. "One can't help but notice when every other bedroom gets fresh sheets so regularly, but not that one."

Louisa hadn't noticed the sheets, but she had noticed that whenever her parents retired, they used the door that led to the duke's sitting room, never the duchess's. She'd noticed the duchess's hairbrush beside the ducal bed of a morning, and she'd noticed that her mother's reading glasses could often be retrieved from the duke's nightstand.

"There are eight of us born to them," Louisa observed. "Mama and Papa could hardly have arranged that without spending some time in the same bed."

"Bed." Maggie snorted the word and stroked a hand over her rounded belly. "Our firstborn child was conceived on a picnic blanket. Benjamin gets adventurous notions with wonderful frequency."

"In coaches?" Sophie asked, sounding as if this was merely a husbandly peccadillo.

Maggie waved a hand. "Coaches, saddle rooms, gazebos... I dare not close the door to the billiards room or find myself in a private pantry with the earl. His creativity on short notice is truly astounding."

The billiards room?

"We have a piano that is just the perfect height," Sophie mused. "Valentine would be scandalized. And Sindal claims the term 'folly' originates in the most appropriate use for a secluded little building."

Valentine would be scandalized? Louisa was scandalized—also intrigued.

"So you do not attempt to gainsay your husbands when they become...creative?"

Maggie started the chair rocking slowly. "Amorous, you mean? Oh, maybe in the first few weeks after the wedding. I had some fool notion propriety entered into things."

"It doesn't," Sophie said simply, firmly. "If Sir Joseph can't bring some imagination to that part of the marriage, then it's up to you to inspire him. Sindal positively goggles at me when I'm in the mood to inspire him. I love to make him goggle too."

Louisa goggled. She'd known these women all her

life; she loved them and would have said they were her best friends in the entire world.

In the context of this discussion, they'd become complete strangers to her.

"If propriety has no place in these matters, then how do you know how to go on?" Jenny asked the question Louisa had been burning to voice.

Maggie stopped rocking. "You love your husband. He loves you. You puzzle it out together, and that's half the fun."

"Half the pleasure," Sophie added softly.

They were smiling secret, dreamy, thoroughly female, *married* smiles, leaving Louisa to wonder two things.

How did one go on if love were not a factor for either husband or wife, and how on earth was she to explain her indisposition to Sir Joseph?

❧

"Your brother should hire out as a toastmaster," Joseph said, shifting the skirts of Louisa's wedding dress to tuck himself beside her on the coach's front-facing seat. "Westhaven has the gift of a light, warm touch with his sentiments."

Louisa got up and switched to Joseph's right side, which necessitated more arranging of frothy forest-green skirts. "He also has the gift of brevity, though I'm sure Valentine and St. Just were hoping to get a word in, as well."

"And Sindal and Hazelton, and His Grace Your Papa, and His Grace My Former Senior Commanding Officer, and old Quimbey, His Grace At Large."

She grinned at him as Joseph rapped hard on the

roof. "We were lucky to escape our own wedding breakfast before spring. We're expected to call on my parents ere we leave for Kent tomorrow morning."

"Does your mama need to make sure you survive the wedding night?"

Her smile died, but she didn't move away. "Perhaps it's your survival they're concerned for, Sir Joseph."

There was something different in the way she addressed him as "Sir Joseph" now that they were married. As if he were *her* Sir Joseph, knighted by his wife rather than the Regent. She stripped off her gloves with a similarly self-possessed air and turned a little toward him.

"This leg is paining you."

Before he could brace himself for the pleasure and discomfort of her touch, she was applying a sure, steady pressure up the length of his thigh.

"Louisa, you don't have to… Just because you have four sisters who love to dance… God in heaven…" He gave up on a sigh. "And your mother."

"Who is saintly but not in heaven." Louisa dug in a little harder, and the bliss of it, the sore, aching bliss of it had Joseph closing his eyes.

"And don't forget my aunt Gladys. Have you ever considered laudanum for this leg, Joseph?"

"I have not, or rather, I was given enough laudanum when I was injured to know its limits. I rather think I should have tried marriage to you instead."

Except he'd been married at the time, and the thought let a hovering shadow join Joseph in the coach.

"You needn't toss out compliments, Husband. I'm married to you whether there's flattery to be had from it or not."

He wrapped an arm around his starchy new wife. "And you need not flinch from sincere appreciation. My first wife could not stand the sight of my injury." Louisa's hands paused but did not leave his person. "I'm sorry, Louisa. I should not have brought her up. I did not mean to make mention of her now, of all times."

The blessed stroking of her hands on his thigh resumed. "She is the mother of our children. Of course you will make mention of her. Lionel said she would have been relieved to see you happily remarried, but I concluded he was demonstrating his wedding-day manners."

What he'd been, was standing too close to Joseph's wife, but there had been no point in taking exception to it in front of all of Polite Society. Louisa's brother Valentine had appeared at her elbow long before Joseph could have hobbled to her side, in any case.

"Lionel was a favorite of Cynthia's. He was probably being honest."

As soon as Joseph made the comment, he wished he hadn't said his late spouse's name, much less in conjunction with dear Lionel's.

"Do you miss her?"

The warm glow of the wedding day evaporated with four little words, bringing instead all the burden and complexity of a new marriage, a marriage undertaken, at least on the lady's part, for less than sentimental reasons.

"Shall I be honest, Louisa? This isn't the most sanguine topic between two newlyweds."

"You shall always be honest with me, and then I will have the courage to be honest with you."

He hadn't lit the coach lamps, because their journey was short, only a few blocks. The darkness allowed him to focus not only on the soothing touch of his wife's hands on his leg but also on the beauty of her voice in the darkness.

When she sang, Louisa would be a contralto. She would excel at the lower, warmer registers of the women's range, and her voice would be both supple and graceful—like her body moving on the dance floor.

Reading poetry, that voice would be divine in its beauty and luster.

And he never wanted to hear deception from her, so—to the extent that he could—he accepted the challenge she'd just laid down.

"My—Cynthia—and I married in a fit of patriotic lust, I suppose you could call it. I was young but well heeled, and she was young and, at least to appearances, smitten by a pair of broad shoulders in dashing regimentals. Her family was happy to pass her off into my willing arms, something I did not understand until after the ceremony."

"You did not suit?"

The prosaic nature of the question, the very bluntness of it endeared Louisa to him. "In the way of young people, we suited well enough to consummate the union, and then I shipped out for the Peninsula."

Louisa was a bright woman. The manner in which she leaned up and kissed Joseph's cheek assured him that she understood: after he'd rejoined his unit, he and his young wife had not suited so very well at all.

"I'm sorry. My family is likely happy to pass me

into your willing arms too, but I am not young, and I do not intend to be an aggravation to you."

"Nor I to you."

What a humble exchange of intentions for a pair of newlyweds to make to each other. Joseph found it appealing, though. Comforting.

Attainable and honest.

The carriage turned into the alley that led to Joseph's mews, and he realized he could have spent far longer cuddling with his wife in the dark and cozy confines of their town coach.

"I must be honest with you too, Husband."

"I would prefer it."

"I am not in a position to consummate our vows tonight."

He felt surprise and disappointment, and for an instant considered that for all her affection and pragmatism, all her passion on his hearth rug several nights past, Louisa was consigning them to a white marriage.

Except...her passion had been honest. Her rejoicing in his coming through the duel unscathed had been honest. The smiles she'd sent him across the hordes of wedding guests in the Moreland ballroom had been blazingly honest.

"Why can't you consummate our vows, Louisa?"

Now she withdrew her hands from his leg, his no-longer-throbbing leg. The horses slowed to a walk.

"Louisa?"

She mashed her face against his throat, and against his skin, her cheek felt unnaturally hot. "...Dratted... Blighted... female... Next week."

Joseph blinked in the darkness. He had been

married before. For several long, unhappy years, in fact, but in that odd moment with Louisa tucked close to him in the darkness, those years of marriage enabled him to decipher her meaning and her problem.

He gathered her close and kissed her cheek, when what he wanted to do was laugh—at fate, at his worst imaginings, even a little at his wife's muttered indignation over nature's timing.

"Next week is not so very far away, Louisa Carrington, and I promise to make the wait worth your while."

She lifted her head, a challenge glinting in her green eyes. "And yours too, Sir Joseph. I promise you that."

And then they did laugh—together.

❧

There should be poetry for the morning after a wedding.

Louisa watched her husband shave. He was careful, methodical, and efficient as he scraped dark whiskers from his face. He kept a mug—not a cup—of tea at his elbow throughout this masculine ritual, shaving around his mouth first so he might sip at his tea.

"You missed a spot on your jaw, Husband."

Husband. *Her very own husband.*

He turned, flecks of lather dotting his visage, and held his razor out to her. Not quite a challenge, but something more than an invitation. The moment called for a shaving sonnet.

Louisa set her tea aside—tea Joseph had prepared for her—and climbed off the bed. She took the razor from him and eyed his jaw. "Were you trying to spare my sensibilities last night?"

"You were indisposed."

They both fell silent while Louisa scraped the last of the whiskers from Joseph's cheek. She appropriated the towel he'd draped over his shoulder and wiped his face clean.

"I know I was indisposed, but you blew out all the candles before you undressed. I've seen naked men before." She'd never slept with one wrapped around her, though. Such an arrangement was...cozy, and inclined one toward loquaciousness.

"You've seen naked men?"

There was something too casual in Joseph's question. Louisa set the razor down and stepped back. "Growing up, there was always a brother or two to spy on, and I think they didn't mind being spied on so very much, or they wouldn't have been quite as loud when they went swimming. I attend every exhibition the Royal Society puts on, and the Moreland library is quite well stocked."

He kissed her, and by virtue of his mouth on hers, Louisa understood that her husband was smiling at her pronouncements. He gave her a deucedly businesslike kiss though, over in a moment.

As Louisa lingered in her husband's arms, sneaking a whiff of the lavender soap scent of his skin, she wondered if married kisses were different from the courting kind.

"I have married a fearlessly naughty woman," Joseph said, stroking a hand down her braid. "And to think I was concerned that I was imposing by asking you to share my bed last night."

"You needn't be gallant. I talked your ears off."

And he'd *listened*. He hadn't fallen asleep, hadn't patted her arm and rolled over, hadn't let her know in unsubtle ways that the day had been quite long enough, thank you very much.

"You had an interesting upbringing. Not many women study astronomy, ancient history, and economics."

"The calculus makes measuring the stars easier. I'm having my telescopes sent over from Morelands—our daughters will have great good fun staying up past their bedtimes, learning the constellations. I don't know who enjoyed the midnight picnics more, His Grace, my brothers, or myself."

His hand on her hair went still, cradling the back of her head. "Do you even know you refer to them as our daughters?"

And with one question, they were on tricky ground indeed. Not the stuff of poetry, but possibly the stuff of marital discord. "I don't mean to presume. I can refer to them as Amanda and Fleur—such pretty names."

He pulled back enough to frame her face with his two warm hands. "Because you say it is so, Louisa, they *are* our daughters. This is more than a wedding gift, because you give it not just to me but also to two small girls who very much need a mother."

This kiss was different, reverent, tender, lovely... beyond poetry.

Louisa dropped her forehead to her husband's naked chest and, for the dozenth time, silently cursed her female organs for their poor scheduling. "We'll never get to Kent if we aren't on our way soon."

Joseph patted her bottom and stepped back. "We will not let your parents serve us breakfast, or your sisters dragoon you into their private lair. I suspect the worst offenders will be your brothers, though. I've never met such a lot of mother hens."

He splashed on his cedar-and-spice scent, then started laying out clothing, making trips from the wardrobe to the bed. Joseph continued striding around the bedroom in nothing but riding breeches, as casual as you please.

And Louisa did please. Her husband was well endowed with muscle and masculine pulchritude, and he thought her brothers were mother hens. He had listened to her in the dark, and he had held her and rubbed her back when she hadn't even known she could ask for those considerations.

Maybe love was not a matter of ringing declarations and rhyming couplets. Maybe it wasn't blood-red roses and dramatic sentiments. Maybe love was a pat on the bottom and a tender kiss, a shared good night's sleep, and a man considerate enough to build a quick stop by the ducal mansion into the start of the wedding journey.

❧

"You get her for the rest of your life, Carrington. At least let us say a proper goodbye."

The musical brother—Lord Valentine—delivered this observation with a paucity of good cheer as Joseph watched Louisa being hugged yet again by St. Just, Westhaven, and each sister in turn. In an odd display of diplomacy, Their Graces had retired inside the mansion after wishing Joseph and Louisa safe journey.

"You had your sister for the first twenty-five years,

my lord, and I'm starting to wonder if you've waited until she's leaving to appreciate her."

Dark brows rose in a gesture very like the duke's. "What is that rudeness supposed to mean?"

"She's studied practically every modern European language, but her only opportunities to speak them have been when your parents entertain diplomats. She can do math in her head you and I couldn't follow even on paper, and yet she's lucky if Westhaven lets her tag along to the occasional economics lecture. She summarized half a millennium of Roman military strategy for St. Just—knows Caesar's letters by heart in the original and in translation—and yet St. Just's epistles back to her from the Peninsula dealt with ladies' hats. You compose little bagatelles for her when what she needs is to be working on a translation of *The Divine Comedy*."

Lord Valentine blinked, and then his lips curved up in a rueful smile.

"I suppose when it comes down to it, we haven't known what to do with Lou. I realized early on that as much passion as I have for music, she has that passion too, but she can turn to practically any intellectual pursuit. I would have been sent down my first term if not for her."

He fell silent while Louisa accepted a small parcel from St. Just and tucked it into her reticule. Lord Valentine had passed her a similar present, as if little tokens made up for a quarter century of fraternal neglect.

"You should have been sent down. She should have been allowed to matriculate."

"She went through much of the curriculum by

correspondence with me. I struggled in every class mostly because I spent too many hours at the piano. Latin was the worst. She did my translations for me and for a few of the other fellows, though it was cheating. Once she understood what we were about, she put a stop to it, but by then…"

Lord Valentine went quiet again, his smile nowhere in evidence.

"By then you'd learned enough Latin or Greek or mathematics from her to limp along yourselves, while she was left to rusticate in Kent and stare at the stars as her sisters embroidered their stays and drew nude sketches."

"Merciful heavens. Nudes?"

"Miniatures, I'm thinking, because the only models they had were the brothers they spied on."

On that parting shot, Joseph stepped forward, waiting just long enough for Louisa to slip yet a third parcel—this one from Westhaven—into her reticule. Lady Genevieve passed along a small packet of documents tied with twine, which also went into the reticule, and then at long, long last, Joseph was bundling his wife into the traveling coach.

"One has a sense of escape every time one departs from your family, Louisa."

She switched sides so she was again on his right.

"Husband, you say the most comforting things. When Sophie stole a few days of solitude for herself last Christmas, I finally realized I am not the only Windham sibling longing for peace and privacy. I love my family, but they are just so…"

She turned her head to peer out the window.

Joseph passed her his handkerchief, thinking she'd wave it at them in parting.

"I am being ridiculous." She did wave the handkerchief, but then she dabbed at the corners of her eyes. "I'll see them all again in just a few days at the Christmas gathering, and the children too. I suppose an excess of sentiment can be forgiven. I hadn't seen St. Just in months, and Maggie is expecting, but I'll see a great deal of Sophie—"

He hauled her against his side and gently pushed her head to his shoulder. "We'll visit all you like, all over the realm, even the perishing West Riding if St. Just insists on ruralizing there. I did want to take you to Paris in the spring, however, and you'd like Lisbon too, even if it gets quite hot. I'm not as fond of Rome, though Sicily has all manner of ruins you might find interesting."

Her head came off his shoulder. "May we take the girls? Children need exposure to the greater world, you know. One can't learn everything sitting in some dusty schoolroom."

No, one could not.

While Louisa started fashioning an itinerary for summer travels, Joseph cast around for a way to explain to her that journeys beyond a certain duration would be difficult for him. There were a dozen children in Surrey from whom he did not want to be too far away for any length of time. His children.

Not *ours*, not yet. Likely not ever.

❧

"How is a man to enjoy a proper drink when his hand is bandaged like this?" Grattingly waved a swaddled right hand. Lionel barely glanced up from the meager fire doing battle with the chill in Grattingly's smallest parlor.

"How is a man supposed to think when you're whining about a stoved finger, for God's sake? It's all over the clubs that Sir Joseph refused to blow a hole in your hide as well he should have."

Like a hound hearing a puzzling sound, Grattingly cocked his head at Lionel. "You didn't tell me that limping simian was Wellington's personal marksman. Not well done, Honiton. A friend risks his life for you, puts his very existence on the line, and you—"

"You're the one who changed the plan. Wellington's staff did not include a personal marksman, though I'll grant you, Sir Joseph is a dead shot. I tried to preserve you from the folly of dueling with him, and you were the one who insisted on meeting him."

"And this is the thanks I get? Any girl who's been the cause of a duel won't find a decent husband. I hand Louisa Windham to you on a platter, even when you can't manage to be the one interrupting her scandalous behavior. I put a fat dowry within your grasp, and you can't be bothered to thank me."

Lionel remained silent, which was as much thanks as Grattingly was going to hear from him. The original idea had been simple: Lionel was to rescue Louisa from a compromising situation and accept her grateful hand in marriage immediately thereafter. No duels had been contemplated—until Grattingly thoroughly bollixed up the matter.

"I should be the one swiving the fair Louisa," Grattingly muttered. "I like a woman who fights back."

Lionel took another sip of inferior wine. "You like

a woman who pretends to fight back. Louisa Windham would have gelded you in another moment."

Grattingly's chair scraped back. "Mother of God, what is *wrong* with you? You need coin. For a small sum certain, I make it possible for you to acquire the same and a wellborn wife into the bargain, and when you can't manage to take what's offered, you turn up nasty on me."

"My apologies. Impending poverty has quite soured my disposition, this drink isn't helping, and I hardly regard a percentage of Lady Louisa's dowry as a small sum. When did you stop stocking decent libation, anyway?"

And where were the other half dozen or so young men who usually ensconced themselves in Grattingly's town house of a late evening?

Grattingly went to the sideboard. "Madeira isn't cheap, I'll have you know."

It was not, particularly, being fortified with brandy, but it was cheaper than imported spirits. "I haven't seen that pretty little upstairs maid about lately either. Are you attempting to economize, Grattingly? It's a plebeian turn of mind that stints on the necessities."

Lionel finished his wine and did not join Grattingly at the sideboard. In his cups, the man could be mean as well as stupid—witness the challenge to Carrington—and goading Grattingly served no purpose other than temporary distraction from Lionel's own difficulties.

"The trades have cut me off," Grattingly spat. "The pretty little maid disappeared last week, and I won't see another quarterly until the New Year. Happy damned Christmas from dear old Pater's solicitors."

"One does usually pay off the trades in December," Lionel drawled. "At least the Quality do."

"My grandfather is as wellborn as yours, Honiton, and you've no more coin to show for it than I do."

Lionel knew better than to take that bait—he knew better, but he took it anyway.

"There you would be in error."

"What is that supposed to mean?"

"You put all your eggs in one basket, so to speak, expecting to dip your fingers into Louisa Windham's dowry without doing the hard work of wooing or marrying the woman. I am not as shortsighted as you and thus have other plans in train."

Grattingly paused in the act of swigging from a decanter. Lionel had to look away, lest he gag at the sight. "You speak in riddles, Honiton, and riddles that don't even amuse."

"Ah, but the tailors still accept my custom, don't they? And because I am more resourceful than you, they'll continue to do so, as will the farrier, the coalman, and all the other petty actors whose contributions to a comfortable existence are mandatory, if tedious."

Grattingly belched, a slow, wet eruption of vulgarity punctuated only by the soft hiss of the fire. Had that indelicacy emerged in the company of a pack of similarly inebriated young men, it might have provoked a round of ribald comments—or no comment at all. As Grattingly's sole companion, however, that Lionel should be subjected to such rudeness struck him more as a reflection on himself than on his host.

"Grattingly, the hour grows late. My thanks for your hospitality, but I must be leaving."

Lionel rose and—there being no servant on hand—attired himself in gloves, scarf, hat, and greatcoat, and all the while, Grattingly watched him.

"Did your housemaid take the footman with her when she left?"

"Quite possibly. I don't suppose you'd like to step around to The Velvet Glove?"

He would—Lionel liked swiving as much as the next fellow—but he took in his companion's stained cravat, his thick fingers wrapped around the neck of the decanter, the way the man's mouth went slack at the thought of visiting a brothel.

Those fingers had been thrust into Louisa Windham's bodice, and those slack lips had been aiming for her mouth when Grattingly had been detailed merely to embrace the woman or slobber churlishly over her hand. "Afraid I can't. Perhaps another time."

Grattingly saluted with the decanter. "Suit yourself. And best of luck with those other plans."

He waggled his fat fingers in a parting wave, and Lionel took his leave. The night air was frigid but fresh, considering all the coal fires gracing myriad London hearths. From some nearby street, a vendor chanted cheerfully about roasted chestnuts and Christmas blessings, and at the end of the block, a Christian rang a bell and importuned passersby to Remember The Less Fortunate.

Somehow, Lionel himself had become less fortunate, though he hadn't quite sunk to the level of Grattingly—Grattingly, whom it was time to cut.

Grattingly's dishonorable behavior—and what could be more dishonorable than compromising a young lady of good birth then firing early upon her champion in the subsequent duel?—had cost Grattingly the company of even those fellows too poor to afford their own drink.

Lionel turned his steps toward the Earl of Arlington's mansion, several blocks away in Mayfair proper. The women at The Velvet Glove were delightful, inventive, and generous with their time. They were also professionals who expected hard coin at the time services were rendered.

Until Lionel's other plans bore fruit—or pawning paste jewels became profitable—the free food and drink at a Mayfair ball would take precedence over the more enjoyable offerings to be had of an evening. As snow began to fall through the darkness and both the vendor and the Christian fell silent, Lionel sent up a small prayer that his other plans bore generous fruit, and soon.

Eleven

THROUGH THE LONG DAY OF TRAVEL, JOSEPH HAD KEPT Louisa company inside his capacious traveling coach. Each time they stopped to change horses, he'd insisted she have a hot cup of grog, and she'd insisted the bricks in the floor of his traveling coach be reheated while she did.

The distance wasn't long—Louisa had often ridden it in a day—but they'd gotten a late start, and freezing and melting had made the roads miserable. As darkness had fallen, Joseph had given her the option of putting up for the night at a decent hostelry rather than pushing on.

"Will Amanda and Fleur fret if we don't arrive until tomorrow?"

"Amanda and Fleur had best be sound asleep at this hour," he replied as a maid set their meal out on a small table in their sitting room. "Their governess will answer for it if I find otherwise."

This was the cavalry officer in him, a part of her husband Louisa had had occasion to study in the progress of their journey. With her, Joseph was polite and deferential, never demanding.

With others, he was also polite and never unreasonable, but like Louisa's father and brothers, he expected to be *obeyed* by those in positions of service. Before God, she had vowed to obey him, as well, though she hoped, for a new wife, the Almighty—and Sir Joseph—made allowances for a period of adjustment.

Joseph sat back a half hour later, having demolished a substantial meal and two servings of plum pudding. "Shall I have a bath sent up?"

"I bathed within an inch of my life yesterday. Some warm water will do."

"Then perhaps I will have a bath...if you don't mind?"

Louisa paused with her teacup halfway to her lips, searching her husband's gaze for a clue as to the slight innuendo she'd heard in his words.

"Of course you should. I stayed tucked up in the coach the live long day with hot bricks and my favorite books, while you were freezing your attributes off in various inn yards."

One corner of his mouth kicked up. "My attributes? I suppose they are attributes, if I'm to be saddled with a title."

"Does this truly bother you?"

For all they'd been in company for much of the day, they'd conversed little. Joseph had been nose-down in a ledger book of some sort, while Louisa had been reading a French tome on social philosophy and enjoying the novelty of traveling without a lady's maid glued to her elbow.

Joseph hunkered to poke up the fire. "The prospect of a title daunts me. I hardly know how to organize my own affairs, Louisa. What business have I taking a seat in the Lords?"

"If more fellows in the Lords had that degree of humility, they might be making better decisions and more of them."

A knock on the door interrupted the moment as servants appeared to clear up the remains of the meal then wheel in a sizable copper bathing tub. Screens were delivered next, then footmen and maids alike trooped through in a bucket parade, until Louisa was once again alone with her spouse.

She rose and started unknotting his cravat. "Hold still. The sooner you're in that water, the hotter it will be."

His lashes lowered as if he were veiling amusement, but he made no protest as Louisa went on to unfasten his sleeve buttons and unbutton his waistcoat and shirt.

When Joseph stood bare from the waist up, Louisa gestured toward his knees. "Boots next."

He took a seat and stuck his left leg straight out, parallel to the floor. "Do you ever think of Their Graces engaged in such mundane domesticity?"

Louisa bent to tug off one boot. "Not much. One takes for granted that one's parents are a married couple, but they're very protective of their privacy. I've probably seen Her Grace remove Papa's boots twice in my life. Other one."

And yet, this domesticity with Joseph did not feel at all uncomfortable. A trifle strange or novel, maybe, but not uncomfortable. Louisa set both boots outside the door for the boot boy then turned to find her husband clad only in his riding breeches.

And abruptly, the situation was novel, indeed.

"I can blow out the candles, Louisa."

Louisa pushed up the sleeves of her nightgown and robe. "Nobody bathes in the dark, Husband. Get in the tub."

He smiled at her peremptory tone, which was fortunate, because Louisa hadn't *meant* to issue an order. "Perhaps you'd help me with my falls?"

And clearly, from his wicked grin, Joseph wasn't asking a question so much as he was issuing a challenge.

"Of course." Louisa marched up to him, and the smile died even from his eyes. By firelight, his eyes no longer looked blue; they simply looked dark and intently focused.

"My falls, *Wife*?"

He hadn't called her that before—Dearest Affianced Wife not being the same thing at all. The word—and his tone of voice—sent a jolt through Louisa, of warmth and something else. Possessiveness, possibly. Whatever it was, she liked it. Rather than waste time analyzing her emotions, Louisa started undoing the buttons down the flap of Joseph's breeches.

"There are rather more buttons than simple modesty requires."

"Perhaps that's to ensure a man truly wants to lose his breeches, or a woman truly wants him out of them."

"The water is getting cool as we…"

Her fingers brushed a bulge in the fabric, a solid, sizable bulge. When she glanced up into her husband's face, he'd dropped his lashes again and dipped his chin, as if watching her undress him.

He shucked his breeches and turned in one move,

so he climbed into the tub with his back to Louisa. Once in the water, he made quick work of his ablutions, but even when Louisa had sluiced rinse water over his hair, he seemed reluctant to get out.

"If you stay in there any longer, the water will be cold, and so will you, Husband. I am not inclined to share a bed with a block of ice."

He remained leaning back against the rim, eyes closed. "Maybe cold water is a good idea, Louisa. Next week isn't here yet."

"Next week...?" She paused in the middle of folding his clothes into a tidy pile. "What does next week...? Oh."

He rose from the water, climbed out, and stood dripping on the bricks before the hearth. "Next week, when I swive you until we're neither of us able to walk." He faced the fire, so Louisa had a marvelous opportunity to admire the wet musculature of his back, legs, and yes, of his taut male fundament.

She would not be able to walk? "Surely, you exaggerate." *Or did he?*

He glanced over his shoulder, as if to make sure he had her attention, then turned to face her.

He had not exaggerated. With firelight limning his wet skin in rosy gold, Joseph stood six feet away from Louisa in a condition clearly conducive to procreation. She'd read about this, but nothing in any language could have prepared her for the sudden galloping of her heart at the sight of her unclad, aroused husband.

"You need to see what you married, Louisa. The flesh is willing but far from perfect."

He spoke in earnest and remained where he was,

his *membrum virile* arching straight up along his belly in intimate emphasis of his uncompromising posture. Louisa studied his arousal until her fingers itched.

"Say something, Wife."

"I want to touch you."

His expression shifted for just a blink, from unreadable to unsure, then back to unreadable. "About the scars, Louisa."

Her eyes swept over him, over the muscled thighs and chest, the curiously elegant architecture of big, bare male feet.

"Don't be ridiculous." She closed the distance between them. "I have seen scars before. I have a few myself, but I have never seen... What do you call this business?"

She drew her fingers up the length of him, surprised to find both how firm his flesh was and how warm. "It must have a name." She dropped to the hearthstones, the better to inspect him. "I know some Latin terms, of course, but regarding their persons, men are not without a certain inventiveness—"

Louisa felt Joseph's hand land on her hair, not heavily, more of a benediction. "We can make a list if you like, Wife. Later."

"Before next week, if you please." She sleeved him with her palm then traced one fingertip around the crown. "So soft."

"We'll make the list directly after I've regained the ability to think."

His voice had gone dark and smooth, as if he were reading poetry to her, but he said nothing more, which Louisa took for permission to continue exploring him.

"This hair is different, not like the hair elsewhere on your body or on your head." She sifted her fingers through it then traced them over the soft sacs below. "I'm supposed to kick a fellow here if he ever menaces me. That was Devlin's word—menace."

On impulse, she ran her nose over those same parts. Joseph drew in a sharp breath but didn't flinch away. The scent of lavender was here too—thank God her husband was not shy about using the soap—but even damp and fresh from his bath, there was a different quality to his intimate scent. Masculine, maybe, or just Joseph Carrington.

"Louisa, don't you dare…"

Some knowledge that didn't come from books told Louisa he wanted her to dare, he *longed* for it, though he'd never, ever, ask her for what she was about to do. Before her courage could desert her, she ran her tongue up his shaft, a slow, wet tasting of his male parts.

He shuddered and sighed, which she interpreted as surrender of a sort. The notion was precious and… intoxicating. Physically intoxicating.

She did it again, lapping the blunt, velvety end of his erection in cat strokes, learning him with her tongue in a way she didn't yet know him with her hands or eyes.

"You must stop…soon."

From him, that was a parody of an order. Louisa wrapped a hand around the base of his shaft and took him in her mouth, lest he stop her before she'd been permitted that liberty. Phrases of Catullus and his naughty ilk finally made sense, even as Louisa's own body became mysterious to her.

When she drew on her husband just a bit, her breasts felt heavy and tender. The urge to weep and the urge to laugh mixed with a wanting that coursed through her from some location in her vitals for which she hadn't even a Latin name.

"Louisa..." Joseph had two hands threaded into her hair now, and his hips moved so he was rocking slowly, slowly in and out of her mouth. She drew on him again, less gently, and he eased away.

He hauled her to her feet, wrapped one arm around her, and fused his mouth to hers. With his free hand, Louisa could feel him stroking himself, the intimacy of it nearly making her knees buckle.

"Joseph..."

His tongue insinuated itself into her mouth in the same slow rhythm he used on himself.

She kissed him back, wrapped her arms around him, and held on, until he shuddered against her and his hand went quiet, though his chest still heaved in slow, deep breaths.

"Holy *God*, Louisa. Holy..."

He wasn't disapproving. She deciphered that much over the subsiding tumult in her body. And he wasn't turning her loose, either. Shyness warred with a sense of accomplishment, of having shared a milestone with her new and naked husband.

"Holy..." He kissed her again, softly. "That was... How on earth...? Jesus." Another kiss, even more tender. "I need to hold you. To bed, if you please."

He *needed* to hold her, and he'd said as much in plain English. Admitted a need *for her* as if...as if he couldn't help himself and didn't care if she knew it.

Louisa turned to comply and felt his hand stroke down over her derriere and finish with a soft pat. There had been affection in that caress, also possessiveness and some male appreciation.

"You like my bottom."

He paused in the act of toweling off his stomach, his smile sweet and masculine. "I *adore* your bottom. I am also more than fond of your derriere."

Bottom—a cavalryman's term for grit, staying power, or heart. Louisa discarded her night robe and climbed on the bed, watching as her naked husband banked the coals, blew out the candles, and pushed the hearth screen right up next to the fire.

"Husband? I like your bottom too."

He prowled over to the bed and climbed onto the mattress. "One suspected this was the case. I rejoice to hear it, though."

"I wouldn't dissemble about something so important."

She expected him to come back with another dry retort, but instead he spooned his body around her, laced his fingers with hers, and kissed her shoulder.

And that was answer enough.

❧

"How many does that leave?" Valentine ran his hand along the mantel of the hearth in the estate office at Westhaven's country seat in Surrey. The wood was satin smooth and gleaming with a beeswax-and-lemon-oil shine—a nice symbolic comment on the happily married man who owned the premises.

Westhaven, seated at a desk worthy of a ducal heir, consulted a ledger then pushed his glasses back up his nose. "Twenty-seven remain unaccounted for. Our progress has slowed as the number dwindles."

St. Just blew out a breath and glanced upward, as if appealing to the heavens, then his lips quirked. "Your countess has been busy, Westhaven."

"Anna is the soul of industry," Westhaven began, but rather than treat Val and St. Just to a paean of husbandly appreciation, Westhaven's gaze followed the line of St. Just's finger to where it pointed at the lamp hanging over the desk.

"That is enough to keep a man diligently at his paperwork for the entire Yule season." Westhaven's smile was a slow, naughty grin.

Not a sprig, not a branch, but a sheaf of mistletoe rife with white berries dangled from the lamp.

Valentine regarded his brother, who was looking pleased and serene at the vast desk. "There's just as much hanging over your entry hall, a good deal gracing your library, and I've no doubt the kitchen rafters are hard to spot for the bundles and bales of mistletoe hanging all about."

"Anna likes a cheerful staff."

"I like a cheerful sister," Val said, returning to the purpose for their gathering. "Could Victor have destroyed some copies before we got involved?"

St. Just's smile disappeared. "He would have told us, or he would have told Louisa, at least. If Westhaven says there are twenty-seven copies still to locate, then twenty-seven copies we shall find."

"Valentine has a point." Westhaven rose from his desk to answer a tap on the door then admitted his wife bearing a tray.

"Sing ye wassail, gentlemen. You look like you're dealing with matters far weightier than the season permits."

Val and St. Just watched while Westhaven, in an exercise of the patience for which he was legendary, waited for Anna to put her tray down on the desk before he pounced.

"Happy Christmas, Countess."

The kiss was long, thorough, and so lacking in decorum, Val met St. Just's gaze rather than gawk for its duration. There was humor in St. Just's eyes, and also something else—approval or relief. Whatever the sentiment, Valentine shared it: Westhaven deserved his happiness, even if it meant his brothers had to endure unseemly displays as a result.

Though Anna's smile suggested she hadn't regarded Westhaven's behavior as unseemly at all.

"Christmas is still a few days off," Val noted to no one in particular. "I think you're going to have to cut more mistletoe." He reached up and plucked a berry from the bouquet then pitched it in the fire.

"We've plenty," Anna said, eyes dancing. "Drink your toddies, you lot. Whatever you're dealing with, the fortification can't hurt. Westhaven, will you be visiting the nursery as usual?"

Westhaven accepted a mug from his wife's tray. "Gentlemen, is anybody up for a game of skittles?"

"I can still beat you both," Val said. "Somebody has got to show the lad how it's done."

Anna brought a drink to St. Just and another one to Val, murmuring a quiet "thank you" and kissing Val's cheek as she did.

When she'd taken her leave, her husband's gaze fixed shamelessly to her retreating form, St. Just spoke. "Your countess always smells like a spring garden, Westhaven. There's warmth in the scent of her."

"Honeysuckle," Westhaven said, looking besotted.

"Which is lovely," Val allowed, "but what do we do about twenty-seven missing books, and given that Louisa has a husband now, and a rather capable fellow at that, isn't this more properly his quest?"

The besotted look vanished from Westhaven's face to be replaced by a more familiar stern expression. "She's our sister, Victor charged us with this task, and something tells me Carrington and Louisa will have their hands full without adding this problem to their adjustment as newlyweds."

Val and St. Just exchanged another glance, one that confirmed they'd both heard the undercurrent in Westhaven's tone.

"Enough coyness, Westhaven." St. Just settled into a chair before the desk. Val took an arm of the couch. "What do you know that you've been keeping under your hat, and how can we help?"

Westhaven slid into the seat behind the desk and looked from Val to St. Just, then up at the mistletoe hanging over his desk. He studied the kissing bough while he spoke. "Carrington owns a property not far from here. A pretty place in excellent repair with some nice acres. I've had occasion to make a discreet call when Sir Joseph was not in residence. You would not believe what I found."

❧

A husband who was not shocked at a lady's grasp of certain French philosophers, a husband whose lips turned up in the sweetest smile when he ought to *be* shocked, was a worthy husband indeed.

As a father to his small daughters, however, Joseph Carrington seemed slightly at a loss.

Louisa came to this conclusion the moment she was introduced to her daughters, or rather, the moment when she should *not* have been introduced to her daughters. As Joseph's offspring, Amanda and Fleur ought not to have been made to stand outside, their little faces pinched with cold while they waited among the servants to welcome the new lady of the house to her abode.

"And whom might we have here, Sir Joseph?" Louisa went down on her haunches in the snow. "A pair of your prettiest maids, perhaps?"

"Fleur and Amanda, make your curtsies." He rapped it out like an order. "You do not want to keep your stepmama out here in this chill when dirty weather threatens."

They bobbed identical curtsies, and even those gestures looked cold to Louisa.

"Greet your father." That command was issued by a stern-faced nanny, one whose chest preceded her like the bow of a black-clad ship.

"Good day, Papa." Two more curtsies, two pairs of eyes trained on Joseph with something like trepidation.

"What lovely manners," Louisa said, extending a hand to each child. "I'm Louisa, and I will be relying on you entirely as the ladies of this house to show me where everything is. Come along, and I'm sure your father will arrange some hot chocolate to help us warm up."

The nanny drew in a breath through her nose, her eyes darting to Sir Joseph. Joseph, fortunately, was regarding his daughters and could not see the appeal. "Chocolate, is it? I suppose that wouldn't go amiss."

He offered his arm, but Louisa didn't drop the hand of either child. "Chocolate and some cakes," she said, beaming a smile at him. "I do adore cakes."

"So do I," said the younger child, just as her sister hissed her name in warning.

"You do not address adults unless spoken to," the nanny interjected, great cargoes of disapproval in her reminder.

Louisa turned, offering a smile intended as a different kind of warning. "I'm sure your admonition is well intended, miss, but our daughters are meeting their stepmother for the first time. This is not an occasion for strict discipline." For good measure, Louisa hoisted Fleur to her hip then grabbed Amanda's hand again. Louisa moved off, hoping Joseph would fall in step rather than placate the damned nanny.

Without looking back, Louisa sailed on toward the house. The uneven crunch of footsteps in the snow told her Joseph was indeed joining the progress of his womenfolk.

"What's a stepmama?" Fleur asked in the too-loud undertones of a curious child. In the next moment, she was plucked from Louisa's grasp and tucked onto her father's back.

"A stepmother," Joseph said, "is your father's new wife. Lady Louisa will be living with us now unless you two drive her off with your wild behavior."

He sounded convincingly serious about the possibility.

Fleur's downy little brows knit, while Amanda remained silently clutching Louisa's hand.

"I like the occasional bit of wild behavior," Louisa informed the company. "And nothing and no one will drive me off. Depend upon that."

Joseph said nothing, though his lips quirked in the hint of a smile. He remained quiet when they gained the library, and other than barking at his daughters not to spill their chocolate, he tolerated twenty minutes of their company over tea, sandwiches, and slices of apple.

"Having seen that you've both grown more than is decent, and having introduced you to your step-mama, you will now take yourselves off to the upper reaches, please."

Joseph was polite with his daughters, true enough, but it wasn't the same kind of mannerliness he showed Louisa.

"I'll take them." Louisa rose and had two little hands grasping her fingers before the words were out. "And then, Husband, perhaps you'd be willing to show me some of the house?"

He nodded and said nothing while Louisa took the children from his company.

"I'm glad Papa's back," Amanda said. "Did you make him come back, Stepmama?"

"Nobody makes your father do anything he doesn't like. It's one of the privileges of being a grown-up." *In theory.*

"We make him punish us," Fleur said. "It's wicked of us."

"But not very often," Amanda added. She dragged

on Louisa's hand as they approached the stairs. "Not very often at all."

"That's not so," Fleur retorted. "The whole time Papa was gone, we had to be punished. Bread and water is punishment, Manda. It is. And we had to do all that kneeling, and no fire, and why should I hush?"

Amanda stopped gesturing frantically with her finger to her lips and turned miserable eyes up to Louisa. "We're not bad. *We're not.*"

What on earth? The first step to solving any puzzle was to gather as much information as possible about the problem. Louisa stopped on the top step, turned, and sat. "Come here, the both of you. Tell me how it is when your papa's not here."

She wrapped an arm around each child and listened. She listened for a long time then took them to the nursery. There, she ordered that the fire be built up and kept roaring, that the children's menus be sent to her in the next hour, and that their lesson plans be made available to her by nine of the clock the following morning. She also warned the nursery maid that she'd be tucking her daughters in each night and likely stopping by frequently during the day, as well.

She'd be inspecting their wardrobes, taking them out for regular doses of fresh air, and inviting the children to the occasional tea below stairs. Breakfast or luncheon at the family table was not out of the question, and—Louisa glanced around the nursery, which bore a faint coal-smoke odor—Sir Joseph would be consulted about regular audiences for their daughters in the family parlor after tea.

While the maid's eyes bugged rounder and rounder,

Louisa felt a pang of homesickness for her parents and siblings. They'd each have an appropriate curse to rain down on the blasted nanny. The old besom should have been protecting Sir Joseph's esteem in his daughters' eyes, not eroding it.

Her Grace's set down would be the most telling. Something dignified, understated, and knife-edged with gracious disdain.

Louisa kept that example in mind and went in search of her husband.

A woman's reticule was a mysterious thing, alike unto Aladdin's Cave of Wonders. Joseph's first awareness of this phenomenon had come to him as a small boy who could count on his mother to produce anything from a handkerchief to a spinning top to a shiny red apple from the depths of her various purses and pockets.

The aunts-by-marriage who'd taken over his upbringing had continued the tradition, though their treasures were more likely to be books, chocolates, or flowery sachets that imparted curious flavors to the chocolates.

And Louisa's reticule proved no less fascinating.

He'd drawn the thing open in search of a lowly pencil. Following that impulse hadn't struck him as a violation of her privacy. Rather, it had been a means to make a correction in the ledger open before him on the estate desk.

And he had not read his wife amiss, for she had two pencils lurking in the bottom of her purse, but a man had to dig past a hairbrush and comb—why carry both?—three books of very good erotic verse—why carry three copies of the same volume?—two hand-kerchiefs, one wildly embroidered, the other simply monogrammed—one for show, one for utility?—a packet of letters bound with red ribbon—did the red ribbon signify old love letters?—an unpeeled orange, and his former best flask.

Joseph opened the flask and, by olfactory divina-tion, concluded it contained his private blend of hazelnut liqueur and rum, which might make an interesting complement to the orange, should a lady become peckish.

Or perhaps, given the brew she carried, these last provisions were stowed not for herself but for her husband.

Joseph restored the contents to the reticule, including both pencils. The idea of Louisa carrying supplies for him put his rummaging in a different and less attractive light, so when Louisa rejoined him in the library, he was ensconced at his estate desk, whittling a point onto a pencil taken from his desk.

"They tried to take you prisoner, didn't they?" He rose, dumped the pencil shavings behind the fire screen, and peered at his wife. "They are like barnacles, wanting stories and tales and conversation. When they're a little older, there are boarding schools that will take them."

The idea made him ill, but the words could not be unsaid, and Louisa was regarding him very intently.

"Boarding school might not be a bad idea."

His heart sank. In his chest, it felt like the organ physically lurched south several inches, constricting his lungs and upsetting his digestive processes as well as his breathing.

"When the time comes, we'll discuss it with Miss Hodges."

"No, we shall not."

Louisa's spine had become militarily straight. The unease in Joseph's chest spread to the sort of physical sensation a soldier recognized as battle readiness— mostly dread and a little hope that a man could acquit himself honorably in the coming affray.

"You do not regard the governess's opinion as worth consulting? Louisa, Miss Hodges was Cynthia's choice for the nursery, and both Fleur and Amanda are receiving an excellent education as a result."

His wife wheeled away from him, which only increased his unease. They were apparently to have a difference of opinion, and he wanted to be able to see her eyes when they did. Louisa wouldn't lie to him, but her eyes would give him truths her lips might not.

"Your daughters are slight, Joseph."

"They are little girls." Though he had wondered if they were littler than other girls their age. He handled them carefully because of it. For the same reason, he stopped by the nursery to watch them sleep.

"They are subsisting on bread and water, did you know that?"

"Bread and water?"

"Bread, water, and the kindness of the kitchen staff, who likely know very well your children are forced to raid the larder after hours to keep body and soul together."

"My children are not starving, Louisa Carrington."

He spoke more sharply than he'd intended, but Louisa's accusations were preposterous. "You saw them. They are hale and lively. I have no doubt their high spirits lead to the occasional exercise in discipline, and bread and water is a time-honored means of enforcing same."

"For days? For two straight weeks? What infraction could those two little girls commit that merits such severe retaliation?"

Weeks? "They have not been subjected to weeks of bread and water. You have allowed them to tell you a tale designed to gain your sympathy, nothing more. One can excuse their scheming, because they are young, but one certainly isn't going to encourage it."

She whirled around to face him, and for an instant, Joseph thought she might be getting ready to raise her voice to him. Were the subject under discussion not so disquieting, he'd almost enjoy seeing his wife in high dudgeon.

Louisa crossed her arms. "Summon the undercook."

He sauntered close enough to see the gold flecks in her green eyes. "Isn't the cook typically queen of the entire kitchen? If you're going to ask for an inventory of the larders, her word might be the most reliable."

His wife took a step closer, glaring up at him. "The cook, the butler, and the housekeeper run your household, Sir Joseph, particularly in the absence of a house steward. The governess ranks comparably but has no staff, so her power is limited to the nursery, though the nursery maids technically answer to the housekeeper. Some governesses dine with the family, go on holiday with the family, and are otherwise informally elevated over other staff."

"What has this to do with a pair of little girls who are occasionally badly behaved?"

Louisa closed her eyes, as if summoning her last reserves of civility. "The cook will not cross the governess, not unless she wants to start a war. If the governess takes the cook into dislike, dishes will be sent back from the nursery repeatedly as unsuitable or poorly prepared. When the children sicken, as they inevitably do, the poor food will be blamed. Nothing will arrive from the kitchen quickly enough above stairs, and at meals, the governess will make a great show of being unable to stomach what's on her plate."

He could not entirely dismiss these odd predictions, because an army camp operated with the same sense of an invisible hierarchy enforced with unlikely and subtle weapons. Wellington had had no patience for it but had respected the reality of camp politics nonetheless.

"Go on."

"If we interrogate a scullery maid, the cook might well turn the girl off or make her life hell for starting trouble with the governess, but the undercook is a different matter. She's the cook's replacement, for one thing, and it's understood she cannot lie to us and keep her position."

Louisa whipped away again. "If you don't send for the undercook, Joseph, I will make an inspection of the kitchen myself and ask some very difficult questions of the entire staff. You cannot stop me unless you tie me to a chair, or—"

"Louisa Carrington, come here." Her head came up at the imperious note in his voice. "Allow me to rephrase that: Dearest Wife, would you let me hold you?"

He held out his arms, willing her to accept his embrace. Her first steps were tentative, but he held her gaze and waited until she was bundled against his chest.

"I want to shout at you, Joseph. I am very like my father in this."

"Go ahead and shout. I think better when I'm holding you. Perhaps you think better when you shout."

She heaved a mighty sigh, a sigh of relief, he hoped. He was certainly relieved to have her in his arms.

"Please don't be angry with me, Joseph. When I am like this, when I can see problems and solutions others can't, it makes other people angry. I realize that it's not enough to identify the difficulties and know what must be done. One must convey the proper course to those who have the problem, so they might see the way as if they had discovered it themselves. Jenny explained this to me, but I lack the ability to accomplish her ends, try though I might."

He gentled his hold, because she'd guessed correctly: he was angry, but not at her. "And if you cannot defer to those of lesser insight, Wife? Are you to keep silent and do nothing?"

Another sigh followed by a silence. Silence at least suggested Louisa was considering Joseph's question, and it meant he could hold her a while longer.

"I used to wish I would wake up one day and be less intelligent," she said, sounding very weary. "That is, of course, blasphemy, but I don't like making people feel angry and stupid, and I like even less when they must try to impose those emotions on me in retaliation."

The resignation in her tone broke his heart. He'd thought Louisa Windham—Louisa Carrington, God be thanked—was bored, and perhaps she was much of the time. She was also bewildered and lonely, and that he could not abide.

"Heed me, Wife: I do not feel angry or stupid because you understand household politics better than I. Watching your mind is like watching a billiards player who knows exactly the force, direction, and trajectory of every possible shot. What husband would not be proud of such a wife?" She went still, even her breathing paused, but she said nothing so Joseph tried again.

"Louisa Carrington, *I am proud of you*." And while he'd been a blockhead regarding the state of his nursery, he could be a little proud of himself too, for earning the hand in marriage of such a woman.

Her body shuddered minutely. Joseph braced himself for her tears—she was certainly entitled to tears—but then she smoothed her hand over his chest.

"I am very good at billiards," she murmured to his cravat. "It's just physics."

"Perhaps you'd teach me some of this physics. We could play for kisses."

She kissed him on the mouth then subsided against his chest, which Joseph took as confirmation that he'd read her situation correctly. Still, he did not want to let her go.

"I used to wish I was not such a reliable marksman," he heard himself say. He'd forgotten this wish—stuffed it out of mental reach along with the rest of the misery on the Peninsula.

Another slow, smooth stroke of her hand over his chest. "Because," Louisa said, "when you hit your targets, widows and orphans resulted."

Her words landed in his heart, near the guilt and sadness every soldier dealt with one way or another, though her tone had been one of sorrow rather than judgment. He nuzzled her hair, fortifying himself with the scent of her.

"The other officers used to stage demonstrations, set up targets so I could impress the new recruits. The officers would tell the men: 'This is the level of skill Wellington expects of us.'"

"Brutal of them, but, Joseph?" She angled back so he could see her eyes, which were steady and serious. "I am proud of you too. He who protected the duke protected the entire realm, which included many widows and orphans. By reputation alone, your marksmanship protected Wellington."

Those words landed in his heart as well, laying over the guilt and sorrow like a bouquet on a grave, lending peace and beauty to what had been so very difficult.

Whatever words he might have given her back, whatever poetry, would have been inadequate. He framed her face and kissed her with all the tenderness in him, a prayer of thanks for the heart and courage that went with Louisa's grasp of physics.

This is what it should feel like to be married.

"You don't need to fight every battle by yourself, Louisa. If there's a problem in the nursery, we'll deal with it together."

This nursery, in any case. Joseph tried not to consider what Louisa might make of the establishment in Surrey. That household boasted four separate dormitories.

"There is a problem in the nursery, Joseph. Trust me on this." She nuzzled his throat. "I begin to realize now how hard it was for my mother, raising two children to whom she had not given birth."

"And yet, she managed, and we will manage too, Louisa."

Another prayer, as fervent as the earlier one.

"I'll summon the undercook." Louisa patted his chest and drew away. Joseph let her go, though he had no need to confirm Louisa's conclusions by interviewing the domestics.

While she spoke to the footman, Joseph missed the feel of his wife in his arms. Holding her, even briefly, had settled down all the battle nerves and uneasiness and tight lungs their altercation had engendered. He prayed she was still willing to allow him the privilege of holding her when she learned of those dozen other children.

If she learned of them.

Twelve

"SHOT THE BASTARD'S GUN RIGHT OUT OF HIS CHEATING, dishonorable grasp!" The Regent gestured toward a footman, who made haste to pour His Royal Highness another medicinal tot of cognac. "It's enough to make Us forget this damned dirty weather, Hamburg. Have you those letters patent?"

Hamburg shuffled a stack of beribboned vellum. "A viscountcy for Carrington, Your Royal Highness, and that bit of land to go with it in the West Riding."

"Every gentleman needs a grouse moor, particularly a fellow who's a dead shot."

His Royal Highness surveyed the proffered document, which fortunately was written in a hand large enough that no glasses need be affixed to the royal proboscis simply to read the words.

A tidy little viscountcy, complete with grouse moor. The boon was…fitting but unimpressive, no more than what a gracious monarch would bestow.

No *style* to it.

Not like shooting an opponent's gun from his hand after the wretched vermin had fired early.

"How many urchins has Sir Joseph been supporting all these years on that baronial estate, Hamburg?" Supporting without even knowing it, which rather made a Regent cringe.

Hamburg looked pained but cited a number fairly in excess of the mere dozen the Regent might have hoped for. Urchins as a species seemed to proliferate like rabbits, which they oughtn't to be able to do on the basis of tender years alone.

"The cousin isn't doing well?"

"Not well at all. The man's affairs are thoroughly in order, and he's leaving a good deal to Sir Joseph as his only heir."

Well, then. Sir Joseph was to be quite, quite wealthy, and a canny Regent did not make unimpressive gestures toward loyal subjects who had served bravely on the Peninsula, acquitted themselves masterfully on the field of honor, earned Wellington's praise, and the hand in marriage of no less than Moreland's most exotically appealing daughter.

Much less those fellows who achieved the foregoing in addition to knowing how to raise a very tasty pig.

"A marquessate might be a bit too much," the Regent reflected. "It wouldn't leave Moreland enough room to maneuver on behalf of family, in which the old boy delights."

"No, Your Royal Highness."

"Oh, for God's sake, Hamburg. You'd think I was asking you to bring the damned plague back to London."

"But that leaves only an *earldom*, Your Royal Highness. Surely, for a gentleman pig farmer, regardless of his acumen with a pistol, surely..." Hamburg trailed away, eyes downcast. A few beats of martyred silence went by, then, "I'll see to it."

"An earldom and a grouse moor, and perhaps Baconer to the Regent. That has a nice ring to it. We like that last bit, about the baconer. Indeed We do. Fair puts Us in a holiday mood, it does."

"Of course, Your Royal Highness."

By the time Hamburg had backed from the Royal Presence, the Regent had heaved himself to his feet and started on a progress about Carlton House, noting all the locations from which a kissing bough might still be hung.

❧

"You don't hold with the tradition of keeping the greenery out of the house until Christmas Day?"

Joseph cast a dubious eye on the kissing bough above the entrance hall. Louisa planted a smacker on his cheek. "That isn't greenery. It's mistletoe. Her Grace says it's good for morale among the staff, and His Grace says traditions ought to be upheld where they don't impede progress or contradict common sense."

She kissed him again.

"Was that for morale or tradition?"

"Both. Will you stay more than the night in Surrey?" Louisa was trying to be brisk and unsentimental, trying to tell herself that being left in charge of their home so soon was a sign of Joseph's trust in her.

"That depends on the weather. You'll manage?"

"We'll be fine, won't we, girls?"

Amanda and Fleur popped down from the step where

they'd perched. "We'll be good, Papa. Stepmama says we're to have a tree with decorations, and we'll make snowflakes of gold paper, and bake stollen if we can winkle Aunt Sophie's recipe from her."

"Winkling." Joseph's brows drew down. "I do not believe winkling can be regarded as a ladylike pursuit. Perhaps I will remain in Surrey for a bit after all."

"If you're in the vicinity, I'm sure Westhaven would make you welcome." Louisa had sent a note to her brother just to make sure. "Say goodbye to your papa, ladies, and then I'll walk him to his horse."

Joseph knelt awkwardly and held out his arms to the girls. They ploughed into him like a pair of small whirlwinds, clinging to his neck with ferocious affection. "Goodbye, Papa. We'll be good, and we'll save you some stollen."

He kissed two little noses. "You'll eat all the plum pudding, turn Lady Ophelia loose, and no doubt polish the banisters in my absence. Wife, send to me if the *mobile vulgus* threatens to overrun the house."

The girls thundered off in the direction of the kitchen, leaving Louisa to slip her arm through Joseph's and escort him from the foyer. His horse was being held at the mounting block by a groom, which disappointed Louisa just a bit.

Time to steal a few more kisses would have been nice.

"You will catch your death, Wife." Joseph opened his cape and enveloped her in its folds, which— happily for her—necessitated that he hug her to his chest. "I will be back as soon as possible."

"We have much to do in your absence."

"I've never seen this house so thoroughly decorated

for the holidays. I can't believe there's another thing to be done." Louisa felt his chin come to rest on her temple.

"We have a great deal of baking to do if we're to send baskets to the tenants and neighbors. I must write to the agencies to find us another governess, and you've set me the task of finding a charity worthy of your coin. Then too, I am behind on my correspondence, and if all else fails, I have your library to explore. I will stay busy."

"While I will freeze my backside off, haring about the realm without you." He did not sound joyous to contemplate his peregrinations, which pleased Louisa wonderfully.

"I could go with you."

He drew away, taking the warmth of his cloak with him. "I'll travel more quickly without you, and I think you and the girls will benefit from a brief time without me. And Louisa?"

He tugged on his gloves and turned to face the drive. "Husband?"

"When I return, it will be next week."

"Two or three days does not—" Louisa felt a blush creep over her cheeks as the implication of his words sank in. She went up on her toes and kissed his mouth this time. "Safe journey, Husband, but swift journey too."

"Indeed." He tapped his hat onto his head and left her standing there at the foot of the front steps. Louisa remained where she was until Joseph had swung up onto Sonnet's back, set the horse into a careful bow in her direction, then cantered off down the snowy drive.

Being married was difficult in many ways, ways not even your mother or sisters warned you about. You worried for your husband when he was doing nothing more than checking on a property an hour's brisk ride to the east. You worried for your daughters, watching day by day to see them recalling how to smile and laugh in their father's presence.

You worried a little for yourself too, particularly when there were still two-dozen little red books to be located, and you were now under your husband's watchful eye, making retrieval of those books a great deal more difficult.

Louisa marched back into the house, intent on catching up on her correspondence before she took the girls over to call on Sophie and her baron at Sidling. To that end, she went to the library, deposited herself in her husband's chair, put a pair of his glasses on her nose, and withdrew the packet of correspondence she'd brought down from Town.

The first epistle was several days old, having arrived the same night as Valentine's warning regarding Grattingly's crooked pistols. Seeing no return address and no franking, Louisa slit the seal.

> How much will you pay to keep your champion ignorant of your facility with filthy verses, once you've wed him and become his lady?

Dread lodged in Louisa's middle, a tight, cold brick of anxiety that obliterated the warmth Joseph's parting reminder had created. She crumpled the letter up in a small, tight ball and pitched it into the fire, hard. Twenty-seven books was not so very many, but she wished Joseph were there in the library with her. As frightening as that letter was, as much mayhem as it threatened, not just for Louisa but for her family, she wished Joseph were with her.

Not that she could confess her folly to him yet. Please, God, let her find the books first, and maybe then… *Certainly* then. But not yet.

꩜

"They are notoriously resourceful, the womenfolk."

One of Sonnet's black ears flicked back, as if he were considering his rider's conversational sally. Joseph had been having a one-sided discussion with his horse since turning off his property more than an hour ago.

"They won't miss me. That's as obvious as the nose on your face, old boy. They'll contrive. Witness how my daughters contrived to bear up under the tyranny of a vindictive witch."

Sonnet flicked his ear forward and then back again, while Joseph silently pushed away a mental deluge of rage. To think that dreadful woman had been depriving his children of food and warmth…and worse, undermining the mutual regard of father and daughters.

Guilt and anger tore at him, so he urged his horse into a rocking canter. In the crisp winter air, Sonnet seemed all too happy to comply.

"I'm going to tell Louisa she has not two stepchildren, but fourteen. She's pragmatic, and her own father wasn't exactly a saint prior to his marriage."

Though Moreland had only two illegitimate children. Two was considerably fewer than twelve. Louisa, being good with figures, was likely to note this.

"Stop leaning right. You're as bad as a crooked

pistol." He had the horse execute a series of flying changes of leg, and still the damned beast leaned on the right rein.

"Surrey is that way, you fool. At least pull in the direction of your next meal. London is dirty with coal smoke, devoid of proper company, and no place I want to be without my wife—and daughters."

Sonnet didn't even flick an ear, nor did he falter in his pace.

Rather than wrestle with his horse, Sir Joseph fell to musing again. "I did not get her a morning gift. This is remiss of me."

A quarter mile later: "Very remiss. I intend to consummate the marriage thoroughly, and I do apologize for bringing such a matter up to a fellow who's in want of his ballocks."

Though the lack hardly seemed to bother the beast. "I could not have spent one more night with that woman driving me mad, and nothing to be done about it. I shall have my revenge on her, see if I don't."

Thoughts of erotic revenge were not comfortably pursued when a man occupied a saddle, much less a cold saddle.

"And something else has been bothering me. Lady Ophelia had no insights to offer on the matter: Why does my wife have three copies of the same little book of naughty verse I found in Westhaven's possession? A remarkable little volume, if I do say so myself." A very remarkable volume. Long study had told Joseph that to call it naughty in no way did it justice.

He could find his wife a book of poetry in London.

The thought crystallized in his busy mind like the

Concert-A tuning note of the oboe, around which an entire orchestra organized its performance. A detour into Town didn't necessarily mean an extra day away from home, but it meant a fellow needed to make haste.

London lay off to the right. At the next crossroads, Joseph set his horse in the direction of Town, whereupon Sonnet commenced leaning on the left rein.

⁂

"What are you doing, Stepmama?" Fleur was trying to shuffle a deck of playing cards with little success.

"Do you want to play the matching game with us?" Amanda asked from their playing field on the hearth rug in the library.

Louisa eyed the foolscap before her on Joseph's desk. "I'm looking over a list sent to me by my sister Sophie."

Fleur passed the deck to Amanda. "She's our auntie now, isn't she?"

"We have lots of aunties now," Amanda observed. "Is it a list of presents?"

In a manner of speaking, it was. Sophie had kindly listed the charities she knew of that met Louisa's criteria: not too geographically distant, without substantial patronage, and devoted to children.

"I'm choosing a charity for your papa. When you're done playing cards, shall we try Aunt Sophie's stollen recipe?"

Fleur was on her feet in an instant. "Can we, Stepmama?"

"May we?" Amanda chorused, organizing the cards into an untidy pile.

Louisa glanced at the clock on the mantel, wondering

where Joseph was at that moment. She missed him. She missed him, and she *enjoyed* that she did.

She'd never had a husband to miss before, never had a husband expecting her to maintain the household in his absence before, never been tasked with selecting a charity before.

The organization Sophie was recommending most enthusiastically was about an hour's hard ride east, in Surrey. The children were orphans of the Peninsular campaign, whose "English relations" had not the means to care for them.

A child born in Spain with indifferent English relations was probably an officer's bastard. Louisa drew a circle around Sophie's first suggestion. A jaunt to Surrey would make for a fine Christmas outing, and Joseph would approve of her selection—she just knew he would.

Louisa drew a line under the circled suggestion and rose. "Come along, my dears. We're off to bake up a special holiday treat to spoil your papa with when he comes home."

❧

"I need a book." This was the third location at which Joseph had opened negotiations with that statement. "I need a special book, preferably a book of verse, preferably in English, but French or Italian would do, as would Latin or classical Greek."

With each language, the shopkeeper's bushy white brows climbed farther toward the pink dome of his head. He stroked a snowy beard that flowed down his chest in contrast to the climbing eyebrows. "Are we looking for a contemporary tome or something from antiquity?"

"I don't know. This book must be special. Beautiful." Joseph frowned at the hodgepodge of volumes shelved every which way from ceiling to floor, the books so abundant they lent the entire shop a leather-and-paper mustiness. "The words have to be beautiful, but it wouldn't hurt if the binding was nicely done too."

The shopkeeper rocked back on his heels then rocked forward, laying a finger to the side of his nose in thought. He was a rotund fellow, attired in a green velvet waistcoat and a green morning coat worn shiny at the elbows. "Is this a gift, then, good sir?"

"For a woman." The fellow's brows came down. "For a *lady*. A very intelligent lady of sophisticated literary sensibilities."

And because her sensibilities were so sophisticated, Joseph was not frequenting the usual genteel haunts on the better streets of Mayfair. He was instead freezing his backside off in the narrow alleys and lanes of Bloomsbury.

"You present a challenge, my friend, but Christopher K. North is your man if it's a book you're seeking."

The old fellow extracted a green handkerchief with a flourish, polished his spectacles as if polishing a shield prior to battle, and ascended one of several ladders about the room.

"I have a nice collection of French works up…" The ladder creaked ominously, but Joseph said nothing. North's backside was well padded. If the man were to fall from a broken ladder, injury to anything other than pride was unlikely.

"Or perhaps Italian." With a rattling slide, the ladder glided several feet to the side, leaving Joseph to realize the thing was on runners.

"Or even Flemish. Not many acquainted with Flemish hereabouts." The ladder caught on a volume protruding from one of the lower shelves, all but pulling the little book out and flinging it to the floor at Joseph's feet.

"Dear me." North came gliding back to Joseph on his ladder. "I thought that one had gone to Moreland last week. I'm afraid that volume is not for sale."

Joseph and this particular little red book were old friends, and the book was apparently on good terms with Joseph's relations by marriage, as well.

"Not for sale?" Joseph retrieved the book from the floor. "I know somebody who appears to be collecting these verses."

Amid creaks of wood from the ladder and groans originating from the proprietor, North descended. "When I come across a copy, I'm to put it back. There's a duke who snatches up all I can find. It's got quite a following, that book. My competitor, Mr. Heilig, says he has an earl pestering him for copies, and we've an acquaintance in Knightsbridge who claims he too has an earl *and* a baron asking regularly after those poems."

Joseph opened the book to a random page, finding one of his favorites, where old Catullus was making wild claims to his mistress about bringing her off nine times in a row.

Maybe the man hadn't been so old when he'd written that one. Maybe he'd been in love for the first time, lying before a blazing fire with a woman whose gaze carried more wonder and passion…

Sir Joseph stopped seeing the books around him. North's jovial homilies about the pleasures of finding the right book faded to silence, to be replaced by Louisa's voice, full of curiosity and redolent with sexual enthusiasm.

"*Can one do this repeatedly? Successively? Nine times in a row?*"

The three volumes in her purse.

The copy in Westhaven's library, which had been summarily removed from Joseph's notice.

The sheer brilliance of the translations and the odd innocence of the terms chosen for the most vulgar concepts.

The passion conveyed in the words, despite the occasional innocent phrase.

Joseph stared at the little book. "Oh, my dearest, most brilliant wife."

"Getting an inspiration, are we?" North was back to polishing his glasses. "It's a work of genius, I say. Others aren't so *liberal* in their appreciation, no pun intended. I'm sorry I can't let you have it."

Joseph considered telling the man Moreland was his father-by-marriage, but North was apparently the chatty sort, and these were racy poems indeed.

"How much does Moreland pay you?"

North's eyes narrowed as he named a figure.

"I'll pay you ten times that amount, and I can assure you I will never let this book leave my family's possession."

North studied him, all vestiges of a shopkeeper's bonhomie falling away. "For whom did you say you were buying this present?"

"I didn't."

North crossed his arms over his chest, widened his stance, and lifted his bearded chin. "For whom do you procure this verse, good sir?"

The shopkeeper had gone in an instant from a cheerfully vague, slightly bumbling old fellow to the embodiment of the north wind, ready to obliterate the unwary in a sudden gust of disapproval.

"I want to give it to my lady wife. Her tastes are learned and unusual, and she would delight in this volume for all her days. She would delight in *me* for having found it for her."

The north wind slipped away from the old man's visage, to be replaced by a twinkle in his eye. "I confess my own wife has borrowed a copy of this little tome from the shop on occasion. I refuse to allow the loan at my peril. In her honor, I make you a gift of this book—for your lady wife."

Joseph scrawled the direction of his Surrey property on the back of a calling card and extracted a promise from the bookseller to alert him to any copies of the little red book that might turn up in future.

"I'll not be out to Surrey until Christmas Day at the earliest," Joseph explained, "but you'll have payment in full before the New Year if you direct your invoices to that address."

Booksellers were apparently an odd lot. As Joseph visited one obscure little shop after another, one jovial old fellow in holiday velvet after another pressed little red volumes into his hands, and with a wink or a smile, wished him and his lady wife felicitations of the season before imparting exact directions to the next shop.

By the time he left for Surrey in the morning,

Joseph had a dozen copies secreted in his saddlebags, though by the time he'd arrived home in Kent—by way of a clandestine sortie to the Earl of Westhaven's carriage house—he'd made sure his saddle bags were again empty.

Thirteen

So many insights had come barreling at Louisa in the course of a few days that she'd resorted to a tactic she'd given up five years previously: she resumed keeping a journal.

How had her parents raised ten children? Of course, His Grace shouted occasionally. Of course, Her Grace had learned how to quell adolescent rebellion with a single raised eyebrow—and how to encourage with a quiet smile.

Of course, her parents were close allies, there being no sensible alternative when that many children required love and care.

And this prompted a recollection that was truly amazing: Louisa's first dream, before she'd wanted to run the observatory at Greenwich, before she'd longed to join the Royal Society, before she'd aimed her sights at lectures for the scholars at Cambridge—doomed aspirations, all—her first dream had been to have a large family of her own.

The details had always been vague, involving bedtime stories in the nursery, little tales written for her by her small children, letters sent home to Mama from visits to aunts and uncles—always books, always writings—but mostly, always family.

A large, loving family.

When had she cast this simple, prosaic dream aside for things no woman could realistically aspire to?

Louisa wanted not only to raise Joseph's daughters with him, not only to be a dutiful wife and helpmeet, but also to be his partner in the rearing of more children.

Their children.

"Fleur and Amanda are our children," Louisa informed a rotund cat that went by the name of Limerick. The beast's fur was mostly black but shot with enough red to make her coat gorgeous.

"I've added their late mother to the list of people for whom I pray each night," Louisa said. "I will love those girls all my days, but I'm coming late to the ball with them." She fell silent, while the cat rose from its place on the corner of Joseph's desk and stalked close enough to bop the underside of Louisa's chin with the top of its head.

"I never held them as babies, never rocked them to sleep. I had nothing to do with choosing their names. I never paced the floor with them, or saw them smile at me even before they had teeth."

Louisa glanced at the slim epistle that had arrived from her husband by messenger after sunset:

Ended up in London for a day. Off to Surrey in the morning, missing the ladies of my household. Stay warm until next we meet.

> Love,
> Joseph

Love. Love could mean many different things, from the long-suffering patience Her Grace frequently exhibited toward the duke, to the shy smile Maggie wore when she admitted she slept in the same bed as her earl every night. Love could be the smoldering passion for his wife Westhaven was unable to conceal, or the quiet glances Valentine earned from his baroness.

From Joseph, it was a single, unadorned word in a terse epistle, but how fitting that he should convey the word to Louisa for the first time by putting pen to paper. There was boldness in wielding his pen for such a purpose. Louisa of all people knew how long the written word could linger in evidence.

And he had written that word *for her, to her.*

Good God, *she wanted a baby—ten babies—with Joseph.*

"I miss a man to whom I've only been married for a handful of days, cat. What do you suppose that signifies?"

She hefted the cat to the side, opened her journal, pulled Joseph's dressing gown closer around her shoulders, and fished in a drawer to find a penknife.

Only to find a ledger. The same ledger she'd seen Joseph poring over all the way through Kent. A ledger she might even have seen on his desk in Town, a thick green volume with red bookmarking ribbons sewn into the binding. Embossed on the cover in gold lettering was an address.

The cat settled on the desk, its front paws resting over Louisa's open journal.

"I shouldn't."

Except Joseph would no doubt show her the contents if she were to ask. He'd been forthcoming to the point of bluntness regarding their finances generally, and the desk drawer was hardly a place to keep secrets.

She peered more closely at the book where it lay in the drawer. "This address..." *Was familiar.* She bestirred her tired brain for where she'd seen it before, written out in a flowing, feminine... "This is the same address as the orphanage Sophie put at the top of her list earlier today, the one in Surrey."

The cat began to purr, a soft rumbling that made a contented counterpoint to the snap and crackle of the nearby fire. Louisa lifted the book from its resting place and opened it on her lap rather than disturb the cat.

The entries went back more than five years and recorded myriad household expenses drawn against a substantial monthly deposit. The household was large, complete with footmen and maids. The expenses for coal were prodigious, as were the outlays for food, bedding, clothing, shoes, copybooks, pinafores...

Pinafores?

Pinafores?

"That man." Louisa flipped a page and ran her fingers down the entries as something warm coursed along her spine. "That dear, dratted..." She paused at the entries from the previous December. Any Windham daughter knew well what it took to make a Christmas pudding, and the amount of candied fruits and sugared almonds procured for the household was staggering.

"Jump ropes—the boys love those—and dolls, spinning tops, oranges, two complete cricket sets—likely one for the boys and one for the girls—quilts of flannel and down—and shoes. Gracious God in heaven, the place must keep an entire workshop of cobblers busy."

She closed the ledger and went to put it right back where she found it, except a single sheet of foolscap fell from between its pages. The hand was not Joseph's neat, bold script, but a backhanded scrawl:

Assuming you survive the field of honor, what would you be willing to pay to keep your new wife in ignorance of your profligate adultery in Spain?

"What on earth?" She picked up the page between thumb and forefinger, as if it bore a noxious scent. Reading it again did nothing to change the vile sentiments the words communicated.

"Somebody is threatening my husband."

The cat squinched up its eyes in response.

"Some fool, probably the same fool who sent me that execrable epistle last week, is attempting to threaten *my husband*."

She put the nasty little paper back in the ledger and the ledger back in the drawer, then got up to pace. On her feet, Joseph's wool socks slid along the polished wood floors at each corner of the room.

"I cannot believe the effrontery... Joseph has enough to manage with duels and orphans and marriage to me... The nerve... The gall... The..."

She picked up the cat and cradled its heavy, furry body close. "We must begin as we intend to go on, cat. These threats and secrets simply will not do. For Christmas, I will give my dear husband nothing less than complete honesty, and we will sort through our difficulties as a proper couple."

Which sounded like a fine sentiment indeed, particularly when her dear husband was in the next county over and Christmas still several days off.

⟡

Westhaven considered himself a reasonably bright fellow, but the circumstances causing him to put pen to paper puzzled him exceedingly.

> *Gayle, the Earl of Westhaven, to Their Lordships, the Earl of Hazelton, the Earl of Rosecroft, Lord Valentine Windham, and Wilhelm, Baron Sindal…*
>
> *Gentlemen,*
> *Have received an anonymous gift of twelve copies of a certain small book left by stealth in my carriage house. Will confer with you further at Morelands on Tuesday next.*
> *Westhaven*

"Husband, you do not look happy."

Westhaven looked up to find his countess eyeing him from the estate office doorway. "I am happy but flummoxed, as well."

"Then it has to do with family, doesn't it?" Anna crossed the room to peer over his shoulder, which meant the dear, sweet, trusting lady was of course pulled onto his lap. The door was closed, after all, and Westhaven's son was in the midst of that most blessed of familial institutions, The Napping Hour.

"My bewilderment has to do with Louisa's books," he informed a tender spot just below his wife's delectable ear. "The number of circulating copies was just cut by about half, but I've no idea whom to thank for this development. Perhaps Father Christmas is taking a hand in Louisa's affairs."

Anna looped her arms around his neck, bringing to his nose the scent of honeysuckle and luscious female. "I have an idea," said his fragrant, warm, and curvaceous countess. She whispered a few words in his ear, words that made his eyebrows knit.

"By God, Wife, you do astound me. I'll send along to him, something ambiguously worded but comprehensible, if he's our benefactor. Intriguing like this would be just like him too."

She leaned in and whispered something else to his lordship, and he was astounded all over again—so astounded he rose with his wife in his arms, deposited her recumbent on the sofa, then locked the door.

⌘

Sonnet picked up the pace as Joseph turned him up the drive, which proved the gelding was in better condition than his owner. Rather than be sensible and tarry another night in Surrey, Joseph had pushed himself and his horse to get home, taking advantage of the illumination of a waxing moon on snow.

He'd promised a return to the Surrey household on Christmas Day—which would be a delicate undertaking, indeed—or on Boxing Day. Boxing Day was more likely, but his Christmas visit was something of a tradition—one he'd miss sorely should he have to sacrifice it.

The grooms took the horse, leaving Joseph to stand for a minute on the back terrace and consider what awaited him inside.

Tarrying at the door yielded a pretty moment, for all it was also nasty damned cold. The world was silvery white, still, as only a winter night could be, and profoundly quiet. Peaceful.

Inside, there might not be peace. Inside, Joseph was going to have to explain to his very new wife that even though matters in Surrey proceeded without any more threatening correspondence, if a nasty note was any indication, there *was* a threat. A threat to the family's peace of mind, and possibly to the safety and wellbeing of the children.

"Joseph?" Louisa appeared at the back door, wrapped up in one of Joseph's old dressing gowns. "Come in here this instant, Husband. You will catch your death, stargazing on such a chilly night."

She crossed the terrace and went up on her toes to kiss him.

Warmth, sweet and unstinting, greeted his chilled lips. She sighed and slipped her arms around him, laying her head on his shoulder. "I trust your journey was uneventful?"

Uneventful. The same word His Grace had used to convey the All's Well to his duchess. And yet as Joseph greeted his wife, looped an arm over her shoulders, and escorted her into the house, matters were not entirely uneventful.

Joseph's nose was greeted by the scent of cinnamon and fresh bread, the fragrance wafting through his blessedly cozy home. As Louisa led him through the ground floor, beeswax joined the olfactory bouquet, the scent coming from a pair of tall candles standing on either side of the main entrance and decorated with red ribbon.

The house was festooned with greens, even to the banisters on the presentation staircase in the front hallway. Wreaths hung in the windows, alternating with cloved oranges, while sprigs of mistletoe dangled in strategic locations.

"Husband, at the risk of boring you with sentiment, I have missed you." She led him into the library as she spoke, which was even warmer than the rest of the house. Not stifling, but...snug.

As soon as the door was closed behind them, Louisa plastered herself to Joseph again. "I didn't even let you get your coat off."

His arms came around her, and the pleasure he felt just to hold her, safe and warm and content, was almost another event in itself. In his chest, something unknotted; in his mind, something eased. "I have missed you too, Wife. You are well?"

She pressed her nose against his throat. "I am well."

Too late, the implications of the question sorted themselves out in Joseph's tired brain. He resisted the urge to lock the library door. "And the girls?"

"Thriving. I told them they could come down to breakfast in the morning if they're on their best behavior."

"Of course."

"There's a tray for you on the sideboard."

He did not want to let her go, not even to fill the gaping abyss that was his belly. He sneaked a kiss to her cheek and let her lead him by the hand across the room.

"I typically raid the larder, Louisa. I don't expect you or the staff to wait up for me when I'm from home."

She paused with him before the sideboard and started unbuttoning his coat. "I can read poetry for hours, Joseph, and were you not home by midnight, I would have sent to Morelands to get a pigeon to Westhaven."

"What could your brother do?"

"He's in Surrey. He could track you to your property and send word by pigeon that you fared well or were set upon by bandits." She had his coat off, a literal weight falling from Joseph's shoulders as she eased it away from him. "I gather you did not pause to call on him?"

"I did not." Though getting on and off his property unseen had been an exercise to rekindle thoughts of slipping behind enemy lines in Spain. "Louisa…"

She started on his cravat, her hands quick and competent, and damned if it didn't feel good to be rid of his neck cloth.

"Come eat." She headed for the hearth, setting the tray on the low table and pitching a pair of pillows onto the raised hearthstones. "You're limping, you know."

He'd been trying not to.

"Cold weather is not my friend." She turned back to retrieve a tea service from the sideboard, but Joseph caught her around the waist. "You really did not have to wait up for me."

What he had meant to say, what he'd challenged himself to say, was simple and true: *I love you.*

This was his kind of loving, this pragmatic provision of comfort and company. There was nothing romantic about it, nothing grand or earthshaking, but it met a need more profound than Joseph could have conveyed in words.

Perhaps Louisa, with her turn of phrase and polyglot capability might have the right words, but all Joseph could do was hold his wife and make simple declarations.

"Thank you, Wife. Your hospitality is much appreciated."

Soon enough, they'd have to have difficult discussions about threatening letters and decisions made years before in Spain, but not yet.

Louisa remained quiet in his embrace, her hand stroking absently over his chest. "I did not repair to my own bed in your absence."

Neither did she make use of her own dressing gown, nor her own socks—which gave Joseph inordinate pleasure. He let her go and patted her quilted bottom. She fetched the tea service while Joseph managed to get himself situated before the roaring fire.

"Your leg is paining you. Shall I fetch some laudanum?" She set the tray down, saw to removing Joseph's boots—bliss beyond imagining—then lifted the quilted warmer off the teapot.

"Is that warmer new?" Of course his leg was paining him, but less so for being in a cozy house— or something.

"I embroidered it for my trousseau. Eve and Jenny do better fine work, but it's the first thing I made I liked well enough to want for my own household."

She seemed pleased that he'd noticed, but it was the only warmer he'd ever beheld that bore the medieval image of the unicorn and the maiden. "I like it too. It's original."

"Odd, you mean." She reached forward to pour him some tea, her dark braid falling over her shoulder.

"Lovely, I mean." He tucked her braid back over her shoulder. "Unique, unusual, the only one I'll ever find of its kind."

"Have a sandwich."

He took the sandwich and the next two sandwiches, eating in a contented silence while Louisa plied him with tea and absently stroked her hand down his thigh.

When he'd eaten his fill, completing the meal with grapes—no doubt procured from Morelands and fed to him by his wife, one by one—he realized Louisa had been waiting for him to finish eating.

"Are we expected to call at Morelands over the holidays?" He wrapped his arm around his wife as he posed his prosaic question, a peaceful lassitude stealing over him.

"We can. I've yet to take the girls there, though they did very well at Sophie's. Sindal said to tell you you've an ally in him. I expect Hazelton will make the same proffer."

"I have an ally in you, I hope." Hoped it desperately, in fact.

Something curious flickered through Louisa's pretty green eyes. "Never doubt that." She laid her head on his shoulder, and left to his own devices, Joseph might have fallen asleep right there on the hearth. "The girls are giving you a cane for Christmas."

He needed a cane. A cane would make heaving himself to his feet from cozy hearths a less undignified proposition. "I have not found them ponies, though I suppose the thing is easily accomplished."

They fell silent, while behind them, a log fell amid a shower of sparks.

"Husband, will you come up to bed with me now?"

He blinked, wondering what all her question might entail. He could dodge and spend time making journal entries to update the Surrey ledger. He could tell her he was tired—he *had been* tired, very tired, when he'd climbed off his horse. Or he could struggle to his feet, get his wife into bed, and consummate their marriage vows.

"Will I come to bed?" He nuzzled her hair, which smelled of flowers, freshly baked bread, and cloves. "Gladly—provided I can find the way to my feet."

She boosted him smartly to a standing position, and before he knew it, Joseph was beside their bed, the door locked, and his wife unbuttoning his shirt.

❦

"This thou perceivest, which makes thy love more strong / To love that well which thou must leave ere long."

His Grace looked up from the Bard's melancholy if tender sentiments to find that the duchess was not exactly riveted by a recitation of her favorite sonnet. She was instead frowning balefully at a small stack of little red books sitting on the table, each volume the same as the other.

"They seem such innocuous little things." His Grace set Shakespeare aside while he made this observation and crossed to the half-dozen decanters sitting on the windowsill beneath a fragrant green wreath. "Just another book of verse among many books of verse."

Her Grace held up a crystal glass and allowed the duke to refresh her drink. "Some of those poems are brilliant." She sounded sad, which tore at his heart.

"If Westhaven's note means what I think it does, we might very nearly have the lot of them, Esther. I should have known Victor would set the entire family to the task."

Her Grace took a sip of her drink, her nightcap a concession to the deepening grip of winter on the countryside. "And then nobody will ever expose our daughter's folly—or her genius."

Hence, the sadness.

"You blame yourself. Madam, I tell you Louisa's odd starts cannot be the result of her getting hold of a few old letters from that Lady Mary Whomever Montagu. Victor's goading had a great deal to do with it, and the teasing from the others."

"Louisa read that entire book about traveling around Constantinople, Percy, and those wretched, damned poems. I should not have lent her the book."

Her Grace never swore. That she'd give vent to her feelings now was a measure of her despair as a mother—and perhaps a function of having made a substantial inroad on the contents of the decanter, albeit abetted by her husband.

"Lady Mary's poems are lovely, some of them." Naughty *and* lovely. His Grace took a sip of his drink, which was fine libation indeed. "Louisa's brothers have much to answer for, expecting her to do translations for them and half their forms at university. Young men are a blight on civilization."

"You were a young man once." She sent him a look

of such limpid approval, His Grace made a mental note to break out the cognac more frequently, and bedamned to the dolorous old Bard.

"And you, my dear, still resemble the lissome girl who had the good sense to snabble herself an arrogant young officer much in need of a wife."

They shared a moment of quiet reminiscence, while an eight-day clock on the landing sounded the hour.

"We should retire, Percival. Christmas will be upon us, and there is yet much to do. The boys will be joining us, and then comes the open house on Christmas Eve, for which a great deal of baking is to be done tomorrow."

"The house is looking quite festive, my dear. One couldn't ask for a more welcoming domicile. Will you call on Louisa tomorrow?"

Her Grace contemplated her glass. "I'm waiting for Louisa to call here first. She and Joseph have some things to sort out."

Her gaze strayed to the damned books, which His Grace would have loved to have tossed into the fire, though that would not serve. Victor had been very clear that each volume was to be returned to its author. For several years, His Grace hadn't known quite how to accomplish such a thing without embarrassing his daughter terribly.

Westhaven had apparently solved that dilemma. If they could get their hands on a few more books, then Louisa's little difficulty might finally be surmounted—and without casting a ruinous shadow over her new marriage.

◦⁓◦

Now that the moment was upon her, Louisa felt a curious hesitance, and Joseph, ever observant, must have sensed her faltering resolve.

"Louisa?" He stood by the bed, gazing down at her, his face wreathed in fatigue and something grave and intimate Louisa could not bring herself to look upon. She fell back on the bed and drew her hand across her brow.

"Have you the headache, Wife?" He stayed right where he was, standing by the bed.

She shook her head, when what she wanted to do, what she ought to do, was undress her husband.

"'Why dost thou shade thy lovely face?'"

Her head came up. "Who is that?"

"Old John Wilmot, Earl of Richmond in Charles II's day. Why don't you warm up the sheets while I wash off?"

Of course he would toss out a line of poetry then turn to the practical. Louisa accepted the suggestion though, because she was fresh out of suggestions herself. In a very few minutes, their marriage would become irreversible fact, and doubts assailed her.

What if she was no good at this, this... *This?* What if Joseph's first wife had been his exact mate regarding the marital intimacies, a precedent Louisa could never compete with? What if Louisa could not give her husband sons, which was, after all, the point of the instant proceedings?

She realized Joseph had filled the copper warmer with coals and was holding it out to her by its long handle.

Louisa rose from the bed and took it. "My thanks."

"They've more snow west of here," Joseph remarked

as he finished unbuttoning his shirt. "Though it didn't feel any colder."

Louisa pulled back the covers and ran the warmer over the sheets. "And the roads?"

"Passable. Sonnet is not fussy about the footing." His sleeve buttons came next, and those he deposited in a tray on the clothespress. "Should I get the girls ponies, do you think?"

"I'd wait for spring. We can take the children up before us if we get some mild days. A puppy will do for now."

He whipped off his shirt and paused in the act of pushing his breeches down over his hips. "A damned dog. They make noise, they stink, and they track all manner of dirt into the house. You are suggesting we procure a dog?"

"Possibly two if the girls can't share well."

"They share me well enough." Wearing not one stitch, Joseph ambled over to the fireplace and picked up an ewer Louisa had left to warm next to the fire. In defense of her nerves, Louisa went behind the privacy screen and used the tooth powder.

God in heaven, her husband was a beautiful specimen. Even the limp seemed somehow virile on him.

Louisa heard the sound of a rag being sopped in a basin.

"I can ask your father if he knows of any recent litters in the area. Is tomorrow too soon to call on your parents?"

Tomorrow. Tomorrow Louisa's marriage would have been well and truly consummated. How was she supposed to focus on socializing when that reality filled her entire awareness?

"Tomorrow will suit. The girls are looking forward to meeting Their Graces."

More wet, splashing sounds. Louisa peeked around the screen to see Joseph, one foot up on the hearth, running a flannel over his chest. His wet skin gleamed golden in the firelight, and the line of his naked back and flank...

Louisa hadn't known a man could *be* poetry. Oh, she'd seen the Elgin marbles, she'd seen her brothers as adolescents, but Joseph...

"The sheets will get cold, Wife. Get you to bed."

The sheets were going to spontaneously combust if Louisa deposited herself thereon, but whether from anticipation or mortification, she could not have said.

On the strength of sheer self-discipline, she crossed to the bed. "You are very matter-of-fact about your exposed person, Joseph Carrington."

He shrugged muscled shoulders—more poetry. "I don't believe I married a missish woman—and somebody has purloined my dressing gown."

Louisa tried to keep her gaze focused on her husband's chin. "You have others."

"That one is my favorite... *Now*. I might like it even more did you let me remove it from your person."

As he prowled over to her where she stood near the bed, she could not help but notice he was becoming aroused.

"Louisa, we need not be intimate tonight, but I see no point in further delay."

"Of course we shall be intimate." The words did not come out sounding precisely calm or inviting. She'd squeaked them, in truth.

He considered her, his mouth kicking up on one corner. "Into bed, then." He patted her bottom. "I'm for the tooth powder."

He was being matter-of-fact, but also, Louisa suspected, considerate. She unbelted the sash of his dressing gown, hung the robe on the bedpost, climbed under the covers, and listened to her husband brushing his teeth.

This was a sound she'd become familiar with, just as she'd learn the sight of him shaving each morning. Just as she'd see, time after time, Joseph moving around the room naked, blowing out the candles and banking the fire.

"You scented my wash water, Louisa. Do you know how long it's been since anybody heated or scented my wash water?" He lifted the covers and joined her in the bed. "I begin to suspect that marriage to you will have a salubrious effect on my physical well-being."

He kept moving, not reclining on his side of the bed but shifting and rocking the mattress as he maneuvered himself to Louisa's side. "Hello, Husband."

She was on her back. He was plastered against the length of her, a particular part of him prodding her hip.

"Greetings, Wife, and as much as I admire the embroidery on your nightgown, I will wish that article of clothing farewell without a pang—at your earliest convenience."

She covered her face with both hands. "Must you sound so merry?"

"A merry season is upon us." He peeled her hands away and kissed her nose. "'Oh why does that eclipsing hand of thine deny the sunshine of the Sun's enlivening eye?'"

"You have that Wilmot fellow on the brain."

"No, I do not. I have something else entirely—someone else—on my brain." He spoke gently, but there was happiness for him in what he contemplated. Louisa could hear it in his voice.

"Joseph, there are things we must discuss."

He untied the top bow of her nightgown. "We can discuss them naked." A second bow came free. "We can discuss them tomorrow." A third, a fourth. "We can discuss them naked tomorrow, but, Louisa, you are my lawfully wedded wife, and the time has come for me to pleasure you to the utmost, which I am enthusiastically willing to do."

Those were not lines penned by any long-dead earl. More of Louisa's bows came undone, until there were no more bows to undo. Joseph pulled the covers up around her shoulders and slid a hand across her bare belly. "I did not feel the cold in Surrey, Louisa, not as long as I thought of what these moments with you might hold."

God in heaven. "Joseph, what am I supposed to *do*?"

He shifted back to regard her, his dark brows drawing down. "You do whatever you please, with one exception." He kissed her collarbone, a sweet little tasting that might have involved the tip of his tongue. "You do not think your way through this, Louisa Carrington. A plague on me if you're able to cling to ratiocination at such a time. You put your prodigious mind with all its thoughts, languages, ciphering, and blasphemy aside, and let the damned thing rest while I love you."

The words—*while I love you*—were muttered against Louisa's neck. She liked the sound of them, even if the meaning in context was more biological than romantic. The idea of allowing her intellect to remain idle, however, was novel and vaguely disquieting.

"You still haven't told me what—"

He kissed her, and just like that, she did put her mind aside, except in as much as she perceived her husband shifting over her, straddling her, and surrounding her with the naked, lavender-scented length of him.

"You are such a lovely, warm sort of wife. I suppose you could kiss me back. Just a suggestion."

He slid a hand under her head and recommenced with the kissing, but he was devilish about it, making a slow, kissing inventory of her features so she wasn't *able* to kiss him back.

She drew her toes up the back of one hairy, muscular calf, reveling in the feel of Joseph's skin against the bottom of her foot. He paused in his kissing. She repeated the caress with her foot, and at the same time, arched up to join her mouth to his.

He growled. She smiled, and he retaliated by tracing her bottom lip with a slow, wet stroke of his tongue.

Sensations and intentions piled up, collided, and scattered in Louisa's awareness.

Joseph's erection, rigid and hot between their bodies.

Louisa's nightgown disappearing down between the covers.

A groan—his—followed by a sigh—hers.

And his weight, his lovely, blessed, utterly enchanting weight, pressing Louisa down into the mattress, anchoring her as arousal lifted in her blood.

"Husband, I want…" She pulled on a fistful of his hair at the back of his head and pressed up against him.

"Kiss me, Louisa." His lips swooped to cover hers, and Louisa's tongue charged into his mouth, intent on plunder and victory.

His hand, big and warm, settled on her breast, and the sensations resulting were so exquisite—comfort, pleasure, shock, anticipation—that Louisa broke off the kiss entirely.

He applied the slightest, most wonderful pressure to her nipple. Louisa gripped his buttocks with an answering squeeze. "That is… That is… Again, please. More, Joseph."

Her body recalled this, recalled the pleasure and wonder of Joseph's ability to tease and soothe and delight—also to shock, as when he bit her nipple gently and began to nudge at her sex with his cock.

"Louisa?" He put the question to her as he dragged his nose up her sternum. "Wife?"

"Yes, Joseph. Please, yes. *Now.*"

He straightened his arms, which meant their bodies touched only where he would join with her.

"I want your weight…" Louisa tried to drag him back down to her, but he was steadfast.

"In a moment."

The words were tight, grim almost, warning Louisa that for Joseph, the immediate demand was for reserves of self-restraint. She closed her eyes and put one hand over his heart. The other she wrapped around his wrist and held on.

"Breathe, Louisa."

Yes, breathing, something she'd been neglecting for

some moments. She drew in a deep breath and let it out on a sigh. Joseph snugged himself right up against her sex. On the next gusty exhale, he pushed his hips forward, and on the third, he was penetrating her heat, bringing with him strange and pleasurable sensations.

"Husband…"

He held still, their bodies barely beginning to join. "You're all right?"

"I want you so. More, *please*."

But the damned, dratted, dear man would not hurry. Louisa's nails were anchored in his buttocks, her breathing was ragged, and her body was silently roaring with desire for completion of this joining with her husband.

"Joseph Carrington…you are tormenting me."

He lowered himself to his forearms. "I am loving you." He got his hand under her head again and cradled her closer. "Move with me, Louisa. I'll hold off… Holy *God*."

She gave one glorious, sinuous roll of her hips, gloving him and retreating. "Like that?"

"Jesus have mercy. Exactly like that."

His voice was harsh against her ear, harsh and… awed? She slowed her movements, the smooth counterpoint of their bodies contrasting with their increasingly ragged breathing. He did not increase the tempo. For lovely, long minutes, Louisa moved with her husband, learning his rhythm, learning how to withstand an onslaught of pleasure from several directions at once.

"Louisa, I'm not sure I can…"

Something inside her gathered tightly, then more

tightly still. She laced the fingers of one hand with his against the pillow, and like a bolt shot from a crossbow, pleasure pierced her being. The feelings were much, much more profound than what she'd known with him before the wedding. Much more intimate, more...

Her mind could not form thoughts. Her body took over, begging her husband to prolong the bliss then join her in it, to sunder them both from everything except the pleasure to be had in each other's arms.

She felt the moment when he stopped fighting his own completion, when his thrusts became just a little wild, a little more fierce and pleasurable to them both.

Loving him like this, being loved by him, it was beyond description, beyond...poetry. Beyond everything.

Fourteen

WHEN THE PASSION EBBED AND JOSEPH LAY QUIETLY IN Louisa's embrace, there was more pleasure. The pleasure of stroking her hand down the muscled plane of his back, the pleasure of matching her breathing to his, the pleasure of smoothing her fingers through the silky tangle of his hair.

"I should move." A soft, possibly awestruck growl accompanied by some teeth applied to Louisa's earlobe.

She patted his bottom and kissed his cheek. "Not yet." Not when she was still so overwhelmed with intimacy that the idea of turning loose of him struck like grief.

He kissed her temple a few minutes later. "Louisa, we'll make a mess if somebody doesn't find us a damned flannel."

"My thoughts are a mess." And she did not mind that in the least—another novelty. She dropped her arms from around him, and he eased up, his cock leaving her body in a soft, damp caress.

"Don't look so woebegone, my lady. The night is young."

She watched as he strutted over to the basin, wrung out the cloth, and made brisk ablutions in the region of his genitals. "You are not delicate with yourself."

"I need not be. You are another matter." He looked positively piratical as he surveyed her in the bed. "A cloth, madam?"

"For?"

"To deal with the mess of your husband spending his seed."

No poetry there, but she approved of the bluntness of it. This was how she wanted her husband to speak of intimate things with her—openly, with one eyebrow lifted in challenge. "A cloth would be appreciated. A husband under these covers to keep me warm would be appreciated more."

"There's bound to be a husband around here some-where." He *swaggered* back to the bed. "He'll probably accommodate you for a bit, if you promise not to steal all the covers."

She wanted to steal his heart. "The cloth, if you please." Something damp was indeed making itself felt in an intimate location. How…curious, and *married* the sensation was.

Joseph passed over a soft, dry flannel and climbed on the bed while Louisa tended to herself.

"I take it you intend to linger in this vicinity, Wife?" He was peering at her in the gloom. Louisa pitched the cloth to the night table and had the sense Joseph was trying to see her without revealing much of himself.

"I had planned on sharing this bed with you for the next forty years or so, Joseph Carrington. If the notion does not appeal—"

He was over her in an instant. "*Sixty*," he growled. "Sixty at least, or seventy. There are people who have lived to be a hundred, though much more of this conjugal bliss, and five-and-thirty might be a stretch. I sustained wounds on the Peninsula, you know."

Louisa wrestled the covers up over him. "I married a ridiculous man."

He sighed and dropped his forehead to hers. "A ridiculous brute. Are you all right, Louisa? We became more impassioned than was perhaps wise for a first encounter."

"No, I am not all right."

He pulled back, real concern—even panic—showing in his gaze. "Wife, I am abjectly sorry. We'll rouse the servants and order you a hot, soaking bath. I most humbly beg—"

She put her hand over his mouth. "You are being ridiculous again, Joseph Carrington. I am not merely all right. I am most pleased. I am most definitely pleased."

And besotted. She was most definitely besotted with her husband too, though that was hardly convenient, dignified, or worth mentioning.

He subsided against her on a grand sigh. "I am most pleased, as well."

Some moments later, when Louisa was drowsing on the pillow that was her husband's chest, a thought occurred to her.

"Is there more to that poem by Wilmot?"

At first, she wasn't sure Joseph was awake enough to reply. His hand passed over her hair in a slow caress, though, then his fingers traced her facial features, one by one.

"Thou art my life—and if thou but turn away
My life's a thousand deaths. Thou art my way—
Without thee, Love, I travel not but stray.

My light thou art—without thy glorious sight
My eyes are darken'd with eternal night.
My Love, thou art my way, my life, my light."

He fell silent, his hand stroking over her hair. Louisa leaned up and kissed him, lest she say something besotted to a man who gave her both poetry and pleasure in the darkness.

And in the measured, sonorous lines of sentiment he offered her, in the tenderness of his hand caressing her hair, Louisa found hope that even her husband—her dark, limping, occasionally ridiculous husband—might be a little besotted too.

❧

"An embarrassment of feminine pulchritude graces my table." Joseph seated his wife first, then Amanda, then Fleur, bestowing a kiss on each lady's cheek. From his perspective, expecting the children to behave properly at table was likely to ruin both their meal and his, but this morning, if his wife had asked to dine with Lady Ophelia at the table, Joseph would have fetched the sow himself.

"What did Papa say?" Fleur leaned closer to Louisa to whisper her question, glancing at her father uncertainly as she did.

"He said there are so many pretty ladies joining him for breakfast, it makes him wish he were handsomer," Louisa explained.

Which wasn't quite what he'd meant—or was it?

"Papa's handsome." Amanda looked troubled by the idea that he might not be.

"Most observant of you, Amanda. Louisa, perhaps you'd pour us each a cup while I fix plates for our daughters."

But what did children eat? He resented that question, and resented that he did not know the answer. Another father, a truer father, would know.

As he surveyed the sideboard, inspiration struck.

"How would you ladies like to break your fast? We have buttered toast, an omelet with our own white cheese, kippers, beefsteak, oranges, ham, bacon—the best bacon in the realm, if I do say so myself—and are these crepes, Louisa?"

"They are. Let's start with tea, toast, and eggs, and perhaps an orange."

Petty of him, but it was gratifying to know those would have been his choices for the girls, as well. Joseph served for everybody—the footman being mysteriously absent from his post—and sat at the head of the table, intent on ignoring his children's clumsy attempts at manners.

"May I please have cinnamon on my toast?" Fleur's childish soprano interrupted Joseph's effort to rain cinnamon over every buttery particle of his toast.

"Of course." He might have passed her the cinnamon, but she held up her plate.

The entire meal went like that, with near misses, stumbles, and crossed signals that all seemed to right themselves somehow. And yet, breakfast hadn't been an ordeal, exactly… Not in the sense Joseph had expected.

"After riding all day yesterday, Husband, I'm wondering if you wouldn't like to stretch your legs a bit." Louisa patted her lips with her napkin. Fleur and Amanda mimicked her with sober precision.

Husband. She called him that as if it was the only form of address to which he ought to answer.

"I generally do," Joseph said. "Riding out has no appeal today—it looks to try to snow again—but a short visit to the livestock starts the day off properly."

A cavalryman looked after his own horse. For the first time, it struck Joseph as suspect that a proper English gentleman looked after his own children only indirectly.

Amanda speared her father with an expectant look. "May I be excused?"

"Of course. Put on your boots and fetch your cloaks."

"May I be—?" Fleur began.

Joseph waved a hand. "Away with you, both." This was a mistake, a misstep, because Fleur's little face fell, and Louisa's lips flattened.

Nerve-wracking, to be so at the mercy of multiple females.

"Though I do hope you will both grace the breakfast table again soon. I don't know when I've enjoyed a meal more."

Smiles greeted him all around, though it had been a near thing. When the girls had walked to the door then thundered down the corridor to the stairs, Joseph topped up his wife's teacup and his own—his flask not yet being to hand.

"I would like my marks, if you please."

Louisa stirred sugar and cream into both of their cups. "We all managed fairly well, but it wasn't a test, Joseph."

"Then what was it?"

She slid his cup close to his hand and patted his knuckles. "It was breakfast. When they're confident with breakfast, we'll add the occasional luncheon. By the time they're dreaming of putting up their hair, family dinner will be no challenge at all."

His wife was a handsome, even beautiful woman. In the morning light, her skin had a luminous glow, her green eyes sparkled, and the sun caught fiery highlights in her dark hair.

But she was also…lovely. Lovely in the way of a woman who took the time to notice and understand children, lovely like a woman who'd kept her arms around her new husband the entire night. The sense of being protected—

Joseph took a sip of his tea and knew it for the craven stalling it was.

He set his teacup down and glanced out the window to the chill, gray snowscape. "They are not mine, Louisa. Neither one of them."

"They are ours." She patted his hand again, but he turned his palm up and trapped her fingers in his.

"I am not their father. Amanda was born not eight months after the wedding—I was in Spain, and my wife did not immediately notify me of the birth, but I happened to see the parish records. I questioned the midwife and was told Amanda was full term. The midwife also verified the day of Amanda's birth, about which my wife had dissembled by a margin of nearly two months."

Louisa did not withdraw her hand. He loved her for that. For that and for many things.

"And Fleur?"

"I hadn't seen my wife for a year when Fleur showed up. I should not have spent such a long time in Spain without leave—Wellington could be reasoned with in this regard—but it was easier…"

Louisa was gripping Joseph's hand rather snugly. The sensation might have made him feel trapped, but instead it comforted. "Are you blaming yourself, Joseph?"

"Of course I blame myself. Cynthia was desperate to marry me, a fellow she'd known only briefly, a man beneath her socially. I should have realized her situation and spared her marriage."

Louisa's eyes narrowed. "She had family to look after her. Are these Lionel's daughters, Joseph?"

He shook his head. "Honiton denies it, and he was in Scotland when Fleur would have been conceived. I do not know who their father is, and because I never questioned my wife on the matter, she had no opportunity to tell me."

"Well, then." Louisa took a measured sip of her tea but kept her hand in Joseph's.

"I'm sorry. I should have acquainted you with matters before you spoke your vows to me."

And why he hadn't done so was not something he wanted to examine too closely.

Louisa set her teacup precisely in the middle of its saucer and aimed a frown in the direction of their joined hands. "I don't see as it makes a difference, Joseph. They were born to your wife. Legally, you are the only father they will ever have. You love them. They love you. What matters anything else?"

He reviewed her words in his mind to make sure he had the sense of them, for sense there was, in abundance.

"I am the only father they will ever have." He brought Louisa's hand to his lips and kissed her palm. "And you are the only mother they will ever need."

"Exactly. More tea?"

He did not want to swill more tea. He wanted to take his wife upstairs and make love to her all over again. He wanted to thank her for easing a weight he'd carried on his heart for years; he wanted to go down on his creaky, unreliable knee—

Above stairs, a door banged. "No more tea, thank you. We'd best be donning our mittens and scarves lest we delay our scheduled outing."

She nodded, smiling faintly, and let Joseph assist her to her feet. He paused with her by the door, mindful that two pairs of small, booted feet were making a racket on the main staircase.

"Louisa, thank you."

She peered up at him. "Their manners were quite up to the challenge, Husband. All I did was issue an invitation and provide a few reminders."

He couldn't say if she was deliberately misunderstanding him or if the fact that they were raising some stranger's children was truly of so little moment to her. *You love them; they love you. What matters anything else?* He made one more try.

"Thank you for that, as well."

When he offered his escort, she twined her hand onto his forearm and let him lead her out of the breakfast parlor. Outside, snow threatened, and the sky was a leaden gray, but in Joseph Carrington's heart, the sun was trying to break through the clouds.

❧

Louisa boosted Fleur over a board fence then clambered over in her wake, only to find her husband glowering at her when she jumped to the ground.

He was handsome even when he glowered, and he was handsomer still when he confessed, his blue eyes full of bewilderment and hesitance, that he'd provided a home to children not of his blood.

"You must not worry." She held him back when he would have gone stomping off in pursuit of the children.

"The pond may not be frozen solid, Louisa, and at their ages, warnings are pointless."

"We will keep the girls within eyesight and earshot, but that's not what I meant." She looped an arm through his to keep him from striding off across the snow. "In a proper merchant's household, such a thing as a cuckoo in the nest would never be tolerated."

"I am a merchant, a purveyor of fine pork, in case you hadn't noticed."

"You are soon to be a baron, you married a duke's daughter, and among titled families, these things are taken in stride."

He looked at her in some consternation, as if the subject of their conversation were only now dawning upon him. "God preserve me from any baronies—and that would be two cuckoos in the nest. I married a woman who needed a friend, not a husband. I abandoned her to go play soldier, and you are suggesting one need not be concerned about the consequences."

Play soldier? "You've been tormenting yourself over this since Cynthia's death, haven't you?"

He remained silent, his gaze on Fleur and Amanda

shrieking with glee as they tried to pelt each other with snowballs.

"I should not have left any wife of mine to shoulder her burdens alone, Louisa. That isn't what marriage means. It can't be."

"It certainly shouldn't be." And yet, despite the burden they'd created, Louisa was not going to tell him about the poems in that little red book. Not yet. Compared to the lives of children, children who bore no responsibility for or control over their circumstances, a passel of naughty poems meant little.

She would examine that interesting thought later, in private.

"I owe my life to a child." Joseph's gaze was glued to Fleur and Amanda, and Louisa had the sense the words had been wrenched from him.

"Tell me."

She led him to a bench some conscientious servant had dusted clean of snow and seated herself, keeping her gaze on the children rather than on the awkward business that was Joseph lowering himself to sit beside her.

"There isn't much to tell. I frequently carried orders from one general to the other, or dispatches headed back to Portugal. Spain was…difficult. Napoleon's court had spies everywhere, territory changed hands with each campaign, and the people were left to shift with whatever armed authority was in the vicinity. We tried not to involve civilians, but an army must eat. It must drink. It must sleep somewhere."

Fleur wadded up a snowball and aimed it at Amanda, but it flew high into the branches of a pine tree over Amanda's head. The resulting shower of snow put Amanda in pursuit of her younger sister, both of them screaming bloody murder as they darted around bushes and shrubs.

"I was bringing orders back from the coast— arguably a dangerous proposition—when I stopped by a village that was frequently on my route. The good sisters there ran an orphanage out of their convent, and everywhere one saw children doing men's jobs. They worked the gardens, they dug the irrigation ditches, and they served up the food at the cantina. I was famished, the food there was cheap and nourishing, and as it lay on my path that trip, I stopped at Vera Cruz."

Each girl had taken shelter behind a bush, and the air rang with their taunts about how many snowballs they were making and where they would aim each one.

"I rode a fine gelding, though he wasn't much to look at. The damned horse never let me down, never put a foot wrong, but the stable boy—Sebastian—he insisted my mount had a loose shoe. I told him to find the farrier and tack the thing on tightly while I ate. I had territory to cross where no sane Englishman lingered, and I wanted badly to rejoin my unit before nightfall."

Louisa tightened her gloved fingers around her husband's hand—when had she linked her fingers with his?

"The farrier was taking his siesta, according to Sebastian. Then the fellow had to find his tools, and then he had to settle an argument between his wife and his *abuela*—his grandmother. Grandmothers are holding Spain together as we speak, trust me on this.

I wasted half the bloody afternoon while Sebastian manufactured one delay after another."

Fleur promised to bury Amanda in snow; Amanda promised to dig herself out in time to see what Father Christmas had brought and to make sure the dear old gent knew what a fiend her younger sister was.

"By the time I got to my unit, they'd been slaughtered to a man."

Louisa slipped an arm around her husband's back and laid her head on his shoulder.

It made sense. It made sense that a man who owed his life to a child would reciprocate that grace many times over, to many, many children. Louisa waited for Joseph to explain this to her, for him to share with her the wonderful beneficence he was capable of, but Joseph sat there on the cold bench, as unmoving as an ice sculpture, while Fleur and Amanda laughed and played in the snow.

Louisa remained beside her husband until the lowering sky and an increasingly chill wind forced her to gather up the children and return inside.

❧

"You females and your silences." Joseph scratched Lady Ophelia behind her ear and was treated to a blissful porcine grunt in response. "I almost told her, almost informed her we have not two bastard children but a small regiment of them."

He switched ears, and Lady Opie obligingly shifted her great head. "I ought to take a journey, lest more time in my wife's presence turn me into a man with no dignity, no pride."

No secrets.

He wanted to be a man without secrets, without secrets from Louisa, in any case, but what sort of holiday would they have if he put all his cards on the marital table and even Louisa's pragmatic, generous heart were overtaxed?

"I have become that most pathetic of creatures, a man in love." The situation was dire indeed, because he felt not just enthusiasm for Louisa's company and desire for her intimate attentions—a younger man's version of being in love—but also...respect, affection, protectiveness, and a possessiveness that was foreign to his nature.

"And then there's the matter of what I should get her for Christmas, my last shopping spree in Town having been thoroughly derailed by other priorities." Joseph peered at his friend. "A pet pig would be a novelty. If your progeny grow to your size, then I might be spared the purchase of ponies."

Lady Ophelia apparently took offense. She wandered out from under Joseph's hand and rooted in the straw of her pen.

"Don't go into a decline. Perhaps love will find you again in the spring, my lady. We all sit out a dance occasionally."

She ignored him. Joseph put a little more feed in her dish, wished her a good day, and considered taking himself back to the house. The ladies were preparing to go calling at Morelands, and Joseph would not allow them to face such a challenge without his escort.

Christmas was still a few days away. He did not want to endure that holiday with secrets remaining in his heart, but the right moment for a disclosure of the situation in Surrey was going to have to present itself.

He was encouraged, though, to think Louisa hadn't batted an eye to know his daughters had been sired by another. A cuckoo or two in the nest hadn't daunted his wife in the least.

Fourteen cuckoos might be another matter altogether.

∽∾

"He's visiting Lady Opie," Fleur confided as she tugged Louisa toward the house. "She is Papa's best friend. Sonnet is his friend too but Sonnet is a gelding, and he sometimes gets cranky. Lady Opie never gets cranky."

"Ophelia is a formidable lady," Louisa replied. The hog was enormous, though placid for all her size. "Do we need a Christmas present for her ladyship and Sonnet?"

"Oh, they would like that," Amanda said, kiting around on Louisa's other hand. "They both eat carrots, and we've tons and tons of carrots in the root cellars. Papa doesn't like carrots."

"However would you know such a thing?"

"We don't know such a thing," Fleur said. "But *we* don't like carrots, and if you think Papa doesn't either, you won't put them on our menus."

Amanda turned big blue eyes on Louisa. "That will mean more for Sonnet too."

"You are a pair of minxes. Their Graces will adore you, but nothing will preserve you from having to eat the occasional carrot. You must accept your fate with dignity."

Mention of Louisa's parents occasioned many questions and much what if-ing—"What if the *dewk* and the duch-*ess* want us to come live with them?"—but Louisa wasn't about to make her first post-wedding call on her parents in the cozy old dress she'd worn to the barn.

She sent the children up to the nursery to make lists of appropriate presents for Sonnet and Lady Ophelia, picked up the day's mail, and headed for the library.

Only to stop short outside the library door.

The handwriting gave away the nature of the missive. Louisa shuffled the offending note to the bottom of the stack, locked the library door behind her, and went to Joseph's desk.

Before she slit the seal on the letter, she got out the nasty note she'd found in the Surrey ledger and compared the handwriting.

"Somebody seeks to bedevil us both. Somebody with execrable penmanship."

She opened the note and scanned it quickly, lest Joseph find the door locked and become alarmed.

Won't your husband be surprised to find he married a lady with the imagination of a whore? Won't all of polite society be surprised? And to think, a little coin might spare you this shame…or perhaps a lot of coin.

Louisa did not toss the note in the fire, much as she wanted to. Instead, she put it in her pocket and unlocked the door, then sat back down at Joseph's desk.

Thinking productively was, for the first time in

Louisa's experience, heavy going. There were only a dozen or so of the books left unaccounted for according to Westhaven's last reckoning, but all it would take was one copy of the dratted thing, and Louisa's future—and very likely the future of her marriage—were done for.

Soon, after a few more notes intended to unnerve her and make her desperate, she'd find a demand for money. She had money—Joseph's allotment for the household was generous, and she'd been saving back from her pin money for years—but money would not solve the problem, because there would always be another demand and then another.

The difficulty admitted of two solutions. The first was to identify the blackmailer and put him to rout. The second, no easier than the first, was to locate each and every copy of the book and destroy them all.

And either solution required nothing less than a miracle to effect.

❧

"I'm looking for a specific book."

Christopher North raked his customer with an assessing look: decently turned out, though the cuffs were threadbare, the seam near one elbow of the fellow's greatcoat was starting to unravel, and the toes of his expensive boots showed wear and want of care.

Quality but without *quality*.

"I pride myself on knowing my inventory, good sir. What book do you seek?"

"*Poems for Lovers*. It's a small volume in stitched red leather, very pretty, and I know you have it, because I pawned my copy of it just two weeks past, along with a box of other books of a similar nature."

The young nob had gotten the title wrong. If a man was going to own something as precious as a rare volume of poetry—and very good poetry at that—he ought at least to know the book's proper title.

"I'm afraid you're laboring under a slight misunderstanding, my friend." North beamed a smile at his customer, though the fellow looked like he hadn't an ounce of seasonal good cheer to his name. "I am the proprietor of a book shop. I sell books. I do not own a pawn shop, and were I to hold myself out as the owner of same—"

The man made a slice through the air with one large hand. "Spare me the commercial details. I need that book back, now if you please."

Felicitations of the season to you too.

"The book has been passed into the hands of another customer, and I doubt he'll be bringing it back."

While North tried to make his voice sympathetic, in his heart he knew that little volume had ended up exactly where it ought to be. A purveyor of fine books had an instinct about these things.

"Describe this other customer. Was he a city man? I need that book."

"Is the book to be a gift?"

The fellow's eyes took on a shifty humor, presaging an attempt to dissemble, unless North was much mistaken. "In a manner of speaking, it shall be a gift. I've tried every bookshop within ten blocks to find another copy, and nobody has a single one to sell. I know it was in the box my man brought here to you.

Tell me where this other customer can be found—a name would be very helpful, or a crest from his ring or carriage—and I'll trouble you no further."

The fellow wasn't offering to pay for the information, wasn't even pretending to peruse the shop as if in anticipation of making a purchase. Mrs. North would have a few choice words to say to such a person.

"I'm afraid the gentleman you seek wore no signet ring, nor did he arrive by carriage such that I might have seen a coat of arms." Sir Joseph had, of course, left his card and his exact direction, not that North would divulge either to this miserable specimen.

"What about a name? If he purchased a book, then he either gave you his particulars or a bit of the ready."

"He paid in cash, and I have no other information from him other than that he was off to rusticate for the holidays." North aimed a smile across the shop at the Misses Channing, regular customers, and both of the old dears were avid readers in several languages.

"What else did he purchase?"

From the scowl on the fellow's face and the way he slapped his gloves against his thigh, North concluded this customer was not simply determined, he was desperate. The book must not fall into the hands of such a one. Even Mrs. North would agree a spot of prevarication was called for.

"He appeared a very learned gentleman, choosing three volumes of Spanish poems of a similar ilk, three copies of *Gulliver's Travels*, and a book regarding the history of horse racing in Surrey."

The young toff seized on the only glimmer of fact in the entire recitation. "Surrey?"

Drat the luck. "A last-minute purchase. The gentleman was clearly not a Corinthian, if that's the direction of your thoughts." Though he had had the look of a seasoned horseman.

The scowl became considering. "Why do you conclude that?"

What North concluded, was that he wanted this aggravation gone from his shop. He mustered an expression of abundant geniality. "What Corinthian needs three copies of *Gulliver's Travels*?" Sound reasoning, and a deuced fine improvisation. North tossed in a dash of truth for good measure. "Moreover, the man was plagued with a slight limp. I doubt risking further injury with equestrian sport would have much appeal to him—then too, he enjoys poetry. What Corinthian spouts poetry in Spanish?"

The scowl cleared, but the conniving look was back as the fellow muttered to himself. "He limps, he spouts poetry, he's conversant in Spanish, he has a place in Surrey, and he bought three copies of *Gulliver's Travels*. No signet ring or displayed coat of arms."

"And no name or direction that I can give you." A truth, that, and yet, North had the uneasy sense he might not have done enough to throw this mongrel off Sir Joseph's scent. "Might I show you some other volumes of poetry, sir?"

The swell was already yanking on his gloves and tossing his scarf over his shoulder with the kind of sartorial panache young fellows thought passed for manly grace. In place of the conniving look, he now wore a smile that caused North the beginnings of dyspepsia.

"You needn't plague me with volumes of poetry,

but if you find any other copies of *that* book, you are to hold them back for me."

The door banged closed with a merry tinkling of the sleigh bells affixed to it, leaving North to hope Sir Joseph and his lady passed their holidays without having to suffer a visit from the useless bounder exiting the shop. North had done what he could to ensure same—Mrs. North would agree.

He turned his smile on the Misses Channing and held out his hands to them. "My dear ladies, it's a fine day when you grace my shop with your custom. What has caught your fancy on such a lovely Yuletide afternoon?"

Fifteen

A MAN HAD REACHED A SORRY CASE INDEED WHEN HE worried that his favorite pig might have fallen victim to the megrims. Lady Opie was not her usual sociable self, and yet she was in good weight—in spectacular weight, come to that—and she did not appear in want of anything.

As Joseph left her rooting desultorily in her straw, Sonnet wuffled at him from the adjoining paddock. Joseph ambled over to the fence and scratched the gelding under his hairy chin. "Shameless beggar. I suppose you want a carrot too?"

Visiting the horse afforded an opportunity to delay by another five minutes the visit to Louisa's parents, so Joseph headed to the supply of carrots stored in the saddle room.

What would Their Graces say about Joseph's clutch of stray children? Moreland hadn't been a saint prior to his marriage—few ducal sons were—but he'd limited his by-blows to two and raised both under his own roof.

Joseph had selected a decent-looking carrot and was

chomping on the end of it when he spied a small, folded missive laid on the seat of Sonnet's saddle.

"Bloody hell." He recognized the handwriting. The damned thing had been lying where any stable boy might have seen it and brought it up to the house.

No address, just his name—conspicuously lacking the honorific too.

> Carrington—
>   The last fellow to sire a dozen bastards at least wore a crown and conferred titles on his progeny. What can you bequeath yours but scandal and notoriety? And to think, a little coin might spare you this shame…or perhaps a lot of coin.

"Bloody, *bloody*…" He crumpled the note viciously in his fist and fought the urge to roar out a stream of curses. There would be more notes, more threats, and when the sniveling coward trying to exploit innocent children for gain finally showed himself, there would be another duel, at least.

The thought gave Joseph pause as he stalked out of the barn. He took aim and pitched the carrot so it landed directly at Sonnet's big, feathered feet.

There was only one person who knew both the extent of Joseph's considerable personal wealth and had some inkling of the nature of the household in Surrey. That person also had a need for coin and some arguable grounds to bear Joseph a grudge.

Tomorrow was Christmas Eve, and Joseph was not going to spend his holidays chasing Lionel Honiton down and thrashing the miserable sod within an inch of his lacy, mincing life, but Joseph silently vowed that Honiton's New Year would begin memorably indeed.

✑

"Wife, that note looks to be troubling you."

Louisa glanced up to find her husband regarding her from the door of their private sitting room. "It's from Sophie." She crossed the room and held the note out to him. "She says there's to be a baking day at Sidling, both to prepare for Their Graces' open house tomorrow and to get my brothers out from underfoot at Morelands."

And Louisa wanted to see her siblings, wanted badly to see them, though she also wanted to tuck herself into her husband's embrace and bare her soul to him.

He scanned the note. "I cannot believe your brothers are any help whatsoever in the kitchen."

"Rothgreb will keep the fellows gathered in his study, drinking spiced eggnog and listening to his tales."

Something in Joseph's expression became harder to read, and he remained in the doorway. "Then you will not need my escort?"

It had been a question, but barely. Louisa drew him into the room by the wrist. "Of course I will need your escort. My sisters would keep me prisoner until spring, interrogating me about married life and our daughters and what will I name our firstborn."

"Intimidating lot, your sisters."

Louisa threaded her fingers through his and kissed his mouth, just because they were married and she could. "A lusty lot. Papa claims we get it from him, but I've seen the way Her Grace looks at him when she thinks they're private."

"Louisa Carrington, you'll scandalize my newly married ears."

He was teasing, but the word "scandalize" jarred. "Come with me to Vim and Sophie's, Joseph. The girls will be disappointed not to go to Morelands, but they'll stay busy cutting out snowflakes and stars and making wishes."

"Wasting expensive paper, you mean."

The remark was not characteristic of him. "Is something wrong, Joseph?"

He hesitated, and for one instant, Louisa was certain he knew of the books and the poetry and the whole mess.

"Your family en masse puts me in mind of facing a French cavalry charge. I suppose the gauntlet must be run, though, and Rothgreb won't let them maul me."

"My sisters' husbands won't either, and come to that, I rather thought you enjoyed getting mauled last night." She had certainly enjoyed mauling him.

He closed the door and turned the lock with a quiet click, his expression becoming abruptly very focused. "You call that a mauling, Louisa Carrington? You call those sweet, tender caresses imparted by a blushing new wife a mauling?"

He started unbuttoning his waistcoat, and Louisa's heart began to beat faster.

"You have much to learn, Wife." Joseph's boots hit the floor in two thumps. "It shall ever be my pleasure to teach you."

"Joseph, it's not halfway through the morning, I'm fully clothed—"

"Which can be remedied posthaste—should the need arise." His shirt came off over his head, and

Louisa saw a button go flying across the room to land on the windowsill.

"Sir Joseph Carrington, you cannot seriously be contemplating—ooph!"

He scooped her up into his arms and hefted her against his chest. "Not contemplating, my love. Contemplation is for scholars and penitent school-boys." He strutted with her into their bedroom and dropped her onto the mattress, then covered her with his semiclad length.

They did not leave for Sidling until another hour had passed, in which time both Sir Joseph and his new wife were thoroughly, tenderly, and wonderfully mauled.

∾

Louisa tucked herself against Joseph's right side, hoping her body heat was some comfort to his leg in the chill confines of the coach. Hauling her about their chambers—hauling and mauling—could not have been wise for him.

"We should have the kitchen keep bricks heating at all times as long as my family is nearby. There will likely be a deal of visiting going on in the next fortnight."

"Shall we man the garrison?" He looped an arm over Louisa's shoulders, but she heard the disgruntlement in his voice.

"You aren't used to family, are you?"

He let go a quiet sigh, probably the reaction of a man who wasn't used to being questioned either, much less by a wife. "I lost my parents early, and then I was raised by two maiden aunts, for whom Fleur and Amanda are named. Family is dear, doting, elderly relations, and I can't see that the Windhams sport a single one of those."

"Give it a few decades."

Louisa felt him nuzzling her temple, which resulted in a sigh of her own. Joseph was surprisingly affectionate when they were private.

"Have you started looking for a charity to endow, Wife? Westhaven would be gazing pensively down his nose at me for the next five years did I renege on that bargain."

"He does that, doesn't he? Gazes pensively down his nose. If he's gazing at Anna, he shifts about in his seat and *almost* smiles."

There followed a review of the family tree: Anna and Westhaven, Emmie and St. Just, Sophie and Sindal, Válentine and Ellen, Maggie and Hazelton, and—as yet unwed—Eve and Jenny, both of whom Joseph had danced with. Time enough before the open house to start on Uncle Tony, Aunt Gladys, and the cousins.

"And the forlorn hope charges forth," Joseph muttered as he handed Louisa out of the carriage.

"The forlorn hope was the first battery of men into a breached wall after a siege," Louisa said, regarding him curiously. "That is a grim analogy, Joseph."

"Suppose it is." He tucked her hand over his arm. "But those who survived the charge were usually field promoted and got first crack at the spoils."

"I believe we've already enjoyed the spoils," Louisa observed as they approached Sidling Manor. "What will you be promoted to?"

"Brother-by-marriage."

He did not seem sanguine at the prospect, but Louisa had to admit, the throng of Windhams within the old house was imposing indeed. She hugged and kissed and was kissed and hugged for a merry age before her sisters tried to pull her off in the direction of the kitchen.

Westhaven appropriated Louisa's hand before the abduction was well and truly under way.

"I need a word with Sir Joseph's lady, assuming she can spare a moment for her dear old brother?"

Westhaven *was* dear. He would never be old, not in the harmless sense he was implying. Louisa tucked her arm around his. "Since my husband has been dragooned into the study to serve out his sentence among other dear old fellows before the fire, I can spare you a minute."

Westhaven escorted her to a small, unheated parlor. A comfortable room, full of embroidered pillows, winter sunbeams, and framed sketches of smiling people—probably the family parlor.

"You look well, Louisa. I trust marriage is agreeing with you?"

A fraternal interrogation, but Louisa also gathered Westhaven was truly concerned and trying not to show it.

"Marriage to Sir Joseph agrees with me very much. I expect we'll be producing the requisite grandchildren for Their Graces posthaste as evidence of how well we suit." She slipped her arm from his. "Need you question me further, Westhaven, or might I go and snitch my allotted portion of batter while I endure the same treatment from my sisters?"

He tapped her nose, a very un-Westhaven-like gesture. "Not quite yet. I have a present for you." Westhaven reached behind a chair and produced a linen sack.

"There is a growing fashion, Westhaven, of wrapping presents in decorated paper or cloth." The sack was tied closed with a red bow—a brother's gesture in the direction of seasonal trappings, no doubt.

"Open it, Lou. Happy Christmas from all of us, and from Victor too, I think."

Mention of the brother who'd lost his battle with consumption several Christmases earlier had Louisa studying Westhaven's face.

"You needn't have gotten me anything, you know. If it weren't for my family, two hundred volumes of potential scandal would still be at large. As it is, only twenty-seven—"

He shook his head slowly from side to side.

A blend of holiday cheer at seeing her family and mild irritation at Westhaven's theatrics vanished, leaving Louisa with a sense that the moment had grown significant.

She tossed the ribbon onto a chair and peered into the sack. A bounty of small red volumes lay within, some worn, some pristine, and all bearing the title of her potential undoing.

Louisa Windham Carrington comprehended many languages, including both the ancient and the modern. She corresponded with learned minds regarding astronomy, mathematics, natural science, and economics. She had read more Latin than most of the top scholars at Cambridge, and she could recite more poetry than the literary prodigies at Oxford.

But she had only two words for her brother: "Thank you."

"They are all there, save one," Westhaven said. "We can safely assume that one is at the bottom of some river, buried with a worthy cavalryman on the Continent, or otherwise gathering dust in an old curmudgeon's attic. Your troubles are over, Lou. It took years, and the efforts of every sibling and even some relatives, but—thank the Deity and His Angels—we found them all."

His smile was doting, triumphant, and affectionate, and as Louisa let him hug her, she admitted they were sharing a fine, fine moment full of gratitude, familial love, and loyalty.

All of which would have portended very well, had Louisa thought the last little red volume was indeed rotting in the bottom of some obscure river.

She, however, knew quite the contrary to be true. That last, most important copy of the infernal book was in the lily-white hands of a man with whom Louisa had waltzed. A man to whom she'd shown every courtesy, and a man who had to be stopped by any and all possible means.

❧

"We do so enjoy the holidays," the Regent declared, jowls working around a mouthful of plum pudding. "Nasty weather, true, but good food and good friends abound. Let me see that menu one more time."

He waggled pudgy fingers in the direction of his senior footman, who procured the requisite document—the thing ran to five pages—from a delicate escritoire several feet farther from the fire.

His Royal Highness glanced up from his tray. "Humbug, you're eyeing my pudding like a starving mud lark. Bad form, old boy."

Hamburg directed his gaze to the cherubs gleefully sporting about on the ceiling.

"Do you think eight desserts is—oh, this will not do. There is nothing chocolate among the desserts. Our friends are very fond of their chocolate."

His Royal Highness's friends were of the female persuasion, one female in particular. Hamburg exchanged a glance with the footman that confirmed their shared opinion of altering the menu when the kitchens had long since started preparing the Christmas meal.

"Perhaps Your Royal Highness might gift the guests with chocolate drops, or serve them between the dessert courses?"

More plum pudding disappeared down the royal gullet. "I suppose We could at that. When you go, send Mortenson to me. He'll whinge and whine about the expense, but it's Christmas, what? The shop-keepers will boast for years of having Our custom."

"For decades." Given the magnitude of that custom when it came to sweets.

"Humbug, are you attempting to curry Our favor?"

Well, yes, he was, because the sun would soon set, and Hamburg Senior believed in getting into the spirit—or spirits—of the season nightly unless some-body was on hand to curb his Yuletide zeal.

"Of course not, Your Royal Highness."

"Not the preferred answer, though We will allow you're honest. You've been too conscientious, however, and so must be punished for your virtue."

Only in the royal household would a good man be punished for his virtue.

"I live to serve Your Royal Highness."

The Regent's smile was sardonic. "You live to complain about serving, so We will indulge your propensities. You're to scare up Sir Joseph Carrington and inform him of his honors on Christmas Day. We would like to make it clear that We feel an especial affection for Our loyal servant on the day of the holy birth, particularly if the dear fellow is going to keep a regiment of urchins off the charity of the parishes."

Hamburg watched despite himself as the royal fundament was heaved up out of a well-padded chair. "The letters patent are…" The Regent scanned the room. "Ah, on that mantel." He snapped his fingers. "If you please."

The footman who'd fetched the menu handed the sovereign the relevant beribboned documents.

"I'm to understand Your Royal Highness wants this delivered on *Christmas Day*?"

"Boxing Day wouldn't make quite the same impression, now would it? One rewards the trades and the lower orders on Boxing Day."

"Of course. Christmas it is."

"There. You see? You are perfectly miserable, and you have your high and trusted office to thank. Sir Joseph has likely taken his bride out to the family seat in Kent. If you leave now, you stand a chance of making a splash at Moreland's annual open house. Mind the punch, though. Her Grace never lets a guest go thirsty, and while the libation is delightful, it also kicks like a mule."

As if the Duke of Moreland would be swilling punch with a Carlton House lackey. The footman gave a slight, commiserating shake of his head while the Regent settled in to annihilate more plum pudding. "You can take one of the coaches. A four-in-hand ought to do. A six-in-hand can be tedious when the roads are sloppy. Two postillions, full livery, you know the drill."

"Of course. A four-in-hand, two postillions." Which made the journey an altogether different proposition. The royal coaches were nothing if not commodious, and Kent was not so very far away. Then too, when the Prince of Wales's coach came galloping up the lane, *everybody* stopped to stare.

"Be off with you." The royal hand flapped languidly. "Happy Christmas, Humbug, and Crenshaw has a little something for you to keep the chill off while you travel."

A strapping young specimen in periwig and footman's livery stood by the door, holding a wooden case that looked to be full of…bottles.

"Your Royal Highness, I'm going only to Kent."

"Shoo. We need peace and quiet to consider Our menu."

"Happy Christmas, and thank you."

"Happy Christmas, Humbug, and mind you don't get the coachman drunk. We value Our cattle."

❧

The only thing saving Joseph was the messenger's timing. He arrived while Louisa was above stairs, putting the finishing touches on her toilette. Twenty minutes either way, and she would have known at the same moment Joseph himself learned of old Hargrave's passing.

"He did not suffer at the end, sir—I mean, my lord."

"Sir will do. Nothing's official yet." Pray God the legalities would take months to untangle. A title did not often come out of abeyance, and Joseph certainly wasn't going to hurry the process.

The old fellow looked like he'd argue with Joseph for declining more formal address, but one glance at Joseph's visage, and no more was offered on the subject.

"You are, of course, welcome here for the holidays," Joseph said. The man had the look of an aging jockey—not much over four feet tall, wizened and somehow boyish at the same time. "Cook will feed you within an inch of your life, and I'm sure the punch bowl was set out in the servants' hall several days ago."

"A tot of grog wouldn't go amiss, your—sir. The old, er, Mr. Sixtus Hargrave Carrington give me a letter for ye and a message."

Joseph accepted a single folded sheet of foolscap, sanded and sealed, his name scrawled across the outside.

"My thanks. What was the message?"

The little fellow tugged on one red ear. "He said to be sure to tell you, 'Happy Christmas,' because his is likely the best one he's had for fifty years."

"And his widow?" To lose a spouse in the Yule season could not be an easy thing.

"You shoulda seen the bachelors circling her at the wake, my—sir. She'll bear up, and Mr. Carrington wouldn't begrudge her her fun, neither. She stood by him while he lived. He wouldn't expect more."

Joseph nodded and frowned at the letter. "Off to the kitchen with you, and my thanks for bringing the news in person."

The little fellow bobbed in parting, leaving Joseph alone with Sixtus Hargrave Carrington's final missive. Joseph slit the seal reluctantly, because having something of his relation yet to read meant Hargrave's business in the mortal sphere was not quite concluded.

My Dear Joseph,

As you read this, I am cavorting about the celestial realm with the naiads and muses, my form once again restored to the youthful vigor you yet enjoy. The Deity has granted me my fondest Christmas wish and put an end to my suffering—you will not presume to castigate Him for His timing until you yourself are wracked with illness and relieved of every dignity for years on end.

I regret my passing without issue means you are now burdened with the deuced title, as you referred to it, but I think you'll find the barony comes with more blessings than you might have anticipated.

Be kind to Penelope, please. For all her youth, she was a good wife to me. She's been left well set up, consistent with my wishes and her desserts. I trust you will not allow the fortune hunters to exploit her generous nature while she grieves my passing.

The seat of the barony is a lovely place I had occasion to visit just a few years past. Don't wait until grouse season to see it for yourself. My dying wish, Joseph, is that you collect your newly acquired lady wife and make a journey North to what is now your family seat. Yorkshire in spring is glorious, a perfect complement to a new marriage.

Trust me on this, dear boy. Wear the title with pride and honor, and I shall ever be,

Your loving relation,
Sixtus Hargrave Carrington

Damned if it didn't hurt like blazes.

It hurt to think Joseph would never again hear the old fellow's raucous, irreverent laughter, it hurt to think there would be no more holiday epistles exchanged between two relics of an old and not very illustrious family. It hurt to think Amanda and Fleur, in some way, had lost what little family remained to them, as well, regardless of the lack of any blood tie.

And it hurt to know that after centuries of carefully mapping generation after generation of Carringtons, with the elders from age to age charting which branch of the family might yet revive the title and when that happy day might arrive, only one Carrington remained standing—a lame pig farmer with more money than was decent.

"Joseph?" Louisa had come into the library without making a sound. Joseph held out a hand to her, drinking in the sight of her in red velvet with gold trim, white lace at her wrists and across her bosom.

"My dear." When she took his hand, he pulled her in closer, wrapping her in his embrace and resting his cheek against her hair. "You are a vision."

She wound her arms about his waist. "You are

quite handsomely turned out yourself, which is fortunate. Mama and Papa will inspect us, so we must be
properly put together and graciously cheerful."

"Cheerful." *What a notion.* "Sixtus Hargrave
Carrington is gone." And when had marriage meant
a man had no control over his moronic mouth? "I
hadn't meant to tell you until after the holidays."

She hugged him closer. "I am sorry for your loss,
and I know you dread assuming the title, Joseph, but
it need not be a burden."

"Dread." He considered the term. "That is not
putting it too strongly. I must vote my seat, I must
wade through all the courtesy invitations. I must leave
cards all over creation when I arrive to Town. My
daughters must now have a come out—"

She kissed him into silence. Put her mouth right
over his and didn't desist until he was kissing her back.

Joseph felt her sigh against his throat.

"You will be in a position to steer the course of events
in the Lords, Joseph. You are a caretaker by nature, and
better you should have the responsibility than some
gouty old marquis concerned only with protecting his
own privileges and oppressing the Catholics."

"But Town, Louisa?"

"We'll have family there. Maggie's husband bides
there frequently. Sophie's husband will soon be
invested. His Grace's influence will put you on any
committee you choose, and you and I will host the
most scintillating political dinners seen in ages."

A shaft of light pierced the gloom of Joseph's mood.
"You aren't in the least daunted by this, are you?"

"I have no gift for small talk, Joseph, but the

political types haven't either. You and I both have a complement of brains, and your common sense is the equal of anybody's. We shall contrive." She was confident in her complement of brains and well she should be. While Joseph was by no means as confident of his own intellectual gifts, in this, he was confident of his wife.

He purely hugged her, drawing in her clove-and-citrus scent and silently thanking heaven that this woman had consented to be his spouse.

And then he recalled his dependents in Surrey.

Could a baron weather the scandal of multiple bastards any more easily than a lowly pig farmer could?

"Shall we stay home, Joseph?" Louisa was cuddled close, close enough that while Joseph was lamenting a fate most men would have celebrated riotously, Joseph's body had begun celebrating something else entirely. "We can plead mourning, and it will be the truth."

"I would as soon not cast a pall on anybody else's holiday." Still, he did not turn her loose. "My cousin was old, he welcomed his own passing, and he had a long, jolly life. We've acquired another fortune, by the way. Best be about picking out that charity, Louisa."

She went still against him, her hand pausing in a slide over his backside then resuming its journey. "Shall we be a bit late, Joseph?"

At first he didn't comprehend her question, but she followed it up with a soft, friendly kiss on the mouth and a little squeeze to his fundament. An image popped into his mind, of Louisa's back pressed to the wall, her skirts hiked up all around, and Joseph's cock buried in her sweet heat.

She was tall enough to make it workable, provided he could—

His leg would never withstand the languid joining he wanted to offer her.

"Drawers off." He let his hand slip over her breast as he eased from her embrace and locked the door. Her smile was an entire Christmas of female good cheer in a single expression, and it brightened more as Joseph settled into a chair and started undoing his falls.

"We will be more than a little late if you leave me by my lonesome over here, Wife, waving my parts in the breeze for your amusement."

His parts weren't entirely ready to receive callers, but as Louisa slid off her drawers and tossed them onto the desk, the knocker was definitely going up.

"I had wondered about this." She eyed him where he sat. "How does one…?"

"You put a knee on either side of my hips for starters, as if you're straddling my lap. I expect some kissing will follow, and very likely some marital intimacies."

Louisa hiked her skirts and climbed into the chair, positioning herself exactly as Joseph had suggested. "Or perhaps," she whispered in his ear, "we could recite poetry to each other."

She beamed at him, not at all at a loss to contemplate an impromptu coupling by the fire in a reading chair. Her gaze held mischief and tenderness and a hint of determination, as well.

"My dearest wife, you *are* poetry."

Which should have sounded like fatuous rot, but as a cloud of velvet and Louisa eased over Joseph's lap, it was the truth as he knew it. She moved on him like poetry, breathed through him like poetry, and brought him comfort more intimate than any words ever had.

Their joining was unhurried and a profound consolation. Joseph held off his own completion until Louisa had found hers at least twice and possibly a third time—he wasn't sure about those last few happy shudders—and then he let pleasure flood his awareness as he spilled his seed deep in his wife's body.

When the tide ebbed, his face was pressed to Louisa's fragrant bosom, her fingers were stroking gently through his hair, and Joseph's body felt better than it had in…better than it had *ever*.

"I haven't dissuaded you from attending Their Graces' open house, have I?" She spoke with her lips against his temple, their position making Joseph feel a protectiveness from her embrace she probably didn't intend.

"Your parents haven't seen us since the wedding, Louisa. They'll fret if I don't show you off to them soon."

He *wanted* to show her off. Wanted the entire realm to marvel at his wife, and yet, he did not hustle her away to retrieve her drawers. When Louisa did gain her feet, Joseph passed her his handkerchief and took his time putting himself to rights.

Louisa turned to face him as he rose awkwardly from the chair. "Is my hair a fright?"

Such a tedious, wifely question—though in his previous marriage, Joseph could not recall being asked such a thing even once. Joseph liked the inquiry nonetheless. They'd been married a week, and already Louisa assumed she could rely on Joseph to be honest with her about something so personal.

He liked that she made the assumption he'd be honest with her. Had he been worthy of her trust, he would have liked it even more.

⊷

The carriage ride to Morelands went more slowly than it might have otherwise because a light snow was falling, obscuring the ruts that identified the frozen road. Louisa wondered if every couple arriving "fashionably late" detained themselves with similar sport.

Except it wasn't sport. Joseph had been so...*tender* with her, his touch reverent, his kisses a benediction upon her flesh.

My dearest wife, you are *poetry.* The words landed in her heart like a rose tossed from a gallant to his lady, but a thorny rosy.

"What are you thinking, Louisa?"

She slipped her hand into his, and he squeezed her fingers. "I am thinking a man with a title is at once held up to public scrutiny more than his untitled neighbor, and yet above scrutiny too."

"You are not philosophizing fifteen minutes after I've loved you witless, Louisa Carrington. My pride will not allow it."

"Fifteen minutes after I loved *you* witless, Joseph Carrington."

He kissed her fingers. "Not a wit to be found between us. An enviable state."

Though a temporary one. Louisa recalled her intention to give her husband the truth for Christmas, and now Christmas was almost upon them. Before her courage could desert her, she posed a question.

"Joseph, are you amenable to a short journey tomorrow?"

He hadn't lit the coach lamps, so Louisa had the blessing of darkness in which to make her query. "On Christmas Day, Louisa? Where are we going?"

"It's a surprise. We can easily get there and back in time for Christmas dinner."

He was quiet for so long Louisa wondered if he was going to answer, but then he patted her hand. "Weather permitting. I cannot make myself available to you on Boxing Day, though, and I hope you haven't beggared your pin money to procure me this surprise."

"I have not." Though *she* hoped offering to spend her dower funds on his private charity might allow her to broach other, more difficult matters involving a small red volume of verse.

"Shall we take the girls on this journey, dearest Wife?"

"I think not. They'll want to take the puppies, and I cannot recall a sanguine experience involving both a puppy and a traveling coach, much less two puppies, two little girls, and a traveling coach."

The carriage slowed to turn up Morelands's drive. "Then I shall enjoy having you to myself, Louisa Carrington. I have a small token to give you in honor of the holiday—very small."

"Can I see the stars with it?"

She heard him chuckle in the dark. "You did not see them earlier, did not soar among them in my arms?"

"I have married a fanciful man—a fanciful baron."

"None of that, Louisa. You promised we'd keep quiet until the Regent has done something official."

The reproof was casual, nothing in it hinting that

Joseph was as burdened as he'd been when Louisa had found him in the library. That he'd trust her with this secret, rely on her to protect his privacy this way was…a gift. It bespoke a marital bond that had flourished in a short time, a bond another man might never have built with her.

She loved him for it. Loved him for raising his wife's by-blows and not even inquiring into their paternity. Loved him for defending the honor of a lady who had both father and brothers arguably better suited to the task. She loved him for introducing her to Lady Ophelia and for naming his daughters for his maiden aunts.

She loved him for being himself, for raising the happiest pigs in the realm, for taking on a title as a weighty honor, not an excuse to live an idle and selfish life.

"Why the sigh, Louisa?"

"I am cataloguing your virtues. The list is lengthy."

The carriage slowed on the grand circular driveway before the Moreland mansion. Torches lined the walk, and the falling snow looked like so many tiny stars against the illumination.

"Put at the top of your list that I had the great good sense to marry you when I had the chance, would you?"

He meant it. For that alone, Louisa would somehow find the courage to tell him that a stupid, schoolgirl tantrum might land the newly minted baron and his family in the middle of a nasty scandal.

Tomorrow—she would find the courage tomorrow.

Sixteen

"I THOUGHT LOUISA WAS LOOKING SPLENDID. FOR pity's sake, St. Just, leave some bacon for the rest of us." Maggie, the Countess of Hazelton, glared at her brother, who obligingly held up a strip of crispy pork, from which she took a ladylike nibble.

"Mags, you missed his fingers," Valentine said from her other side. "I agree with you. Lou was in splendid good looks, except when her gaze fell upon her spouse, and then she was positively radiant."

"Matrimony becomes all of you Windhams," Anna, the Countess of Westhaven, remarked as her husband topped up her tea. Westhaven set the teapot down and patted her hand right there in front of all his hungry, gossipy siblings.

"Were anyone to ask my opinion—" he began.

"Which we have not," Sophie pointed out.

"—I would have said it's Sir Joseph who was in fine form. I don't believe I've ever seen Louisa so competently partnered at the waltz."

Valentine paused in the act of snitching bacon from St. Just's plate. "They did look splendid. He has that tall, dark, and handsome business going for him that others have enjoyed to such good advantage."

Valentine's wife, Ellen, lifted her teacup in salute across the table, which his lordship acknowledged with a section of orange.

"It's a fine thing when Sir Joseph must arrive late and leave early rather than enjoy the hospitality of the household overnight like the rest of us," Maggie said. "But then, they are newly wed."

"That has little to do with it," Valentine said. "Westhaven, stop goggling at Anna long enough to send that teapot around." As the teapot started working its way about the table, he went on. "Lou was going to take Sir Joseph on a tour of the charity of her choice today, and they needed to make an early start of it."

"There's a worthy charity hereabouts that Her Grace and Sophie haven't already endowed hand-somely?" Westhaven asked.

"Not here," Vim, Baron Sindal, said from Sophie's side. "Louisa told us it's over in Surrey, not that far, but the snow might make the going tedious."

Westhaven did not stop ogling his countess, but he did pause with his teacup halfway to his lips. "A charity in Surrey?"

"A home for Peninsular orphans whose English relations cannot see fit to take them in." Rather than elucidate further, Sophie peered into the teapot. "Empty. May you lot all find a lump of coal among your presents today."

Sindal passed her his teacup.

"Our sister lives to castigate us," St. Just said,

spreading a liberal portion of butter on his toast. "We mustn't deprive her of her few pleasures."

"And what would you know of my vast and varied pleasures?" Sophie asked, but then she frowned over at the earl. "Westhaven, one cannot find that look at all encouraging over one's breakfast. Anna, kiss him or find some handy mistletoe and offer the man some holiday—"

"I know of only one charitable establishment in Surrey that caters to unfortunate children from the Peninsular excursion." Westhaven pushed back his chair. "Sir Joseph has cause to know of the same establishment, but I fear Louisa has not yet been apprised of her husband's lamentably close connection to it. If we hurry, perhaps we can catch Louisa and Joseph before they depart."

Amid a few soft curses, "oh dears," and a muttered "heaven help us," the mood at the table abruptly shifted.

"Go with your brother," Emmie, the Countess of Rosecroft, said, laying a hand on St. Just's arm. "We were going to call on Louisa today in any case."

"Ladies"—Westhaven's gaze swept the table— "perhaps you'll follow in the coach. Valentine, St. Just, I'll meet you in the stables in ten minutes."

A general scraping of chairs followed, leaving only two people at the table: the handsome, blond Baron Sindal, whose greatest honor was to be married to Lady Sophie, and the darkly attractive Earl of Hazelton, who'd won Lady Maggie's hand in marriage.

"We can't leave Carrington to deal with the rabble on his own," Hazelton remarked. "Wouldn't be sporting."

"And worse yet, we'd have to listen to our

brothers-by-marriage tell the tale for years to come, their heroics growing with each rendition."

"Can't have that." Hazelton's dark brows twitched up. "One wonders whom they're rescuing, Joseph or Louisa."

"Or both?"

Both men rose, crammed their pockets with cinnamon buns, and headed directly for the stables.

❧

Joseph looped an arm around his wife as the coach lumbered along. "You still won't tell me where we're going?"

"It's a surprise." Her smile was smug, pleased with whatever this surprise was and pleased with herself.

"I'm coming to enjoy surprises."

Louisa said no more and cuddled into his side. She had started his Christmas morning off with a lovely surprise, her hand wrapped around his burgeoning erection while he'd spooned himself around her.

And then he'd had the pleasure of surprising *her*, taking her gently and oh, so slowly from behind...

"What *is* that smile about, Joseph Carrington?"

She missed nothing. Being around such a lively mind was an ongoing pleasure. "Happy memories made on Christmas morning."

"Those were the dearest puppies, weren't they? I wonder what their names will be."

Puppies? Ah, yes, the puppies. "I stand by my vote for Westhaven and Rosecroft. We can name the new donkey Valentine."

This provoked a chuckle from his wife. "How could you not know there was a foal on the way? And what are you doing with a donkey, Joseph? It isn't the sort of dignified animal a peer of the realm and former cavalry officer ought to have."

"Jesus rode a donkey. What greater recommendation does a creature need? Besides, Clarabelle is gentle and patient with the girls. They can learn to drive her this spring and be ready for ponies in the summer."

He let her reference to him as a peer of the realm slip by but knew exactly what she was up to. In the smallest increments, she was preparing him for the day when he would be, not Sir Joseph, but Joseph, Lord Wheldrake. On this fine and frosty Christmas morning, the notion did not inspire anywhere near the dread it had just days ago.

When they had rocked through the countryside for some moments in silence, Joseph brought Louisa's knuckles to his lips. "I rather liked being your chosen knight, Louisa. If we're going to be saddled with a title, a mere barony doesn't seem worthy of you."

"Ridiculous man. The baronies are among the oldest titles in the land. The titles of wife and mother being older, I shall content myself with them."

Sir Joseph considered pleasuring his wife in a moving coach. "Have we much farther to go, Louisa?"

They'd gotten an early start, in part because the girls had been up before dawn, tapping on the bedroom door and giggling their way through breakfast.

"Not much farther. Joseph, can one indulge in marital intimacies in a traveling coach?"

He turned his head to regard her. The look in her eyes suggested the question had not been theoretical. "You tempt me, Wife. You tempt me sorely, but I find myself more inclined to get this errand over with then hasten back to the warmth and comfort of our bed, where I can indulge your whims at our leisure."

She looked disappointed. "You have not given me my Christmas gift, Husband. Perhaps I'll call a forfeit instead." Her hand stroked over his falls, and Joseph retaliated by kissing her soundly indeed. As it turned out, the coachman soon stopped on his own initiative to let the horses blow, but it was rather a long time before the occupants of the coach gave him the signal to drive on.

❧

"Who are you?"

"I am your uncle Gayle, or Westhaven if you're of a more formal inclination."

Fleur looked at Amanda to see if she knew what a *formal inclination* was.

"He must be related to Stepmama. He talks like her," Amanda pronounced. "We were going to go see Lady Ophelia's brand new piglets. There are twelve, and when we went to wish them Happy Christmas, our papa said there isn't a damned runt in the batch, and our mama didn't scold him at all because it's Christmas. You can play with our puppies if you don't want to go to the barn. This one has the same name as you."

"Lou will pay for that," said the other fellow. He was as tall as Westhaven, but he had darker hair, and he was smiling a little. "Our felicitations to Lady Ophelia, whose acquaintance we'll make some other day. We've come to see if you know where your parents have gotten off to. The servants claim not to know."

Fleur peered over at Amanda and visually confirmed that they weren't going to tell. Stepmama had said it was a secret.

"This is a waste of time," the fellow Westhaven said. He looked like Papa before a journey, all impatient and determined.

Yet another tall man strolled into the nursery, one bearing a resemblance to the first two, though a little more muscular, like Papa. "Hello, ladies, I'm your uncle Devlin. Has Westhaven scared you witless with his fuming and fretting?"

This fellow looked to be great fun, with a nice smile and kind green eyes.

"Mama and Papa didn't say anything about getting uncles for Christmas," Amanda observed, but she was smiling back at the big uncle.

The *biggest* uncle—they were all as tall as Papa.

"Well, that's because we're a surprise," the other dark-haired fellow said. "I'm your uncle Valentine, and we have an entire gaggle of aunties waiting out in the coach to spoil you rotten. Westhaven here is just out of sorts because Father Christmas gave him a headache for being naughty yesterday."

"I was not naughty."

The other two uncles thought this was quite funny, judging by their smiles.

"There's your problem," said Uncle Devlin. "I'm thinking it's a fine day for a pair of ladies to join their aunts for a ride in the traveling coach."

Uncle Gayle—it didn't seem fair to call him by the same name as Fleur's puppy—appeared to consider this. "For what purpose?"

"To keep the peace. Emmie and I never haul out our big guns around the children," said Uncle Devlin, which made no sense.

"Do you like to play soldiers?" Fleur asked.

Amanda appeared intrigued by the notion. She was forever galloping up hills and charging down banisters in pursuit of the French.

Uncle Devlin's brows knitted—he had wonderful dark eyebrows, much like Papa's. "As a matter of fact, on occasion, if I've been an exceedingly good fellow, my daughter lets me join her in a game of soldiers."

"I'm not exactly unfamiliar with the business myself," said Uncle Valentine. "I excel at the lightning charge and have been known to take even the occasional doll prisoner."

"Missus Wolverhampton would not like being a prisoner," Fleur said, though Uncle Valentine was teasing—wasn't he?"

"Perhaps you gentlemen can arrange an assignation to play soldiers with our nieces on some other day," Westhaven said. He sounded like his teeth hurt, which Fleur knew might be from the seasonal hazard of eating too much candy.

"You can play too," Fleur allowed, because it was Christmas, and one ought to be kind to uncles who strayed into one's nursery.

"We'll let you be Wellington," Amanda added, getting into the spirit of the day.

"Which leaves me to be Blucher's mercenaries," Uncle Devlin said, "saving the day as usual."

"Oh, that's brilliant." Uncle Valentine wasn't smiling now. "Leave your baby brother to be the infernal

French again, will you? See if I write a waltz for your daughter's come out, St. Just."

Uncle Gayle wasn't frowning quite so mightily. In fact, he looked like he wanted to smile but was too grown-up to allow it. "Perhaps you ladies will gather up a few soldiers and fetch a doll or two. We're going on a short journey to find your mama and papa, so we can all share Christmas with them."

Fleur noticed his slip, and clearly, Amanda had too—but it was the same slip Amanda had made earlier, and one Fleur was perfectly happy to let everybody make. Uncle Gayle had referred to their papa's new wife not as their stepmama, but as their mama.

What a fine thing that would be, if for Christmas they got a mama again for really and truly. Amanda fetched their dolls, Fleur grabbed their favorite storybook, and the uncles herded them from the nursery, all three grown men arguing about whose turn it was to be the blasted French.

⁓

"Percival, were we expecting Wales to join us this holiday?"

His Grace came over to the window, and—because the children had all gone on a mad dash over to Louisa's—slipped a hand around his wife's trim waist.

"By God, that is his coat of arms, isn't it? Best ready the state rooms, my dear—" His Grace broke off as down in the drive, a footman dropped the steps on the elegant conveyance and a diminutive fellow emerged, swaddled in scarves and mufflers.

"Not the Regent, then," Her Grace muttered.

"Is this one of your eccentric compatriots from the Lords, Percy?"

The woman had a way of referring to affairs of state as if they barely merited the same notice as a tippling parlor maid. His Grace occasionally shared her perspective, as when those affairs of state interfered with the little peace and quiet a man could cadge with his own wife on Christmas Day.

"Damned if I know what's afoot. Prinny and I aren't exactly bosom bows."

A footman read a card for the Honorable Mister Somebody Whoever Hamburg, Special Whatever to the Something Committee of His Royal Highness's Select Commission on Whatnot.

His Grace's hearing was not what it used to be—sometimes. "Show him in, Porter, and send around the holiday tray if you can find anybody in the kitchen sober enough to put one together."

Her Grace's lips twitched. "If there's punch left over from the open house, it should hardly go to waste."

"My dear, I assure you it does not go to waste. We have a spate of housemaids in an interesting condition every autumn to show for the vigor with which we celebrate the holidays here at Morelands each year."

A bustling was heard from the main hall below, while the duchess lowered her lashes. "Four of our children were born in the autumn, Moreland. I have many fine memories of the Yule season."

Oh, it was a delight, a positive delight, to be married to this woman, and each decade—each year—the delight grew more profound. But of course, in the few hours when the house was free of children, grandchildren, nieces, and neighbors, the damned Regent would have to send out some damned holiday greeting.

The footman announced Hamburg, who bowed deeply to the duchess and then to the duke.

"Your Grapes, Your Grazes—Your Graces," he enunciated. The little fellow blinked owlishly then peered around the main parlor, a lovely room at the front of the house, with enormous windows overlooking the snowy expanse of the Moreland park.

"Mr. Hamburg, felicitations of the season, and of the day." Her Grace offered Prinny's man the smile that had felled many a lord, and Hamburg did indeed weave a trifle on his feet. "Perhaps we should be seated?"

Her Grace took a seat while Hamburg continued to blink. Then, several moments later, "Yes, Your Grace."

He marched over to a pretty little gilt chair finished in pink velvet, flipped out the tails of his morning coat, and all but fell into his seat.

"I come in hopes of locating your daughter, the Lady Louisa, and her spoush." Hamburg's brows drew down amid the pink expanse of his pate. "Her *husband*, that is, because I bear tidings for Sir Joseph from the Regent himself. Tidings"—the man wiggled his eyebrows at the duchess and stabbed a pudgy finger toward the ceiling—"of great joy!"

Porter appeared at the door with a wheeled cart, which was never bad news in His Grace's estimation.

"You haven't far to go, Mr. Hamburg," Her Grace said gently. "Though surely you can tarry long enough to take some sustenance with us? Your journey from Town in this weather could not have been easy."

"It was not, my good woman."

My good woman? His Grace didn't care what committee of which commission the little sot hailed from, nobody addressed the Duchess of Moreland as my good woman…except Esther appeared amused by it.

"The roads," Hamburg went on, leaning forward to rub his posterior as he spoke, "the roads are deplorable. If it weren't for the good inns and the fine libation provided by them, travel throughout this sceptered isle would not be possible, not even in support of His Royal Highness's most dearly held fancies."

Her Grace passed their guest a cup of tea. "And is it a fancy that brings you to Kent, Mr. Hamburg?"

"Nothing but. My thanks. I say, did you put at least two sugars in this? Can't abide tea that isn't properly sweetened."

"Three," said Her Grace solemnly. "My vow on it."

The duke began to really, truly enjoy himself, because his duchess was enjoying herself. Tidings of Great Joy was probably enjoying himself too, and wasn't that what Christmas was for?

Hamburg took a sip of his tea. "Well, that's all right, then. A man could use some tucker, though. Haring about in the dead of winter, leaving earldoms in people's stockings where they ought to find baronies is surely famishing work. A barony would not do, you see, nor a viscountcy. I do favor the cakes, missus."

Missus? Her Grace's eyes began to sparkle.

His Grace took a seat beside the duchess. "Hamburg, do we understand you to mean Sir Joseph Carrington is going to be created an earl?"

"We this and We that," Hamburg said, banging his

teacup down. "The livelong infernal day, it's We, We, We... Do *We* go to the privy? Do *We* break wind? I lie awake at night in my cold and lonely bed—well, actually, I take a few hot bricks there with me—and I *lose sleep* wondering if *We* scratch *Our* arse, or have the bloody footmen—"

"Some cakes, Mr. Hamburg?" Her Grace was nigh shaking with suppressed laughter, while Hamburg heaved out a long-suffering sigh.

"If you please, ma'am. Cakes would work a treat. Damned cold in that coach. A man must contrive on the crumbs of consideration *We* throw at him."

Her Grace did not serve her husband a cup of tea, but she did pass him a plate with two cakes on it. His Grace considered it a measure of Hamburg's riveting performance that he'd rather hear what Prinny's herald had to say next than eat the cakes.

"Are you looking to inform Sir Joseph of his great good fortune?" His Grace asked.

"Well, what else would have me racketing about on Christmas Day, I ask you? Himself wouldn't have it otherwise, and I do live to serve. Good cakes, sir. I commend your wife on her kitchen."

"My thanks," Esther murmured, which was all that stopped His Grace from having Porter show Good Tidings out the door and back into the Regent's traveling spirit shop.

"You have only a short way to go to find Sir Joseph's home, Ti—Hamburg," His Grace said. "And your timing is well chosen, because all of the Windham siblings are gathered there and will make a proper fuss over Louisa and her earl."

His Grace aimed a look over Hamburg's head at Porter, who stood bloodshot eyes front, shoulders back, and wig slightly askew at the drawing room door. Porter nodded and slipped from the room.

"More tea, Mr. Hamburg?"

Hamburg peered at his empty cup. "*We* prosed on at great length about the punch to be had here. I missed your open house. Apologies for that, but there was a maid at the inn where we—not that *We*, just the coachman, the grooms, postillions, footmen, and myself—stopped to rest the grays…"

Watching a man who was so very bald succumb to embarrassment was an interesting natural phenomenon. The color crept up from neck to cheeks to brow and kept on going, until Hamburg's entire head was a lovely shade of pink His Grace had heard referred to as Maiden's Blush.

"We do have comely tavern maids here in Kent," His Grace said.

"But terrible roads!" Hamburg expostulated. "*We* ought to do something about it, if you ask me—which he never does. Not unless he wants to know if the puce waistcoat is more flattering than the salmon, for God's sake. The man is fat, I tell you. Fat as a market hog, and his stays creak abominably. One has to pretend one doesn't hear them, and that is trying in the extreme."

Amid grumbling, grousing, and more contumely flung at the royal person, Hamburg finished his tea and cakes and then stuffed a cake in his pocket while beaming cherubically at his great good friend, missus.

Porter was told to explain to the coachman exactly

how to locate Sir Joseph's estate, and then Hamburg was reswaddled in his scarves and poured into the coach.

"Percival," Her Grace said as they waved a muttering Hamburg on his way, "was it kind to tuck that bottle of punch into his satchel?"

His Grace spied a handy sprig of mistletoe not six feet away and kissed her cheek. "The man is suffering, *missus*, surely you don't begrudge him a medicinal tot?"

"For Christmas, I acquired my first drinking companion. I can begrudge such a rare good friend nothing." Her Grace was nearly grinning, then her brow knit. "Percival, the children are already over at Louisa and Joseph's, you don't think we'd be intruding…?"

"The sleigh is being hitched as we speak, my dear, and because we know all the lanes and shortcuts, I'm sure we'll beat Hamburg's conveyance handily."

"That is splendid of you, Percival. Just splendid."

And then, without even a sprig of mistletoe to provoke her into such a display, the Duchess of Moreland planted a thorough smacker on His Grace's cheek. Five minutes later, they were bundled into the waiting sleigh, hot bricks at their feet, robes over their laps, and a flask or two of punch warming the ducal pockets.

✼

"Seems Prinny's coach came through earlier this morning. All the stable boys are too busy gossiping about it to fill a bucket of water. How much farther have we to go?"

St. Just held the bucket for his horse while Westhaven did what Westhaven did best: frowned pensively down his nose.

"Not far. Sir Joseph's holding is only a few miles from my own, as the crow flies. I can water my own horse."

St. Just moved down the line. "General officers must be free to see to any aspect of the march requiring attention. How are the ladies bearing up?"

"You never heard more giggling coming from one coach. I believe they've broken out their flasks."

Valentine took the bucket from St. Just, dumped the remaining water into the snow, and dipped fresh from a trough before watering his own mount. "It's cold enough to merit the occasional nip. Has anybody figured out what we're going to say to Louisa and Sir Joseph when this cavalcade shows up on their doorstep?"

"We'll start with Bloodshed Solves Nothing," Westhaven informed him, "and go on to Not in Front of the Children, and finish with an observation that A Cup of Tea Wouldn't Go Amiss."

St. Just exchanged a look with Valentine. The horses remained wisely silent.

"Westhaven," St. Just began, "Sir Joseph dueled for Louisa's honor, which often results in bloodshed. If what you say is true, there will be at least a dozen children on hand, and the little dears are expert at hearing and seeing what they ought not to hear or see. The tea tray is a stretch—this is Louisa whose hospitality we're imposing on."

"But she's going to be upset when she finds out her husband has a collection of bastards," Westhaven said, reaching out to brush a hand down his horse's shoulder. "Carrington will be upset because Louisa's upset. We're their family. We can't *not* try to help."

Valentine set the bucket aside. "We feel guilty

because of that business Sir Joseph raised when he whisked Louisa off to Kent, about not appreciating her."

Westhaven rubbed a hand across his chin. "The man had a point."

Before anybody could elaborate on that thoughtful observation, St. Just swung up into the saddle.

"The man has a wife, and she's our sister—a sister who might be about to get her heart broken for Christmas, so let's ride."

❧

Of all the counties, Surrey was the most congenial to forestation. Fields, manors, and pastures were represented in abundance, but whereas other parts of the realm might revert to moor or fen if uncultivated, Louisa's sense of Surrey suggested the trees would cheerfully take over and turn the place back into the England of the forest primeval.

"Had I known we were going halfway to London—" Sir Joseph broke off as Louisa trailed a hand up his thigh.

"Husband? You were saying?"

"Had I known we were traveling halfway to London, I would not have let you button me up quite as quickly."

"Were we not almost at our destination, I would at this moment be unbuttoning you again." She meant it too, yet another revelation courtesy of the married state. "I wonder how my siblings stand to behave themselves in public."

"They very often don't." Sir Joseph spoke with his lips against Louisa's temple, lazy affection suffusing his voice. "Westhaven is the master of the subtle buss, St. Just's hands are seldom off his countess's person, and Lord Valentine excels at the visual caress. Your sisters are more discreet but no less affectionate with their spouses."

The coach was rocking along, and Louisa knew she and her husband would soon be having a difficult discussion. It would go well. She was determined on that and optimistic enough to pose her next question.

"Joseph, would you be averse to having a large family?"

In some subtle way, he drew her closer. "Childbirth is not without risks, Louisa."

"I'm built for it, though, and my mother never had difficulties, and neither did Sophie. I want children, Joseph. We have a great deal of material security, and we can afford to give our children every advantage. That thinking is what guided me in the selection of the charity I'd like to endow."

He straightened. He didn't exactly set Louisa on the opposite bench, but just as he'd gathered her close at the mention of having babies, he withdrew into himself now.

"Is that what we're about today? Inspecting the charity of your choice?" He did not sound pleased.

"It is, and then there are matters upon which I would like you to give me a fair hearing."

He took to studying her bonnet, which reposed on the opposite bench like a figurative lady's maid. "You would like a large family, Louisa? You want lots of babies of me? They'll grow up, you know, and turn into shrieking, banister-sliding, pony-grubbing little people, all of whom must have shoes and books and puppies. They'll eat like a regiment and have no thought for their clothes—which they'll grow out of before the maids can turn the first hem. They'll skin their knees, break their collarbones, and lose their dolls. Do you know what a trauma ensues when a six-year-old female loses her doll? I have a spare version of Missus Whatever-Hampton Her Damned Name Is, but Amanda found her and said a spare would never do, because the perishing thing didn't *smell* right—you find this amusing?"

"I find you endearing."

His brows came down. "I will never understand the female mind."

"I am coming to understand something about you, though." She cradled his jaw in one hand, wishing they indeed had time to get unbuttoned. This was an unbuttoned sort of topic, one of many. "You were raised by your widowed mother, and then by maiden aunts. You have little familiarity with a normal family life—siblings, cousins, uncles, grandparents, you never had them."

He turned his head and kissed her palm—she hadn't gotten around to putting gloves on again. "What you say is true, Wife, and then by the time my aunts finally let me go up to university, I was the common fellow among a bunch of lordlings. Books were my companion of choice by then, and beasts."

"And it was more of the same on Wellington's staff."

He was silent for a few minutes while the coach slowed and swung around a turn. "I will give you all the babies you want, Louisa, gladly, enthusiastically, but just as you have matters to discuss with me, I have matters to discuss with you too."

That was fine. Louisa hoped his matters would sort themselves out easily enough when he saw where they

were. The coach slowed further, and Louisa raised one
of the shades from the nearest window.

"It's very pretty here, what with all the snow on the
trees. I can see why Westhaven enjoys these surrounds."

Sir Joseph handed her gloves to her. "We are near
your brother's holding?"

"It's not far at all."

Something passed through Joseph's eyes, something
bleak. "Louisa, before we see this place…"

The coach lurched to a stop, the footman dropped
the steps, and Louisa pulled on her gloves. "We're
here, and this is the charity I've chosen, Joseph. You
can do nothing to change my mind on the matter, not
one thing."

He looked like he'd say something, then preceded
her out of the coach and handed her down. When
Louisa would have withdrawn her hand from his
grasp, he closed his fingers around her palm. "Louisa,
there are things you don't know about this household.
Things I would be the one to tell you."

She looked around, never having seen the property
before. "It's lovely, isn't it?" Her gaze traveled over
the huge old Tudor dwelling, which like the barn
still sported a thatched roof. Mullioned windows
graced the lower floors, and a venerable growth of ivy
climbed the north wall.

"I can see pots and pots of geraniums here in
spring," Louis said, not liking Joseph's silence. "And I
can see us spending a lot of time here. Say something,
Joseph. Please say something."

He looked so grave, and on a day that should have
been so happy.

"Louisa, I am sorry. I meant to make sure you never knew, and then I meant to explain. Maybe I always meant to explain, but then—"

A door banged open at the front of the house, the wreath on the door pane bouncing with the impact, its harness bells shaking merrily. A thunder of feet, small and not so small, followed along with a chorus of happy shrieks.

"It's Papa! We knew you'd not miss your Christmas visit! Papa has come to see us!"

Louisa felt stunned, confused, and not a little off balance. As a dozen children swarmed Joseph where he stood, she raised curious eyes to him. "Papa?" she mouthed over the happy din.

He wrapped his arms around as many children as he could gather close but held her gaze almost defiantly. "Papa?" Louisa asked again, quietly, as something odd turned over in her chest.

Joseph nodded emphatically, once, then bent to greet the children.

Seventeen

A COMMOTION ON THE DRIVE HAD TIMOTHY Grattingly shoving a book back onto the shelf from which he'd taken it.

There were volumes of poetry here by the score, but none of them small, red, and filled with some of the most vulgarly glorious erotic verse ever written. No matter—the thing had been quite popular among the scholars at Oxford, and Sir Joseph apparently had a copy. The irony of this was as delicious as a well-spiked Christmas punch.

Grattingly peered out the window and saw that Sir Joseph and his lady had arrived, and—wasn't it just fitting?—the man's bastard offspring were swarming him, Louisa Windham was looking puzzled, and the groom walking Grattingly's horse was staring at the lady with something like foreboding.

The staff had tried to keep Grattingly penned up in a pokey little parlor, but he had insisted a book would pass the time while he waited for Sir Joseph to make his predictable Christmas visit.

And Grattingly had waited, and waited, and *waited*.

Now, finally, it was time to make an entrance, or an exit, as the case was. Grattingly took one last glance around the library and showed himself from the premises. /

"What a touching reunion." He couldn't help but sneer a little as he came down the front steps.

The lady recovered first. "Mr. Grattingly, you are not welcome here, and if you think holiday sentiment is going to stop my husband from finishing what you started prior to our wedding, you had best mount up and think again at a dead gallop on the way down the drive."

"Louisa—" Carrington disentangled himself from his bastards, a delightfully uncomfortable look on the man's face.

"Won't you introduce me to your children, Sir Joseph? I'd like to be able to boast that I met every one of your by-blows before we turn to the equally interesting topic of your wife's naughty poetry."

Ah, that had Carrington's dark brows twitching down and Lady Louisa's chin lifting a half inch. Before either one of them could launch into questions, accusations, or denials, a trio of riders appeared at the foot of the U-shaped drive.

"So much the better. We'll have an audience for our little chat, unless, of course, you'd like to part with some valuables and coin in the very near term? Lady Louisa's ring might be a nice overture. With that ring and her earrings in my possession, along with some cash, of course, I could forget a lot of poetry and forget I came across what looks to be a dozen illegitimate progeny, as well. What a vigorous fellow you are, Carrington. You may thank Honiton for mentioning that your soldiering had produced some interesting additions to the Crown's loyal populace."

Honiton had also mentioned this location in Surrey weeks ago, though Grattingly didn't see a need to share that.

Both Carrington and his wife glanced down the drive, while the children quietly heeded Sir Joseph's gesture and filed away to the side. A coach followed the three riders around the turn onto the property.

Better and better. Grattingly couldn't help smiling at the children. "Happy Christmas, you lot—for me."

☙

Louisa wasn't panicking. Joseph understood that with one glance at his wife, but it was no reassurance at all.

She was *thinking* instead, plotting and planning with that slight frown forming between her brows that meant she'd just sprung her mental horses and was galloping off to conclusions mere mortals wouldn't be reaching for days.

And yet…reinforcements were on the way. Surely she had to know those were her brothers outriding for that enormous traveling coach. And behind the traveling coach there lumbered some other conveyance Joseph did not recognize, though the four matched grays were impressive beasts.

"Grattingly." Joseph raised his voice in hopes the approaching riders would hear him. "I am unarmed, else I'd shoot the ballocks off you even before my wife and children."

"We'd cheer," Louisa interjected. "Heartily and at length."

Joseph didn't dare take his eyes off Grattingly, but her show of support was heartwarming.

Grattingly cocked his head and considered Louisa, which had Joseph's fingers itching for a weapon—any weapon. "Your loyalty to a man who single-handedly swived his way from one end of Spain to the other is touching. Must be a function of the Moreland blood."

"It must be." That quiet comment had come from Devlin St. Just, who'd swung off his horse and come to stand behind his sister. Grattingly was fool enough not to know he'd just insulted one of Moreland's illegitimate offspring—or perhaps Grattingly had a wish to die on Christmas Day.

"Sir Joseph." Westhaven sauntered up to stand on Joseph's right. "Is this man trespassing? And on a holiday? That would be the height of bad form, would it not?"

Lord Valentine came up on Joseph's left. "Almost as bad form as threatening our family before these children."

"What an impressive bunch of saber rattlers you are," Grattingly said, slapping his gloves against his thigh. "Sir Joseph is just about to round me up some valuables and wish me a Happy Christmas, lest I start bruiting about, not just the existence of his miscellany here, but also his wife's propensity for prurient poetry. That would be an example of alliteration, *would it not*, Lady Louisa?"

"Lady Carrington, if you're fool enough to address my wife directly," Joseph said. And as if there weren't audience enough to this little drama, behind the coach drawn by the grays, a sleigh came tooling up the drive.

"Whatever her name," Grattingly sneered, "it will

be dragged through the gutters along with yours, Carrington, unless you produce some blunt and produce it now."

"Joseph." Louisa's gaze bore a world of banked emotion. She'd scooped up a handful of snow and was patting it into a hard, round ball. "Perhaps Mr. Grattingly hasn't seen the crest on that coach."

"I care not if the Regent himself catches wind of the folly you two have been up to. I was sent down because of you, Louisa Carrington. It was fine for all the other fellows to have you doing their translations, but when I needed help, your damned brother said you would no longer oblige. I'd already seen some of your Catullus, though, and when that naughty little book came out, I knew exactly who'd authored those poems."

"Well, the Regent *isn't* here," said a sniffy little pink-headed man. "But I am, so let's have done with this nonsense, and I'll be on my way just as soon as I've dispensed with my Good Tidings."

"Who the hell—?" St. Just was scowling at the grays and the coach behind them.

"And Father Christmas himself," Valentine said, lips curving up as a sleigh completed the parade assembled in the drive. "Their Graces, rather."

"This is Mr. Hamburg," the Duke of Moreland announced as he led his duchess away from their sleigh. "He's bearing letters patent to bestow on a certain deserving and loyal subject of the Crown." His Grace pursed his lips. "And that would not be you, Grattingly. Be off with you—you're bothering my family, and my duchess has taken you into dislike."

"I most assuredly have, Timothy Grattingly. Your

poor mother cannot show her face in society because of you," said Her Grace, her profile looking to Joseph exactly like Louisa's.

"Grattingly will just be going," Joseph said, "with all possible haste, preferably to board a packet for the Continent."

"Now why would I do that?" Grattingly said, swiveling his gaze over the assemblage. "We can keep this in the family, so to speak, Sir Joseph, and I'll just hope nobody else ever learns of how diligently you carried out your military duties while in Spain—assuming you found the occasion to don your uniform from time to time."

"Mr. Grattingly," Louisa rapped out. "You grow tiresome. Children?" She turned to the silent knot of anxious faces huddled on the steps and tossed her snowball from hand to hand. "Which of you is Sebastian?"

The tallest boy stepped forward. "I am Sebastian Carrington." His voice was plagued with the *cambiata* huskiness of midadolescence, but he spoke evenly.

"I am pleased to make the acquaintance of the fellow who saved my husband's life," Louisa said. "What is your date of birth, Sebastian?"

Bless the boy, he cited a date fifteen years in the past.

Louisa speared Grattingly with a look. "Are we to conclude my husband nipped down to Andalusia on his way to university, Mr. Grattingly? That he summered in Spain for his own entertainment before he was legally of age?"

"Most of them are younger," Grattingly spat, "plenty young enough. I'm told Sir Joseph is legally their father, and what about all that nasty, dirty, vulgar poetry, *my lady*? Surely your devoted knight would pay handsomely to keep that tripe from the ears of Polite Society?"

Before Joseph's eyes, Louisa's confidence crumbled. Defending her husband's decisions in Spain, she'd been magnificent, assured, and unfaltering. One mention of her literary talent, and she wilted like a tender plant in a frost.

And that, Sir Joseph would not permit.

"A devoted knight offers to his lady the most beautiful verse he can find," Joseph said. "'How do I learn the number of kisses needed to satisfy my longing for you?'"

Louisa's head came up. Shock registered in her gorgeous green eyes. "Joseph? *You know?*"

He wanted to declaim the entire poem, the entire volume of poetry, but settled for one more line: "'So many kisses that no intruding eye could count them, nor any gossiping tongue accurately fix their total, much less their precious worth to me.'"

"Joseph, you know? You knew?" A smile was trying to break through her incredulity. One of Louisa's brothers chuckled, another started swearing cheerfully, and the duke apparently had something caught in his throat.

"It makes no difference if he's memorized the entire lot," Grattingly said, but to Joseph's ears, there was a slight tremor in his statement. "I *know* too. I know, and as long as that book exists, as long as I know who wrote it, you'll be handing over coin when I tell you to, Sir Joseph."

Westhaven spoke from Joseph's right. "My recollection of my terms reading law is growing blessedly dim, but I do believe you're attempting blackmail, Grattingly—albeit not very successfully. Few of the books were printed, and between Sir Joseph's efforts and those of the Windham family, we've retrieved every copy you might get your filthy paws on. Now, Mr. Hamburg's earlier comments have me in a state of uncomfortable curiosity, and those children have to be getting a bit chilled."

"We're fine," said a little girl.

"Ariadne, hush," Joseph said, but he smiled at his youngest daughter for sheer pride at her pluck.

Grattingly whipped his gaze to Louisa. "You have every last copy of that damned book?"

Louisa's gaze could have chipped ice, and Joseph had never been more proud of her. He wanted to swing her against his chest and dance up the steps with her, wanted to laugh out loud, and yet...

"My wife does not converse with scoundrels, Grattingly. Neither will she associate with cowards, nor with a person so craven he'd exploit the unfortunate circumstances of children left orphaned by war." Joseph flicked a glance at St. Just, who caught Lord Valentine's eye.

"It's coal in your stocking today," Valentine said as he and St. Just started toward Grattingly. "Or perhaps a very long jump rope once the magistrate finishes with you and your pathetic attempted felonies."

As they closed in on Grattingly, Joseph held out a hand to Louisa, needing in the marrow of his bones to put himself between Louisa and the miserable cretin responsible for almost ruining their holidays, and their lives.

But he'd not figured on Grattingly's desperation, or on how much speed that desperation could impart. Grattingly whirled away, snatched the reins of his horse from the startled groom, scrambled into the saddle, and was off toward the curve of the drive.

While Joseph could only watch. No gun, no knife, no bow, no—

"Joseph!" Louisa slapped the snowball into his hands. "Into the trees above him!"

While Joseph had focused on Grattingly, Louisa had apparently been figuring trajectories and angles and options. Visions of Fleur raining snow down on her hapless sister snapped into Joseph's mind. He didn't have to aim; he just let his ammunition fly into the boughs so that Grattingly's horse was showered in the face with a huge lot of snow. The animal propped, whinnying its indignation, while Louisa slapped another snowball into Joseph's hand and Valentine and St. Just leapt onto their mounts.

The second dump of snow had Grattingly's horse rearing and Grattingly tumbling ignominiously into the snow, while Joseph—with a silent apology to the animal—fired a third snowball hard, directly at the beast's quarters.

"Mind if I have a go?"

Westhaven's aim was good enough to bring more snow down on Grattingly, and by the time St. Just and Lord Val were marching the man back up the drive, even Louisa had taken a turn pelting the miscreant with snow.

"I might grow to enjoy marksmanship," Louisa said, beaming at her husband.

Joseph caught her close, barely resisting the temptation to hug the stuffing out of her. "You've a wonderful mind and a good arm, Wife."

"I have a wonderful knight. I cannot believe you knew."

"And you knew. Let me introduce you to the children."

"Our children." She corrected him so gently, so happily, Joseph's heart just about beat its way from his chest.

"My wife is ever correct. Our children."

"Not so fast." The little pink-headed fellow came careening through the snow. "You'll be taking these, and I'll be heading for the nearest inn, by God. I don't know yon miserable sod there"—he jerked his chin in Grattingly's direction—"but I'll be telling the Regent how cavalier that fellow attempted to treat an earl and his countess."

"An *earl*?" Joseph cocked his head and glanced at Louisa, who was looking as puzzled as Joseph felt.

"You, my lord, are created the first Earl of Kesmore. Here." Hamburg pushed some papers at Joseph. "You'll tell the Regent I delivered the documents Christmas Day with all due pomp and ceremony, or I'll see that you end up on as many committees as I have myself."

Joseph stared at the vellum in his hand. "*An earl?*"

"Mr. Hamburg, I do thank you," the duchess said quietly, and this for some reason had the man beaming from one pink ear to the other.

Joseph passed the document to Louisa, who scanned it quickly and came up smiling like all of her Christmas wishes had just come true.

"You must not fret over this, Husband. It's a mere few lines on a piece of paper, and probably some more property that you will turn to good advantage. Let the Regent say what he will. You will always be my perfect, gentle Christmas knight."

In recent months, Joseph had grown complacent. His injury had well and truly healed, and not since the previous winter had his perishing damned knee gone out on him. Before the entire army of his wife's family, his children, and the Regent's representative, Joseph was bowing to his lovely wife one moment only to find himself down on one knee before her in the snow the next.

As he made an ungainly descent, he heard the sound of gloved hands applauding from all sides, almost as if he were making a grand, intentional romantic gesture. The children cheered, the men whistled, and little Fleur—where had she come from?—could be heard exclaiming over the din:

"Oh, Manda, look! Just what we wanted for Christmas, a tidy lot of friends to play with!"

❧

Two burly footmen wrestled a cursing Timothy Grattingly off to be confined in the groom's quarters until the magistrate could be fetched.

"Good riddance," Her Grace muttered, sending a glare of maternal protectiveness in Louisa's direction.

Louisa could only smile back at her mother, at everybody, like an idiot, drunk with the happiness of knowing her husband, her siblings, and even—she suspected—her parents had for years been tirelessly protecting her interests, and that these children, these beautiful dark-eyed children, had Sir Joseph's protection.

"Arise, Knight," she said, beaming down at her husband, "lest thy riding breeches get soaked and thy wife take thee to task before these good people."

"Can't have that," St. Just said, boosting Joseph to his feet. "Happy wife, happy life."

"Esther, I swear I never told the boy such a thing," the duke began, but he was smiling and so was the duchess.

"No, Percy, that advice came from me."

The ladies hooted merrily at the duchess's riposte, while Louisa tucked herself against her husband's side. "Shall we repair to the house? I'm sure you could all use food and drink after journeying here from Morelands."

While Louisa waited for her family to file ahead of her into the house, Joseph silently passed her a small silver flask. This one was engraved with a rose in full flower, and held the exact blend of heat and comfort Louisa might have asked for, had her husband not already guessed her preferences. That Joseph kept his arm around Louisa suggested he also, thank God and all the angels, understood her other needs as well.

As she stood beside her husband, snow flurries began drifting down from the heavens, and Louisa decided a woman had never, ever had a better Christmas.

❧

"I thought they would never, ever leave." Joseph closed the door to the library—the only room in the Surrey house big enough to hold the impromptu Christmas party. "Wife, please come here."

Louisa went into his arms, grateful for the quiet, grateful for her family, and grateful beyond words for the man she'd married.

"I love you, Lord Kesmore. I love you so much, but we really must talk."

He held her for a moment, then Louisa felt his embrace tighten. "And by heaven, Lady Kesmore, I love you. You were magnificent, you were breathtaking. I could almost write a damned poem—"

"Husband, you are squashing me. May we sit?"

He did not let go of her. Instead, he turned her under his arm and escorted her to a huge reading chair beside the fireplace. Next to the chair sat an enormous basket of fruit sent by Lord Lionel and his recently acquired bride, Lady Isobel Honiton.

Joseph settled himself into the chair. "This chair holds eight children and one adult. We had a contest last Christmas."

Louisa was pulled into her husband's lap, a very fine place to find herself. "I don't think I am capable of counting to eight," Louisa said, trying to arrange her skirts. "This is your fault, Husband." Though how marvelous, to be unable to count, cipher, or calculate for a time. Louisa kissed her husband for bestowing upon her yet another Christmas gift.

Joseph drew her head down to his shoulder and stroked her hair, leaving Louisa content in a way she hadn't been yet that day—perhaps yet in her life— except for one detail. "About the poems, Joseph. My brother misspoke."

"Alert *The Times*. The Earl of Westhaven misspoke. In anybody else we'd call it an out-and-out bouncer, perhaps even a falsehood. Never say your brother lied on Christmas Day."

Joseph was nuzzling Louisa's neck in a distracting and thoroughly endearing manner, so she got the words out quickly. "He did not lie, but he was mistaken. There's one volume of that dratted book still extant. I have no idea where it is if Grattingly doesn't have it. Victor dared me to see if I could get my manuscript published, never dreaming one can deal with the literary people entirely through the mails. I was too stupid to know publishing anonymously would hardly protect me once I used some of the same translations for Valentine and his friends at Oxford. I am sorry. Victor was horrified when he realized I'd taken his dare."

Joseph did not desist with his nuzzling. "Victor should have known better than to underestimate you. It's lovely poetry, Louisa, and the work of a woman as beautiful in her intellect as she is in her heart. Why didn't you believe at least some of the younger children here could be mine?"

Louisa followed the change in topic with a little difficulty, because Joseph was, in addition to running his nose along her jaw, petting her breast, cupping its fullness and generally creating mayhem with Louisa's ability to speak.

"You were married at the time, and you are a man who keeps his vows."

"Even to an unfaithful wife? I doubt society would see it as you do. In fact, I know they wouldn't."

"Cynthia had your compassion. You would not have played her false because she was young, lonely, and weak."

"Louisa Carrington, what am I to do with a countess such as you?"

"Make babies?"

His smile was both tender and radiant, a Genuine Article of a smile if ever she'd beheld one. When Louisa thought he'd reach into her bodice, he instead reached into his waistcoat and withdrew a small red volume.

"Your brother Bartholomew asked me to hold onto that when he went on leave in Portugal. He said if he bet it in some inebriates' card game or lost it to a light-fingered drinking companion, he would never forgive himself."

Louisa took the little book with shaking fingers.

"*You* had the last volume? All along, *you've had this*? And it was Bart's?" She clutched the book to her chest and hid her face against Joseph's shoulder.

"He'd bought it, not knowing it was yours, but one of your brothers must have told him. Some of the notes in it are his, but the rest are mine. I've carried that thing across the entire Peninsula, I've read it to Lady Opie, and I look very much forward to reading it to you. You're brilliant, Louisa Windham Carrington, and those poems are brilliant too."

For so long, Louisa had viewed this printed evidence of her creativity and learning as a shameful, stupid expression of a good education, as an adolescent rebellion gone very far amok. Joseph didn't see it that way, and while Louisa could not agree with his assessment entirely—some of the poems were vulgar indeed—she also couldn't cling to her own character-ization of the book.

"This is my present to you," Joseph said, prying the book gently from Louisa's grasp. "Happy Christmas, beloved Wife."

He kissed her, sweetly and gently, not enough to start anything, but not enough to put Louisa off the notions gathering momentum in her heart.

"Joseph, I cannot... I cannot..." She sighed. "I cannot get out of this dress fast enough. I would like to make love to the Earl of Kesmore."

"And he would like to make love to the Countess of Kesmore, but, Louisa, I have one more request of you this holiday."

He sounded not serious, but not playful, either. Louisa peered at her husband. "Is the door locked, Husband? Is it that kind of request? You've been a very good fellow, after all, my wonderful Christmas knight, and a serving of plum pudding just isn't reward—"

He put a finger to her lips. "The door is locked, but what I want you to do is reprint that book."

"*What?*"

Louisa tried to pull away, but sitting in a strong man's lap—a strong and determined man's lap—didn't give a woman who'd had several servings of punch much leverage.

"Edit out the truly risqué offerings if you must, polish up the erotic language where it makes you uncomfortable, but leave all the love songs, sonnets, ballads, and odes, Louisa. They're enchanting, and I would have the world know of your talent. You're married now, not a prodigy in the schoolroom, and if anything, your rendering of those poems will only be more lovely for your maturation."

She opened her mouth to argue then shut it.

He was right. Louisa was not only married now, she was happily married, married to a man who loved her, who didn't flinch or look away when she said she loved him.

A man who was proud of her.

"I could do it." She hadn't meant to speak aloud.

"And I can be an earl, so my countess tells me. It's much the same thing, a matter of keeping things in perspective and maintaining the right associations."

Louisa sensed he wanted her to do this, to publish, to cast her work before all of society, and to take her place among those with literary talent.

"I'll use a pseudonym," she said, finding joy in the idea of reworking the poems, taking her time, and getting them exactly, wonderfully right. She had missed the pleasure of creation, missed it desperately. "I'll use a publisher up in York—there are several good ones—and correspond, like I did last time. It might work."

"That is all entirely up to you, but as your partner in this venture and several others, I think you might want to use your own name, or the titled version of it common on publications."

"Joseph, I'm flattered beyond words that you'd support me in this…" Flattered didn't begin to convey the relief—the joy—coursing through Louisa's veins, but she fell silent at the expression on her husband's face.

He was smiling, a naughty, lovely, wicked smile—even better than a Genuine Article smile. "Dedicate this volume to *me*, my love, and get the credit you deserve from all and sundry. Louisa Windham was not appreciated for her talents, but as long as I am her knight, the Countess of Kesmore will be."

And so it came to pass that in the following Christmas season, Louisa found under her pillow another small volume bound in red leather, a beautiful book full of enchanting verse, dedicated to a wonderful man. Louisa's husband lay beside her, reading words of love in the voice Louisa adored to hear rendering her poems, until the baby started fussing, and all thoughts of poetry—at least the kind in that little book—had to be temporarily set aside.

But only temporarily.

Author's Note

Joseph recites the following poem by William Wordsworth to Louisa while they're riding by the Serpentine in Hyde Park early one winter morning:

Composed upon Westminster Bridge,
Sept. 3, 1802

Earth has not anything to show more fair:
Dull would he be of soul who could pass by
A sight so touching in its majesty:
This City now doth like a garment, wear
The beauty of the morning; silent, bare,
Ships, towers, domes, theatres, and temples lie
Open unto the fields, and to the sky;
All bright and glittering in the smokeless air.
Never did sun more beautifully steep
In his first splendour, valley, rock, or hill;
Ne'er saw I, never felt, such a calm so deep!
The river glideth at his own sweet will:
Dear God! The very houses seem asleep;
And all that mighty heart is lying still!

Feeling a little bleak before Christmas, Louisa mentally runs through some lines by Blake about chimney sweeps:

The Chimney Sweeper

A little black thing among the snow,
Crying, "'weep! 'weep!" in notes of woe!
"Where are thy father & mother? Say?"
"They are both gone up to the church to pray.

"Because I was happy upon the heath,
And smil'd among the winter's snow,
They clothed me in the clothes of death,
And taught me to sing the notes of woe.

"And because I am happy and dance and sing,
They think they have done me no injury,
And are gone to praise God & his Priest and King,
Who make up a heaven of our misery."

Her Grace refers to Lady Mary Wortley Montagu, a woman ahead of her time in many ways, though perhaps best remembered for bringing the smallpox inoculation with her when she returned from Constantinople, and for penning the following:

Between Your Sheets

Between your sheets you soundly sleep
Nor dream of vigils that we lovers keep
While all the night, I waking sigh your name,
The tender sound does every nerve inflame,

Imagination shows me all your charms,
The plenteous silken hair, and waxen arms,
And all the beauties that supinely rest,
…between your sheets

Ah, Lindamira, could you see my heart,
How fond, how true, how free from fraudful art,
The warmest glances poorly do explain
The eager wish, the melting throbbing pain
Which through my very blood and soul I feel,
Which you cannot believe nor I reveal,
Which every metaphor must render less
And yet (methinks) which I could well express
…between your sheets.

Joseph quotes a few lines of the following to Louisa on the night when they consummate their vows:

To His Mistress
By John Wilmot, Earl of Rochester

Why dost thou shade thy lovely face? Oh why
Does that eclipsing hand of thine deny
The sunshine of the Sun's enlivening eye?

Without thy light what light remains to me?
Thou art my life, my way, my light's in thee;
I love, I move, and by thy beams I see.

Thou art my life—and if thou but turn away
My life's a thousand deaths. Thou art my way—
Without thee, Love, I travel not but stray.

My light thou art—without thy glorious sight
My eyes are darken'd with eternal night.
My Love, thou art my way, my life, my light.

And His Grace reads the following Shakespeare Sonnet (No. 73) to his duchess, and Joseph quotes just a few lines from the same to Louisa early in their story:

That time of year thou mayst in me behold
When yellow leaves, or none, or few, do hang
Upon those boughs which shake against the cold,
Bare ruin'd choirs, where late the sweet birds sang,
In one thou see'st the twilight of such day
As after sunset fadeth in the west;
Which by and by black night doth take away,
Death's second self, that seals up all in rest.
In me, thou see'st the glowing of such fire,
That on the ashes of his youth doth lie,
As the death-bed whereon it must expire,
Consumed with that which it was nourished by.
  This thou perceivest, which makes thy love
    more strong,
  To love that well which thou must leave
    ere long.

I first came across the quote from Aeneas in college: "*Fortran et haec olim meminisse juvabit.*" This encouragement appeared in a venerable restaurant/diner/watering hole (the place has had many incarnations), where I hope it remains today. The sense of the phrase is: Someday, we'll look back on even this and smile.

And as for Catullus… My dear sister Gail taught

Latin for many years, and by the time you read this, will be well on her way to a PhD in comparative literature, her focus being in the realm of classics. She loaned me enough of Catullus's translated poetry that I understand why much of his work cannot be studied prior to college, at least not in a school setting. *Naughty* puts it mildly.

But treat yourself to a few of his more genteelly impassioned offerings, and you too will appreciate that like Louisa, his genius was not limited to the proper and staid.

I hope you've enjoyed this story—I certainly enjoyed writing it, and I wish you and yours the happiest of holidays.

Grace Burrowes

Lady Maggie's
Secret Scandal

"The blighted, benighted, blasted, perishing thing has to be here somewhere." Maggie Windham flopped the bed skirt back down and glared at her wardrobe. "You look in there, Evie, and I'll take the dressing room."

"We've looked in the dressing room," Eve Windham said. "If we don't leave soon, we'll be late for Mama's weekly tea, and Her Grace cannot abide tardiness."

"Except in His Grace," Maggie replied, sitting on her bed. "She'll want to know why we're late and give me one of those oh-Maggie looks."

"They're no worse than her oh-Evie, oh-Jenny, or oh-Louisa looks."

"They're worse, believe me," Maggie said, blowing out a breath. "I am the eldest. I should know better; I should think before I act; I am to set a good example. It's endless."

Eve gave her a smile. "I like the example you set. You do as you please; you come and go as you please; you have your own household and your own funds. You're in charge of your own life."

Maggie did not quite return the smile. "I am a disgrace, but a happy one for the most part. Let's be on our way, and I can turn my rooms upside down when I get home."

Evie took her arm, and as they passed from Maggie's bedroom, they crossed before the full-length mirror.

A study in contrasts, Maggie thought. They were the bookends of the Windham daughters, the eldest and the youngest. No one in his right mind would conclude they had a father in common. Maggie was tall, with flaming red hair and the sturdy proportions of her mother's agrarian Celtic antecedents, while Evie was petite, blonde, and delicate. By happenstance, they both had the green eyes common to every Windham sibling and to Esther, Duchess of Moreland.

"Is this to be a full parade muster?" Maggie asked as she and Evie settled into her town coach.

"A hen party. Our sisters ran out of megrims, sprained ankles, bellyaches, and monthlies, and Mama will be dragging the lot of us off to Almack's directly. Sophie is lucky to be rusticating with her baron."

"I don't envy you Almack's." Maggie did, however, envy Sophie her recently acquired marital bliss. Envied it intensely and silently.

"You had your turn in the ballrooms, Maggie, though how you dodged holy matrimony with both Her Grace and His Grace lining up the Eligibles is beyond me."

"Sheer determination. You refuse the proposals one by one, and honestly, Evie, Papa isn't as anxious to see us wed as Her Grace is. Nobody is good enough for his girls."

"Then Sophie had to go and ruin things by marrying her baron."

Their eyes met, and they broke into giggles. Still, Maggie saw the faint anxiety in Evie's pretty green eyes and knew a moment's gratitude that she herself was so firmly on the shelf. There had been long, fraught years when she'd had to dodge every spotty boy and widowed knight in the realm, and then finally she'd reached the halcyon age of thirty.

By then, even Papa had been willing to concede not defeat—he still occasionally got in his digs—but truce. Maggie had been allowed to set up her own establishment, and the time since had seen significant improvement in her peace of mind.

There were tariffs and tolls, of course. She was expected to show up at Her Grace's weekly teas from time to time. Not every week, not even every other, but often enough. She stood up with her brothers when they deigned to grace the ballrooms, which was thankfully rare of late. She occasionally joined her sisters for a respite at Morelands, the seat of the duchy in Kent.

But mostly, she hid.

They reached the ducal mansion, an imposing edifice set well back from its landscaped square. The place was both family home and the logistical seat of the Duke of Moreland's various parliamentary strategems. He loved his politics, did His Grace.

And his duchess.

One of his meetings must have been letting out when the hour for Her Grace's tea grew near, because the soaring foyer of the mansion was a beehive of servants, departing gentlemen, and arriving ladies. Footmen were handing out gloves, hats, and walking sticks to the gentlemen, while taking gloves, bonnets, and wraps from the ladies.

Maggie sidled around to the wall, found a mirror, and unpinned her lace mantilla from her hair. She flipped the lace up and off her shoulders, but it snagged on something.

A tug did nothing to dislodge the lace, though someone behind her let out a muttered curse.

Damn it? Being a lady in company, Maggie decided she'd heard "drat it" and used the mirror to study the situation.

Oh, no.

Of all the men in all the mansions in all of Mayfair, why *him*?

"If you'll hold still," he said, "I'll have us disentangled."

Her beautiful, lacy green shawl had caught on the flower attached to his lapel, a hot pink little damask rose, full of thorns and likely to ruin her mantilla. Maggie half turned, horrified to feel a tug on her hair as she did.

A stray pin came sliding down into her vision, dangling on a fat red curl.

"Gracious." She reached up to extract the pin, but her hand caught in the shawl, now stretched between her and the gentleman's lapel. Another tug, another curl came down.

"Allow me." It wasn't a request. The gentleman's hands were bare and his fingers nimble as he reached up and removed several more pins from Maggie's hair. The entire flaming mass of it listed to the left then slid down over her shoulders in complete disarray.

His dark eyebrows rose, and for one instant, Maggie had the satisfaction of seeing Mr. Benjamin Hazlit at a loss. Then he was handing her several hairpins amid the billows of her mantilla, which were still entangled with the longer skeins of her hair. While Maggie held her mantilla before her, Hazlit got the blasted flower extracted from the lace and held it out to her, as if he'd just plucked it from a bush for her delectation.

"My apologies, my lady. The fault is entirely mine."

And he was laughing at her. The great, dark brute found it amusing that Maggie Windham, illegitimate daughter of the Duke of Moreland, was completely undone before the servants, her sisters, and half her father's cronies from the Lords.

She wanted to smack him.

Maggie instead stepped in closer to Hazlit, took the fragrant little flower, and withdrew the jeweled pin from its stem.

"If you'll just hold still a moment, Mr. Hazlit, I'll have you put to rights in no time." He was tall enough that she had to look up at him—another unforgivable fault, for Maggie liked to look down on men—so she beamed a toothy smile at him when she jabbed the little pin through layers of fabric to prick his arrogant, manly skin.

"Beg pardon," she said, giving his cravat a pat. "The fault is entirely mine."

"WHAT YOU SEEK TO ACCOMPLISH, MY LORD, IS arguably impossible."

Earnest Hooker shuffled files at his desk while he sat in judgment of the Marquis of Deene's aspirations. When the ensuing silence stretched more than a few moments, the solicitor readjusted his neck cloth, cleared his throat, and shifted his inkwell one inch closer to the edge of the blotter centered on his gargantuan desk.

Two of his minions watched the client—whom they no doubt expected to rant and throw things in the grand family tradition—from a careful distance.

Lucas Denning, newly minted Marquis of Deene, took out the gold watch Marie had given him when he'd come down from university. The thing had stopped for lack of timely winding, but Deene made it a point to stare at his timepiece before speaking.

"Impossible, Hooker? I'm curious as to the motivation for such hyperbole from a man of the law."

One clerk glanced nervously at the other when Hooker stopped fussing with his files.

"My lord, you cannot mean to deprive a man of the company of his legitimate offspring." Hooker's pudgy, lily-white hands continued to fiddle with the accoutrements of his trade. "We're discussing a girl child, true, but one in her father's possession in even the simplest sense. The courts do not exist to satisfy anybody's whims, and you can't expect them to pluck that child from her father's care and place her in…in *yours*. You have no children of your own, my lord, no wife, no experience raising children, and you've yet to see to your own succession. Even were the man demented, the courts would likely consider other possibilities before placing the girl in your care."

Deene snapped the watch shut. "I heard her mother's dying wishes. That should count for something. Wellington wrote me up in the dispatches often enough."

One of the other men came forward, a prissier, desiccated version of Hooker, with fewer chins and less hair.

"My lord, do you proceed on dying declarations alone, that will land you in Chancery, where you'll be lucky to have the case heard before the girl reaches her majority. And endorsements of a man's wartime abilities by the Iron Duke are all well and good, but consider that raising children, most especially young girl children, should not have much in common with battling the Corsican."

An insult lurked in that soft reply, but truth as well. Every street sweeper in London knew the futility of resorting to the Court of Chancery. The clerk had not exaggerated about the delays and idiosyncrasies of that institution.

"I'm sorry, my lord." Hooker rose, while Deene

remained seated. "We look forward to serving the marquessate in all of its legal undertakings, but in this, I'm afraid, we cannot honestly advise you to proceed."

Deene got to his feet, taking small satisfaction from being able to look down his nose, quite literally, at the useless ciphers whose families he kept housed and fed. "Draw up the pleadings anyway."

He stalked out of the room, the urge to destroy something, to pitch Hooker's idiot files into the fire, to snatch up the fireplace poker and lay about with it, nigh overcoming his self-discipline.

"My lord?"

The third man had the temerity to follow Deene from the room, which was going to serve as a wonderful excuse for Deene's long-denied display of frustration—a marquis did *not* have tantrums—when Deene realized the man was carrying a pair of well-made leather gloves.

"My thanks." Deene snatched the gloves from the man's hand, but to his consternation, the fellow held onto the gloves for a bit, making for a short tug-of-war.

"If your lordship has one more moment?"

The clerk let the gloves go. The exchange had been bizarre enough to penetrate Deene's ire, mostly because, between Hooker & Sons and the Marquis of Deene, obsequies were the order of the day and had been for generations.

"Speak." Deene pulled on a glove. "You're obviously ready to burst with some crumb of legal wisdom your confreres were not inclined to share."

"Not legal wisdom, my lord." The man glanced over his shoulder at the closed door behind them.

"Simple common sense. You'll not be able to wrest the girl from her father through litigious means, but there are other ways."

Yes, there were. Most of them illegal, dangerous, and unethical—but tempting.

Deene yanked on the second glove. "If I provoke him to a duel, Dolan stands an even chance of putting out my lights, sir, a consummation my cousin and sole heir claims would serve him very ill. I doubt I'd enjoy it myself."

This fellow was considerably younger than the other two, with an underfed, scholarly air about him and a pair of wire-rimmed glasses gracing his nose. The man drew himself up as if preparing for oral argument.

"I do not advocate murder, my lord, but every man, every person, has considerations motivating them. The girl's father is noted to be mindful of his social standing and his wealth."

Vulgarly so. "Your point?"

"If you offer him something he wants more than he wants to torment you over the girl, he might part with her. The problem isn't legal. The solution might not be legal either."

If there was sense in what the young man was saying, Deene was too angry to parse it out.

"My thanks. I will consider the *not legal* alternatives, as you suggest. Good day."

About the Author

New York Times and USA Today bestselling author Grace Burrowes's bestsellers include *The Heir*, *The Soldier*, *Lady Maggie's Secret Scandal*, *Lady Sophie's Christmas Wish*, and *Lady Eve's Indiscretion*. Her Regency romances and Scotland-set Victorian romances have received extensive praise, including starred reviews from *Publishers Weekly* and *Booklist*. *The Heir* was a *Publishers Weekly* Best Book of 2010, and *The Soldier* was a *Publishers Weekly* Best Spring Romance of 2011. *Lady Sophie's Christmas Wish* and *Once Upon a Tartan* have both won RT Reviewers' Choice Awards, *Lady Louisa's Christmas Knight* was a *Library Journal* Best Book of 2012, and *The Bridegroom Wore Plaid* was a *Publishers Weekly* Best Book of 2012. Two of her MacGregor heroes have won KISS awards.

Grace is a practicing family law attorney and lives in rural Maryland. She loves to hear from her readers and can be reached through her website at graceburrowes .com.

Also by Grace Burrowes